The True Faithen's Plight

K-A Russell

Dedicated to my God, who adopted me as his own.

MAP

A'theria

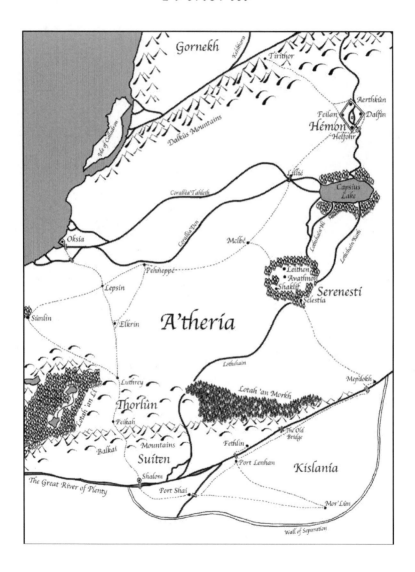

MAP

Serenestí

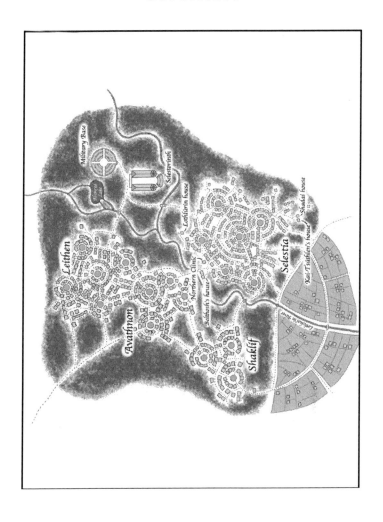

Hémon

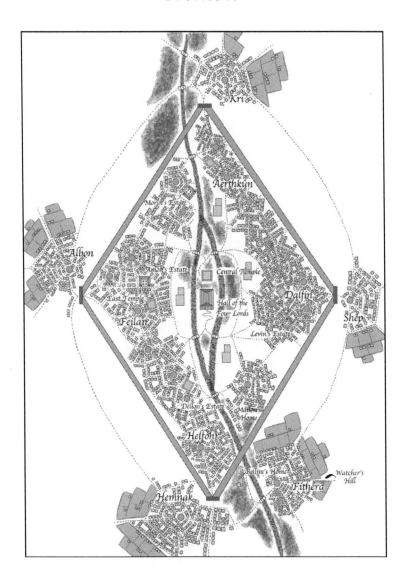

Part 1

CHAPTER ONE

Memories

It was dusk by the time Yosef saw the city of Shalom. Colours strewn through the sky set a dazzling backdrop for the golden city, making for a serene sight that lifted his spirits. A city like that meant good food and kind people, not to mention a place to rest his tired legs that by now felt like jelly from having walked all day.

With a rejuvenated skip in his step, he crossed a wide, sturdy bridge over a voluminous river. He got the feeling he used to know the name of the bridge, but it slipped out of his recollection along with the other memories of his life. They'd all been swallowed up into a big black hole in his mind. Where was he? How did he get to where he was in the first place? Those were the questions tumbling through his head when he found himself in the wilderness on a long, straight road. Only two things remained in the chasm of his mind. One was an image of creepy yellow eyes in the midst of a black, wispy haze. The other was a single voice spoken by a young girl:

Follow this road…

That was it. With nowhere else to go and fear of the yellow eyes spurring him on, he heeded the girl's words and ended up within sight of the golden city.

Buildings sprung up on either side of him as he stepped off the bridge and engulfed him as he plunged into the heart of town. Their huge, angular shapes cast enormous shadows on the ground that made it seem like night had already devoured the city. Cobblestones under his feet swallowed up the light of the crescent moon. The small, deserted alleyways and the smell of industry gave an unwelcoming feeling. So much for a golden city on the outside. Within, Yosef got the impression that strange things were at work here, and a tingling sensation on the back of his neck added to his unease.

He hadn't walked very far when he saw a bearded man standing on a high ladder. The man fumbled with a flimsy match so he could set a street lamp ablaze. Similar street lamps glowed dimly in a row lining the street, though they hardly illuminated the growing darkness of fast-approaching night.

Yosef walked up to the man even though his insides churned and twisted. Were he not famished, he wouldn't have approached him.

"Excuse me…" His small voice came shrill like a mouse.

The man peered down at him.

"What do you want?"

"Um…I'm kinda looking for a place to stay? And some food?"

"Nothing here. Leave me alone."

He returned to his work. Yosef continued to look hopefully at him.

"I said leave me alone, boy!" the man spat.

Yosef dropped his chin and walked on.

He tried knocking on a few doors where glowing light streamed through the cracks of curtained-covered windows. Those who answered wore weary or melancholic expressions. Yosef cringed at one lady in particular whose face bore the scar of a burn. Her left eye was gone, and her right barely poked through wrinkly bags of fatigue.

"Do you have food?" he asked.

The scarred woman stared at him blankly. Maybe she didn't understand Common.

"Food?" he repeated. "You know." He made a gesture of scooping imaginary spoonfuls into his mouth.

The woman continued to stare at him.

Yosef slumped his shoulders. "Never mind." He turned and slowly trod away.

"What you doing talking to my wife!?"

3

Yosef jumped and spun to see a man now standing in the doorway. He caught a whiff of strong spirits caught in a gust of wind.

"Just hungry," he squeaked.

"You got no business here!" the man boomed.

Yosef had two ways to react and only a split second to choose which one to act on. He could stay and confront the man—which would probably end badly because Yosef was just a boy and the man was twice his size and breadth—or he could run away.

He chose the latter. His legs protested, but he darted down the street, turned left, then left again, and ran until the road ended at a T. A dusty path marked its end. Across the path, the ground dipped and fell into the wide river.

Yosef skidded to a halt before flying over the bank.

"What's wrong with this city?" he questioned aloud. His stomach grumbled, reminding him he hadn't eaten anything all day. Or at least not since he found himself in the wilderness.

"Got no business here, boy."

Yosef jumped. Tingling senses on the back of his neck tumbled down his spine.

"Got no business here," the voice repeated.

That wasn't the angry man. In fact, Yosef couldn't tell what the voice belonged to. No one was around. But he could *feel* someone—or some*thing*. Someone somewhere was watching him, like invisible eyes in the dark.

"Got no business here, should leave," came the voice again.

Its raspy tone silenced the wind and in its place came a biting cold that gripped Yosef's limbs.

"W-Where are you?" Yosef called back.

"Not your business. Got no business here, boy," the voice replied.

"Then leave me alone! All I want is food and a place to stay."

"Got no place here."

Yosef trotted down the riverbank path. The voice never left him, echoing variations of "got no business here" and "leave now".

Yosef had had enough. "Shush it, creepy voice thinger!"

He covered his ears.

Got no business here.

4

The voice didn't ring in his ears, but in his mind.

Flesh, living flesh!

Laughter thundered all around him. Other voices joined in the cackle until their shrieks rose into a tumultuous gaggle.

Flesh, living flesh! Devour it, devour it we shall! Got no business here!

Yosef crouched down on the bank facing the river, trying to ignore the mocking laughter.

It was no use. The voices tore at his sanity. What were these things? Why couldn't they just leave him alone? All he wanted was to find a nice home with nice people, eat food and sleep in a comfy bed.

Got no business here!

"Leave me alone."

He peered into the fast-flowing current below. Little ripples gave hint of fish. Yosef could just make out shapes underneath the surface of the water.

A breeze blew at his back like hands trying to push him forward.

Go on, jump in! the voices wailed. *Free yourself, free from the mess. Join the fishes! Go on, jump in, and away we shall be. We shall disappear!*

That was a foolish idea. Yosef couldn't swim. He'd drown. The voices were trying to kill him!

But he wouldn't let them. He stood up, spun around and yelled into the blackness of night.

"Leave me alone! If anyone's got no business here, it's you!"

Speaks, it speaks, they said. *Strong, it is. Resilient, yes. Come, let us feast! Flesh, living flesh!*

Yosef felt a tug within his chest coupled with lifeless cold.

"No! Get away!"

Invisible hands pushed him over the bank. Yosef tumbled down. 'I'm gonna die. But I don't wanna die!'

A splash erupted from the river and massive arms wrapped around him before he hit the water. Before Yosef could fully grasp what was happening, he was plunked down safely on the path again. Shaking, he looked up to see an enormous figure whose skin glistened silver-blue in sheets of scales. Fins jutted from its joints, and three large slits on either side of its neck fluttered slightly as it took in heaving gasps of air.

Curses, the foul! rasped the voices.

The creature bellowed back. The voices screeched just as loudly, then all went quiet. Yosef's tingling sense gradually faded. Were they gone? He looked around. Even though he couldn't see what the voices belonged to, he knew he'd been left alone with the massive river monster.

"What are you?" he asked.

The creature didn't answer, instead pointing up the path. Yosef followed his direction and saw an old, rundown house a fair distance from other buildings. The upper windows glowed yellow, indicating people were inside.

"You want me to go there?" he asked.

"*Jadai-nal jal dúr,*" the creature said.

"What's that mean?"

"*Jadai,*" the creature repeated. "*Jadai magar.*"

Yosef stared up at the creature, then shrugged and started heading toward the house. Halfway there, he stopped and looked back.

The creature was gone.

"Did you hear that?" Ninthalas asked.

He went to the doorway on the top floor of their shabby inn. The building was more like a two-story shack, but finding better accommodation in Shalom was like trying to find the point of a needle in a mountain range where the weather caused him to lose track of his bearings. And the extravagant effort it took just to come up with that correlation was as tedious as finding someone considerate enough to offer a place to stay. To think this was normal for the city of Shalom.

"I hear nothing," said Kai-Tsúthlen. He had his journal open on his lap and was scribbling down details of what they had witnessed that day.

"A patter of feet," Ninthalas noted.

"Are you certain you are not hearing things, brother?"

"I could have sworn I heard something."

"Then I know you are lying, for you seldom swear without reason."

The door downstairs clanged shut. The twins glanced at each other, then Kai-Tsúthlen sprung to Ninthalas' side, sword in hand. Ninthalas clumsily retrieved his own weapon, sliding it out of its sheath so loudly Kai-Tsúthlen shot him a disgruntled look.

"Do not tell me it is that man from earlier today," Ninthalas said, ignoring the scowl. "I meant him no harm, yet it seemed every word I spoke sent him into a wild rage."

"He was also drunk. Hush now and listen."

They crept to the top of the stairs on soft feet. No sound came from the first floor.

Kai-Tsúthlen leaned toward his twin and spoke in a whisper Ninthalas strained to hear. "If we hear footfalls on the stairs, be ready to catch him off guard."

"You would not kill a man, brother."

"No, but I would wound him should he thieve from us, and more so should he assail us."

They fell silent. The sound of a cup tipping over echoed from downstairs and then what seemed to be the sound of rustling cloth.

"Should he take our trading goods…" said Ninthalas.

"Let us see what he is about."

They descended the stairs, each step creaking though they tread as carefully as they were able. Ninthalas cringed at every squeak. Any thief would have heard them and fled before they even got to the bottom of the stairs.

Yet he heard no sounds of flight.

He and Kai-Tsúthlen stepped onto the cold, hard wood floor and rounded the corner into the living room. Both froze when they saw the intruder: only a boy who lay curled up on a bean sac. A wooden cup lay on the floor beside the table, and bags that had once been tied shut were now open, though the boy must not have been interested in their contents.

The brothers relaxed and lowered their swords.

"How peculiar," said Ninthalas.

"This is…unprecedented," Kai-Tsúthlen commented.

Ninthalas glided over to the boy and knelt by his side.

"Why, Kai-Tsúthlen, he is adorable!"

"You speak like my wife," Kai-Tsúthlen returned, joining his brother by the boy's side.

"He sleeps deeply for how loud we are speaking, and he most

certainly fell into a slumber quickly. How strange his features are. Blond hair, yet tanned skin like a Kislanían. And…"

"What is it?"

"Are those wounds?"

Ninthalas gently pulled down on the back of the boy's shirt. A scabbed scar poked through.

"This boy has seen ill times."

"Indeed."

Ninthalas pulled back his hand as the boy stirred. The child breathed in deep and shifted, but didn't wake up.

"How old do you suppose he is? I would say eight, though his ethnicity bewilders me."

"Eight sounds about right for a Common child," said Kai-Tsúthlen. "Perhaps ten if he were True Faithen like us."

Ninthalas gently brushed the boy's cheek. "How precious he is. Say, brother, we should bring him with us."

"Are you mad, Ninthalas? Do not tell me another nightmare plagues you. How troublesome you were when you went insane in Luthrey."

"I am not, I assure you. Yet I have a feeling about this boy…"

"You and your feelings," Kai-Tsúthlen scoffed. "We do not even know where he is from."

"Please, brother, you must trust me. I know what I feel, and I believe this boy's destiny is great."

"You have only just seen him."

"True, yet I believe it is not by chance that he crossed our path. Come now, would you leave a poor, tattered boy stranded in the middle of this accursed city without any care?"

Kai-Tsúthlen sighed, shaking his head. "He will need new clothes."

"I will purchase a tunic tomorrow."

"Very well. I am to bed. This has already been a tiring day, and my nerves are failing me."

He left while Ninthalas continued to study the boy. "What wonders do you hold for us, little one? What a mystery you are, and I do enjoy mysteries."

The next morning, Ninthalas went to the market early. The sun beat down on him like a welcome friend. It didn't feel like autumn this far south. Back home, the leaves would be beginning to change colour and the air would be growing cool. Though he had made this trip with his brother and father several times in his twenty-three years, he still longed for the forest of his home country—the scenery, specifically, and his family as well. Most other people he did not particularly care for, which reminded him why he somewhat enjoyed his profession. Aside from those few cities where muggers roamed wild, he enjoyed visiting the smaller villages. The city of Shalom, however, did not make his list of favourable locations.

The early morning saw plenty of activity. Fishermen flooded the riverside, their catch to be a popular exhibit at the evening market. Farmers tended their fields, anticipating a promising harvest in the following months. Other peasants strode to and fro, most wearing faces of determination and focus. Busyness flourished as Ninthalas entered the city's centre where locals had already set up their market booths. Shops of charms, clothes, tools and every other trinket native to that region lined the street.

Ninthalas walked up to one booth selling children's clothes. Every item dazzled him with their many colours and elaborate designs in a size that would have fit the Kislanían boy, but they wouldn't have suited the terrain. Ninthalas needed a plain tunic and pants so the boy wouldn't stand out in the south. He soon realized that finding such garments would prove difficult in a society as colourful as Shalom's citizens.

"Excuse me," he said to the booth clerk.

The middle-aged lady looked up. A mountain of colourful clothes lay in a heap in front of her, which she happened to be folding before Ninthalas interrupted her. Her wrap-around dress blended in with the other garments in the booth, making her almost impossible to distinguish among the merchandise.

"No sales to True Faithens," she replied and went back to work.

"I need only a tunic for a boy of about eight. Do you have any bland colours or know of a place that does?"

"No bland. Just the play clothes," she said.

Ninthalas was about to leave when he spotted a corner of beige cloth sticking out from her hefty pile.

"What about that one?" he asked.

He walked over and carefully pulled out the plain cloth. It was a tunic.

"This would work," he said. "Now if I had a sash and pants—"

"No, no, no," the woman said. She snatched the tunic out of his hands. "Is not for sale."

"Yet it is in your pile."

"I said is not for sale. Why you True Faithens not understand rules?"

"Please, lady, I seek only that tunic. I beg of you to sell it to me."

She looked him up and down with a critical eye. "Why you so pushy?"

"I have a boy under my care. He arrived at our inn last night and I am charged with caring for him."

"A True Faithen?"

"No, this boy is from Kislanía."

The woman continued to stare at him, one eyebrow raised in a quizzical expression. Then without a word, she went to another table and pulled out matching pants and soft-soled shoes. Ninthalas watched as she ran her hands fondly over the fabric, a sorrowful expression drawn on her face.

"My son wore these," she said at length. "Drowned in the river not two months ago."

"I…had no idea. I am truly sorry. Please, forget that I pushed you to sell it to me. I will find another booth."

The woman shook her head. "No, no. They were not his. Belonged to other boy, but husband beat him."

"Beat him? What do you mean?"

"Strange things here. Men go mad, beat the wives and children."

She handed him the clothes. "You take your boy away."

Ninthalas bowed. "May Yahlirin look favourably upon you."

The woman returned to her desk. "Your God left us. He not see us. Left to evil spirits."

Ninthalas saw tears in the corners of her eyes. Without anything else to say, he left her alone, making his way back to the inn.

"Evil spirits," he said under his breath.

He glanced around at the people flocking the stalls. Though their colourful duds might have expressed a more vibrant ethnic group, many of them seemed melancholic, remorseful even. He spotted one lady whose face was half scarred by a terrible burn. Some others had seen similar suffering. What was going on in this city?

His mood would have remained downcast, but when he got back to the inn, he found the boy awake and sipping on a bowl of warm milk. Crumbs on the table in front of him were the only evidence that he had also eaten bread.

The boy looked up at Ninthalas as he walked through the door. The True Faithen gave him a warm smile, but the boy didn't seem convinced. And why would he be? He had come to a stranger's house a long distance away from his hometown. That begged the question of how the boy ended up in Shalom in the first place.

"Is that you, brother?" Kai-Tsúthlen called down from the second floor in the twins' native language.

"Indeed, we are all bought for and ready," Ninthalas replied. "Yet come down now and meet our little guest."

He went over and knelt at the low table on the floor. The hard wood proved more comfortable than the bean sacs, which he could never find a suitable position on.

The boy continued to study him, eyes wide and attentive. He had probably never seen a True Faithen before, and True Faithens were visually distinct compared to other nations of A'theria. For one, they wore their hair long and it was always black. Ninthalas and Kai-Tsúthlen tied theirs halfway down their backs like others of their profession. The brothers wore wrap-around tunics held in place by thick sashes. The billowing sleeves cut short at the elbows. Their pants were short-legged and tied just below the knees. Underneath, tight, dark garments provided a little warmth, although this far south the brothers hardly needed them.

"Fair greetings, young fellow," Ninthalas said in the Common language known to most ethnic groups in A'thería. "I am Ninthalas Líran Shadai, a News Bearer from the far north in the central part of A'thería from the country of Serenestí."

The boy blinked, a dumbfounded expression on his face.

"Blue eyes," he muttered.

11

Ninthalas chuckled. "Indeed, and so are my brother's. What colour did you think they were?"

"I dunno," the boy replied. "Yellow maybe?"

Ninthalas burst into laughter, which ultimately made the boy shyly lower his head.

"Yellow eyes. Now there is something I have never heard in my short years in A'thería. Where do you get such ideas?"

"I remember yellow eyes," the boy replied sheepishly.

Ninthalas stopped laughing. That sounded awfully strange. He had never known anyone to have such an eye colour. Unless...

Kai-Tsúthlen appeared at the bottom of the stairs. He neither looked surprised, nor happy, nor any emotion in particular for that matter. The boy, however, exuded his bewilderment as he gaped at the sight of him and glanced back and forth between the brothers several times.

"Well, he is up then," said Kai-Tsúthlen. "And I see he has also taken the liberty of eating the breakfast I prepared for him."

"This boy claims we should have yellow eyes," Ninthalas told him. "And that by memory. 'Tis the first thing he said when he saw me."

"*Joldashlí*," Kai-Tsúthlen commented. He came over to the table and took a place beside his brother on the floor.

"What's that mean?" the boy asked.

"Never you mind, dear boy," Ninthalas reassured.

Despite the sincerity in tone, the boy still gave him an unconvinced look.

"Why do you two look the same?" he asked.

"We are twins," Ninthalas answered matter-of-factly. He was about to properly introduce his brother, but Kai-Tsúthlen cut him off.

"What is your name?" Kai-Tsúthlen's face hadn't changed from stoic.

"Yosef Mathíus."

"And where are you from, Yosef Mathíus, and how did you come upon this place?"

"I'm from Mor'Lûn," said Yosef. "I...don't know how I got here exactly. Well, it's just that I was on this road, so I walked. And then I walked and walked some more and..."

He paused, his face contorting into a comical thinking

expression. Ninthalas struggled to keep himself from chuckling. "Mor-Lûn is a long journey from here," Kai-Tsúthlen went on. "Did you not come with anyone?"

"Well, no, I…" He hesitated. "I just can't remember. Like I try to, but my head's all empty-like. Why do you look so different?"

"Our people are quite distinct in both appearance, language and culture," said Ninthalas.

"We are lingering too long, brother," Kai-Tsúthlen noted.

Ninthalas nodded. "Well now, Yosef Mathíus, what are your motives here? Will you stay in this dusty place by yourself? We are leaving this morning and would be more than willing to bear you back to your hometown. Would you like to come with us?"

"You're going to Mor'Lûn?"

"We are headed that way. More precisely, we are going south to complete our errand. Port Shai is our next destination, but we will bring you to Mor'Lûn if need be so you may find your parents."

"My…parents."

"Indeed. Come now. We cannot leave you here alone. Time is against us, you see, for we must return to our home country to report what we have seen."

The brothers stood in unison. Kai-Tsúthlen walked away and out the front door. Ninthalas reached for Yosef's hand.

The boy jerked back.

"You have nothing to fear," Ninthalas reassured.

"You look strange-ish."

"Do I now?" He chuckled and went to retrieve the tunic he'd received from the woman at the market. "Fair enough. My people are quite outlandish compared to your own, and I am the strangest of them all."

"That doesn't sound like something I'd be proud of," said Yosef.

Ninthalas shot him a grin and headed for the stairs. He heard Yosef follow on the creaky steps behind. 'Good. He at least trusts me enough to follow.'

On the second floor, he handed Yosef the clothes. "Go change into these in the other room. They should fit you fine until I can find you something more suitable for a journey."

Yosef disappeared into the other room.

"Is it very far to Mor'Lûn?" he asked.

"Far and far again, dear boy. It is a day to Port Shai providing we leave quickly, and from my understanding another three to your hometown."

He heard painful grunts from Yosef.

"Are you alright, Yosef Mathíus?"

"Fine-ish yeah. My body hurts all over."

Ninthalas remembered seeing the edge of a cut on the boy the night before. Perhaps Yosef had more. His question was answered when Yosef came out holding his tattered garments. Blood stained the clothes in places. Whatever had happened to him, his people had not faired well, and trauma had likely given the boy amnesia.

Yosef wrinkled his nose. "What?"

"'Tis nothing, Yosef Mathíus. Nothing at all. You may leave those here. On the floor is fine."

Yosef dropped them in a heap and then followed Ninthalas back downstairs.

"How come you always call me Yosef Mathíus and not just Yosef?"

"It is the most respectful way to address you. If you had a middle name, I would call you that instead of your first. Take my name, for example: Ninthalas Líran Shadai. The most respectful way to address me would be Líran Shadai."

"Should I call you that?"

"Oh, no. You may call me Ninthalas if it suits you. Though it is most respectful the other way, I will not hold you to it since you are not of my people."

"Sounds complicated."

Outside, Kai-Tsúthlen was waiting with the horses. Yosef gaped at the beasts, and Kai-Tsúthlen smiled, the first sign of emotion Ninthalas had seen on him all morning.

"How much it cheers me that my brother has finally woken up," Ninthalas teased in True Faithen.

Kai-Tsúthlen's face turned sour.

"We're riding on that?" Yosef exclaimed, turning the conversation back to Common.

"Indeed, we are," Ninthalas replied. "Have you not seen horses before?"

"I can't remember."

"Ah...of course." He cleared his throat. "These are Fellas and Hallas, raised in the plains surrounding our country."

"They have journeyed with us on many errands," Kai-Tsúthlen added.

Ninthalas helped Yosef up onto the back of Hallas.

"Your weapons, brother," Kai-Tsúthlen noted.

"Will I truly need them? It is only a day to Port Shai."

"From the trouble that happened upon us yesterday, we should be wary. I will not be found dragging my injured brother back to Serenestí."

Ninthalas sighed. "Very well."

He strapped his two swords, one long and one short, to his sides, and clumsily shouldered his quiver. He'd rather not have worn them, but Kai-Tsúthlen was right. Bandits had sought to assail them just a few days after they left Serenestí, and another gang had chased them through the mountain pass before they passed into the country of Suíten. The previous day, a large, crazed man taller than the twins pursued him and his brother. It took all of Kai-Tsúthlen's cunning for them to escape. Kislanía was known for being a peaceful country with pleasant townsfolk who kept to themselves, yet with the rotten turn of events the twins had endured on this fall's errand, more could follow.

When he had slung his bow over his shoulder, he hopped up behind Yosef.

"Can you fight?" the boy asked.

"Kai-Tsúthlen is more skilled than I," Ninthalas replied.

"Every man teaches the way of the sword to the sons of his household," Kai-Tsúthlen explained.

"Can you teach me?"

"I am not so sure you will need the skill where you are going."

"But I want to Kai—Kai-Tsú—what's your name again?"

Kai-Tsúthlen's complexion turned pink. "It is Kai-Tsúthlen, and if that is too hard to pronounce, then you should call me by my middle name, Okran."

"So Okran Shadai. But why can't I just call you Kai-Tsú or something?"

"Oh, you would do well not to, my little friend," Ninthalas said with a chuckle. "Shortening his name is reserved strictly for

15

his wife."

"Does your wife shorten your name?"

"I am not married."

"Oh. Sorry."

They rode out of the city and across the bridge into Kislanía, following the road that gradually curved east and then straightened out along the flat terrain. Along the way, Yosef pestered Ninthalas with questions, and Ninthalas answered using many words and extravagant stories that he knew from reading and rereading the historical texts of his home country. As the road curved east, Ninthalas caught sight of the Wall of Separation to the west. It continued south before curving east and then north up toward Mepdokh, the longest manmade structure bordering A'thería and the forgotten land beyond.

"Why's there such a big wall?" Yosef asked.

"Many years ago during the First Age of the world, there was a terrible quake in the earth that drove our ancestors away. They fled west and north, all the while fighting back against an onslaught of *malshorthath*. After the Great War of the First Age, our ancestors built this wall to keep out any evil intruder from passing. To this day, no man has crossed it. That is the gist of what the historical records tell anyway."

"Why hasn't anyone crossed it?"

"It is rumoured that if you do, you will never return," said Ninthalas, "for the malshorthath would seek you out and end you."

"What's a malshorthath?"

"A malshorth, you mean?" Ninthalas clarified. "Malshorthath is more than one malshorth in our language. I suppose the best explanation would be a monster. Its skin is often charred black, rugged, its hair as dark as the night sky, and eyes malicious. To tell you the truth, I have never seen one, though I have some hint as to their appearance..."

His voice trailed off as he remembered a recurring dream he had had where a host of malshorthath had attached the city of Luthrey. In the dream, Ninthalas had seen his cousin die in the battle. Though Ninthalas had found peace after delivering the message to the city's king, he often thought about his cousin. Of Ninthalas' relatives, Lamnek was one of the most dear to him besides his brother.

"They have not been seen since the Great War," he went on.
"Yet the ancient writings are detailed in their description."
"If you wanted to cross it, how would you do that?" Yosef
kept asking.
"Why? Do you wish to pass over it? You could always go
around if it suits you. The wall does not go on forever. Yet people
simply do not go that way because they are often caught up in their
own dealings. Exploration is no one's dire quest, no one of
importance anyway."
Kai-Tsúthlen cut in. "Indeed, you would be the one to say that
brother."
"I truly wonder what is on the other side…" he mused.
"Do not start. If you venture beyond it, I will not come save
you."
"I think there are hills on the other side," said Yosef.
"Why do you say that?" Ninthalas asked.
"I remember hills."
"Yet you told us that you do not remember anything regarding
your past."
"That's right. But I just remembered it now. That's the Wall
of Separation, but there's supposed to be hills. I remember them.
That and the yellow eyes."
"Can you tell what the eyes belonged to?"
A pause fell between them before Yosef answered.
"No. But I remember being scared."
Ninthalas would have continued the conversation, but the lull
following Yosef's comment prevented him from doing so. Despite
acquiring a single memory, the boy had only provided another
riddle to add to the already perplexing mystery behind his
appearance in Shalom. What had happened to Yosef's village?
And more importantly, who was this character with yellow eyes?

CHAPTER TWO

Port Shai

The companions stopped to rest only once that day. By the time they reached the next town, dusk had come and gone and only the moon and stars lit their way. Black silhouettes of the first straggling houses of a town obliterated the stars as they neared.

"Port Shai," Ninthalas announced. "'Tis a far more pleasant place than Shalom."

"Why's that? Have you been there before?" Yosef asked.

"Indeed, several times in the company of our father. Twice a year, we send word by News Bearers who journey before us to make ready the inn, and the townspeople more than generously clean it and fill it with provisions."

"Sounds like some nice people."

"They truly are," Ninthalas agreed. "Even Kai-Tsúthlen appreciates this town."

"You say that as if I seldom appreciate anything," Kai-Tsúthlen remarked.

The hulking shapes of simple stone houses became more numerous as they entered town, but by no means were they as compact and towering like the buildings in Shalom. Those houses would have made for a pleasant setting under normal circumstances, but there was something eerie about the way the stagnant air clung to the ground. A growing silence overwhelmed them and Yosef wondered if Ninthalas felt the same as he did.

"It is quiet," the foreign man said as if answering the boy's thoughts.

Silence. As Yosef listened, it sounded as if the silence had a voice. It spoke to him, not necessarily with words, but with a feeling, a sense. He closed his eyes to focus, drowning out the sound of his own breathing and the clopping hoof beats of the horses. The silence grew louder, as audible as a person speaking directly to him.

Come this way, it told him.

Yosef's sense of curiosity followed it into the ground. It took hold of him like a friend, guiding him through a sea of earth. A river crossed their path and the silence veered right until Yosef felt the impact of treading feet as if he were actually touching them. Several feet. Most crowded around a lump of a figure. Three other lumps lay in scattered locations nearby. One by one, those three lumps lifted from the touch of the earth until only the one remained, and Yosef guessed by the shuffling of feet where they once lay that they were being carried off somewhere.

"Shadai twins!"

The voice of the silence ceased. Yosef's head swirled as he snapped back to reality. Four people dashed out of the shadows in front of them: a woman, two men and a boy not much older than him.

"Fair greetings, good people," said Ninthalas. "And a very good evening."

"Good nothing," barked one of the men. "Yer both late."

"We are terribly sorry. We had some delays upon the road."

"Which one are ya?"

"I am Ninthalas Líran Shadai and no other," Ninthalas answered. "What is this flitty business about? My heart leapt as suddenly as my horse."

"Yer askin' me!" the man spat.

"No matter, Mr. Ninthalas," the woman cut in. "Come quickly. You might be able to save the last one."

"Save the last one? Who is he and is he ill or injured?"

"A refugee!" exclaimed the second man whose jaw grew more hair than his head.

The twins dismounted and Ninthalas pulled Yosef off the horse. Both brothers proceeded to rummage through their bags. Ninthalas pulled out a small handbag. Kai-Tsúthlen retrieved a leather-bound book. Yosef had no idea how either items would be useful to an injured man.

"Take us to him," Kai-Tsúthlen commanded. "Boy, take our horses to the usual stable and provide them feed and water."

The older boy nodded, grabbed the reigns of both steeds and led them off.

"Now, show me this man so I may help him," said Ninthalas.

The villagers darted off in a hurried walk between two houses from where they'd sprung out. The twins followed close behind. Even on uneven ground, their movements were as graceful as in midday. The party disappeared into the shadows, leaving a confused Yosef in the middle of the road.

Without any instructions for himself, Yosef followed them. The shadows swallowed him up like a dense fog. He shivered from a chill in the air that seeped into his skin and emptied his limbs of life. There was something odd about this place, something not right.

Loud voices guided him into the light of campfires. Whatever pleasantness Ninthalas had spoken of about the townsfolk, none appeared to be kind-looking. Some gathered in small groups around the fires. A man carrying a large pot trailed behind two women who visited each campfire group. They were serving a watery soup that emanated a strong fish odour.

A sharp cry caught Yosef's attention. The leaders marched over to a small crowd, saying, "Make way, them Faithens 're here."

People parted to let Ninthalas and Kai-Tsúthlen through. Yosef could hear the twins speaking to the townsfolk amidst pained cries.

"What is the matter with him?" one of the brothers asked.

"Dunno, think it's the cut on 'is belly."

Yosef trotted up to the crowd and pushed his way to the centre. As he squirmed and shoved, he heard people around him talking about him.

"Is that—?"

"It cannot be."

"Bless my beard, it *is* him."

"Yer eyes ain't seein' straight. Them kids were taken south."

He ignored them and wiggled his way to the middle where

Ninthalas and Kai-Tsúthlen knelt by a man lying on the ground who was crying out in agony and terror. Two villagers, one red-headed and the other dark-haired, both wearing tattered garments that fit loosely around their angular bodies, struggled to hold the wounded man down.

"Water," Ninthalas ordered as he searched his bag.

He pulled out a vile of translucent liquid and a jar of cream. A withered, skinny woman brought him a bucket and cloth, and he began cleaning the wound, all the while singing a soft melody Yosef could barely hear over the man's deafening cries.

Kai-Tsúthlen knelt at the man's head next to the two restraining villagers. He flipped his book open and began to read in a foreign language.

The man continued to lash about in violent spasms of pain. Despite the severity of the scene, the brothers went about their work as calm as a still pool of water. One sang while applying a mixed ointment to the man's abdomen where a nasty cut festered with black decay. The other placed a gentle hand on the man's forehead as he spoke in a foreign language.

Yosef stared at the scene with wide eyes, wondering what exactly the twins were doing. Gradually, the sounds of the screaming, singing and speaking died down until Yosef couldn't hear them. The intensity of the scene hadn't changed necessarily. It was just that Yosef couldn't hear them.

It was the silence. Tired of the screams and commotion, Yosef focused on it. The silence, in turn, pulled his special sense away from physical things.

And toward something else.

Leave it be! Leave me to devour!

Yosef shivered. He couldn't see them, but he knew they were there, watching, laughing. The voices! But where were they coming from?

"Evil voice thingers," he whispered.

It burns! Leave me be! Leave me to devour!

"Evil voice thingers!" Yosef exclaimed.

It senses us, the voices hissed. *Feels us like the elder ones it does. What is it? Where did it come from?*

Yosef stood up and closed his eyes, allowing the silence to lead him.

The sense! It has the sense!

Just then, the injured man fell silent.

Nethi'ním! An Other! Burns, it burns! Curse the Faithna'him!

"They're inside of him," Yosef said.

A sharp screech lit up the sky. The silence died down, vanishing along with the voices. Yosef opened his eyes and froze. Everyone in the crowd was staring at him with wide, almost fearful expressions, including the foreign brothers.

"What is inside of him, Yosef?" Ninthalas asked.

Yosef looked around at the many faces. Some whispered amongst themselves. Others said nothing at all, but their judgmental faces spoke wonders. He shrunk under their stares.

A groan diverted their attention and everyone turned to see the wounded man's eyes flicker open. The crowd gasped.

"It's a miracle," a woman said.

"Truly amazing," said another.

"Can't believe my own eyes," a man added.

Kai-Tsúthlen removed his hand from the injured man's forehead and snapped his book shut. "By Yahlírin's grace, he is saved." Even he couldn't hide the surprise in his tone.

Ninthalas gently wrapped a dressing around the man's abdomen. Yosef crept over to his side, just as surprised as everyone else that the man was alive.

"How'd you do that?" he asked.

"Do what, Yosef? I merely applied cream and dressed his wound. Kai-Tsúthlen spoke a prayer over him from the holy book which in times past has eased people's senses."

"That's it? But what about the voice thingers?"

"What voice thingers are you talking about? I heard nothing but the man's own cries and my singing."

"You didn't hear them?" said Yosef. "There were voice thingers inside him. They were saying, 'Leave me be! Leave me to devour!' and 'It burns!' and all that. Then they screeched like some bird thinger and flew away into the sky."

Ninthalas gave him a peculiar look. "That is odd. I have never heard of such a thing. Yet perhaps—No, perhaps not. I do not know. Yosef, my dear boy, you do none but plague me with riddles."

"I'm sorry."

He chuckled, something Yosef figured he always did even if the situation wasn't funny.

"It is not a bad thing, little friend. I enjoy a good riddle."

"You sure are strange-ish."

"As are you—"

"Yosef?"

The injured man was now looking at him, as well as his two friends who had been holding him down.

"Yosef?" said the one with red hair and beard. "Is that really you?"

A murmur broke out over the crowd. Those outside elbowed their way to the middle to see.

"It is you!" exclaimed the black-haired, black-bearded man. "Mark my breaches, he's alive!"

Several shouts of "Yosef's alive! Thank the stars, he's alive!" circled through the gathering. Yosef didn't recognize any one of them, least of all the three men. But they all knew him, and that wasn't necessarily a comforting thought. Yosef already didn't like the idea that his memories had disappeared, but it was far more unsettling that people actually remembered him. He didn't want the attention. A lump grew in his throat and a heavy weight fell on his chest. He wanted to cry, but he had no idea why.

A gentle arm wrapped around his shoulders. Yosef looked up to see Ninthalas smiling down at him. The outlandish man pulled him close. Yosef welcomed the embrace. For some reason, that simple gesture comforted him, though he hadn't known the foreigner very long.

"Do not be afraid, Yosef Mathíus," Ninthalas spoke gently in his ear. "I am here for you. You are safe with me."

Yosef believed him.

"I don't know any of them," he said.

"You do not have to. I will not hold it against you, nor will any of these people." He turned to the three men. "I am afraid your Yosef Mathíus has no recollection of times past. He does not recognize you."

"What?!" the dark-bearded man exclaimed, scrambling toward Yosef on hands and knees. His coal eyes lit up with an intensity so strong they might have burrowed a hole in Yosef's face.

"Don' cha remember us, lad? I'm Ruter. Worked with yer father. He took ya to work one time…"

Yosef sank back as far as he could into Ninthalas' embrace. How come he could remember the freakish yellow eyes but not his father's coworker? And he couldn't even remember his father, either.

"Please, good man Ruter, do not distress him," said Ninthalas. "We found Yosef in the golden city of Shalom."

The man Ruter heaved a sigh and retreated to his friends.

"That far north?" said the red-headed man. "Them grey thingers took the kids south. What'd they do to ya, Yosef? How'd you escape the Black Assailant?"

Yosef's chin dropped shyly.

"Poor boy's lost it," said Ruter.

The red-bearded man shot his friend a cross look.

"Ya can't remember anythin'? I'm Doken and this here's Paden."

"I worked with yer father, too," the injured man added. Sweat dripped from his brow, but there was an alertness in his eyes that defied his predicament.

"They did anyway. I'm a smithy," Doken explained.

"Where is Yosef's father?" Ninthalas asked.

All three averted their eyes, melancholy capturing their faces.

"Ah…I see."

"He's gone?" said Yosef.

"You were there, kid," Paden told him. "You saw him die."

Yosef didn't know what to feel. His father dead? He didn't even remember who his father was, let alone what he looked like. But a deep well of sorrow grew in Yosef's heart, bubbling in his chest like a heated tea kettle. He clenched his fists tighter as his tension rose into a raging fire. Even though he couldn't remember his father, he felt the pain of losing him. He felt the anger!

A hand lightly touched his shoulder. Kai-Tsúthlen knelt beside them now. His aspect didn't show as much emotion as his brother's, but there was a sadness in his eyes that told Yosef he cared.

"It is time we retired to the inn."

"Indeed," Ninthalas agreed.

He shifted and Yosef reluctantly got off his lap.

"What's gonna happen to me?" Yosef asked.

Ninthalas gave him a warm smile. "Whatever you would like. You could stay with your people here, or you could come with my brother and I to the inn. It is your choice."

Yosef looked back and forth between the villagers from his hometown and the foreigners. Which should he choose? Sure, those refugees knew him, but Ninthalas and Kai-Tsúthlen were kind. Yosef got the impression that he could trust them.

"I'll go with you."

"You sure lad?" Doken asked.

Yosef nodded.

"Ah, probably better that way," said Ruter, throwing his hands up in the air. "Probably safer with those outlandish fellers."

Ninthalas took Yosef's hand and started to leave.

"Healer…"

They turned to see Paden struggling to sit.

"Do not move lest you aggravate your wound," Ninthalas warned.

Paden ignored him. "See me tomorrow. If Yosef's gonna stay with you, then you'd best hear what his father was about."

"He was of your profession. Do we need to hear more?"

"He was a giant."

Yosef looked up at the brothers. The twins looked at each other.

"Well, now we know where Yosef's mixed lineage comes from," Kai-Tsúthlen commented.

"Hardly so, brother. We still do not know his father's ethnicity."

Yosef lay on his back on a cold stone floor, his body frozen in place like a boulder half submerged in earth. Thick blackness enveloped him. Silence stripped the air of any sound, drowning out his breathing.

Where was he? He remembered meeting the outlandish brothers and riding with them from a golden city to a small town. He remembered the villagers who knew him by name and freakish voices who recognized his ability to feel them.

Flesh, living flesh.

Their voices dug into his ears and down into his soul.

"Ninthalas! Ninthalas, where are you?"

No one answered. Had the twins left for their northern homeland already? But that would mean they'd left him alone!

A light shown and there was the sound of a long, slow stride. He strained his neck to see small slits of yellow glowing in a wall close by, the outline of a door. A latch clicked and the door opened. Light flooded the room, revealing ominous cracks and shapes on the walls. Yet not as ominous as his visitor. A ghostly hand held a torch in its icy grip, suspended in the air like a puppet without strings in the midst of a black void. From the blackness, two eyes peered down at him.

"Yellow eyes…" Yosef managed to say, his voice shrill.

Two voices spoke to him from the void. "Where is your courage now, boy?"

A chill crept through Yosef's body. He squirmed, but couldn't lift himself off the ground. Black mists seeped out of the void and wrapped their spidery arms around him. And the eyes got nearer…nearer…

"How helpless you are," the void chided. "Yet in time, you may become like me."

"Go away!"

"Oh, I would, yet you are too valuable to let alone."

"No! Ninthalas, help!"

The void laughed. "You cannot escape. You shall never be free."

Yosef's voice trickled to a whimper. "No. Ninthalas. Help…please."

"Yosef! Yosef, my child, wake up!"

Yosef opened his eyes, inhaling massive gasps of air, his heart racing. He lay in the arms of the delicate-featured man with the sky blue eyes—one of the twins, though he couldn't tell which one.

"Are you alright?" the man asked. "I heard you calling for

me."

Yosef stared at him, unable to move. Had that all just been a nightmare? Yet it had been so real! The two voices that spoke as one still echoed in his mind.

You are too valuable to let alone.

Yosef didn't understand. How was he valuable? Was it because he had escaped? He didn't even know how he managed to do that. He was just a boy. He didn't even know how to fight.

"Blue eyes…" He reached up and touched the man's face. "Ninthalas?"

"Indeed, 'tis me," the man replied. "Do you remember? We met yesterday and travelled from the city of Shalom here to Port Shai."

"The yellow eyes," Yosef said.

"You told me of them yesterday. Did you dream of them?"

"I…" he drifted off. "I dunno. I…"

Ninthalas pulled him close and started singing a song in another language. It was a sweet melody. Gradually, Yosef's sorrows began to melt and a deep peace sank from his head to his feet.

"Ninthalas?"

"What is it, dear boy?"

Yosef backed away and looked up into the man's eyes. They were definitely blue, not yellow like the ones from the nightmare. What did the yellow eyes belong to? And the two voices that came from the black void. What did that…*thing* want with him?

He leaned against Ninthalas' chest.

"'Tis alright," said Ninthalas, rubbing his back. "It was just a nightmare."

"Ninthalas?"

"Yes, what is it?" Ninthalas replied. His voice rose and fell like a song.

"What's wrong with me? Why can't I remember anything. Only the Wall of Separation and the golden city and you. That's all I remember." He pulled away and looked straight into Ninthalas' eyes, blue like the sky, otherworldly but friendly. "Nothing before that. Not my ma, my da. I don't know how I got here, either. I just…" He sighed. "I wish I could remember what happened."

"Perhaps you have endured much suffering and have forgotten it all," Ninthalas replied. "Many things are yet a mystery to me, despite my deepest musings. Yet what I do know, Yosef Mathíus, is that you are with me, and that is enough."

Yosef rubbed his eyes from straggling tears threatening to tumble down his cheeks. He didn't know why, but he got the impression he could trust this man. Though he'd only known Ninthalas for a day, the man already become a friend.

Ninthalas swished his hand in a dismissive gesture. "Enough of this talk now. I have readied the bath for you and I."

Yosef jolted back.

"For both of us?" he exclaimed.

"Indeed so."

Yosef couldn't stop his jaw from dropping.

"Have you not bathed with your father before?" Ninthalas asked. "'Tis a common practice among my people for parents to bathe with their children."

"That's strange-ish like there ain't no strange!"

Ninthalas laughed. "Is that so? I do not think it so odd. And I should know, for I am an oddity of sorts! I guarantee you it is a grand experience, one to be enjoyed in the company of family. Come now, we are both grimy from the long day yesterday."

Yosef didn't know about grand. He trusted Ninthalas, but to bathe with him—that was just pushing boundaries.

"I...don't know."

"No? Well, if it comforts you, Kai-Tsúthlen will be there as well. He bathes with his children often."

"That's strange-ish, too."

Ninthalas chuckled again. "Well, how about this? You may bathe with us once and if it does not suit you, then I will not press you to bathe with us again. Is that fair? I also wish to take a look at that cut on your back."

"Are you gointa put cream on it like you did with the Paden man?"

"If it needs it, then yes."

Yosef still wasn't sure. Still, he had no reason to refuse. He slid off Ninthalas' lap and they walked hand in hand across the living area to the bath room. A large tub full of steaming hot water sat in the middle. Kai-Tsúthlen was already there, half naked and brushing his hand in the water.

"So you persuaded him to come," he said.

Ninthalas grinned. "Am I not the persuasive one?"

He closed the door and proceeded to undress. The brothers exchanged a few words in their own language, apparently unabashed to be naked in front of each other. Yosef just stared at them. He was beginning to be able to tell them apart. Ninthalas had a slimmer frame than his brother and he looked even skinnier without his clothes on. His face always showed some kind of emotion while Kai-Tsúthlen wore the same expression he had when Yosef first saw him the previous day.

"Staring is rude, little friend," said Ninthalas.

Yosef averted his gaze and reluctantly proceeded to peel off his clothes. When he slipped off his tunic, he noticed the brothers giving him an odd look. The boy followed their line of sight to his own body, which was covered in cuts, scrapes, and scabbed remnants of greater wounds. Every inch of him had some cut or scratch, though the abrasions had missed his hands, feet and face.

The three stood staring at each other, one because he felt exposed in front of two very white-skinned naked men, the others because of a beaten little boy.

Ninthalas' expression melted. He knelt down to Yosef's height and ran his fingers along the more prominent cuts, occasionally applying pressure.

Yosef winced. "Ow!"

"My apologies."

Kai-Tsúthlen came over to see. "Your speculations were correct, brother."

Ninthalas nodded and spoke to him in the foreign language. Kai-Tsúthlen wrapped a towel around his waist and left the bath room.

"These are strange wounds. They should be closed by now, yet this one in particular is festered. 'Tis a shame you do not remember what caused these." He glanced over at the bath. "They may not do so well in hot water. Shall we see?"

"I guess so," said Yosef.

Ninthalas took a cloth, dipped it in the water, and dabbed one of the scabs on Yosef's back.

"How is that? Does it hurt?"

"No," Yosef said, though he really meant 'yes'.

Ninthalas scanned the rest of Yosef's body. Yosef, in turn, couldn't help but look the man up and down as well. Ninthalas had more the physique of a scholar than a traveller. Why he carried swords around was perplexing in itself.

Ninthalas continued to muse, mostly to himself. "What a strange wound it is. The edges are...decaying I suppose, like charred flesh. I cannot tell if it is infected or not. Let us try the bath now, shall we? Can you get in yourself?"

Yosef nodded and stepped into the large tub, one foot at a time. The water wasn't scalding hot, but warm enough that his supposedly open abrasions stung.

"Can you bear it?"

"It's not so bad," he lied.

"Your face says otherwise."

Moments later, Kai-Tsúthlen re-entered the bath room, carrying the small bag Ninthalas had had earlier.

"You are running low on supplies," he said.

"Then let us hope it lasts the last week of our journey."

"Should it take us that long."

They stepped into the tub and began scrubbing the grime off their white bodies. Ninthalas sang a merry tune as he slathered his body with suds. Kai-Tsúthlen, as usual, said nothing.

By this point Yosef, had grown a bit more comfortable being naked in front of them. Almost anyway. He began scrubbing dirt off his own body, staying well clear of the cuts and bruises. Pretty soon his whole body stung, even his hands and feet which had somehow evaded whatever beating he had received. It was probably the yellow-eyed thing's fault. What else could have hurt him?

Every now and then, he glanced at the white-bodied foreigners who were absorbed with their own hygiene.

"Wash your hair as well," Ninthalas said as he removed the tie from his own long, black hair and proceeded to soak it.

Kai-Tsúthlen had already dunked his head.

Yosef lathered up his hands using a thick liquid Ninthalas gave him and slapped it on his head. As soon as he did, his head swirled in a dizzy pool of agony.

"Ow!" he whined, grasping his head. "Ouch! It stings!"

In a fluid motion, Kai-Tsúthlen took hold of Yosef and leaned the boy back to rinse out the soap. A flush of pain rattled Yosef's skull, and he cried louder.

"It hurts!"

Kai-Tsúthlen ran his fingers roughly through Yosef's hair, then propped him up again.

"That is troubling," Ninthalas commented. He rummaged through Yosef's hair and prodded an area on the side of his head.

"Ow!"

"My apologies. There is a cut on your scalp surrounded by a fading bruise and stained roots. It isn't bleeding, thankfully." He continued to feel the cut, occasionally applying pressure.

"Ah!"

"I am sorry."

"The ointment?" Kai-Tsúthlen suggested.

"Do you know which one?"

Kai-Tsúthlen hopped out of the tub and fished through the small bag.

Ninthalas turned to Yosef. "Lean back."

"But it'll hurt," Yosef whined.

"I will be careful.

Yosef obeyed and tried to relax as Ninthalas gently ran his fingers through the boy's hair. His head throbbed, but he strove to bear the pain. To take his mind off the numbing pain, he studied Ninthalas' face. The man had smooth skin, his jaw line masculine, but soft enough to make him appear gentle. Yosef reached up to touch it.

Ninthalas smiled. "What are you doing?"

Yosef barely heard the muffled words with his submerged ears. "Do you shave?"

Ninthalas laughed, propping the boy up.

"I do not. We True Faithens do not grow facial hair as other men do."

"What's a True Faithen?"

"Why that is what Kai-Tsúthlen and I are. We are men of the Faith."

"What does that mean?"

"I would tell you, but I would rather not preach to you. There are those who become finicky when we mention our beliefs."

"Huh."

Ninthalas checked him over and scrubbed a few places where stubborn dirt clung to his tanned skin, then helped Yosef out of the bath. Yosef sat down. A pool of water gathering on the floor around him.

"Here." Kai-Tsúthlen handed his brother a glass jar of white cream.

Ninthalas handed Yosef a towel. "You can dry yourself while I prepare some curing ointments. Can you manage?"

Yosef nodded and patted his body dry as he watched the brothers converse. They were bickering about something or other, probably about Kai-Tsúthlen having retrieved the wrong cream. The stoic man raised an eyebrow as Ninthalas as showed him a vile of clear ointment and proceeded to mix the two together in his hands.

Before long, Ninthalas was back at Yosef's side, slathering the boy's stinging cuts with the mixed cream. As he worked, he sang in that ethereal language that was so soothing Yosef found himself able to relax. The ache in his head faded and in its place rose a sensation of peace.

When the last wound had been treated, Ninthalas stopped singing, closed his eyes, and whispered some strange words. Yosef heard his name being mentioned and couldn't help but wonder what the man was saying about him, and why he was saying those things out loud.

Finally, he opened his eyes. "I fear many of these scars will remain for the rest of your days."

Kai-Tsúthlen handed Yosef a set of clean clothes. "I purchased these in town for you."

"Thank you…" Yosef muttered. He pushed his arms through the short sleeves and poked his head out the hole at the top. The tunic fit well, and the pants even better than the ones Ninthalas had given him the day before.

"How peculiar you do not recall how you received those wounds," Kai-Tsúthlen mentioned.

"I should think not, brother. A blow to the head and terrible trauma? It is no wonder our little friend has amnesia."

Yosef didn't comment. The yellow-eyed thinger had hurt him.

At least that's what he assumed. In the back of his mind, he saw the yellow eyes and the black wisps, memories from his nightmare. For some reason, he got the feeling that the horrid void monster would find him again.

CHAPTER THREE

The Refugees' Tale

"If I do recall, you told that boy that staring is rude. Should I remind you of that since you seem so taken by him?"

Ninthalas looked back at his brother. Yosef had retired from the table after breakfast and went to the bedroom while the twins remained at the table enjoying a fresh pot of one of their mother's black teas. Ninthalas could see the boy sitting on one of the beds, his eyes transfixed until Kai-Tsúthlen's statement stole his attention.

"I cannot help it, brother. I am rather fond of the boy."

"Though you have known him only a day."

Ninthalas ran his thumb over the rim of his handleless cup. The green-coated pottery was a luxury item for a village like Port Shai.

"What do you suppose we do with him?" Kai-Tsúthlen asked.

Ninthalas sighed. "That is the question, I suppose."

"What are you thinking then, that we bear him to Serenestí?"

"The thought had crossed my mind…"

"That would be ill conceived."

"Did your wife not say something similar before we left on this errand?"

"She was referring to adoption," said Kai-Tsúthlen, "though I would think you brash to say that that, too, had crossed your mind."

"Do not be absurd, brother. As you said already, I have only

34

known him a day."

He took a sip of tea and swished the liquid in his mouth before swallowing.

"Then speak to me."

"Why are you so persistent? You normally gawk at my musings."

"I do not enjoy seeing my brother upset."

Ninthalas sighed again and took another sip from his cup. "I am curious about him. He is a cavern of riddles and I am not fit enough a riddler to know them. Yet there is something more—a compelling if I could put a term on it—some desire to be by his side. How I wish I were a man strong enough to protect him, to tell him all is well and bring him to a haven where he might live and grow in peace."

"Our country is no haven for foreigners. You know this."

"He is a foreigner here as much as he would be there."

"My statement remains true," Kai-Tsúthlen stated. "If you do this, think of the implications it will have on our family's name."

Ninthalas studied the teacup, his thoughts mulling over the strong views of his people regarding integration. Thankfully, Kai-Tsúthlen diverted his thoughts.

"Well, if you are so curious, then you might as well speak to that Paden fellow."

"Ah, I almost forgot!" Ninthalas exclaimed. "He mentioned Yosef's father was a giant. Now tell me, my dear brother, do you know of any being that is a giant that is not also a malshorth? Who was this man? Was he truly as tall as they make him out to be? For men larger and thicker than any True Faithen, I wonder just how massive this fellow was."

Kai-Tsúthlen smiled. "There is my brother again and the fire of his curiosity. If you are indeed going to meet them, you might as well bring Yosef with you. I am certain our companion will want to hear of his own past."

"I commend that idea."

Kai-Tsúthlen sipped his brew. "That is why I am with you."

Ninthalas finished the last of his tea and went to the bedroom. Yosef sat on the bed cross-legged, his eyes closed and his breathing steady. Ninthalas walked over to the bed and sat down beside him. Yosef opened his eyes and jolted when he saw the

True Faithen.

"My apologies for startling you," said Ninthalas. "What were you thinking about?"

"Trying to remember," Yosef replied. "But I felt the ground instead."

"What do you mean?"

"I dunno. It's just sometimes I can feel stuff and hear voices. It's like a tingling on the back of my neck."

"You are most certainly a puzzle, little friend."

Yosef sighed. "I wish I wasn't."

"I am to visit those three men this morning," said Ninthalas. "Would you join me? They may be able to remember things that you cannot, and they have some clue as to who your father was."

Yosef shook his head. "I dunno if I wanta know."

"The knowledge may do you well. If you know where you came from, you may discern what course you may take in the future."

"What does that mean?"

"It means you should go with him."

Both turned to see Kai-Tsúthlen in the doorway.

"It would be good for you to get to know each other."

Ninthalas stood. "Indeed. Come now, let us partake in this new adventure. I am eager to stretch my legs and speak with the townsfolk. You would do better with some fresh air as well."

"I guess so," said Yosef. He followed the True Faithen to the door.

The day was bright and clear, and the atmosphere of town much more cheery than the night before. For a small town, the busyness of Port Shai rivalled any urban centre. It seemed the entire population was out and about, mostly gathered in groups of five or less talking about the recent course of events. Children ran in every direction, sometimes in circles around the gossiping adults.

"Oh, Mr. Ninthalas!" a woman called as Ninthalas walked by. She had an apple-shaped figure whose size made the True Faithen appear little more than a twig. She stood with three other women, two older and one not much younger than Ninthalas.

"Fair greetings, ladies," he said with a slight bow. "How are you this pleasant morning?"

"Almost midday now, Mr. Ninthalas," said the younger girl. Ninthalas had seen her several times, but her name escaped him, as well as the names of the others in their little group. Normally he would make a habit of learning them, but with so many places he visited, that proved an impossible task. He usually resorted to learning the names of prominent figures such as elders, noblemen and kings. Even medicine men.

"Once again, your sense of time is much different than mine."

"Yes, yes," the plump woman interjected. "What's the news in Shalom?"

Ninthalas chuckled. "Do you truly wish to know the dealings of the golden city?"

"Just if they're crazier than last year."

"What's it matter how crazy they are?" barked one of the other women. "Crazy's crazy. End of story."

"Truly, there is something amiss," said Ninthalas. "Though I am no man to judge, for I may have begun it."

"Nothing against you. They're just strange-ish folk with strange-ish customs," the young girl said.

"They most certainly do not take too kindly to me in any case."

"Freakish fellers! What'd I tell you?" spat the plump woman. Her two counterparts nodded.

"Who is your friend there?" The younger woman leaned forward. "Hello there, little boy."

"...Hullo," Yosef replied, dropping his chin.

"My, you're a cute-ish one," she said.

Ninthalas clasped his hands on Yosef's shoulders. "I would love to shower you with stories, but my little friend and I must find one of the refugees."

"I'd like to hear your stories," the younger girl swooned.

"Another time, I am afraid."

Just as soon as he left the group, a gruff man in another waved him over.

"Mr. Ninthalas! What news from the north?"

Another man spoke back. "Mr. Healer's more like it. How'd ya save that Mor'Lûn feller?"

Ninthalas smiled and stopped to address him. "The news is

much the same as before, my friend. And I did not heal that man. It was by Yahlirin's grace that he lives."

"God or no god, that was some miracle like I ain't never seen."

Ninthalas would have expounded on how it truly was his God, but faith was a touchy subject to speak of. It wasn't that the town elders forbid such explanations, it was that Ninthalas never gave explanations unless specifically asked. And those opportunities were few.

"I'm looking for that wounded man," he said. "Do you know where he is staying?"

"The elders took 'im to Barkov's. Third house on the south side of the bridge. Right as you get off it."

Ninthalas bowed and headed for the bridge.

"Why do you always bow like that?" Yosef asked.

"It is a form of greeting or to show someone respect," Ninthalas replied.

"Strange."

"How so? How do you greet people?"

"Not like *that*," Yosef purported.

"Well, you already know I am from a different culture than yours. You saw as much from our bath."

"I guess maybe."

They crossed the bridge and turned right. The house wasn't much of a house, just a stone, circular hut with a thatched roof. Ninthalas looked the place up and down. The townsfolk could have picked a nicer dwelling to accommodate the injured man.

Paden. That was his name. And his counterparts were Ruter and Doken.

"Barkov is the medicine man, a rather queer fellow," he said.

"Queerer than you?"

Ninthalas smiled, but said nothing.

He pushed open the flap of fabric for a door. Paden lay in the middle of the only room in the hut, his two friends sitting on stools by his cot. Barkov wasn't present, probably off in town buying herbs or whatever the crazed old man did. Ninthalas figured the only reason he achieved "medic" status was because of his understanding of the plants and flora that grew in the area, and which ones were good for making teas and which were poisonous.

The three refugees looked up at Ninthalas as he entered. Their expressions turned painful when they saw Yosef come in behind.

"You came, Healer," the red-headed man said.

"Of course, friend Doken," Ninthalas replied. "Where there is a mystery, I am close at hand to learn of it."

"You northern folks sure have a strange-ish way of speaking," Ruter muttered.

"Is that so surprising?"

"Er...no." He flustered.

"Nothing we're not used to," Doken clarified.

"Yosef's father," Ninthalas guessed.

They heard a grunt. Paden struggled to sit.

"Don't go stressing yerself for a wily man, Paden," Doken urged.

"I'm fine," he said, propping himself up on his side. "He's got ta know."

"About my da?" Yosef questioned.

"You said he was a giant," said Ninthalas.

"A foreigner. Came into town one day. Thought we were seein' a moving mountain. And he said he was one o' the small ones!"

"Did he say where he originated from?" Ninthalas asked. "In all my journeys to distant lands, I have heard of no giants dwelling in the entirety of A'thería."

"We don't know. He just showed up, started helpin' the lead carpenter after Maggun n' Nilly's place burnt down. Then he married Terga and had Yosef and, well, not much else to him."

"Did he ever speak of his homeland?"

"No, but he did journey to the Wall o' Separation plenty times. Ne'er told us why, just went for a week or two. Then he'd be back with some beastie not found in these parts and we'd squander what's in it for the town."

"A beast?"

"Always different, every time," Ruter explained. "He couldn't 've gotten it around these parts."

"Then he must have ventured beyond the Wall."

"Was my da a fighter?" Yosef asked.

"Best I ever seen, but we're no fighters here to know what's skilled an' not, lad," Doken replied. "You should know—"

"He can't remember nottin', stupid!" Ruter barked.

Yosef's chin dropped. "Just…yellow eyes."

"The Black Assailant!" Ruter exclaimed.

"He called himself somethin' else," said Doken. "It was some foreign-ish language or somethin'."

Paden stroked the stubble on his chin. "Emkala-Mor'Lûn? Nah, that can't be it."

Ninthalas' eyes widened. "*Emkalaf'Morlúrnan.*"

Amazed but puzzled expressions distorted the men's faces.

"That's it!" Paden exclaimed. "How'd you know that?"

"It is the language of my people. *Emkalaf'Morlúrnan* means Black Assailant in True Faithen. But that would mean this new foe has some relation to us." He paused, then added, "Tell me what happened to your village."

"I remember it like yesterday, though it's been three weeks or so gone past now," Doken began. "It was a normal-like day. Yosef's da'd been out for a couple weeks. All of a sudden, he runs back yellin' 'Run! Malshorthath 're coming!' Next thing we know, a band o' foul creatures enters town. Never seen anything like 'em. Big, black an' strong brutes. An' they just start killin' men and dragging our women and children off. Then there were these…ghost thingers o' some sort that went inside o' people an' turned 'em mad. Made good fellers come after us with knives an' pitchforks…" He drifted off as tears welled up in his eyes.

"My wife an' daughter 're gone," said Ruter.

"My condolences for your loss," Ninthalas sympathized. "And this Black Assailant was with them?"

"Fierce-ish man," said Doken.

"Describe him to me."

"He looked like you," said Paden. "Human-ish person clothed in black and dark wisps of clouds swirling all around 'im. Eyes golden yellow, skin on his fingers pale like yours. Couldn't make nothin' of his face, though, what with that hood pulled low an' blackness all around him."

"Small feller, but a real fighter," Doken added. "He killed Yosef's da. We didn't think the giant could fall. We lost hope after that. Some of us escaped, but, well…" He nodded to Paden. "He's one of the only wounded ones who's still alive."

"How many escaped?"

"Thirty-somethin', but we lost ten or so on the road and five more when we got here."

"I am sorry for your misfortunes. If only I could provide for you, but I have nothing that might ease the pain."

"You saved my life, Healer," said Paden. "I owe you one."

"You owe me nothing, friend Paden." He sighed. "Well, that answers a few of my questions, but creates new ones for me to ponder over. What would a raiding party of foul murderers want with women and children? It makes no sense to me. Surely men are the better subject to twist and bend into mindless soldiers. And who is this new leader of malshorthath?"

"You know what them grey thingers were?" asked Doken.

"Oh, indeed. They are oft written of in the historical accounts of my people, though they have not been seen for an age or two. Why now do they choose to attack, I wonder...?"

"I don't wanna know," Ruter stated, crossing his arms. "I'm in enough pain already."

"Maybe they'll turn our young 'uns into soldiers," Doken guessed.

"No!" Ruter exclaimed. "I don't wanna hear it! My daughter ain't gonna be no grey thinger monster."

Doken threw up his hands. "Fine, man. I won't go bursting yer eardrums. Just tellin' the new guy straight since he's guessing what's happened to 'em is all."

"There's only one question on my mind."

They turned to Paden.

"What do we do with lil' Yosef?"

"He could stay in Port Shai—" Doken offered.

"Here? Them townsfolk barely have enough food for us even!" Ruter refuted.

"What else can he do? We're his people, aren't we?" Paden argued.

"*Half* his people," said Ruter. "Sorry, kid, but you got nothin' here but pain and sadness. No hope nothin' neither."

Yosef lowered his gaze. Ninthalas could see the helplessness in his eyes. Compassion welled up within him for the boy. No place would truly be his home, not even if Ninthalas brought him to Serenestí. What a brash idea, as Kai-Tsúthlen said. Yosef would be an outsider wherever he went.

"I will take him with me," he said at last.

41

"Come again?" said Doken.

"I will keep him with me today until we can decide what to do with him."

What he really wanted was to bring Yosef to Serenestí, but he had to speak to Kai-Tsúthlen about it. His brother was a hard one to convince of hasty plans, and he often questioned the effects of integration on True Faithen society.

"Best to be in your hands since I hear yer good fellers," said Paden. "At least, that's what these here folks say about you. Wish they were as nice to us."

Ninthalas bowed his head. "I thank you for telling me this. I know it must be hard."

"Don't worry yerself silly," said Doken.

"I must away then to think of these things and report to my brother. I bid you good day, sirs, though I wonder how good it can be when you are going through such sorrow. I have nothing else to say."

He bowed, then turned to leave. Yosef followed, even giving a little bow himself before they exited the small hut.

"So I'm staying with you now?" the boy asked as they retraced their steps back across the bridge.

"If you are willing, dear Yosef," Ninthalas replied.

A pause fell between them. So many things were running through Ninthalas' mind.

"I aim to take a stroll to process what I have heard. You may return to the inn if you like."

"I wanna stay with you."

He hesitated for a moment, then nodded. "Very well."

They veered left and walked along the riverbank. The river slogged along at an easy pace. Come spring, it would be twice the size and rushing in full force, carrying along it a wealth of fish. This was the *Thinshah'Kúl*, the only river that defied logic and diverted from the Great River of Plenty. It was a fitting location for Ninthalas to rummage through his thoughts, which seemed to be a swirling mass of events that diverged from the norm.

A malshorthath raid. After two thousand years, the demons had returned. Understandably, they had come from beyond the Wall of Separation from a land long forgotten by the Common folk of A'thería. A land full of mystery.

Now Ninthalas had clues as to what lay beyond. Yosef's father had hunted wild game on the other side, and had somehow managed to scale the wall with a huge catch and haul it back to Mor'Lûn. Malthorthath had scaled that same wall and attacked Mor'Lûn, carrying away its women and children. How far past the Wall had those vile creatures established their cities? Perhaps all these years their populations had flourished and now they were returning in full force, conquering little by little like they did in the elder days.

"What are you thinking about?"

Ninthalas blinked a few times, recalling where he was and whose presence he was in. They had walked far enough that they were on the outskirts of town. Aside from a few scattered houses and patched farmland, before them stretched golden fields, grass strands blowing in the breeze.

"I was musing about history and its relation to the present," he replied. "Come, let us sit for a moment."

They sat down on the high riverbank. Again, Ninthalas let his thoughts run free like the current below him.

"How do you sit so still like that?" Yosef asked.

"The same way you sat still back at the inn. Ah, that is right. You said you could feel the earth. How about you try to focus now? Feel the breeze; hear the water."

He watched as Yosef closed his eyes and smiled as a series of discomforted expressions crossed his face. Not long after the boy shut his eyes, he opened them again.

"I can't."

Ninthalas chuckled.

"What? Why're you always laughing?"

"You give me such joy, dear Yosef. I cannot tell why."

"I feel the same around you," the boy admitted.

"That is encouraging. Tell me, now that you know what has come to pass, what course do you wish to take?"

"I dunno. I don't wanta stay here, but I don't know where I'd go. Like, I'm angry and sad and confused, ya know? But staying here, I'd always feel that way. Are you going back to your home?"

"Indeed, I am. It is a News Bearers job to journey to distant lands, trade with people and gather information about the other peoples of A'thería."

"Do you get paid a lot?"

"Serenestí is based on peoples' needs and the trade business rather than coin."

"That's different."

It truly was. True Faithens were the oldest people group known in the world and no other culture was quite like it. Ninthalas considered it a blessing that he was born into such an ethnic race. After every journey to other nations, he always delighted in coming home to the lush forest country where he didn't stand out, at least not in the way of appearances.

"Ninthalas!"

He looked up to see Kai-Tsúthlen walking toward them at a quick pace.

"What is it, brother?" Ninthalas replied in True Faithen.

"Come quickly! Tahlen Dían has arrived."

Ninthalas stood. "Tahlen? When?"

"Recently. He is injured."

"Take me to him."

"What's wrong?" Yosef asked.

"Our friend has come down from the north," Kai-Tsúthlen explained.

"Come, Yosef," said Ninthalas.

All three hurried back to the inn. Inside, they found a young man waiting for them. Tahlen Dían was younger than the twins, though he had similar straight, black hair and pale skin. His attire spoke of his military rank of Captain, which he had attained earlier that year on his very birthday. Since his promotion, he constantly wore a rigid expression similar to his regimented father, his emerald green eyes neither friendly nor sour. He stood as they entered the inn, and Ninthalas could see a crude bandage around his arm through torn fabric.

"Ninthalas Líran, greetings to you," he said.

"Stay where you are, Tahlen," Ninthalas urged. "I hear you are wounded."

"'Tis nothing compared to the injuries my Company suffered," the young man said. However, he still obeyed.

Ninthalas retrieved his medical kit and went to work on his arm.

"I will ready some tea," Kai-Tsúthlen offered. He disappeared into the small kitchen.

"You are right. This is no serious wound. 'Tis a wonder your good arm is unscathed. It fairs ill with Luthrey, I am guessing. When did they attack?"

"On the night of *Jímen'Lúra*, the fifth day of this month," Tahlen replied. "It seems your dream was indeed prophetic, and a good thing that you warned us. Only a small group attacked, unlike the legions I supposed from your description of the dream, yet they still outnumbered us. We managed to defeat them, but the cost was great. Many of Luthrey's own soldiers were slain, and the first two levels of the spiral city laid waste. Many of our own perished, including Lamnek Eflan, your cousin." He bowed his head; his voice wavered. "May he find his way to Yahl's Realm and dwell there in peace."

Tears stung Ninthalas' eyes. He knew this would come. His cousin's death had been part of the atrocity of his recurring dream.

Kai-Tsúthlen returned to the table with a tray laden with a teapot and four cups. He stopped dead in his tracks when he locked eyes with Ninthalas.

"So Lamnek is gone then," he said sombrely.

"We shall mourn for his passing tonight," Ninthalas said in a hushed tone.

He thought he was over his grief after they had passed through Luthrey and warned its king of the malshorthath attack, but now that his dream had come to pass, an excruciating agony reverberated in his chest.

"I cannot believe it," Tahlen went on. "I can, but I cannot. He was my closest friend."

He continued with the details of the battle, using the jargon of a military officer. Neither of the twins had a mind for war tactics, yet they listened attentively to the description of formations taken, advances and retreats, as well as Tahlen's own prowess that alone triumphed over a significant number of malshorthath.

"We saw giants among them, but none were Dethshaiken himself. I am not sure why he would not assist in a battle."

"The Third is a master of legions, not a small band," said Kai-Tsúthlen.

"So they were truly malshorthath then," Ninthalas mused. "I do not know whether to consider it an honour or a curse that you fought them."

"You do not want to meet one, my friend," Tahlen said, sticking his nose up in distaste. "Black, menacing creatures they were, some strong, some thin like ourselves. And yet some of them resembled men that had long since been twisted and turned into foul creatures. There were spirits also. They numbered only a few, but they turned Luthrean soldiers on us. We had only but to band together—True Faithens and Faithen converts alike—to defend the city."

"And how do you fair?"

"Must I answer?"

Ninthalas didn't press him. He finished bandaging the Captain's left arm and set his things aside. As he went to take a sip of tea, he felt a tug on his sleeve. Yosef sat on his knees beside him. He hadn't even noticed the boy since leaving the riverside, and now he realized that the whole conversation since they had returned to the inn had been in True Faithen.

"Who's he?" Yosef whispered in his ear.

"That is Tahlen Dían Lothlúrin, the Captain of a company of warriors known as the Denedrúath."

"I thought warrior leaders were supposed to be older with grey hair and wrinkles," said Yosef. "He looks younger than you."

Ninthalas grinned. "He is the son of a high official and a very skilled swordsman, the best in our country. He is also a most remarkable leader, and his knowledge of formation attacks is unmatched among the younger soldiers."

"Oh," Yosef said, drawing out the word and exaggerating with a slow, single nod of his head. "Is that why he's so serious?"

Ninthalas grinned. "He is like his father."

"I would hope so," Tahlen interrupted.

Ninthalas took the opportunity to introduce his small companion. "Tahlen, may I present to you Yosef Mathíus. We met in Shalom the night before last and thus far, he has accompanied us on our journey."

"'Tis a pleasure to meet you," Tahlen greeted in a far from cheery tone. "You hardly resemble those in the golden city from what I saw of those sorry lot."

"He is from Mor'Lûn," Kai-Tsúthlen explained.

Yosef opened his mouth to speak, but Tahlen turned the

conversation back to True Faithen.

"How strange of you, Ninthalas Líran, to take an outsider's child under your wing."

"My business with him is my own, though I am willing to tell you of it later if you wish. I have had...thoughts concerning him."

Tahlen raised an eyebrow. "Have I missed something since last I saw you?"

"You have not," Kai-Tsúthlen intervened. "Ninthalas has become fond of the boy, is all. He even mentioned this morning the possibility of bringing him to Serenestí."

"It is all too rare of our people to accept a foreigner," Tahlen stated.

"Rare, but not illegal. I know our laws, Tahlen Dían."

"You support this behaviour? The High Lord states—"

"The High Lord is only ever submersed in rules and regulations, most of which are his own making and not the law of Namthúl Shadai. Now if Ninthalas wants to bear the boy north, then I have no right to condemn him. Nor do you, Captain Dían. Our people are tried with aiding those who are in need. Yosef is such a case, and his people no less."

Tahlen fell silent, casting his line of sight to the teacup in front of him.

Ninthalas glanced at his brother, who met his gaze. One look was enough. Kai-Tsúthlen supported him. Now Ninthalas just had to ask Yosef if he would like to come along.

"My apologies—" Tahlen started.

"Are accepted," Kai-Tsúthlen finished. "You may look like you are in control of yourself, my friend, but Ninthalas and I know you. This is not a conversation about the laws of integration in Serenestí, but a question of what you have just witnessed."

"Indeed, Tahlen, we see you breaking," Ninthalas added. "You mourn for our cousin, Lamnek. We do as well, and we shall remember it well into the night. Yet do not let that sorrow drive us apart."

Tahlen heaved a sigh, his posture relaxing like a weight had been lifted from his shoulders. "What of this boy then?" he asked. "What makes you so drawn to him, Ninthalas?"

"I cannot tell entirely. His parents are no more on account of men who worked with his father."

He told Tahlen about the raid on Mor'Lûn and the leader of the malshorthath.

Tahlen stiffened.

"Not only is Yosef a mystery, but he is a valuable piece to the puzzle should his memories awaken," Ninthalas went on. "Although, I almost feel he should not remember, for I fear for his soul."

"I should wish that he *does* remember," Tahlen stated.

"And expose him to trauma?"

"I know trauma, Ninthalas Líran. It can be overcome."

Ninthalas disagreed, but he knew better than to aggravate his friend further. Tahlen wasn't over his past. His sorrows had been suppressed, and something told Ninthalas that the horrors his friend had witnessed had caused those memories to resurface.

"What is our next course of action then?" Tahlen asked.

"The Captain is asking this of News Bearers?" Kai-Tsúthlen mused.

"You know this road. I have only just travelled to other lands for the first time in my life."

"Let us discuss this tonight when we are less weary and more even tempered."

"Agreed."

Ninthalas didn't argue. Grief for his cousin gripped his heart in a vice and information about Yosef's village clouded his mind. He wanted to cry, which he more than felt comfortable doing in front of his brother and friend. They expected it of him. But in front of Yosef? No, he would wait until the boy was asleep.

His thoughts drifted as Kai-Tsúthlen and Tahlen changed the conversation to other matters. First Luthrey and then Mor'Lûn. Who knew where the Black Assailant and the malshorthath raiders would attack next. And Yosef's buried memories were key to understanding more of what was going on.

CHAPTER FOUR

Mysteries

"Alas that we should have to travel today!" Ninthalas exclaimed.

The three men had been conversing in their own language the following morning, and the sudden use of Common startled Yosef. He had heard melancholic singing the previous night, and that coupled with the reddening of Ninthalas' eyes this morning told him that something bad had happened. Yosef wanted to know what was going on.

"What do you mean?" he asked.

Ninthalas took a sip from his mug of freshly brewed tea. "Today is *Jímen'Híkahl*, the holy day of the week."

Yosef wrinkled his nose. That couldn't be the reason Ninthalas was so upset. Maybe if he persisted. "A holy day? What's a holy day and what's a week?"

"Have you no knowledge of time? A week is six days, and a month is thirty. There are twelve months in a year as well as four seasons. Really, my child, have you no knowledge of this?"

Yosef shook his head. A day was like any other day to him. "No, there's just now. Now's the most important."

He noticed a slight look of discontent cross Ninthalas' face. Even if the True Faithen didn't talk about what was bothering him, he couldn't hide his emotions.

"I suppose time is of little importance to southerners," he said with a sigh. "We True Faithens are the keepers of time. Every day with its name and happenings are vital for the records."

"Sounds complicated."

"I should think not," Ninthalas replied. "The True Faithen calendar is perfect: six days in a week, five weeks in a month, and twelve months in a year, as I have said. The complication arises with their names. Every day of the week has a name, though I would probably confuse you if I told you them. True Faithen law states that we are to work five days of the week and rest on the sixth. That includes travelling."

"And the rest day is today," said Yosef, putting it all together.

"That is correct."

"So we're gointa break the law today."

"Indeed, we are."

"And what happens then?"

Kai-Tsúthlen interjected. "Nothing, dear Yosef. Nothing at all. The law was made for people, not people for the law."

"I don't get it."

"You do not have to. You are yet young and have not been raised in our culture. I, however, have spent years studying the law books trying to decipher their true meaning. As for my brother, he worries needlessly, for we have oft travelled on the holy day. I am certain Yahlírin will forgive us for this minor offence."

Yosef frowned. In his mind, laws were laws and they weren't meant to be broken. Still, he wasn't any closer to finding out what was really wrong with the True Faithens.

"So…what happens now?" he asked. "You're going home, right?"

"Well, that is your decision, really," said Ninthalas. "I have been in deep discussion with Kai-Tsúthlen and Tahlen, and we were wondering if you would like to come north with us."

"North?" Yosef repeated. "Like to your hometown? But I don't speak your language or nothin'."

"I will teach you everything I know. It is as Ruter said: the villagers here have little food to provide you. There is nothing for you here."

Yosef paused to think while the men went on to talk in their alien language. The prospect of living among folk who were so different from him didn't sound too appealing. But really, what else was he to do? Ninthalas was right. He had nowhere else to go.

He didn't remember the refugees from Mor'Lûn, and it'd be awkward staying with them. Maybe he could have a fresh start.

He looked at Ninthalas, the man he'd come to trust. There was a compelling in his soul then, a sensation he couldn't quite describe. An image of the giant fish monster that had saved his life in Shalom came to mind. Amidst the unfamiliar words, the fish creature had said "Jadai", and now that Yosef thought about it, "Jadai" must have meant "Shadai". Perhaps he was meant to find the brothers, and he should stay with them wherever they went.

A vision of the yellow eyes from his nightmare flashed before his eyes. According to the three Mor'Lûn refugees, those eyes belonged to the Black Assailant. That void figure wasn't just a nightmare. It was real. If Yosef went with the True Faithens, he might be protected from whatever the Black Assailant was.

"I'll go," he said at last.

The true Faithens stopped talking and looked at him.

"I'll go with you to your country."

"You will?" asked Ninthalas. His face beamed with a smile that stretched from ear to ear.

He glanced at Kai-Tsúthlen, who gave the same look of appreciation. Tahlen, however, showed no emotion. Yosef smiled back at the twins, happy to see a change in their moods.

He nodded. "Well, I mean, you're strange-looking fellers, but I like being with you better than with those other Mor'Lûn people we met yesterday."

"I will protect you as much as I am able, dear Yosef," said Ninthalas.

"Can you teach me how to fight?"

"Perhaps Tahlen can. He is the warrior among us."

Yosef looked at the Captain.

"If there is time," Tahlen stated. "Yet I highly doubt there will be. We must go with all speed if we are to make it back in due time. We have wasted enough time already."

"Then let us ready for the leave taking," Kai-Tsúthlen resolved.

They came to the next small village in a single day. By then, Yosef regretting his decision to accompany the True Faithens. His rear end hurt so much he begged the men to stop and rest. But that didn't help because when they went to ride again the next morning, his whole mid-section down to his thighs ached. He was tired of all this riding. Horses were thrilling, majestic beasts, but he didn't think it right to be riding them all day long. He'd rather have his two feet on the ground and walk the rest of the way. In fact, he even considered asking them if he could.

He took turns riding with each of the True Faithens, but he preferred being with Ninthalas. Ninthalas told the best stories— stories about himself, stories about others, and much, much more about the First and Second Ages. So extensive and captivating were these stories that Yosef barely noticed the sun setting on the second day of travel. Of course, his body also lost feeling like it'd been squashed into jelly, but at least that way he could focus on what Ninthalas was saying and not achy pain.

The sun set while they were on the road, and the company was forced to camp by the roadside. Yosef plopped on the ground, unable to move.

"How about a fire, Tahlen?" Ninthalas asked. Thankfully, he spoke in Common for Yosef to understand.

"I was about to inquire of your own kindling skills," Tahlen commented. "Though I have no flint to light."

As if on cue, Kai-Tsúthlen handed him flint. "You may use mine."

Tahlen muttered something under his breath and went to work gathering shrubbery and twigs nearby. He didn't have the luxury of tree branches. When he did start a flame, it produced so much smoke, they decided to douse it. Yosef choked on the dense fumes as the brothers ran to and from the river carrying empty jars of water. He had no idea where they could've got the glass from.

When all was quiet and they partook in a meagre meal of nuts and dried food, Yosef curled up in a warm blanket Kai-Tsúthlen had purchased for him.

"It seems our little friend is tuckered out," Ninthalas commented.

Though his tone was light, Yosef saw that old sorrow in his eyes again from two mornings ago.

"What about you?"

"What do you mean, what about me? Do I seem tired to you?"

"No, just sad."

"Ah…"

"Why're you all sad?"

None of the men responded for a time.

"Well…you see, Yosef Mathíus—a"

"Our cousin died in battle," Kai-Tsúthlen finished for him.

"Oh." That explained a lot. "I'm sorry."

"He is in Yahl's Realm now."

"Where's that?"

"Well, since you are coming to Serenestí, I suppose I could tell you."

Ninthalas began to tell Yosef about what he'd refused to back in Port Shai. He talked about Yahlírin, a God—no, the only God—who chose the True Faithen people to uphold the law. Yahlírin had bestowed the law upon Namthúl Shadai, the twins' ancestor. Namthúl became the first High Lord of Serenestí and was a formidable warrior who battled malshorthath hoards in the War of the First Age.

"The calling of Namthúl marked the emergence of recorded time," Ninthalas explained. "The True Faithen people were called out of chaos and were charged with keeping time. Later, at the dawn of the Second Age, we sought to share our Faith with the free peoples of the world and spread the name of Yahlírin through acts of love and generosity toward others." His gaze fell. "Not every nation accepted our teachings, calling the Faith an invasion of their practices and culture."

"So…this Namthúl Shadai person. He was a ruler man and the first True Faithen?"

"The first ruler of our country," Ninthalas clarified.

"And he was called out of chaos?"

"Indeed, as I said."

"What was the chaos?"

"It is recorded as to have been darkness and disorder where great sorrow, trembling and the gnashing of teeth prevailed," Ninthalas explained. "The exact meaning of this is unclear, but we are not so concerned about the nature of chaos. What matters is that we are the chosen of Yahlírin."

"Huh. You'd think that because your people keep time they'd be more specific."

Ninthalas chuckled. "I agree. I am most fascinated with the

holes in history."

"And this Yahlírin person. Just what exactly is he?"

"Well," said Ninthalas. For the first time in his explanations, he seemed perplexed. "He is not so much a person as He is an entity. I suppose…perhaps not. No, He is a person in that He can think and feel emotion." He paused again, rubbing his chin. "How odd. I have never been asked to explain the concept of a god before. All Faithen converts are aware of what a god is, even those who are not of the Faith, so the idea of Yahlírin as a god—or *the* God—is no mystery. And yet in many ways He can be a mystery."

"That doesn't make any sense," Yosef said with a yawn.

"Perhaps so. In time you may come to understand the idea, and you may find for yourself that that Idea, that Person, is very much alive. Yet I have spoken much. Now it is time you lay to rest. Tomorrow is another long day of riding."

Yosef groaned. Not another day of riding. He lay down on a thin blanket for a mattress. As soon as his head hit the rolled up clothes he used as a pillow, he fell fast asleep.

"You are good with him," Kai-Tsúthlen noted.

"How do you explain Yahlírin to a boy who has no concept of God?"

"I thought you answered well enough. It is difficult for us who have lived solely and exclusively in our own Faith to understand another worldview."

Ninthalas sighed, massaging his shoulders from the long day of riding. He had depleted much of his energy by telling stories. This must be what his brother endured on a daily basis with his own son.

"You almost seemed like a father instructing his child," Kai-Tsúthlen went on.

"Did I? How odd of you to mention that."

"I simply state what I see. The boy has taken a liking to you. I am amazed he agreed to come along with us and leave everything behind."

"It is not as if he had much to leave," said Ninthalas. "I hope he will find refuge in Serenestí."

"As do I."

"Where is Tahlen now?"

Kai-Tsúthlen nodded toward the Great River of Plenty. "Away by the river, doing what he does best by keeping a lookout."

Ninthalas hopped to his feet. "I wonder how he is fairing."

"You would do well to leave him alone, brother."

"No man must grieve alone, if that is what you think he is doing."

"Actually, I assume he is brooding. You know Tahlen. He is a fine warrior, yet he struggles under the weight of responsibility."

"Still, I wish to reassure him if I can."

Kai-Tsúthlen sighed. "Ever the compassionate man you are for your friends. Fine then, go. I will watch over Yosef."

Ninthalas left Yosef in Kai-Tsúthlen's care and found Tahlen on the bank of the Great River of Plenty. A full moon cast its light upon a village on the other side of the river, the buildings' shadowy forms lurking on the opposite bank. No lights flickered from the town, but loud voices and laughter echoed across the water. Fethlin, the town of thieves, never slept. Tahlen was right to be watchful. He had his bow in hand, an arrow cocked and ready. Ninthalas didn't doubt that the Captain could fell five men on the other bank if the thieves spotted them.

He grinned, shaking his head.

"You mock my caution?" Tahlen remarked.

"Hardly so, my friend. I welcome it."

Tahlen sighed. Ninthalas could see the strain of that so-called 'weight of responsibility' on him.

He shook his head and turned his attention to the river. His grin turned to a frown. The current slogged along at a pace that contrasted with its usual activity. A chill crept up his spine like the prickling of spider's legs, making him shiver. Even stranger that his senses were amiss. Something was wrong.

Tahlen broke the silence. "It is too eerie tonight for my comfort. A strange chill hangs about the water."

"So you can feel it as well," Ninthalas said.

"Harvest is nearly upon us, so it is rightly cooler, but the cold tonight could suck the life from me."

It truly could. Ninthalas' arms dangled and his legs grew

weary. He took bigger gasps of air as if it was difficult to breathe.

"Are you alright?"

"Heavy," Ninthalas replied. "I feel heavy. And the water is so still."

"My friend, this is the Great River of Plenty. It is never still."

"No, Tahlen, look. It does not stir with life. Even when night passes, there is a stirring in the current from night creatures, some of which are said to be giants from the sea."

Tahlen rolled his eyes. He always exaggerated his disinterest whenever Ninthalas brought up anything remotely close to myth or legend. Ninthalas was used to it. He ignored Tahlen's gesture and scanned the current downriver, then looked up. The river ran black like a sliding, placid slab. How could Tahlen not notice—? He cut the question short as it was still forming in his mind. Of course the Captain wouldn't know. Tahlen hadn't seen the Great River before.

"What is that?"

Ninthalas looked upstream. A white glow hung above the water, growing, expanding. He gasped as the glow divided into various shapes. Human shapes.

"They are people!" Tahlen exclaimed. "Or bodies of people, what is left of them."

"Souls," Ninthalas breathed.

"Are you sure?"

Tahlen ran back to camp while Ninthalas remained, watching, eyes transfixed. The bodies drew near, swimming through the air just above the surface of the water. Some were dismembered, others mangled and disfigured. Whatever they were and whatever end they had met, Ninthalas knew they had suffered a great deal. Yet he was bewildered as much as he was horrified. No passage in the historical records, nor the True Faithen holy book, documented anything remotely similar to this phenomenon, not even during the First Age of the world when malshorthath raids were common. Ninthalas couldn't help but be fascinated, captivated by the mystery behind the souls' existence.

"Ninthalas, get away from there!"

Ninthalas shook his head, eyes widening as he realized he stood inches from the shore. One more step and he would have plunged into the water. Were the souls trying to kill him? No, they couldn't. Every one of their eyes were closed. They couldn't have known he stood watching them, speculating over their origin.

He laughed despite his uneasiness. "'Tis alright, brother!" he called back. "They are...asleep if I am correct in thinking so. And they have a different air about them than the rumoured spirits of *Lotah 'an Morkh.*"

He ran up the bank anyway. Kai-Tsúthlen grabbed his arm and practically dragged him back to camp. They found Tahlen trying to keep the restless horses under control.

"Would you provide a little aid?" the Captain demanded.

The brothers rushed to help. Ninthalas managed to calm both his own horse and Tahlen's, though it took some coaxing. He was no horse master, but he had a way with animals the others did not. He spoke to all three of the steeds in a calm tone and they eased slightly.

"If our mounts are restless, then those souls are a bad omen," he said.

"What does all this mean?" Tahlen asked.

"I am not the speculator," said Kai-Tsúthlen. "Ninthalas, what do you say of this?"

"I say those were the remains of villagers. Mepdokh is no more."

"How can you be sure?" Tahlen asked.

"I am not. As Kai-Tsúthlen said, I am only speculating."

"If malshorthath attacked Mepdokh, do you suppose they would still be there when we arrive?" Kai-Tsúthlen questioned. "We have no extra provisions to provide aid to refugees should their be any left remaining. Yet proceeding on this road seems our best option if we wish to get home quickly rather than retracing our steps to Luthrey."

"I should like to continue," Tahlen stated. "I would like to discover the fate of Mepdokh and learn why we saw the ghosts of the dead. I did not see this phenomenon at Luthrey. "

Kai-Tsúthlen nodded. "I agree. Even if the malshorthath are gone, we may be able to examine the ruins. We must bring word of this to Serenestí in any case, and thanks to Tahlen being in our company, we have a second witness of our accounts for them to be valid."

"Alright, but I have a request," said Ninthalas.

"You wish to stop at the old bridge," Kai-Tsúthlen guessed.

"Indeed, I do."

"That will delay us too much, and I am eager to not only see what has become of Mepdokh, but return home to my family. I know you, brother. You will muse over that twisted thing for a day or more if we let you."

Tahlen interjected. "What in all A'thería are you talking about?"

"Ninthalas is over-enthusiastic about a natural bridge that crosses the river not far upstream from here."

"I would not call it *over*-enthusiastic," said Ninthalas.

"Excessively so then."

"Please, spare me your bickering," Tahlen said, throwing up his hands. "It is late, we are weary, we have witnessed some ungodly nature, and I would rather sleep to forget it if only for a night."

"I could not agree more," said Kai-Tsúthlen.

Ninthalas didn't argue. He only hoped that Kai-Tsúthlen and Tahlen would be in a better mood and allow him to stop and examine the old bridge in the morning.

When Ninthalas awoke, he rushed to the riverbank. The souls had gone, and he found himself a little disappointed that they had left. The river this morning appeared to be normal, except it was still deprived of the life that had once flooded its current. A small breeze picked up, giving him that same chill from the night before that he knew wasn't the brisk winds of the late harvest season.

Dissatisfied and perplexed by the meaning of it all, he returned to the encampment. Kai-Tsúthlen and Tahlen were already up, packing the blankets they had used during the night. Yosef still slept soundly by the remains of their failed campfire.

"There is a stiff heaviness about us," Ninthalas said. "The Great River is yet lifeless. The earth, too, is quiet and still."

"The earth seldom moves unless there is a force that drives it," Tahlen remarked.

Ninthalas frowned at him. "I know what I feel. Even the sun seems dainty today, and the darkness of night needlessly clings to the morning."

"Then let us leave before you are driven mad," Tahlen suggested.

"Indeed, I would not want you to go insane a second time on this errand," Kai-Tsúthlen agreed. "Once is enough."

Ninthalas nodded and went over to wake Yosef. The boy didn't take kindly to being awakened, and his grumpy morning attitude continued throughout much of the morning. Ninthalas tried to cheer him with stories, but unlike the day before, Yosef shrugged them off, instead preferring to keep to his own thoughts.

Ninthalas decided to let him be, though at a cost. His brooding thoughts over the peculiar phenomena of the past few days suppressed his concern for the boy. No matter how many ways he looked at the riddles of two invasions and the appearance of souls, he couldn't find a connection between any of them. How frustrating. He normally enjoyed pondering over the discrepancies of recorded time; those never ceased to bore him. But these current events concerned him—frightened him even. They were a foreboding of what was to come. How much better it would be for odd discrepancies to remain in the past without them hindering the present. Without them hindering him or the people he loved.

"What is that over there, crossing the river?" Yosef asked all of a sudden.

Ninthalas looked to where he was pointing and smiled. "Ah, the old bridge. That, little friend, is one of the most fascinating structures in all A'thería."

"When was it made and who made it?" Yosef asked. The boy appeared to be over his morning bitterness.

"That is truly the question of ages. We do not know. There are a number of holes in A'thería's history and that bridge is one of the most prominent. No account in recorded time tells of how it came to be there. That is what I find so intriguing about it."

He gazed at the massive grey structure that spanned the length of the river. As they got closer, Ninthalas breathed in deeply, anticipating another meeting with this ancient entity. Here was one mystery he could only dream of uncovering!

He glanced over at his brother. Kai-Tsúthlen stared ahead, a stoic aspect drawn upon his face. He met Ninthalas' gaze, rolled his eyes and sighed.

"Alright, Ninthalas. If you truly wish to stop, then stop we will," he relented.

Ninthalas' heart leapt.

When they got to the bridge, they took the time to rest their horses and eat a measly meal of dried fruit and nuts. The wind had picked up, rustling through the grass which added to the sound of the river slogging along nearby. In his excitement, Ninthalas snatched up his food and brought it over to the bridge. Surprisingly, he found Yosef trailing behind him.

'Curious as I am,' he thought, smiling.

Two massive dead trees marked the bridge's entrance, and when Ninthalas neared, he saw two more on the other side. In between, a twisted mass of interconnecting branches and roots jutted out across the water, joining the two banks. Upon them a path of stone slabs lay embedded in compact dirt. Railings of entangled branches spanned either side, preventing whoever ventured onto the bridge from plunging into the current below.

Ninthalas sat down in front of the two trees and Yosef followed suit. Neither said a word as they gazed up at the sentinel trunks while shivering under the watchful stare of knots and holes in the bark that resembled unseeing eyes.

"Why do you like this bridge so much?" Yosef asked after some time. He took a handful of nuts and dried fruit from Ninthalas' cloth bag and shoved them in his mouth, chewing loudly. "It creeps me like I ain't been creeped."

"As I told you, it is one of the holes in history. That is my specialty, you know: to know the lore of the lands."

"Are you a scholar?"

"No, no. I am a News Bearer. Like I said before, I am required to travel to the nations of A'thería. I bear news between the countries, as well as adding to the accounts of recorded time. In times past since the time I first took to this profession with my father, I passed this bridge on my way to Mepdokh. Every time, I would beg my father to stop so I could marvel at its structure and muse over its origin. There is a clear path on the other side that runs from the bridge to the base of the Balkai Mountains—the mountain range you can see in the distance there. According to the historical records, though the terrain has warped and changed over the millennia, that path has remained free of weathering. I know it has to be in use for it to be in such prime condition, but no travellers in this day and age have been said to cross this bridge and take it through the mountains."

"How come no one goes there? Couldn't we just walk over and see where the path goes?"

Ninthalas smiled at him. "Indeed we could, but we would be playing with our lives if we did so. The western arm of the Balkai Mountains are home to tribal folk, nasty creatures who kill whoever trespasses into their land. Few have escaped with their lives."

"I like the story of the evil creatures better than this here bridge," Yosef commented. "At least they move and you can see them. These trees don't do nothing."

"Perhaps so." Ninthalas got up and walked along the bridge.

"Whoa, wait!" Yosef called after him. "What are you doing? Is it safe?"

"'Tis safe, my boy. Do not worry."

He strode to the middle and leaned on the railing. He smiled as he watched Yosef carefully placed one foot in front of the other upon the stone slabs. Eventually, the boy made it to Ninthalas' side and clutched his clothes.

"I told you, you have nothing to fear. I have crossed this bridge on more than one occasion."

He leaned against the railing facing upriver. A breeze beat against his face, the first sign of life—if wind could be considered alive—he had felt since the previous evening. The mangled forms of ghostly bodies drifted to the forefront of his mind, adding to an already growing unease that the bridge emitted.

"You know, I get an uncomfortable sense while I am here, like something terrible happened long ago. It fills me with such sorrow."

"Then why do you bother coming here if it makes you feel bad?"

"My curiosity overpowers my sense of melancholy. Do you feel nothing while you stand beside me?"

Yosef took hold of the vines, staring through the mesh of the railing. "I feel like badness clouding my insides. Like I'm in a cage and the air is cold and my body hurts all over."

Ninthalas didn't answer. Yosef had appalled him, although

this time the True Faithen had some clue as to what the boy was talking about. The malshorthath had taken him, other children and the women from his hometown south. Somehow, the boy had escaped and ended up in Shalom. But how?

Before he could sufficiently mull it over, he heard Kai-Tsúthlen calling. "Ninthalas! Yosef! It is time we moved on!"

"A while longer, brother," Ninthalas called back. He breathed in again, soaking in the thrilling sensation of being on a structure whose hidden secrets drowned his speculations.

"Oh come now, Ninthalas, we have not the time for this."

Tahlen's voice rang after. "Ninthalas, we must press on. Mepdokh awaits us."

"'Tis been half a year since I have had a good look at it."

"Is not one look enough?" Kai-Tsúthlen continued. "You already know its features. Come, I wish to get moving sooner than later."

Sighing, Ninthalas pushed himself away from the railing and began the solemn trek back to land.

"Ninthalas."

He glanced back. Yosef was still staring through the cracks of the railing. The boy's expression had changed, transforming from bewilderment, to shock, then to fear. Before Ninthalas could ask what was wrong, the boy jumped back and dashed to his side, clutching his cloak.

"What is it, my son?"

Son? Where did that word come from?

"Yellow eyes…"

"What?"

"Yellow eyes! The Captor's coming!" He grasped his head and cried out. "The voices again!"

"What? What Captor? Do you mean the Black Assailant?"

"Go away! Leave me alone!" Yosef wailed.

"Yosef, what is wrong?"

Run, run, Líran Shadai…

A wave of shock froze Ninthalas in place. What was that voice? It sounded like his own, but it had an edge to it, like a blade piercing his skin.

He raised his sights to the horizon. Upstream, a ball of dark haze appeared from the direction of Mepdokh.

"What in all A'thería..."

Flee if you will...

Laughter rose in his mind, the sound of his own voice, but it wasn't him laughing. It was someone else, someone speaking into his very soul. Ninthalas looked down. Yosef lay limp in his arms, unconscious.

"Yosef? Yosef!"

His mouth formed the words, but his voice fell short. Silence swept over the bridge, drowning out the sound of the river. Silence that was now laughing at him. Only that shadow of his own tone remained, mocking, chanting.

You shall be mine...and make me whole!

Its laughter flooded his ears. Its words reverberated in his chest. Other voices cried in response, some shrieking, others singing a haunting melody. Ninthalas' chest tightened like a vice clenched his heart. He gasped, failing to catch his breath under the weight of...

What? What was happening to him? He couldn't think, couldn't feel. Life drained from his limbs as if ghostly claws were tearing his soul out of his body. His eyes glazed over, and in the midst of the haze of his mind, two yellow eyes appeared.

Then his world faded to black.

———◉———

CHAPTER FIVE

Flight to the Mountains

"Ninthalas!"

Kai-Tsúthlen ran to the bridge and caught his brother before he fell to the ground. Tahlen wasn't far behind, echoing the same concern as he called Ninthalas' name.

"What is going on?" the Captain asked when he reached their fallen comrades.

Kai-Tsúthlen had no idea. He raised his sights to the horizon where he'd seen the mysterious ball of haze. He and Tahlen had been conversing about the strange aura of the bridge when they noticed the black haze developing on the horizon. Now it was growing larger and as it neared, Kai-Tsúthlen could make out the shape of a horse and rider.

"Mepdokh truly is no more," he said under his breath.

"Then is that the leader of malshorthath? There could be more in his company."

"Which means we cannot flee back to Port Lenhan lest another village be destroyed."

"How about that town across the river?"

"Fethlin? That is a town of brigands and thieves. Should we come nought a fathom's distance from that place, a raiding party would find us, strip us and beat us before escaping with all our provisions."

"Then what do we do?" Tahlen demanded. "The mountains are riddled with skohls. Even I know the accounts of News

Bearers, and yours and Ninthalas' no less."

Just then a raspy voice pierced the air. The bridge creaked and swayed as if succumbing to an unseen weight.

There they are! That brute was right. Now your destiny shall be fulfilled!

Kai-Tsúthlen and Tahlen glanced at each other, then broke into action, carrying their companions back to where the horses waited. Hallas, Fellas, and Tahlen's horse, Jífehl, whinnied and neighed, but didn't run off.

"If our rides are restless, then that is a terrible sign," said Tahlen. "We must choose the lesser of three evils."

Kai-Tsúthlen considered which route to take while they propped Ninthalas up on the horse. The thieving town or Port Lenhan? Or perhaps they should take their chances in the mountains. It was like choosing which method of death he preferred more.

He jumped up behind his brother and waited for Tahlen to fasten Hallas to his own horse. The Captain lifted Yosef into the saddle and mounted up behind.

"The mountains," Kai-Tsúthlen decided.

They sped across the bridge as fast as they were able without their comrades falling off. The unweathered path on the other side led them up over the first hill and up another. At the second hill crest, they stopped and looked back. The rider in black was crossing the bridge.

"He is following us," the Captain noted. "He has no malshorthath in his company. I could very well fight him and win."

"Or lose," Kai-Tsúthlen pointed out. "Let us not forget, my friend, that this leader led an invasion on two villages. He also killed Yosef's father, who was a giant and a worthy foe. You are injured. That dampens our chances of survival."

"This wound is nothing."

"I would rather we not take chances against that *Emkalaf'Morlúrnan*. There is too much risk."

He descended the hill and Tahlen followed. The path wound up the side of the first mountain, the sharp incline forcing their steeds to walk. Dense fog obscured their view. They slogged through it blind until the path disappeared and they were forced to pick their way up the steep slope. Eventually they circled around the mountain and the ground began to descend. Their horses skittered down on uneven rubble. The fog lifted enough for them to see. Unfortunately, that also meant that they could be spotted. Kai-Tsúthlen felt exposed out in solid daylight in such a notorious place. Skohls ahead and the Black Assailant behind. What could be worse? If they were going to evade their enemies, it would take all his cunning to keep them safe.

The slope dipped into a deep ravine. Along its bank a new path appeared that stretched left into a narrow pass through the mountains.

"A skohl route, no doubt," Tahlen guessed.

Kai-Tsúthlen veered right in the opposite direction of the path. Layers of solid stone climbed upwards like a staircase for giants. Fellas strained under the weight of two bodies as it pressed upwards.

"Where are you taking us now?" Tahlen asked. "If we go this way, we will become lost."

"Hardly so, my friend," Kai-Tsúthlen replied. "I aim to press north."

"But that would lead us to—"

"*Lotah 'an Morkh*, I know. Yet it is our best bet. Any clear path will take us to skohls, so I aim to stay clear from them. If we can get to *Lotah 'an Morkh*, we can ride along its border toward Mepdokh and then head across the plains from there."

"Almost wise, Kai-Tsúthlen," Tahlen remarked. "Yet I assume our pursuer has the wit to guess we would veer off trail, and we will leave tracks."

"My friend, you have no idea how many times I have bailed my brother out of situations. When we can find a place to conceal ourselves, you may cover our way as best you can. I trust you know how to do that?"

Tahlen didn't comment.

He led them up another steep slope. On more than one occasion, Fellas tripped up. The horse panted heavily, but Kai-Tsúthlen pushed it beyond its limit. Eventually, the fog returned and he took the opportunity to switch horses. Hallas seemed eager to bear their weight, and bolted forward as soon as Kai-Tsúthlen mounted behind Ninthalas and Tahlen had secured Fellas to his own horse.

"What an energetic steed," Tahlen noted.

"Indeed. He is like Ninthalas. Fellas, however, takes on my personality far more than I give him credit."

Hallas sprang up the slope with ease and zigzagged down the other side. By the time they began climbing again, the land began to grow dark. A new layer of fog obscured their way and inevitably forced them to stop under the cover of a shallow overhang.

Tahlen helped Kai-Tsúthlen lift Ninthalas off the horse. He retrieved the thin blankets they used as bedding and laid them down, then ran off into the night.

Kai-Tsúthlen sat alone with Ninthalas and Yosef, his sword in hand, ready to protect them should anything attack. What had come over the two to overwhelm them enough to faint? Yosef had probably acquired a terrible memory that shocked him into unconsciousness. The reason behind Ninthalas fainting, however, remained a mystery. How frustrating. Kai-Tsúthlen despised things he didn't understand. Mysteries lacked control.

He heard a noise and jumped to his feet, poised to kill. He relaxed when he saw Tahlen appear out of the mist.

"This fog does well to conceal us, yet it is equally a disadvantage. We cannot see anything that might assail us and that rider does not strike me as the type of fellow to belt out a war cry should he find us."

"He did not spot you, I hope."

Tahlen shook his head. "It is hard to tell. I heard no hoof beats. He most certainly has some wit about him. I thought I sensed him on more than one occasion, but it is hard to tell."

"Sense him, now. You do not strike me as one who senses, but perceives."

"Then I *perceive* he has not picked up our trail. I am not like Ninthalas."

Kai-Tsúthlen turned his attention back to his brother. "There are few who are."

"What do you suppose came over them?"

"I cannot tell. It is as if both are succumbing to the power of nightmares."

Shrieks welled up in the night, far off, but close enough to send shivers down Kai-Tsúthlen's spine. Skohls, creatures he'd rather not meet. Kai-Tsúthlen had never seen one. Old accounts spoke of what they looked like, but as for their habitual nature, no one could guess. Did they hunt at night or during the day? How acute were their senses? Worry drowned Kai-Tsúthlen's hopes. For the first time in his career, he questioned whether he was going to return home.

"We will get through this," he declared in opposition to his doubt.

"How optimistic," Tahlen stated.

"We must live. My brother is the blessed of Yahlírin. He will wake up, and Yosef also. We will rid ourselves of that Black Assailant and come out victorious."

"How can you be so sure?"

"I am not. Yet I do know this: the rain may fall on many, whether True Faithen or not, yet Yahlírin protects his children."

He wasn't sure if he even believed his own words, but they did lift his spirits.

"Come back to me, brother. Please, wake up."

The voices never ceased. They wailed, cursing, screaming, reverberating in Ninthalas' eardrums. Eyes glowed in the darkness, blue and green like those of his people, but they were hollow, empty, mournful even. Their sorrow crushed his soul.

"Be still, brethren! Be at peace."

They would not listen. The pain they emanated overpowered any sorrow he had ever known. If he could only break away from them. Yet when he tried to move, his body failed him. His feet became tree trunks whose roots dug into the ground. His hands became withered and worn, and hung like deadweights at his sides. Panic settled in.

Are you afraid, Líran Shadai?

Light burst into the darkness. The voices screeched and fled, taking with them their terrible song. All around Ninthalas was white. He stood suspended in the air, no objects in sight except for one set of eyes, blue and young like his own, yet they held in them the wisdom of the ages. There was a familiarity to them. They harboured the same calculating expression as Kai-Tsúthlen's.

"What are you—or who are you? And where did the other voices go?"

I am Shadai, the eyes replied.

"How is that possible? There are many Shadais."

I am Shadai, it repeated.

"I do not understand."

You do not need to understand. Only know that I am Shadai. Now arise, brother Líran, awake. Your brother worries for you.

"But—"

Go, blessed of Yahlírin. You are free.

Ninthalas shot up, waking to cold—bitter cold. Night had fallen, and a thick fog obscured his surroundings.

"Ninthalas! Are you alright?"

Kai-Tsúthlen knelt by his side, his face ashen and stricken with concern. Ninthalas had rarely seen his brother so upset.

"Breathe, my friend. You are safe."

It was Tahlen speaking. The young Captain knelt next to Kai-Tsúthlen, his aspect almost as grave as his brother's.

"Where…?"

"In the Balkai Mountains, well away from the bridge," Tahlen answered. "Kai-Tsúthlen and I had little time to react when we saw the Black Assailant coming toward us."

"The Black Assailant…chasing us," Ninthalas breathed.

"What happened to you, brother?" Kai-Tsúthlen asked.

Ninthalas recalled the voices, a memory echoing like a far off nightmare.

"There were voices speaking—screaming—but I could not understand them. They were crying out, some in song, some in desperate pleas. Oh, what a wretched song it was! And then…Shadai."

"What do you mean, 'Shadai'? That is who we are."

Ninthalas looked into Kai-Tsúthlen's eyes. He could have sworn he had seen someone else, someone who had called himself Shadai but had the voice and eyes of his brother. But the more he looked at Kai-Tsúthlen, the more he thought that perhaps it had been his brother speaking to him and not some ethereal being.

"Ninthalas?" said Kai-Tsúthlen.

Ninthalas turned away. "I…I have no words. I have no thoughts." He chuckled in spite of his confusion. "Who is Ninthalas Líran if he cannot speak?"

The sound of singing caught his ears. He lifted his head to see Kai-Tsúthlen voicing the lyrics of a well-known hymn.

Oh gracious Yahl
to You I shall
give praise with every breath.
Oh gracious Yahl
I sing a psalm
to declare your holy Name.

Ninthalas smiled and joined in the merry tune.

For You are kind
you ease my mind
so forever I will sing
forever I will sing.

Joy welled up inside him. He jumped to his feet and in a voice that could captivate an audience, he sang to ease his own soul.

Oh dearest Being
to you I sing
for you have blessed me so.
Oh dearest Being
to you I give
the sound of horns in call.

For you are here
forever near
so I will be at peace
so I will be at peace.

"Hush! Keep it down," Tahlen reprimanded.

"Why? Do you not approve of my singing?" He shivered. "*Bai*, am I frigid! Can you not start a fire?"

"Oh yes. Let us start a fire and give away our location to the rider in black, as if your singing would not draw him out of the shadows."

"What do you mean? Is he on our trail?"

"I told you he was chasing us."

"Enough," Kai-Tsúthlen intervened.

They both fell silent and regarded him apologetically.

"Indeed, brother, *Emkalaf Morlúrnan* is in pursuit of us," Kai-Tsúthlen acknowledged in a soft voice. "We saw him coming towards us on the horizon and fled with you and Yosef here to the Balkai Mountains."

"Of course!" Ninthalas exclaimed. He shrunk under Tahlen's frown. "The yellow eyes," he went on, quieter. "I saw them flash in in my mind before my world went dark. I wonder if he has come for Yosef."

"I heard the boy scream 'yellow eyes' and 'the Captor' before you both fainted," said Kai-Tsúthlen.

"Where is he?" Ninthalas looked around frantically, only to find the boy by his feet. He knelt down and brushed Yosef's cheek. "How is he?"

"He seems well, though I am no medic," Kai-Tsúthlen replied.

Suddenly, Yosef sat up, gasping for air, his eyes wide, terrified. Seeing Ninthalas, he dove into the man's arms. Ninthalas fell back and toppled into Kai-Tsúthlen.

"He's gonna kill me!" the boy cried. "Don't let him hurt me, Ninthalas! Don't let the Captor kill me!"

Ninthalas held him close. "Easy, child, easy," he said, stroking Yosef's head. "No one is going to hurt you. You are safe."

Yosef hushed to a whimper, shivering in the frigid air. Tahlen came over and covered him with another blanket.

"How far are we into the mountains?" Ninthalas asked. "Have you spotted any skohls?"

"No," the Captain replied. "Kai-Tsúthlen took us off the path and over rough terrain. When we stopped, I covered our tracks, though it is hard to say how prominent our enemy's skills are in tracking."

"Let us hope he is not so skilled as you," Kai-Tsúthlen commented.

"If it was my brother doing the evading, then I do not think we have anything to fear," Ninthalas added.

He lay his blanket back against a wall of rock and scooted up against it. Yosef came to sit next to him. The boy hadn't spoken once since waking, and the look on his face told Ninthalas he was still living the nightmare. He put an arm around him.

"I feel anger all around," Yosef said.

"How so, my son?" Ninthalas asked. There was that word again: son. Since when did Ninthalas begin thinking of Yosef as his own child?

"I just feel it," the boy went on. "It's the Captor with the yellow eyes. But it's not like he's in one place. It's like he's everywhere at once."

Ninthalas ran his fingers through the boy's hair. "Lay down and get some sleep, my friend. You will need it for tomorrow."

Yosef didn't listen. He sunk as close to Ninthalas as he possibly could.

"He can *feel* anger?" Kai-Tsúthlen questioned in True Faithen.

"He told me that he can feel the ground and hear voices," Ninthalas explained.

"How peculiar." He smiled.

"What?"

"He is odd like you."

Ninthalas looked down at Yosef. The boy was beginning to doze again, probably exhausted from the weight of the dream.

"I suppose he is," Ninthalas said with a grin.

———◈———

CHAPTER SIX

The Captor

The next morning, the company set off into a gloomy world of grey. Yosef shivered in the freezing air. He was already wearing several layers and even had a wool blanket pinned over his shoulders to keep warm, but they did little to suppress the cold. Throughout the day, the company experienced all kinds of unpleasant weather: wind, rain, and sleet, not necessarily in that order. Neither one lasted very long before changing to the next. Yosef hated them all, and he voiced his disapproval on more than one occasion.

He looked at his guardians, the True Faithen men. Kai-Tsúthlen and Tahlen didn't seem as thrilled about their predicament, either, but they took it in better stride. The only one who could be considered to be enjoying himself was Ninthalas, who rode tall and cheerful, ever a story upon his lips of times long since passed. He never seemed to run out of stories, and he never told the same tale twice.

Yet even his mood dampened. While they tread upon a particular incline of uneven ground, his horse tripped, sending both of them toppling over. Yosef would have landed on the ground had Ninthalas not cradled him.

Kai-Tsúthlen sprung to his brother's side, helping both him and Yosef to their feet.

"Are you alright, brother?" he asked, speaking in Common.

"I am fine, 'tis fine," Ninthalas replied, rubbing behind his shoulder and stretching.

"You pathetic liar."

"Yosef, are you hurt?"

Yosef shook his head.

"How is Hallas?"

The horse strutted forward at the sound of its name, limping toward its master. Ninthalas checked its ankle. There were no signs of aggravation, but he figured it might show with the increasing stress of ascent.

"The poor fellow," he said.

"Is he alright?" Yosef asked.

"It is hard to tell, though I would oppose to riding him to prevent further injury."

"If you go on foot, you will slow us down and that Black Assailant will catch up to us," said Kai-Tsúthlen.

"I am surprised he has not overtaken us already," Tahlen remarked. "If I were in pursuit of you two at this speed, I might have caught up to you and assailed you. In any case, we must keep moving. Hand me some of your things, Ninthalas, and Kai-Tsúthlen will take the rest. Our pace is not fast. I could run alongside you."

Kai-Tsúthlen shot the Captain an incredulous look. "You cannot be serious."

"Do you not know who I am, Kai-Tsúthlen Okran? Am I not a Captain of the Denedrúath?"

"I will not argue," Ninthalas commented, taking Yosef by the hand.

Tahlen hopped to the ground and began helping Kai-Tsúthlen distribute the supplies while Ninthalas got Yosef onto the chestnut coloured horse. Soon they were moving again, the twins steering their steeds up the mountain and Tahlen leading Hallas by the reigns behind.

Yosef couldn't take his eyes off the Captain. He hadn't thought much of Tahlen before, but now he marvelled at how well he could keep up alongside the horses. And he never seemed to get tired. He didn't complain either, which made Yosef's fascination with the Captain change to admiration. Yosef decided to mimic that acceptance of circumstances, so he refused to complain about the cold for the remainder of the day. Of course, he did squirm, shift and make grunting noises because his body ached from riding. The day waned without any alleviation from the fog and night descended faster than Yosef could think. By this point, he sat frozen in the saddle, and when the company stopped to rest within the confines of a crevice in the mountainside, he weakly slid down. Tahlen, still showing no signs of fatigue, caught him before he fell to the ground.

"We need a fire tonight," said Ninthalas, rubbing his arms.

"And risk being found?" the Captain challenged.

"I would rather risk it than freeze. Come now, our little friend needs to warm up."

"I agree," Kai-Tsúthlen added.

Tahlen reluctantly went about gathering what damp twigs he could find. He stood the sticks upright in the middle of the crevice, stuffed some parchment in the middle, and began working with the flint. Through much effort, the Captain got a flame flickering, though it did little to warm them. Yosef watched him quizzically.

"It seems our little companion has an interest in the doings of accomplished folk," Ninthalas commented. He sat leaning against a sheer cliff.

"Well yeah," said Yosef.

"And he speaks for himself," Kai-Tsúthlen added. "I am impressed."

"Oh brother, if you could only know. Our boy is one for words."

Yosef frowned at them. "I was just wondering how he did it, is all. Like how'd he do that when it's so cold?"

"Tahlen is a man of solid talent."

Yosef wrinkled his nose, making the Shadai twins laugh. He even got a chuckle from Tahlen.

"Solid talent? What's that mean?" Yosef asked.

"Ah, it could mean many things," Ninthalas mused.

"You make no sense."

"Brother, you do realize you are speaking to a child, do you not? Although, he is right that you are incomprehensible," said Kai-Tsúthlen. "My apologies, Yosef, but my brother has little sense. Even I cannot understand him at times."

"You are one to talk," Ninthalas returned with a wide grin.

Tahlen raised a hand. "Quiet!"

The other three fell silent. Tahlen darted to the edge of the crevice, listening and watching.

"What is it?" Kai-Tsúthlen asked.

He shot Ninthalas a wary glance and grabbed his sword. Ninthalas retrieved his own and stood protectively in front of Yosef.

That was when Yosef felt it: the silence and the tingling sensation running up and down his spine. He couldn't focus enough to pinpoint where the source of the sensation was coming from, but he knew that something, or some *things*, were crouching in the shadows.

Screeching voices erupted in the night sky. Small grey monsters, barely visible in the flickering flame of the campfire, jumped out at them from all sides. Tahlen dropped down just in time to miss a spear to the head.

"Get down!" he yelled.

He withdrew his swords, killing two of the monsters with swift, efficient strokes. Three more fell before he shouted again at the twins.

"Get out of here! I can handle this!"

Too late. Scores more joined the attack. The creatures surrounded Ninthalas and Yosef. Kai-Tsúthlen fought to his brother's side. Ninthalas finally drew his sword and flung it in swooping arcs. The creatures soon had the Shadais pinned to the ground. Tahlen dashed into the mix, thrusting his sword into the back of a monster that was holding Kai-Tsúthlen down. Ninthalas suffered the blows of several claws.

Yosef remained where he was, fear preventing him from taking action. The creatures took no notice of him, as if he wore a garment of invisibility that left them blind to him. His blood boiled. He was no fighter, but he had to save them! He spotted a stick poking out of the embers of the fire. It wasn't a sword but it would hurt. He ran and grabbed it, then rushed at Ninthalas' attackers. He thrust the stick into one of the creature's sides, catching it completely off guard. It screeched and rolled away. Then he dove into another, slamming into it and knocking it over. They rolled around on the ground, grappling with each other. Yosef pushed and punched, trying to fend the creature off, but the monster was stronger than he was. It wrestled him onto his back,

pinning him with its weight. Something hard struck him in the head and everything went black.

When Yosef woke up, his head pulsed with an excruciating ache that blurred his vision. A cacophony of muffled cries penetrated his eardrums. When he could focus long enough, he found himself draped over the shoulder of one of the grey creatures. An entire tribe of the freakish monsters, wrinkly, dry-skinned half-people as dull as the mountain terrain, filled every inch of what he could perceive over his pulsing headache.

"Ninthalas!" he called.

Only muffled sounds escaped his mouth. The monsters had gagged him and tied his wrists and ankles.

His captor carried him through the crowd and tossed him next to a massive bonfire. Beside it, another smaller fire yielded a pot of bubbling brew whose aroma made him sick. Yosef could easily fit inside the pot, and judging by the hungry expressions on the monsters' faces, they were probably going to cook him.

"Ninthalas! Tahlen!" he cried again through muffled sounds.

It was no use. His companions were gone. But they couldn't be! Yosef remembered how Tahlen had run strong and unwavering alongside the horses. The Captain wouldn't let the others suffer. They probably got away safely and were searching for him. Yosef was sure of it. The True Faithens would come rescue him.

The monsters ceased chanting. There was a dispute going on. Two of the creatures, each wearing head ornaments of bones and dried twigs, were arguing. They might be leaders of the group, but Yosef didn't really know. Five others wore similar headdresses, though they said nothing as the first two quarrelled. What they were disputing Yosef couldn't tell. Their speech sounded more like water-gurgling sounds mixed with lazy morning groans made by drowning animals than a real language. Or at least that was how he would have put it if he had to describe it to Ninthalas.

Wouldn't the True Faithens come save him?

The argument ended and all eyes turned to him. Yosef's tingling sense escalated and his hope for rescue vanished. His insides churned as fear consumed him. Without warning, the headdress-clad monsters leaped on top of him. One sunk its teeth into his arm. The other bit his leg. Yosef screamed as pain shot through his limbs. He kicked and flailed, trying to get the creatures off, yet there was only so much he could do with bound wrists and ankles.

"Ninthalas!"

Screeches wailed, and the grey creatures scurried away. Yosef gasped as chaos exploded in the crowd. Monsters scrambled in every direction, only to meet a ruthless blade. Black wisps blurred the sight of a figure clothed in black. Its sword flashed and hacked. Not one monster escaped. Before Yosef could process what was going on, every creature lay slain, and only he and the figure remained. He'd been saved. Unfortunately, his rescuer wasn't exactly the kind of saviour he had hoped for.

The Captor wiped his blade with his cloak in a fluid motion, face expressionless, his skin pale like a corpse come to life and long black hair tied high on his head. Haunting yellow eyes looked down at him, his nightmare come to life.

"How fortunate that our paths cross again, boy." His voice was two-part, one a beautiful melody, the other a raspy, grating croak.

His voice? The more Yosef looked at the Captor, the less masculine he seemed. His jaw was less angular, more delicate. His yellow irises yielded faint strands of green that softened his fierce countenance. Even the shape of his lean body yielded contours unlike a man's. This was no man, Yosef realized, but a woman.

The Captor knelt by his side and cut his gag loose.

"You!" Yosef exclaimed. "Yellow eyes. Who are you?"

The woman regarded him quizzically. "Do you not remember?" She paused for a moment, then added, "Ah, yes. She would have taken the memories from you. You would not remember me, save for my eyes."

"Who's 'she'?" Yosef asked.

"You would not recall her either. She has taken memories from me at times, though I fortunately have the honour of knowing who she is. I have not the slightest idea how you escaped, and that is reason enough to believe she was involved."

Yosef didn't care. He squirmed, trying to break free. "Ninthalas, help!"

She cupped her hand over his mouth. "Quiet, boy! I cannot have you crying out in a place such as this."

Retrieving a knife, she tore off two pieces of the cloak he wore draped over his shoulders. One piece she wrapped around his bloodied arm and the other around his leg. Yosef winced, but held strong. He had to find a way to escape.

As if answering his thoughts, the Captor cut his bonds. On instinct, Yosef bolted. He didn't get very far before she caught him.

"Let me go! Ow!"

"Be still."

"Never! You killed my da! Ninthalas! Tahlen! Kai-Tsúthlen!"

The Captor covered his mouth again. Yosef struggled to no avail. Eventually, he settled down, tears pouring out of his eyes.

"My master told me about the Shadai twins, yet he said nothing about them being in the company of the child prodigy Lothlúrin," the Captor stated.

She loosened her hold. This time, Yosef didn't run away. He knew he wouldn't be able to get away from her.

"*Dahlela*, we must leave." She rose and began walking away. Yosef didn't move.

"I said 'come'," she spat. "Can you not perceive the context of my speech enough to guess that I want you to follow? Such a clueless boy I have tried myself with."

"Why me then?"

She spun on her heels to face him.

"Why me?" He repeated. "Why bother with me? I'm just a boy."

She slowly shook her head. "Oh no, Yosef Mathíus, you are not *just* a boy. You are *korme'khím*, a mountain dweller, and a very special one. You are far more dangerous to my master's purpose than you know."

Yosef was about to speak, but another cut him off.

He is here.

It was the second part of her two-part voice. It echoed among the hills, penetrating the chilly air. Silence fell across the open circle. Nothing but the wind hallowing among the mountains could be heard, but even that Yosef didn't take heed to. He was focussed on a feeling of dread hanging like a lump in his gut, the sense that made him woefully aware of the Captor's presence. That sense was growing stronger. Yosef clenched his fists as emotions of confusion and dread twisted into malcontent. He had a desire to hit something—anything—like the slain bodies lying on the ground.

They are both here, the voice went on. *You can finish them both once and for all, to seal your fate for eternity.*

"I cannot end them yet," the woman spoke back, her voice more the woman's tone than the raspy one.

You can. You are able. Did you not just slay a community of skohls?

"I said I will not engage them. The child prodigy Lothlúrin is in their company."

Yosef gasped. Wasn't that Tahlen's last name? That meant they were close. Did the creepy second voice of the Captor have the sense, too?

Her focus turned back to Yosef, indicating the conversation was short-lived. "Come. We can evade them if we leave now."

"No," Yosef declared, firmly planting his feet.

He didn't have a choice. She was on him faster than he could blink, binding his hands behind his back. Yosef squirmed.

"No! Tahlen, I'm here! Help!"

The Captor gagged him and marched him off, leaving the bloodbath of slain bodies behind. When they cleared the skohls' feast arena and circled around the mountainside, the darkness of night enveloped them. Unable to see, Yosef couldn't help but trip every few steps. If it hadn't been for the Captor's steady hand, he would have fallen.

A bellowing roar sounded nearby. Yosef shuddered under a tremor of terror. He tried to turn and run, but the Captor pushed him forward. It wasn't long before they saw the source of the cry. It came from a black horse—if he could call it that—that had been twisted into a foul vessel of evil. Its red eyes and fierce demeanour vanquished any ounce of confidence and hope Yosef clung to.

The Captor removed the gag, grabbed Yosef's collar and hauled him up onto the beast, nearly strangling him in the process. He choked as he flopped into the saddle. The mighty steed shook beneath him, pounding its hoofs on the ground.

"What is this thing?" he asked, quivering. "It's too evil-like to be a horse."

"There are some things better left unnamed," the Captor replied, hopping up behind him. "For if they were named, they would become too terrible to bear even their riders. Such words hold that kind of power, power to encourage or destroy."

Yosef didn't get it, but he didn't really care. All he knew was that he was in the hands of a nasty person and he wanted to escape. He heaved a sigh, slumping his shoulders forward. There was no getting away, not like the last time. Although he couldn't remember the last time. He just knew he'd escaped because of a 'she' who had the power to take memories away. He wanted those memories back. Whoever 'she' was, he was going to find her and demand she return them.

"Be still," the Captor told him.

Yosef didn't realize he was fidgeting.

"Where are you taking me?" he asked.

"To *Lotah 'an Morkh*."

"Where's that?"

"You will see when we arrive, and I most certainly guarantee you will not like it."

"Why?"

"Those who venture in seldom venture out. A sleepless mass lives there, a haunting ever to linger in the shadows. They hunger for the living, eager to suck them dry. And the one who brought about its demise periodically feeds it wrath and malice, making it ever the more dangerous."

Yosef didn't understand entirely, but he didn't want to. It sounded creepy, and he could pick up just how frightening the place was—whatever it was—from the raspy tone of her two-part voice.

"I still don't know your name," he said.

"You need not know it."

"Then what am I supposed to call you?"

She hesitated before answering. "The Black Assailant will do."

"But that's not a real name."

"Then you may call me *Emkalaf Morlúrnan*."

If you keep speaking to him, you will grow fond of him, the raspy voice cut in.

Yosef shrank in the saddle. He didn't like this raspy voice that spoke without warning.

"You sound concerned," the Captor remarked.

Do not take my comments as pity, the voice scowled.

"Such a shame. I could have sworn I heard heartfelt concern in your tone."

Hardly, wretch!

They quarrelled back and forth, the raspy voice hating and the woman's voice teasing. Yosef sighed. Was he going to have to listen to bickering the whole way to the creepy-sounding place? If only the True Faithens were here. He hoped they would find him.

CHAPTER SEVEN

Pursuit

"Yosef!" Ninthalas called.

The wind howled around their shelter. The surviving skohls were gone, and so was Yosef. They had vanished just as suddenly as they had appeared.

"Oh, that I were a better man so I could have saved him!" Ninthalas cried. Tears blurred his vision.

"You *are* a better man, brother," Kai-Tsúthlen reassured. "We have simply come across ill favour, is all." He put an arm around his twin. There were a few places where his clothing had been torn, but one of his cuts appeared to be deep.

Out of the three of them, Ninthalas had taken the worst beating. He winced from fresh wounds on his arms and legs, as well as a fresh cut on his shoulder. Four grey half-bodies lay at his side. Kai-Tsúthlen had slain more, and Tahlen—well, if it hadn't been for the Captain, Ninthalas would have been dead.

"Skohl filth!" Tahlen cursed, kicking one of the bodies.

Ninthalas watched as his friend paced back and forth. Tahlen hated to lose, despised failure of any kind. Out of the three of them, the Captain was the only one to come out of the squabble unscathed. A number of bodies lay by his feet.

"What do we do now then?" Kai-Tsúthlen asked.

"We go after Yosef!" Ninthalas exclaimed, starting to march off.

Kai-Tsúthlen caught him by the arm.

"Calm now, brother; we must keep our heads. Tahlen, you are the warrior among us. What do you suggest?"

Tahlen turned to toward them, his face wearing the deepest scowl Ninthalas had ever seen on him. "I aim to get revenge, whether you two follow me or not," he replied in a dark tone. "I have enough skill in tracking to find them."

Ninthalas perked up. "We could ride—"

"Our horses have fled, brother."

Ninthalas looked to where their steeds should have been only to find them gone.

"That does put a damper on our situation, especially if we expect to return home," Tahlen said.

"The way home is at least a week off as it is," Kai-Tsúthlen added.

"We will prevail," Ninthalas declared.

Kai-Tsúthlen sighed. "Ever the one to be optimistic, you are."

"Let us go then," said Tahlen.

They grabbed only what was necessary and ran off into the night. For the first time since embarking through the mountains, the sky was clear and the moon and stars bright enough to provide a glowing sheen on the ground. Still, Ninthalas couldn't tell which direction they were headed. He marvelled at Tahlen's skill for noticing the slightest disturbances—an imprint here, a broken twig there, and crushed tufts of grass. Soon they found a skohl path. In places, soft mud yielded small footprints.

"These are fresh," said Tahlen. "Our enemies came this way."

Ninthalas and Kai-Tsúthlen could only nod and follow.

The path curled up a steep slope, eventually becoming wider and well-worn. Other trails converged until the path they were on became a well-worn highway for foot traffic. High ridges rose up on either side of the road, and the odd small cave spoke of skohl dwellings. Those gaping holes were empty. In the distance, they could hear faint chants.

Kai-Tsúthlen grabbed Tahlen's arm. "We need to get off this road."

"Agreed."

Ninthalas pointed toward a nearby ridge. "Look there."

A serious of stairs and rickety ladders climbed up the left side of the ridge.

"Good eyes, my friend," said Tahlen.

They took to the stairs and climbed the ladders up the mountainside. As they went, the cries and jeers ceased. Moments later, shrieks erupted in the air, getting louder. In the gully where the main road pressed on, a few straggling half-men and tiny children scurried by. None took notice of the True Faithens high on the ridge overlooking their flight.

"What in all A'thería," Ninthalas breathed.

"Let us hurry," Tahlen urged.

He sprung ahead while Ninthalas and Kai-Tsúthlen struggled to keep up. Eventually, the ridge plateaued and flat bedrock stretched out before plummeting into a cliff. Tahlen ran to the edge and immediately dropped to the ground on his belly. Ninthalas and Kai-Tsúthlen crept to his side and peered over the edge.

The sight took Ninthalas' breath away. Far below a circular arena provided for a ceremonial setting. Torches lined the ring, and in the middle a large bonfire lit up the whole area. Close by the central fire, a cauldron sat atop another smaller flame. Scores of skohl bodies of family groups consisting of men, women and children littered the entire circle. This was a massacre.

A lump grew in Ninthalas throat and he thought he might convulse. An image of yellow eyes flashed in his mind.

"The Black Assailant," he whispered. "I can…feel him. Such hatred, such anger! He has a wrath so vicious, it would devour me should I let it."

"Even I could not accomplish such a feat," said Tahlen. The look on his face reflected that he, too, couldn't believe what he was seeing. "I caught a glimpse of him."

"And?"

"It was…"

"It was what?"

"…One of our own."

"What do you mean?" Kai-Tsúthlen asked.

"A slender figure with long black hair tied high on his head. He was dressed in black, though every inkling of my perception can guess he was one of our people."

"One of our people?" Ninthalas repeated. His stomach churned again, making him wheezy.

"…I suppose. Though it was only a glimpse. It is hard to tell."

He pointed straight ahead where a far road disappeared behind a bend in two converging mountains. "I saw him go that way. No doubt he has Yosef."

Kai-Tsúthlen scanned the starry sky. "North," he stated.

"But that would mean he is going to *Lotah 'an Morkh*," said Ninthalas. "Is that where he came from?"

"We will not find out by staying here," said Kai-Tsúthlen. He rose, looked around, then strode to the far right. Tahlen darted after him.

Ninthalas lingered at the edge, soaking in the horror of the scene below. Whoever this enemy was, Ninthalas would rather not meet him. Yet Yosef was in the Black Assailant's grasp, and the task of saving him proved daunting. Even with Tahlen in their company, how were they supposed to engage such a ruthless soul who could slaughter almost an entire tribe of skohls?

He joined his companions down the mountain and crossed the grisly death scene to the road Tahlen had seen the Black Assailant go. Ninthalas' wounds festered and he struggled to keep up to his stronger counterparts. How he wished the horses hadn't run away. Not only would he prefer riding, but Hallas had escaped with his medicine bag. Without proper cleaning and treatment, his cuts would surely fester. Not like he had much left. If Ninthalas found a spring, he could use the fresh water instead and save the ointments for when they found Yosef.

If they found Yosef.

The day wore on and the skohl road faded to a narrow trail, then ultimately disappeared. Tahlen crouched to the ground while the Ninthalas and Kai-Tsúthlen collapsed on the ground, heaving gasps of air.

"There is no sign of them," the Captain said at length. "I noticed since we left the skohl village, but it seems they have vanished altogether."

"That is impossible," Kai-Tsúthlen said through gasps of air. "There is no way they could have gone anywhere without making tracks."

"Yet there are none," Tahlen stated. "My only guess is that he is taking Yosef Mathíus to *Lotah 'an Morkh*."

"Going to its border was my original plan to evade him," said

Kai-Tsúthlen. "Yet I do not think they would not survive in that place. It is too dangerous for any living thing."

"If *Emkalaf'Morlúrnan* is too dangerous for us, perhaps he can survive," said Ninthalas. "I am mostly worried for Yosef. How long do you think it would take us to get there?"

"Since we lost the horses, I imagine another two days," Tahlen replied. He crouched beside them. "I cannot believe we were outwitted by that fiend."

"I can," said Ninthalas. "I can only imagine what he plans to do with Yosef."

Kai-Tsúthlen put his hand on his brother's shoulder. "Do not think about it."

"I cannot help it, brother. I care for him."

"It was a terrible idea to begin with coming to the mountains," said Tahlen.

"We must prevail," Kai-Tsúthlen declared. "Come now, Ninthalas, where is your enthusiasm? Who is the chief adventurer of our country and ponderer of all things past and present?"

"I suppose you are right." He stood. "Let us press on while we can, then. My strength wains, but my determination keeps me going. If I can find a stream to clean my wounds, then I will be able to go quicker."

The other two nodded and all three continued on.

They did find a stream, and when Ninthalas had treated his own wounds and those of his brother, the companions trekked as far as they were able before fatigue settled in, forcing them to rest for the night. In the morning, Ninthalas woke up damp and shivering, light rain dressing him with cold. The wind pierced his cloak and sunk into his bones.

Tahlen was already up.

"I scanned the area just before you woke," the Captain said. "There is an old skohl trail leading north. I am not sure where it leads, but it is the direction we are headed and an easier way to take than trying the rugged mountainside."

They heard Kai-Tsúthlen groan.

"Good morning, brother!" Ninthalas greeted. "Did you enjoy your long rest?"

"Ninthalas, allow me time to wake up before you speak to me, if you please," Kai-Tsúthlen grumbled, sitting up.

"Are you always in such a foul mood in the morning, my friend?" Tahlen asked. "I do not recall you ever being this way."

"Nor have you heard him snore, Tahlen," Ninthalas remarked.

"Enough," Kai-Tsúthlen snapped, irritably. "Now which way are we to take this morning? I would very much like to be done with this silly quest and be rid of its uncertainties."

Tahlen pointed north toward a wall of thick fog.

"Let us be off, then."

They rose, stretched, and set off. At dusk of the second day of travelling, hope of finding Yosef dwindled. Ninthalas' mood sank as the light of day faded and thick darkness prevented them from going on. As he lay down to rest, he said a prayer for Yosef. If they didn't make it out alive, he hoped Yahlírin would at least deliver the boy from evil hands. His stomach growled, reminding him he hadn't eaten much in the past two days, and his limbs had long since gone numb from both the cold and physical activity. Drowsiness settled in.

On the brink of deep sleep, he thought he heard footsteps, but his fatigue was far too complete for him to discover if his senses were true.

How in despair you are, brother Líran.

Kai-Tsúthlen's voice rang in Ninthalas' ears as much as it resonated in his soul. White surrounded him again, and he stood suspended in it like a ghost. The man from his previous dream stood before him. Other than his silver hair and glowing complexion, he was the spitting image of Kai-Tsúthlen. Perhaps it was him. When Ninthalas had seen his cousin Lamnek die in a dream, he had also seen him shimmering in life with hair like the sun and splendour like a king. Perhaps this was what would become of Kai-Tsúthlen when he descended into Shíol at the end of his life and ultimately passed into Yahlírin's Realm.

"Indeed, I am in despair, Kai-Tsúthlen," he replied.

The silver-haired Kai-Tsúthlen chuckled. How unlike him.

Do you not remember from before? I am not Kai-Tsúthlen Okran. I am Shadai.

"Yet you have the appearance of my brother."

Yet you know I am not him.

He spoke the truth. This man spoke to Ninthalas like a father speaks to his son.

"So you are Shadai. Which branch of the family are you from? Are you from Leithen?"

Leithen! Oh brother Líran, can you not tell by looking at me that I am not? I came before.

"Before when?"

The silver-haired man shook his head. *Someday soon you may come to understand. Such a destiny you are to fulfill, oh blessed of Yahlírin.*

"Would you tell me what it is? I cannot stand this situation I am in. Please tell me it is great, that I might become a great warrior such as Namthúl, my ancestor."

Some wars are not fought with swords, brother Líran.

"Then what good am I?"

Far greater than you know.

"I do not understand."

Awake. Let your thoughts be of life. You will need courage if you are to brave Lotah 'an Morkh.

"Lotah 'an Morkh!" Ninthalas exclaimed.

He shot up. He was met with the same dreary atmosphere he had fallen asleep in. Dawn crept over the peaks high above and mist clung to the ground. Tahlen and Kai-Tsúthlen lay beside him, still asleep.

Rise and eat, oh faithful man of courage.

"Shadai?"

In the place where someone should have been, he saw a cloth laid out adorned with bread, fruit and water. He stared wide-eyed at the food. Was he still dreaming? No, he couldn't have been. The brisk chill was a sound sign that he was indeed awake.

He shook his companions. "Kai-Tsúthlen! Tahlen! Wake up!"

They groaned as consciousness pulled them out of sleep.

"Look at the meal Yahlírin provided for us!" Ninthalas exclaimed.

They sat up and immediately their eyes widened at the sight of food.

"How…?" Kai-Tsúthlen breathed.

"Even if someone came to our aid, they could not have brought a feast like this into the mountains," Tahlen said.

Ninthalas picked up the bread and took a bite. "It is real. Let us eat before we overthink this blessing and it disappears."

They devoured the food with no amount of finesse. Aside from the bread, the meal tasted like home, yet was as rich and flavourful as a feast. Ninthalas' strength returned and he leapt to his feet when every last crumb was gone, ready to embark. Today was the day, he knew. He would save Yosef and bring him to Serenestí.

A noise shattered his vigour. Tahlen swerved, reaching for his sword. Kai-Tsúthlen had his half unsheathed when the beasts emerged from a sharp bend. Ninthalas' excitement returned when he saw Hallas, Fellas and Tahlen's horse.

"How is this possible?" Tahlen whispered.

"Praise Yahl! They are safe!" Ninthalas exclaimed. He went to the leader of the pack, his own horse, and checked its ankle.

"No swelling or aggravation of any kind. You are in far better condition than me now, dear friend." He patted Hallas' neck.

Kai-Tsúthlen went to his own steed. "Our packs are with them as well. Whoever rallied them must have known we had left our supplies behind."

"How convenient," said Tahlen. He scanned the terrain, but the landscape was bare.

"It is as if the hand of Yahlírin is upon us," said Ninthalas.

"Truly a miracle," Kai-Tsúthlen agreed. "With our steeds healthy, we may be able to catch *Emkalaf'Morlúrnan*."

Ninthalas sprang to grab the blanket that had served as a tablecloth for their breakfast. Yet when he lifted it, his enthusiasm waned. A gold broach was fastened to one end.

"What is wrong?" Kai-Tsúthlen asked.

"This is the blanket I gave to Yosef to keep him warm. He wore it pinned around his shoulders."

"Without it, he will freeze," said his brother.

Ninthalas hoped not.

CHAPTER EIGHT

Lotah 'an Morkh

Ninthalas couldn't be more grateful for the horses' return. It made the travelling much easier. Hallas energetically took the lead, steering them up and down the slopes with ease. Ninthalas could barely control him, but something told him he shouldn't bother trying. Hallas seemed to know exactly where he was taking them.

Ninthalas twisted in his saddle to see the others. Tahlen followed right behind him and Kai-Tsúthlen took up the rear.

"Do you suppose Hallas is leading us astray?" Ninthalas asked.

"I should think not," Tahlen replied. "He is heading north. That is the direction I would go, although he is doing a much better job than I would have done. I wonder what divine creature he met to become so invigorated and knowledgeable about our course."

Kai-Tsúthlen nodded. "'Tis odd for him to be so lively, for I could fail at any moment. The air is chill, and not only from the temperature."

"That is no trickery of your senses, brother," said Ninthalas. "I sense it as well. *Lotah 'an Morkh* draws near."

The rain let up in late morning and the sky remained overcast when the companions emerged from the last bend between two peaks. Ninthalas breathed a sigh of relief, thankful to be rid of those dreadful peaks. However, the real test of his wits stretched out before him as far as the eye could see, the grey, twisted mass of a haunted wood. They had come to *Lotah 'an Morkh*, the Dead Forest.

Ninthalas breathed in another heaping gasp of air. It hung in his throat instead of filling his lungs. The haunted wood gave off an aura that made it come alive. He could feel it sucking him dry even from high on the mountain. Branches like hungry claws reached out towards him, beckoning him to enter and die.

Despite the unease, Ninthalas found himself intrigued by this ancient beast. Meeting this entity was a dream come true. Like the old bridge, *Lotah 'an Morkh* was a rift in True Faithen history. Nowhere was it written about how it came to be, nor did many who ventured in come out alive. It was said that foul things dwelt in that place. None had ever reported seeing anything unusual, but rumours told of ghosts lurking in the shadows. Others mused great malshorthath cities thrived within. Ninthalas speculated that it was once an extension of *Lotah 'an Lí*, Forest of Life, also a mystery, which bordered the western quarter of the Balkai Mountain Belt. Yet he could not tell how or why this forest died while the other flourished.

"I do not like this place at all," said Tahlen. "It is too silent, too empty."

"Perhaps not empty enough," Ninthalas said in a hushed tone. He leaned over his saddle and listened. A faint hum of whispers, the same he had heard when he had fainted days past, hung on his eardrums. He peered up into the leafless, tangled mass, searching for what the voices might belong to. Yet he saw nothing.

Tahlen broke his concentration. "How so?"

"A sleepless terror lives here, or so legends tell," Ninthalas replied.

"You most certainly cannot believe in such myths, brother," Kai-Tsúthlen remarked.

"Myth or truth, I wonder…" Ninthalas whispered. Here was a place he had only dreamed of exploring, though he also valued his life. To live not knowing or die a curious traveller? He couldn't decide which would be more fulfilling.

"Let us go around it," said Tahlen. He kicked his horse's flanks and took position at the head of the team. "There is not much of a way along its border, but I prefer taking time rather than passing through that place."

"What if *Emkalaf Morlúrnan* took Yosef into the wood?" Ninthalas asked.

Tahlen scoffed. "I highly doubt that. That foe was as alive as we are from what I could make of him."

"I am not so sure..."

"I agree with Tahlen," said Kai-Tsúthlen. "Let us go around. That was my original intention, after all."

He and Tahlen strode forward. Ninthalas took up the rear, ever watchful of the neighbouring wood. He searched between the trees for anything that could be deemed unnatural besides what his senses could tell. His mind reeled over scholars' hypotheses of how *Lotah 'an Morkh* came to be. Most musings of ancient scholars were outright silly, but the one that Ninthalas believed had some truth to it was that the only thing that could drain life out of the wood had to be one of the Great Three. These were the great god-like malshorthath of old, their names so terrible, most True Faithens only spoke of their rank. Ninthalas and Kai-Tsúthlen spoke freely of the Third, Dethshaiken. The other two, not so much. There was the Second, who was said to be a hate-filled spirit that could possess up to five men at once. He had assisted Dethshaiken in the Great War. The First, however, was far more mysterious. Scriptures described him as "the harbinger of death" or "the one who wrought death". Nothing more. The First was not present in the War of the First Age. Some people questioned if he really existed.

"Yet he truly must exist," Ninthalas whispered to himself. "Why else would the Scriptures speak of him? Namthúl Shadai knew of his existence and mentioned him, if only briefly. Perhaps he was once a person who turned sour."

Well, that is not far from the truth, my friend.

Startled, Ninthalas looked around. That voice sounded clear enough to be real, and all too familiar. Kai-Tsúthlen's voice? No, the sound spoke into his heart as well as his ears.

To think a fellow Shadai would cross this way once again as in the elder days of chaos. I might consider myself surprised to find there are those who still bear the ancient name, though I remember Namthúl was called and flourished. And here he is, Lí himself, the blessed of Yahlírin, returned to us.

Ninthalas scanned the tree line and gasped, rearing his horse to a halt. In the midst of the trees looking back at him was the silver-haired man from his dreams. Yet he saw him now in his waking moments. How could that be? Ninthalas turned to his companions. They were further ahead now, but seeing them confirmed that he really wasn't dreaming.

He turned back to the tree line. The silver-haired man was smiling at him. *Not a dream, brother Líran*, the man said. *Indeed, I am very much alive.*

"Ninthalas!"

He looked to see Kai-Tsúthlen and Tahlen. They had stopped up ahead.

"What is the matter now?" Kai-Tsúthlen demanded. "Please do not tell me the voices have come back and I will have to carry you again. That is one horror I do not wish to witness twice-fold."

Ninthalas stared at them a while, then looked back to the forest. The silver-haired man was gone. *Not a dream.* Was the silver-haired man a spirit of the forest? To live in such a twisted wood, perhaps this Shadai was evil in disguise seeking to lure Ninthalas into the forest.

He shuddered and hurried to his companions.

They rode east along the foothills of the Balkai Mountains, staying well clear of the forest border. The overcast sky never cleared. Ninthalas couldn't be sure what time of day it was. Even the sun which would normally give off a soft glow couldn't be seen.

The obscure time of day wasn't their only setback. The land dipped and curved, and finally rose in a steady incline until they rounded a sharp bend, only to discover a high ledge overlooking a sheer cliff. On their right, an impassable rock wall blocked them from climbing higher. Before them, filling in the gap between a massive crevice and the next mountain, the treetops crept so close, they could reach out and touch them.

Kai-Tsúthlen stared at the trees, his face wearing a frown. Tahlen clenched his teeth. Ninthalas' spirits plummeted. There was no way around.

Ninthalas brought his horse alongside Tahlen's. If he sat up straight, he could see out over the treetops.

"This must be the long narrow arm of the forest that stretches east," he said. "It is still quite a distance, but we could cross it in one day, I believe."

"It is past high sun. We will not make it out of the forest by nightfall," Tahlen said. "We should backtrack and find a place to rest, then pass through the forest in the morning."

"Have you forgotten our quest?" Ninthalas protested. "Every moment we waste here, Yosef delves deeper into the wood in the hands of evil. One night may mean his last."

"Ninthalas, we do not even know if he is still alive."

"He is! I know it!"

Tahlen through up his hands. "Fine, fine."

"That forest frightens me," said Kai-Tsúthlen. "Yet imagine how much more scared Yosef must be. We are men of the Faith, men of the sword—"

"Save one," Ninthalas corrected.

"Brother, I get the impression that whatever is in that wood, living or not, does not yield to the sword."

"Then you believe the myths."

"I believe my brother is no lunatic. If we enter, you are the only one who can lead us."

Tahlen frowned. "Why?"

"Because he is the blessed of Yahlírin," Kai-Tsúthlen replied. "He always has been. True, that forest's presence makes us all uneasy, but he has more sense than you and I. My brother will venture where no one else will."

"Yet you are always the one to get me out of trouble should I find it," said Ninthalas.

Tahlen looked between both of them several times, then ultimately heaved a sigh. "Very well, my friend. You get your wish. Let us pass through the forest quickly and get it over and done with. I cannot see the end of this 'narrow' arm as you so call it, but it must have an ending."

Ninthalas breathed in, anticipation filling his lungs. The silver-haired man's words came to his mind.

You will need courage if you are to brave Lotah 'an Morkh.

He had no doubt he could make it through. He would prevail.

Simply penetrating the forest proved to be a daunting task. The brush formed an impassible wall of shrubbery along the forest border that Ninthalas hadn't noticed before.

"Does this wood even want us to enter?" Tahlen questioned.

"I will find a way in," Ninthalas declared.

He backtracked to where he thought he had seen the silver-haired man, and grinned when he spotted a trail into the grey wood. That grin of triumph was short-lived. As soon as he passed underneath the twisted canopy of interconnecting branches, despair sank into his bones. Whatever meaning "dead" conveyed in the forest's name, it certainly didn't apply to *Lotah 'an Morkh*. Ninthalas felt more alive than he had ever felt before. Perhaps it was the lack of life surrounding him that made him so aware of being alive, or perhaps there were yet things lurking in the shadows that watched them traverse the narrow paths. Ninthalas guessed the latter. He couldn't see them, but he could *hear* them. Their whisperings flowed through his ears and soul like a restless river, their language sounding like it had once been True Faithen, but the words had become gnarled and twisted over time. What were they saying? Were they talking about him, or were they speaking of times long since past, of days of lush green and sparkling streams crisscrossing underneath a billowing canopy? The now wood seemed frozen in time, stuck in a downward spiral of decay.

"Well, this is not so bad."

"You have got to be kidding me, Ninthalas," said Tahlen.

Ninthalas looked back. The Captain scanned his surroundings, an expression drawn on his face that spoke of paranoia rather than confidence. He batted his arms every now and then as if to swat at some unseen insect prickling his skin.

"Are you alright, my friend?"

"Am I alright. Certainly, if I did not fear for my life."

"How do you fair, brother?" Ninthalas asked.

"Do not speak to me." Kai-Tsúthlen's eyes stared straight ahead at nothing in particular.

"Something is certainly out there," Ninthalas mused. "I wonder what the voices are talking about."

"What voices?" Tahlen asked. "I hear nothing."

"I suppose I am simply going as mad as you two are."

"You seem oddly content with that."

Ninthalas was, although he couldn't tell why. He wouldn't say that he was joyful per se. His resolve was simply set.

He turned his sight back to the trail. Two walls of tangled brush prevented him from going off road. In time, another path crossed his own, coming from the left. Ninthalas' heart tugged left, but his will kept him going straight. Exploration of this wood would have to be for another time. Another time when he was not searching for Yosef.

Hopelessness dawned on Ninthalas as the day began to come to a close. Yosef could be anywhere in this massive forest. He could be dead or worse. Worst case scenarios tumbled through Ninthalas' mind, each one more imaginative and horrifying than the first.

He shook his head. No, he couldn't do this. He had to be strong, to be courageous. But thick blackness descended upon them. He caught a twig in the face and winced.

"Tahlen, a light?"

"If I could see enough to find my flint and stone, Ninthalas," the Captain said in an irritable tone. "This forest is so dry, though, I would not think it wise to start one."

Ninthalas continued moving forward. In the midst of the trees, he caught a glimpse of a faint light glowing a sickly yellowy green.

"What is that?"

"What is what? I see nothing," Tahlen said.

"Look left. Do you see it?"

"No."

"Follow me, then."

"I have a bad feeling about this, brother," said Kai-Tsúthlen.

"Nonsense," Ninthalas declared. "Yahlírin will guide our steps, or that of our steeds."

"We should rest here and continue on in the morning," Kai-Tsúthlen persisted. "What do you say, Tahlen?"

"I hate this forest," the Captain retorted.

"There, see? Tahlen agrees with me," said Ninthalas.

"Tahlen is not himself," Kai-Tsúthlen argued.

"Come now, brother. What have we to fear when Yahlírin is so much greater?"

"This is no adventure over hills and under the trees of Serenestí, Ninthalas. This is *Lotah 'an Morkh*, and should we stray from the path, we will most certainly get lost."

"Did you not say that my sense is as good as any in this forest?"

"Something along those lines."

"Then let us follow the light."

Kai-Tsúthlen heaved a sigh. "Very well. Lead the way."

Ninthalas pushed his steed off the path through a gap in the walls of brush. His horse's hooves crunched loudly on dry twigs. Ninthalas took little notice. His sights were fixed on the glowing light that seemed to elude them. What did the light belong to? Was it a spirit, or perhaps it was the silver-haired man guiding them to safety. On and on he followed it, crossing several paths. After a while, Ninthalas reared his horse to a halt. The light ceased advancing and hovered amidst the trees.

"You know, I am beginning to distrust myself in this endeavour. There is something unnatural about that light."

The other two didn't reply.

"Perhaps we should take one of these paths," he suggested.

No answer.

"Kai-Tsúthlen? Tahlen?"

No one replied.

A jolt of fear ran through his body. Where were they?

"Brother!" he called.

Kai-Tsúthlen didn't answer back.

Flesh, living flesh.

"Who is there?"

His horse whinnied and backed up. Ninthalas struggled to keep it from bolting.

Lost and alone, it is. Feast, let us feast!

A lump formed in Ninthalas' throat. His hands and feet lost their feeling and his breathing fell short. Something was watching him, and Ninthalas didn't think it was alive in the sense of living things.

The murmurings ceased, and the forest fell silent. Ninthalas' vision went cloudy. He couldn't think, only feel. And that feeling was far more dreadful than anything he had ever known. It was the revelation that he was going to die.

Glowing light flashed amidst the trees in front him. They advanced in his direction, illuminating the forest to reveal the dark shapes of trees tainted with shadows. The lights faded in and out from between the great boughs and trunks. Then they emerged, and Ninthalas realized just how much trouble he had gotten himself into. And this time, his brother wasn't there to save him.

They were eyes without bodies, suspended in the air like queer fireflies.

Look what we have found! A feast, a feast!

Ninthalas backed his horse up. "What are you?"

They answered in unison. *What are we? What are you? False Faithen comes in, seeking to be devoured.*

"False Faithen?" Ninthalas repeated. "I am True."

True, False, flesh, living flesh. All the same meal.

"Fly, Hallas!"

The horse sped away. The eyes laughed and flew after. Ninthalas held tight as Hallas bore him as fast as its hooves could gallop. The glow from their pursuers lighted the way. They must be close. He snuck a peek over his shoulder and gasped. The eyes had formed ghostly, translucent bodies. A hungry swarm was swimming after him, gaining ground.

Flesh! Living flesh! Come, let us feast. Let us devour it whole! they screeched.

Hallas gave a sharp cry and jerked to the side, sending Ninthalas flying from the saddle. He landed in a thicket of prickly branches. Thorns tore his clothing.

The souls rushed forward with outstretched arms.

Ninthalas screamed. "Yahlírin!"

The Black Assailant was right. Yosef hated *Lotah 'an Morkh*. A sickening feeling hung in his gut a day before they met it, a loathing sense of despair fell upon him when they stood at its borders, and now in the midst of the grey mass of twisted trees, Yosef wanted nothing more than to curl up into a ball and die. Something—rather some *things* were watching them, floating through the trees. He couldn't see them, but he knew they were there. His sixth sense had been on overdrive since the skohl attack some nights before that made him aware of the Black Assailant, but now that they were in the forest, the sense overpowered all of his other senses. Even his vision grew slightly blurry.

The only thing Yosef could be grateful for was that the Captor and the raspy voice ceased bickering after the first night he'd spent in her clutches. It came at a cost though. Now the silence under the trees tore at his sanity. Whisperings came and went like a breeze. A cold, lifeless breeze that somehow penetrated his layers of clothing.

He shivered. He regretted 'carelessly' leaving behind the wool cloak Ninthalas had given him, but he needed to let the True Faithens know he was alive. When he had begun to feel the presence of the forest, he had feinted escape and hid it behind an outcropping of rock. The Black Assailant appeared not to have noticed. She probably didn't care if he froze anyway.

A shiver ran through his body again.

"Are you cold?"

Yosef jolted. It had been so quiet.

"Kind of."

She shifted. Moments later, she draped a black cloak over his shoulders.

"Thank you," he muttered.

"You should not have shed your wool blanket for the others to find."

He froze. She had known all along!

"Believe me, I would have retrieved it," she added, "only I was prevented, held back. Shadai is hunting me."

"Shadai? You mean Ninthalas and Kai-Tsúthlen?"

The woman chuckled, a laugh that had the opposite effect as Ninthalas' high-pitched voice.

"No, it is not those two. They are no threat to me like this one is. He is the most feared of the Enemy according to the malshorthath, a supreme meddler who never fails to upset my Master's plans. Oh, how my Master despises him! It is rather entertaining, actually."

"Doesn't sound that entertaining to me. Why do you serve him? Sounds like you don't even like him."

"It is a complicated relationship."

The raspy voice filled the air again. It had long since resorted to speaking in that other language rather than conversing in Common. Good riddance. Yosef hated the voice anyway.

"Well, he has certainly proven he is capable of *something*," the Black Assailant replied. She always answered in Common whenever the voice tried to switch the conversation to the foreign language. "How can I be capable of anything when I can't even get away from you?" said Yosef. "Can't trick you nothin' neither. You knew about the cloak."

"A child after my own heart. You will make a fine malshorth."

"Malshorth? Me? No way, I ain't gonna be no malshorth creature." He heaved a sigh. "I hope that Shadai person saves me and brings me back to Ninthalas."

"I highly doubt they will even be alive should you find them. When they come in, they will never come out again. You and I may show resilience to the effect of *Lotah 'an Morkh*, but a True Faithen will suffer greatly."

"No way!"

"You do not believe me? Have you not felt the presence of the undead ones? They watch our every move, eager to 'suck us dry', as they say. They haunt this wood, the dead do, wretched souls forever trapped within its borders, twisted with as much hate and madness as the trees. Even now, I hear them whispering, 'Flesh, living flesh!' as we ride by—you can as well—and it is only that which is in me that keeps them at bay. Yet there is nothing keeping them from devouring your friends. They will die."

Yosef didn't believe her, not after having spent time with the True Faithens. Tahlen was strong enough to get them out because he was the best fighter. Ninthalas had the most sense and a cheerful attitude that didn't waiver. Yosef wasn't sure what Kai-Tsúthlen was good at, but the man's seriousness had to account for something. They would find him and rescue him, and everyone would escape from the haunted wood together. Yosef included. Surely they would come.

Yet they never did. Yosef's hopes plummeted as the sun set and night swept over the forest.

The beast they rode stopped in a small clearing where tufts of dead grass sprouted through hard, compact dirt. The Black Assailant dismounted and helped Yosef down. Yosef didn't try to run. Being held captive was far better than traversing the forest alone.

As his eyes adjusted to the darkness, he saw greenish yellow lights glittering in the deep shadows. Eyes. Yosef knew what the voices belonged to now. He hadn't seen them in daylight, but now they appeared in full view. Yet they didn't come into the small clearing. The Black Assailant was right. Whatever was inside her held them back.

The Captor proceeded to hack dry limbs from the surrounding shrubbery. Moments later, she had kindled a fire with as much skill as Tahlen. Yosef studied her. She wore tight black clothing. A fitted black leather breast plate pressed against her body, held in place by straps and buckles. Upon her hands she wore leather bracers, and matching shinguards outfitted her legs. Two swords dangled at each side and strapped around her thighs were four daggers.

She met his gaze and he quickly looked away.

"Are you impressed, or merely amused?" she said.

He looked back at her. In the flickering light, he saw tinges of green in her yellow eyes that made her seem a lot less threatening than she made herself out to be.

"You look strong," he said.

"Rightly so. I have been trained in survival and strength of arms. What you see is the result of long days and nights spent fighting for my life."

"Against what?" Yosef asked.

"The malshorthath, of course, as well as the odd wild beast."

"I thought you were on the same team," said Yosef. "Of the malshorthath, I mean."

"Like I said before, it is a complicated relationship."

Yosef didn't understand. He rubbed his arm that had been bitten by the skohl a couple days ago. The Captor had found a spring in the mountains and had cleaned the wounds on his leg and arm as best she could. She said the bites shouldn't succumb to infection, but Yosef had taken a peak at his arm wound every now and then and noticed it getting worse. His arm and leg hurt, too. Constantly.

"Can you tell me a story?" he asked.

She gave him an odd look. "The only stories I know are as twisted as this forest."

"Ninthalas told a lot of stories about Namthúl Shadai and how he defeated the malshorthath."

"He would know of those stories," she said.

"Do you know him?"

She didn't reply. A long pause fell between them before she spoke again. "This clearing was once a glade."

Yosef curled his legs up, listening.

"And this forest was once lush and green, the likes of which few have ever seen. It was much larger then, covering the entire border of the Balkai Mountains. Then a corrupt malshorth infected it with the touch of death. Fearing that the entire forest would be overcome with evil, Shadai commanded the *korme'khím* to clear away the trees in the middle of the forest and raise the ground so the infection could not spread."

The Captor looked up amongst the trees. "My possessor was there. He was one of the ones who the terrible malshorth corrupted with the touch of death."

"You mean the raspy voice?" Yosef asked.

Stop telling him about me, wretch!

Yosef shrank. Whatever the possessor was, he didn't like it.

The Black Assailant ignored the reprimand. "I have dived into his mind several times searching for his memories of the past. I had to delve deep. My possessor is very old."

Enough! the spirit rasped. *Those are MY memories. This wretch of a boy has no need to know them.*

She sighed. "I suppose."

She looked back at Yosef. The green strands in her eyes faded until only one or two were left.

"Indeed, enough about the past. What matters is the present."

"What's the touch of death?" Yosef ventured to ask.

"It is a curse. The first malshorth's curse."

"Who's the first malshorth?"

"My first master. I despise him far more than I despise all the malshorthath combined."

"Then why do you serve him if you hate him so much?"

She stared at him a long while, her face neither inviting nor threatening. The break in conversation dragged and her eyes never blinked. Yosef averted his gaze and glanced back at her several times. Her stare never left him.

She was creeping him out. He closed his eyes to avoid that

scary, ghostly face.

"*Fear,*" the two-part voice hissed.

Yosef opened his eyes again. She was still looking at him. The faint tinges of green were completely gone.

"*I will never forgive him. Never.*"

Yosef's breath caught short. The raspy voice, that possessor, that *thing* inside of her was speaking through her.

"W-what did he do to you?"

She twitched and blinked. The green strands returned to her irises, and her expression showed fatigue.

"Tired again?" she said irritably.

Shadai is close, her possessor noted.

She went to sit by Yosef and put a hand on his shoulder.

"Get some sleep."

Then she curled up beside him and didn't move again.

Yosef lay down. This was the second time she'd slept. That he noticed anyway. He lay down, eyes wide open and in no way ready to sleep. The Black Assailant's body offered no warmth, and the cold kept him awake.

Yosef'an korme'khím.

He sprung upright. That sounded like Ninthalas! Was he here? He searched the trees. Among the eyes, a man stood just outside the clearing. His hair fell silver about his shoulders and his clothing was pure white.

Yosef rubbed his eyes. Was he seeing things? True, his sight was still blurry, but the silver-haired man was definitely there.

Mí dafeth, mortehla.

Drowsiness swept over Yosef. The last thing he saw before his eyes closed was the silver-haired man smiling back at him.

Well, this is some errand you have prepared for me, Yahlírin, the silver-haired man said while looking down at the sleeping pair from the comfort of the trees. *What is your plan with this one, I wonder? I so very much long for the eyes you once blessed me with, eyes that could tell what a person ought to be. Yet you have me here as I am, no less different from a True Faithen. The only difference is this touch of life you have bestowed upon me in return*

for my sight. A fair trade, Father.

He paused, listening for a response. A still, small voice returned.

Perhaps so, he said with a sigh. *Alas, for my dealings with my brother did not end with the infection. What of my sister, who so rashly travels and meddles much more frequent than I?*

Again, the voice spoke to him. He could feel the words surging through his spirit.

I know that all too well, he said. *Well, I will do as you say, for I am Shadai and Shadai never faltered. More so now than before. Now how should I go about doing your will since these children are so scattered and lost?*

He waited.

Them? I suppose they might prove useful, for I have already turned many, though their change be temporary. I beg of you to release them, Yahl, when their good work is done. It grieves me that they remain trapped here, consumed by the torment my brother inflicts upon them.

Another pause.

I am well aware of your sovereign decision. Who am I to question? Alas that it is their choice to disobey, and some fall by the wayside and forever live in this tormenting place. Will my grief never end?

No answer returned.

Very well, he said.

He gathered the eyes that surrounded the camp and brushed his hand over them, speaking to each in turn. The eyes became colder, changing into emerald greens and cobalt blues.

Follow and watch, he told them.

Then he singled out one of the sets, a pair of younger eyes less knowledgeable of history than the others.

For you I have something special planned, for your fate was ill earned. This boy will walk and I want you to lead him until your time is up. I will find him when the need is dire.

With that, he disappeared.

CHAPTER NINE

To Suck Them Dry

Kai-Tsúthlen didn't know when he had lost the other two. He had been solely focused on trying to stay sane. Every breath he exhaled, a part of his soul seemed to latch onto it and leave his body. His skin tickled from nerves firing without reason. He could scream at any moment.

At some point, though, he had snapped back to reality. Something like a breath of wind passed over him, bringing his senses back to life, though they had little to sense save the terrible, dying growth around him. The only sounds he could hear were his horse's crunching steps over the dry underbrush and his loud breathing.

"Ninthalas?"

His brother didn't reply.

Kai-Tsúthlen reared his horse in.

"Tahlen?"

The Captain didn't answer either. He was alone, lost in a web of interwoven, tangled branches. *Lotah 'an Morkh*, the last place in all A'thírin he could ever wish to be lost in.

"Of all things distraught!" he cursed. "I knew this would happen. Yahlírin help us."

Knowing he wouldn't get anywhere by staying still, he kicked his horse forward. Eventually, the branches parted and faint moonlight filtered through the trees, revealing a narrow path. He took it. Where the hulking shape of Tahlen had been in front of him, a hollow tunnel burrowed into black shapes, the moonlight reflecting off of compact dirt.

He breathed in, breathed out. He wouldn't panic. His companions probably couldn't have gone far.

"Ninthalas! Tahlen!"

No answer. He breathed in again and slowly let it out, trying to savour whatever life was still left in his soul before it dissipated altogether. A flood of thoughts swamped his head, each one imagining the worst possible scenarios of what had happened to his brother and friend—No! This was no time to mull over possibilities that probably weren't true. He would find them. He *had* to find them.

He sat up straight and peered around often like a nervous pickpocket. His horse tread like a sleep-walking animal. Time crawled. And his brother and friend never showed.

His series of finicky glances resorted to checking the path behind. A faint glow illuminated the path, following him. He reared his horse in and watched as the glow grew larger. Around a bend in the path, two green eyes drifted towards him, floating in the air like fireflies.

He spun forward. Don't panic.

He kicked his horse into a walk. Was he seeing straight? He snuck another peek over his shoulder. His follower was definitely a set of eyes, but they didn't attack him, nor show any signs that they could be evil. They simply trailed behind, maintaining a distance of a couple arms' lengths away. Every myth or legend Ninthalas had ever told of ghosts of the past, Kai-Tsúthlen now believed them.

A cry echoed afar off. Fellas fought to dart into the brush, but Kai-Tsúthlen pulled hard on the reigns to keep the horse from bolting. Veering off the path would get him more lost than he already was. He needed to keep his head. He had to stay in control.

He looked again behind. The eyes stayed where they were a short distance away.

"What are you doing?" he asked.

What am I doing? Dear boy, I am watching you.

Kai-Tsúthlen turned forward again. He didn't expect the apparition eyes to actually talk.

He looked back. There was no body. Only eyes with irises of

a cool green.

"Why watch me?" he asked it.

I am bidden to.

"By whom?"

The one who sent me, who healed me long enough to ease my desire to suck you dry.

Kai-Tsúthlen pondered for a moment. "How long will the healing last before you desire to 'suck me dry,' as you say? Surely it cannot last forever in this place."

Truly it cannot, the spirit answered. *How long, I wonder?*

"If you are going to watch me, then tell me the way out of here."

I watch and watch alone, it stated.

"To what end?"

Whatever end may come.

Kai-Tsúthlen grumbled and kicked Fellas into a trot. He had to get out of this forest and quickly. The atmosphere was gnawing at his sanity.

Another cry tore through the air, this time from the direction he was headed. He sped forward until he came to a wide clearing. Greenish yellow eyes illuminated compact dirt and withered shrubs, but they weren't the ones screaming. The sound came from a figure lying in the middle.

It wasn't Ninthalas. Kai-Tsúthlen knew his brother's voice.

He jumped from his horse and squeezed through a gap in the glowing eyes—he dared not touch those unnatural things. There in the middle lay Tahlen, screaming and writhing on the ground. His clothes tore as if invisible whips were lashing him, and with every tear, he cried out, twisting and turning at every un-seeable lash.

"Get away! Get away from me!" he screamed.

Kai-Tsúthlen dropped to his side and immediately, the eyes retreated. He grabbed the Captain's shoulders.

"Tahlen! Tahlen Dían!"

Tahlen stopped squirming and lay lifeless on the ground, eyes wide open. Then he gasped, breathing hard, eyes locked staring upwards. Kai-Tsúthlen hovered into his line of sight.

"Kai-Tsúthlen?" the Captain breathed.

Kai-Tsúthlen grabbed his arm and pulled him to sit.

"The eyes..." The Captain shook his head. When he looked at Kai-Tsúthlen again, he wore a dazed expression.

"What was hurting you?" Kai-Tsúthlen asked. "I saw your clothes ripping, yet nothing but these eyes surrounded you, and they were silent."

Tahlen looked down at his garments, feeling through the rips. Though they were torn right through, his skin remained unscathed. Kai-Tsúthlen poked and prodded.

"It burns," Tahlen said, wincing. "Even the pain in my arm fails in comparison. It is like an internal burning. And..."

"And what?"

"The memories, memories of my sister. How I wish I could forget—"

"Do not think about it."

Kai-Tsúthlen looked up at the encircling eyes. The pair that had been following him joined them, its cooler hue a stark comparison to the sickly greenish yellow of the others. The other eyes clumped around it until it appeared like a single monster in itself. Kai-Tsúthlen expected it to attack, but the clump didn't move.

"Have you seen Ninthalas?" he asked Tahlen.

The Captain shook his head. "The eyes, Kai-Tsúthlen. They seek to devour me!"

"We must escape. I see your horse has run off."

"Curses the foul!" Tahlen spat.

"Tahlen Dían, even I feel the effects of this forest, yet it is no reason to swear."

The Captain scowled. Kai-Tsúthlen had seen his friend in ill moods, but none compared to the sneer he wore now. It was *Lotah 'an Morkh*. The best way to make his friend well again was to get him out of the forest.

He helped the Captain to his feet and dragged him over to the horse. Tahlen batted Kai-Tsúthlen's arms away and grunted as he climbed into the saddle.

"Curses, curses," he muttered.

"Calm yourself, my friend. We will get out of here."

The Captain fell silent, his expression lifting slightly, but also changing from frustration to sorrow. "Sister..."

Two lost souls trapped in Lotah 'an Morkh.

Kai-Tsúthlen glared at the one set of cooler eyes.

"It talks?!" Tahlen exclaimed. "The eyes talk!"

"Easy, my friend," Kai-Tsúthlen reassured. He climbed into the saddle behind his friend and steered his horse toward the spirit. "I suggest you use what healing you have left in you and tell us how to leave this place, accursed soul," he declared.

Have I not already said that I merely watch? What will you do if I do not heed your request?

"That I shall let Yahlírin decide. There is no way I will let my brethren die here."

You have great courage, living one.

"I have what courage as I need," he said. "Lead us to my brother and out of this forest."

And what will you do for me should I agree to help you?

"Kindness needs no reward."

The spirit laughed. The eyes floated out of the clump until they hovered directly in front of him. Fellas flinched and Kai-Tsúthlen struggled to keep the horse under control.

And why do you, False Faithen, suppose that I am a being who bestows kindness upon others?

Kai-Tsúthlen's blood boiled. "False Faithen? What Faithen is false but you? You said so yourself that you are healed, and I can tell by your eyes that it has not waned. Healing breeds fruit, of which kindness is one."

Wise fellow you are, the spirit hissed. *Wise and courageous. Very well. Follow if you dare.*

The eyes fell away and the clump followed. They took one of several branching paths out of the clearing and into the maze of trees. The canopy overhead blotted out the moonlight, and the light of the glowing eyes created an eerie atmosphere that drained the life from Kai-Tsúthlen's limbs.

"How is it able to talk to you?" Tahlen asked. "What are they?"

"I did not believe they existed before coming here, though now that I see them, I cannot deny it," Kai-Tsúthlen said softly in his ear. "My brother has mused about them many times—he tells me everything whether I wish to hear it or not. They are spirits of those that once were, he says, the undead who have not been granted access to Yahlírin's heavenly realm. Of course, he cannot fathom what they were before, but his musings proved correct. This one claims to have been temporarily healed, though I do not know for how long the healing will last before it becomes one of them again."

"I never knew such vile things existed," said Tahlen.

"Neither did I. Ninthalas has always been convinced such things do, though the accounts of these spirits were written by enthusiastic outcasts."

"Well, the authorship certainly explains why Ninthalas is interested in them," Tahlen scoffed.

"Mad, people thought they were," Kai-Tsúthlen went on, "but it turns out their speculations were more or less correct. How comforted Ninthalas will be to know he is no fanatic fool."

"Comfort. How can anyone be comforted by this place?"

Kai-Tsúthlen didn't comment. He still believed that if anyone had a chance of escaping *Lotah 'an Morkh*, it would be Ninthalas. His brother was the blessed of Yahlírin.

The path twisted and turned. Occasionally, another crossed it and the lead spirit changed directions down the new path, sometimes left, sometimes right. Kai-Tsúthlen couldn't be certain whether it was leading them in the right direction or not, but he didn't have a choice. Those deceiving eyes were his only chance of getting out.

Time crawled until at last, the beginnings of dawn shed light on their surroundings. The scenery was just as bleak as Kai-Tsúthlen remembered it, and a mist covered the forest floor that made the experience that much more unnatural.

Tahlen heaved gasping breaths, wheezing that he claimed was because of his body growing weak and a heaviness about the air. Kai-Tsúthlen had no idea how to treat it, had nothing that might ease the pain in his friend's chest. He, too, felt the sickness. It was like a disease, an infection that made him sweat though his skin was cool, made his soul exhale with every breath he let go.

Becoming like us, they are, prodded the spirit.

"How much longer?" Kai-Tsúthlen asked, his mouth dry and voice cracking.

How much longer indeed?

"Is this what happened to you? Did the forest suffocate you as

111

it is suffocating us?"

The eyes stopped. Their colour had become a solid green, neither cool nor warm.

Suffocated me, yes. Sucked me dry, indeed. Every False Faithen withers at its grasp, breathes its last and fades away.

"How did it come to this?"

How indeed?

It floated into the trees, the other eyes close behind. *There it is, False Faithen. There, you see?*

Kai-Tsúthlen looked ahead. Golden grass glimmered in the distance, the edge of the Dead Forest.

Flesh. Living flesh!

Kai-Tsúthlen turned back. The eyes were changing rapidly, matching the yellowish hue of the others. The healing had passed. Two translucent arms reached forward. Before Kai-Tsúthlen could grasp what was going on, Fellas bolted. The eyes squealed and chased after them, closing ground faster than Kai-Tsúthlen could comprehend.

"Hurry, Fellas!" he exclaimed.

The path disappeared. They twisted and turned between trunks until at last they broke free onto a vast plain. A sheet of golden grass unraveled before them, stretching into the horizon.

Kai-Tsúthlen reared Fellas in and turned around. The eyes hovered within the forest's border, staring hungrily at them. They would not venture into the open.

"We are free," Tahlen breathed.

Kai-Tsúthlen scanned the tree line.

"Ninthalas!" he cried.

He rode up and down the border, calling. The eyes followed left and right, barring re-entrance.

"Ninthalas! Brother!"

Tears stung his eyes.

Tahlen coughed. "He's gone."

"No!" Kai-Tsúthlen exclaimed. "No, I will not abandon him! What man abandons his brother to ruin?"

"It is over."

"Your mind is too far under, Tahlen. He will come out. I am sure of it!"

Kai-Tsúthlen dismounted and walked up to the tree line. The eyes formed glowing bodies, shapes of men similar in appearance to himself yet disfigured like the unnatural shapes of dead trees. *Come back, come in!* they hollered. *Join us and be free, free from the mess, the despair!*

Kai-Tsúthlen gritted his teeth.

"Kai-Tsúthlen, he is not coming out," Tahlen said.

He shook his head. "No...no, it cannot be." He looked into Tahlen's eyes. They offered no comfort. "It cannot be..."

"It is, just as it was when I lost my sister."

"No! My brother is the blessed of Yahlírin! There is no way he would fall in *Lotah 'an Morkh*. He could not! There is no one better suited to survive in there."

"Come now, Kai-Tsúthlen. We must press on."

He held firm. "My brother is alive, and he is coming out! Ninthalas is the blessed of Yahlírin—"

The sound of a horn cut him off and they turned their eyes to the east. Billowing clouds rose from the eastern edge of the forest. A short line of ant-like shapes danced along the horizon, only specks, but they were growing larger.

"Malshorthath," Tahlen breathed. "I am in no condition to fight them."

"Let us flee to the river. If we find Ninthalas further down by the border—"

Another horn sounded to the far right. Out of the trees emerged a group malshorthath.

Tears streamed down Kai-Tsúthlen's cheeks. He couldn't leave his brother behind. But he and Tahlen would be dead before Ninthalas emerged from the forest. His mind raced like a pendulum. To die by the malshorthath or leave his brother to die? It was a losing gamble whichever way he looked at it. But if he and Tahlen could lure the demons away...

"Let us fly," he said. "Yahlírin will save my brother. We can help him by keeping the malshorthath focused on us."

"We could die if they catch us."

Kai-Tsúthlen remounted. His mind was set. He couldn't save Ninthalas this time, but he could help prevent his brother's demise.

"What are we to fear, my friend? Are you not a child prodigy and I the chief evader? We are rid of the threat that plagued us. Now let us do what we do best and show those malshorthath the true strength of Yahlírin's people."

Tahlen was about to speak, but clamped his mouth shut. A new fire burned in his eyes that Kai-Tsúthlen knew well. He drew his sword.

"Give me the opportunity of revenge and I will gladly take it. For Lamnek Eflan!"

"For my brother's return," Kai-Tsúthlen declared.

He kicked his horse into a gallop in the direction of the ants to the east.

CHAPTER TEN

Flight to Freedom

Yosef.

Consciousness tugged Yosef into the living world. He'd had a dream, but as he woke, the dream faded with only the whisperings of his name dancing along his memory. He reluctantly opened his eyes to the dreary shrubbery, thick trunks and boughs of the haunted wood. *Lotah 'an Morkh*, he remembered, that place the terrible malshorth infected many years ago. Would he really have to live here for the rest of his life with the Black Assailant? Or would Shadai rescue him?

Drowsily, he sat up, and rubbed his eyes. And gasped. He sat in a clearing, but the Black Assailant and the beast they had ridden were nowhere to be seen. No ashes marked the campfire. This was a different glade.

Shimmering streams of sunlight played on the forest floor. They hardly eased the bleak atmosphere. The branches reached out in sweeping grasps, threatening to prick anyone who ventured close enough to their sharp tips. The air was still, silent. The voices were gone. The forest now seemed eerily empty.

He stood and turned around, only to come face to face with a pair of cold blue eyes.

At last, you are awake.

Fear petrified Yosef. It spoke in Common, not the evil language of the voices. His limbs sparked into action and he bolted into the trees.

Wait, child! I am not to hurt you!

Yosef dashed as fast as he could, weaving in and out, out and in before a tricky root caught his foot. He tumbled to the ground. "Ninthalas! Ninthalas, where are you? Help me!" His sobs came up short, the empty air smothering their advance.

The pair of blue eyes floated up and hovered in front of him. Yosef refused to look at them. He curled up into a ball and rocked on the balls of his feet with his face buried in his knees.

You certainly run fast for a small fellow with a wounded leg, the eyes said. *You might not want to yell like that if you wish to avoid being caught again and dragged off against your will.*

Yosef looked up at them. Unlike the ones from the night before, these seemed much more sane.

"Who are you?" he asked.

Oh, I had a name once, but it has long since been forgotten. You see, I was a curious young man who took the unfortunate liberty of venturing into this wood. It was here that my body was devoured and my soul corrupted. Yet I have since been repurposed, and now I must lead you away.

"How can I trust you?"

Would you rather be discovered by Emkalaf'Morlúrnan and captured again? I am your only hope now, and that is temporary. I must use what time I have to help you, and that grows short the longer we sit here talking to each other.

"You're freaky."

You are thinking too much. Now come along. We have not the time to sit and converse.

Yosef stayed put, studying the eyes. Could he trust them? They almost seemed friendly with their cooler hue. Maybe this ghost was telling the truth. He certainly didn't want to meet that Black Assailant again. He needed to find Ninthalas and the others, and if following this ghost meant freedom...

"You can get me out of here?" he asked.

I can lead you most of the way until my time is up, the eyes replied. *Though you will have to find the way out yourself. I assume you can in time since you show such resilience to the forest's evil.*

Yosef thought again, then shrugged. "Sure, I'll go."

Then on your feet.

Without turning around, the eyes moved away, taking to a trail in the opposite direction Yosef had been running. Yosef followed, his own eyes shifting here and there on the lookout for the Black Assailant. He kept expecting her to jump out in front of him, or at least spot the sickly eyes of the ghosts of the forest. Yet he saw neither. He couldn't feel anything. The sense had completely shut off even though the silence surrounded him. The silence was a different shape now, like a square instead of a circle. Or maybe a circle instead of a square? In any case, he couldn't focus on it.

Instead he kept his sight fixed on the blue eyes and his thoughts on putting one foot in front of the other. The eyes led him in a zig-zag pattern of interconnecting paths. They turned down this one or went down that; took the right one, veered down the left. Yosef couldn't be sure which way they were going. He had only to trust the blue eyes.

Their colour made him think of Ninthalas and the others. He hoped his companions hadn't ventured into the Dead Forest, or if they had, that they had already gotten out safely. Maybe they hadn't faired as poorly as he had. Perhaps Tahlen had led them through the trees, marching forward at the pace of trotting horses like a super-human. Maybe Ninthalas was laughing and enjoying himself despite the dreary atmosphere. Or perhaps Kai-Tsúthlen was leading them, his head held high and steadfast.

Yosef smiled. He thought of the many tales Ninthalas had told him in the few days they had spent together, stories of Namthúl Shadai, the fearless leader. The stories gave Yosef hope. He would prevail. He wasn't just a boy. He was *Korme'khím* like the Black Assailant had said, a Mountain Dweller. He didn't understand the significance of that, but he knew it must mean something great.

Before he knew it, dusk brought the promise of night. His guide provided enough of a glow that he could see the path in front of him, but the ground ran so smooth and rid of rocks and roots that Yosef wouldn't have had trouble picking his way, even after night devoured the forest in blackness.

Not far now, not far at all.

"You mean out of this freakish place?"

No, not far until the small hollow where you may rest for the night.

Hollow. The way the eyes said it made it sound pleasant.

Yosef's legs were becoming more like jelly than functioning limbs and he thought they would give way at any moment. Fatigue washed over him, and his eyelids were heavy. Maybe the hollow had a bed for him to curl up in.

The eyes steered him right down a short, stone path. At the end of it, a giant tree rose into the sky, its trunk so thick that if Yosef tried to fit his arms around it, he would need ten more of himself to do so. A dusty cloth draped over the near side of the trunk, and grooves resembling stairs curled from the left up around and around, climbing into the treetops.

The eyes floated through the curtain. Yosef brushed the ratted cloth aside to reveal the hollow. The ghost's eyes illuminated the interior, allowing him to observe the remains of a home. Interconnecting vines wove from the ground up the walls, and branches of a small tree within the tree spread across the ceiling. From the centre of the ceiling hung a circular flask. Similar ones lined the walls. They looked like they could have been lamps of some sort. A few small holes in the walls made for windows. A stone slab in the middle of the floor provided for a table, and curved roots rose and fell around it to form stools.

"What is this place?" the boy asked, staring at the interior in awe. Unlike the atmosphere outside, the hollow offered a comforting tone, residue perhaps from times long ago when the forest was lush and green. How wonderful it would have been to dwell in this hollow back when the forest thrived.

It was once home to a blessed family. Now it is haunted by the sleepless ones above.

"You mean there's more of you ghost-ish things around? I thought you were helping me. Those things will eat me if the Black Assailant isn't with me."

I am *helping you. Do you see that groove in the wall over there? You may sleep there tonight. I am afraid I will not be here when you wake.*

"Why not?"

My time is nearly come and I must go far away before I once more become a spirit that devours flesh. You must stay here and sleep. In the morning, take to the stone path and turn right where it ends. Do not speak or utter any other sound. For now, this village lies dormant, but given the dawn of morning, it will be alive again. The souls will smell your flesh and seek you, so you must flee as soon as you sense them. And you will feel them. The one who healed me told me so.

"I don't want you to go! I don't wanta be alone."

Alone? You are never alone, little friend. Yahlírin is with you. Never fear, boy. Do not be afraid.

The eyes departed, fading back through the curtain, and blackness flooded the hollow.

Yosef's eyes grew watery with tears. Being alone in a creepy forest without even the Black Assailant to talk to scared him. Yahlírin was with him? He didn't even know who or what Yahlírin was. What if the hungry souls found him? How would he escape?

He felt his way to the groove in the trunk's inner wall and curled up inside. There he found a tattered blanket perfectly laid out for him. He took it, batted the dust off it, and wrapped himself up. It provided just enough warmth to keep out the chilly night air.

"Good night, Ninthalas, wherever you are," he whispered into the dark.

Out of the emptiness, he heard a still, small voice reply. *Goodnight, my son.*

Sharp tingling. By now, Yosef knew it all too well and it called him out of sleep. He sat up, listening, reaching out with the sense into the darkness. He was not alone. Ghosts floated above, searching, seeking. A faint, yellowy green glow illuminated one of the tiny windows, then faded away.

Flesh, living flesh. Where is it sleeping? Where is it lurking?

Yosef shivered. Quietly, he placed both feet on the floor and got up. Listening, waiting. The glow passed by another window.

Where is it hiding? Come out, living flesh. Show yourself, show.

Yosef kept his eyes on the glow passing from window to window, slowly making its way to the back of the home. He crept to the door and poked his head outside. No eyes, but another glow emanated from above.

Living flesh, it is here. I smell it, I do. Where are you, living flesh?

Yosef dashed out of the hollow and down the stone path. He turned right at the end, just as the blue eyes had told him and ran until he couldn't run anymore. Eventually, the voices faded and the tingling sense died down. He regressed to a walk and glanced back.

No eyes. No pursuers. He could relax.

Almost.

It started as a faint whispering of a sensation, but soon developed into a lump in his gut. He recognized it instantly. The Black Assailant. He stood still to focus. The silence was much more inviting this time, grabbing him by the arm and pulling him into the ground. He swam like a fish through the earth towards the pulses of the Black Assailant's presence until he found her— close, but not close enough that he couldn't escape her.

He broke into a slow jog, going where the path went in a more or less straight line. Gradually, the light of day filtered through the spiny canopy above and forced branches and boughs to cast shadows of grey and darker grey. He stood in a dead sea of trunks and shrubbery. Not like it mattered. By now, Yosef's vision had become so blurry, he only saw shapes and shades of grey. Was there any end to this creepy forest?

The lump in his gut tightened. Dread. He took a peek over his shoulder and jumped. A glow of blue and green lights floated behind him. The eyes! He ran left into the brush, then right onto the path, and odd combinations of both before something caught his foot. He tripped and fell, landing with a hard thud. Pain erupted in his bad arm.

"Ninthalas!" he cried.

Sírola! hissed the voices.

Yosef whimpered, clutching his injured arm with his other hand.

"What do you want with me?"

Bai, sírola, the voices said again.

He grumbled. He was tired of being stuck in this creepy forest. Why couldn't he be free of the haunting eyes?

Through blurred sight, he saw the blue and green clump grow larger and then separate into pairs.

"Stop staring at me!" he cried.

Sírola, kehman. Úrgol'mar. Shadai kúril.

"Shadai?"

They didn't speak again. Not like Yosef cared. He couldn't understand them anyway.

He sniffled and closed his eyes, letting the sense take him into the earth and expand. But then he felt something he did not expect. Not far away, he felt the beats of four clopping feet. And they were headed in his direction.

Was that...?

He let go of the silence and came to, head swirling, and stumbled to his feet just as a familiar sight emerged from the brush.

"Hallas?" the boy said. "Or are you Fellas?"

The horse whinnied. Whichever it was, Yosef knew the horse belonged to one of the Shadai brothers.

"Probably Hallas," he said as he walked over to the horse.

What happened next he could not tell. It was as if he was lifted and set to rest upon Hallas' back. Warmth returned to his body and his vision cleared. With newfound sight, he saw just how menacing the forest really was. The blue and green eyes formed bodies of light with faces that smiled at him. They weren't really that scary. He smiled back.

"Shadai!"

Voices screeched, and the eyes suddenly changed to eerie yellow, the light of their bodies fading to nothing. That familiar lump hung in Yosef's gut and terror flooded his limbs. Black wisps flung out of the shadows, and into view emerged the Black Assailant. She glared passed Yosef. If her yellow eyes were a weapon and had been directed at him, they would have pierced his chest.

"I should have known you had been sent," she sneered.

Who was she talking to? Yosef twisted, but no one sat behind him.

"Only Shadai would have the power to give my body new life." She stuck up her chin. "Hand him over, *hallon.*"

Yosef trembled.

A roaring thunder spoke back. She raged and charged. Hallas dashed into the brush and the Black Assailant raced after. They zigzagged between trunks, over brush, veering left and right like predator and prey. Yosef clung to the saddle's horn, pain shooting through his injured arm with every bump and sharp turn. His wounded leg flapped against the horse's flanks.

But the pain didn't compare to the fear.

"Faster, Hallas!"

Hallas took a sharp right and Yosef's hands slipped. He would have flown off the saddle, but two arms wrapped around him, holding him tight. Who was holding him? When he looked down, he didn't see anything—just himself. But he felt the arms as surely as he could feel a living thing. Was it one of the ghosts? Was it Shadai?

"*Curses, the foul!*"

He looked back. The Captor stretched out her hand, just barely touching his tunic. Hallas swerved out of the way before she could grab a fist full of cloth.

"Come on, Hallas! Faster, faster!" Yosef urged.

Hallas' hooves pounded harder. The gap between pursuer and prey grew and closed as they swerved through the endless maze.

Just then, the trees ended and Hallas raced into a clearing filled with white ghostly bodies. Cold pain numbed Yosef's legs as he was was whisked through them. His vision started to blur again. Drat this forest! Before he could come up with more curses, Hallas hit a ghost dead on. Shock petrified him in burning cold. His sight fell to blurry shapes and shades.

Hallas pressed on until it broke free from the souls on the other side of the clearing. The reigns tightened and Hallas skidded to a stop. It turned around.

Yosef's head spun as he looked up through blurry eyes. The dark haze of the Black Assailant had reared to a halt on the other side of the swarm, cursing in outrage. She could not pass.

"*Curses, Shadai!*"

The rest of her outrage became muffled and incomprehensible. Thunder boomed back, and Hallas steered around, leaving the Captor behind.

Yosef slumped forward. His head fell like a heavy weight on his shoulders. His arms fell loose by his sides. The last thing he saw before falling unconscious was golden light up ahead, filtering through shades of grey.

Part 2

CHAPTER ELEVEN

Responsibilities

The door slid open and Kai-Tsúthlen stumbled in, hauling what he could inside. He was in better condition than Tahlen. They had barely stopped to rest after taunting the two raiding parties of malshorthath. Fear alone kept them riding for two days and nights, a gruelling trek that left them exhausted and sore. Fellas more so. Farmers gleaning the harvest in the fields had seen them and rushed to their aid, going so far as to bring Kai-Tsúthlen right to his house. But when they brought him to the door, Kai-Tsúthlen shrugged them off and stumbled inside himself.

"Father!" a young voice chirped.

Kai-Tsúthlen's son ran down the hall and burst into view from around the corner, wearing a big smile. The smile vanished when he saw his dad.

"Father, are you alright?"

"Go fetch your mother," Kai-Tsuthlen told him.

The boy nodded and ran off.

Kai-Tsuthlen dropped his belongings and leaned against the wall. Exhaustion didn't even begin to describe his fatigue. His body was languid, his mind weary from lack of sleep. But how could he sleep now? How could he even consider rest? He had left his brother behind!

His wife, Arúthíen, appeared around the corner. Her face immediately turned to shock.

"Kai-Tsú, what happened?" she exclaimed.

"Help me to my study," was all Kai-Tsúthlen could say.

"A bed would suit you better."

"No. I need to be alone—"

"I do not see you in over a month and you shrug me off?" Arúthíen demanded.

She threw her arms around him. Kai-Tsúthlen, in turn, put an arm around her.

I cannot..." He drifted off.

"Cannot what? You sound like Ninthalas."

"Please, Arúthíen."

He withdrew. His wife looked deep into his eyes, searching, studying.

"Very well," she said.

She took his arm over her shoulders and helped him up. Kai-Tsúthlen staggered alongside her, walking slowly to his personal study down the hall. It was a small room, having only space for a low table on the left side, a three-shelf bookcase beside the table and another larger one on the far wall. A circular window in the right corner offered light and fresh air during the day. A mural with the family emblem of Shadai woven with fine threads into its long silk cloth hung on the wall over his desk.

He slumped down onto the square cushion in front of the table.

"Are you sure you will be alright? Will you not speak to me?" she asked again.

"I need time to think."

"Time to think, he says. Time to think."

He pulled her close and kissed her. "Arúthíen, my love, I have seen things I do not know what to make of. I will come to you later."

She let out a long sigh. "Of course, my dear."

She left him alone in the small study. Kai-Tsúthlen could hear a pattering of energetic footsteps in the hall.

"Is he alright, mother?" his son chirped.

"He will be fine. But you must be off to bed."

"But I want to see father, first!"

"In the morning. Come now, to bed."

"Arúthíen!" Kai-Tsúthlen called. "Let him come to me."

Moments later, his son came bounding into the room and jumped into his arms. Kai-Tsúthlen held him tight.

"What is wrong, father? Why are you upset?"

"It was a long journey, son," Kai-Tsúthlen replied warmly. He pulled his son off. "Now, off to bed as your mother told you. I eagerly await your stories tomorrow morning."

The boy grinned wide and trotted away. Footsteps sounded down the hall to the children's room.

Kai-Tsúthlen breathed out a deep sigh. He could hardly believe he was home. Home after the very first trek he and Ninthalas had taken without the aid of their father, a true test of their wit. They had been so excited.

Yet that trip had turned out to be a disaster. Ninthalas' recurring dream that had driven him mad. Kai-Tsúthlen had thought that would be the worst part of the trip. However, Ninthalas decided to bring a foreigner to Serenestí. A foreigner! How would his people react? Although, Kai-Tsúthlen had already made up his mind that he would support his brother's decision. This was Ninthalas' choice. He would probably intend to adopt Yosef, which Kai-Tsúthlen had already accepted. It would be hard, but it was doable. It had all just happened so fast!

But then *Emkalaf'Morlúrnan* had kidnapped Yosef and Kai-Tsúthlen had left Ninthalas behind in a forest infamous for erasing people from the living world. Ninthalas *and* Yosef.

Curse those malshorthath! Kai-Tsúthlen had never left his brother's side before, had barely let his twin out of his sight. Ninthalas had a habit of getting into trouble over little things that made him in need of constant monitoring. He and Kai-Tsúthlen were inseparable as twins should be.

Or at least they used to be.

Since Kai-Tsúthlen had married at the age of eighteen and started a family, he and his brother began to slowly drift apart. True, they still had that old connection when they embarked on errand, and Kai-Tsúthlen was ever his brother's keeper. But here in Serenestí he saw Ninthalas in a different light. Whether it was him who changed or Ninthalas, there had been an invisible wall between them, a divide that had continued to grow over the past five years. It just wasn't the same anymore. Kai-Tsúthlen's concerns became more about his wife and children. Was that not the way it should be?

Yet it didn't matter now. Nothing mattered now. He had left

Ninthalas for dead. What kind of brother was he that he couldn't even protect his twin?

In the midst of his despair, a glimmer of hope flickered in his conscience. Ninthalas was the blessed of Yahlírin. Kai-Tsúthlen knew it in his heart, had known it his entire life. Ninthalas was born different, had lived different, had become the type of man people stared dumbfounded at. And Kai-Tsúthlen loved him. He couldn't live with himself if his brother was ever lost. He saw what a lost sibling had done to Tahlen. He couldn't imagine the same happening to him.

A sensation struck him that this wasn't reality, that Ninthalas had actually returned and what they endured had just been a bad dream. No one ever came out of *Lotah 'an Morkh*. Even the bravest of souls who had passed into it had never returned, and that made Kai-Tsúthlen's escape that much more unbelievable. What would his parents say or even his wife?

He shifted from cross-legged to sitting on his knees and began flipping through the book on his desk: the Fehlthan, holy book of the True Faithen people. He had been reading it to his son the night before the twins left on their journey. Even if no one had survived in *Lotah 'an Morkh*, perhaps the Fehlthan had an example of men who had escaped certain death in the past.

He turned to the first section which outlined the major historical events of the First and Second Ages. Most tales spoke of his famous ancestor, Namthúl Shadai, and other figures crucial to the founding of True Faithen faith and culture. These were men of renown, the very image of masculinity, warriors and traditionalist men. Kai-Tsúthlen was grounded in tradition himself, a citizen devoted to his society, yet he felt no connection to any of the great men of old. And even less was there any connection to Ninthalas. His brother was the exact opposite of what True Faithen society deemed masculine, leaving little hope for him returning safe and sound.

But Ninthalas was the blessed of Yahlírin…

He sighed and closed the book. Brooding over his own thoughts was getting him nowhere. When he thought he had control over himself, he left his study and walked—albeit stiffly— down the narrow hall to the bath room. Sliding open the door, he found his wife, Arúthíen, resting peacefully in the large square bath. She looked up at him and smiled. He managed to return a smile of his own. She cocked her head to the side, wearing that look that she knew something was wrong. Kai-Tsúthlen could never fool his wife.

He undressed and made first for the separate soapy basin—a barrel to cleanse oneself before entering the main bath—and stepped into the water, shivering from the initial chill. He proceeded to slather his body with suds, washing away the grime from his travels.

All the while, he kept an eye on his wife, the crown of his pride. The sight of her almost washed away his despair. Arúthien was a typical housewife, average in elegance and grace according to unpleasant gossip. Yet Kai-Tsúthlen believed her beauty worth far more than the expensive stones salvaged from the mines in the north. She was a strong, capable woman, well-versed in cloth making and the trade business, an excellent mother, and a loving, submissive wife. Kai-Tsúthlen's parents adored her and Ninthalas called her the most blessed of all sisters (though the twins had none).

Kai-Tsúthlen's sorrow gradually subsided. Again he questioned whether or not his trials had been real. But they had, hadn't they?

Arúthien leaned back in the larger square tub, letting the warm water and sweet scent of recently added perfumes refresh her senses.

"How was your first trip without your father?" she asked.

Kai-Tsúthlen knew a myriad of questions were to follow. No matter which way the conversation swayed, he wouldn't be able to escape telling the truth.

"It was…trying. A trying journey" he replied as he rinsed the last of the suds off using water from a separate bin. The water was freezing, making him chirp in a shrill cry.

She chuckled at his outburst. "Obviously."

Kai-Tsúthlen didn't comment. After finishing with the rinse bucket, he went to join her, sloshing into the warm water.

"With all the grace of a loon," she teased.

"No playing fun tonight," he said. "I am ill at heart."

The stern tone didn't faze her. She wrapped her arms around him and began stroking his long hair.

"Is it Ninthalas?"

He nodded.

"What happened between you two? And why did you come back the way you did, so terribly upset?"

"I lost him."

"Lost him?"

"Yes, in *Lotah 'an Morkh*."

She shot back. "*Lotah 'an Morkh*? What in all A'thería would possess you to traverse that ground?" She shook her head. "No, you must be lying. I do not believe you."

He offered her his sincerest look and her eyes widened.

"How…why?"

"Our path was altered. We crossed an enemy's path on the way to Mepdokh, and were forced to flee into the mountains."

"But you went together, I imagine."

"Indeed, we did, yet we faced opposition. First, there was a tribe of skohls that attacked us. Then we lost a young boy who was in our company."

"A boy?"

"He is from Mor'Lûn."

"Mor'Lûn. I have never heard…"

"Please, *mí onen'menan*, let me tell you the story with no interruptions," Kai-Tsúthlen said. "Mor'Lûn is a town off the trade route by a good week's travel, not far from the Wall of Separation. We met a boy from that village whose name is Yosef Mathíus, except that we found him in Shalom, several fathoms from his hometown. The boy stumbled upon the inn we were staying at—the unkept one I am not fond of, if you remember. From there, Ninthalas and I bore him with us for the remainder of our travels. He does not remember anything of his village save the name, nor of it being destroyed—it was raided, mind you and we found refugees in Port Shai. Yet we did not find his family. We assume they perished in the attack on Mor'Lûn."

"Mor'Lûn was attacked? I heard about Luthrey—indeed we all did—when the remnants of Tahlen Dían's Company returned. Yet he himself did not return with them."

"Tahlen met us in Port Shai to tell us of Luthrey. He was with us in the mountains when the skohls attacked, and aided us in tracking the kidnapped boy, Yosef, to *Lotah 'an Morkh*. At first we thought to go along the border, but we came upon an obstruction that forced us to enter the forest. Ninthalas led the way. He has taken a liking to Yosef, what he described to me as being 'compelled'. I am not sure what he means by it, but I am sure he will adopt the boy if he can."

"He has oft spoken of adopting, though I did not expect he would take in a Kislanían. Did I not say—"

"Indeed, you said that it would be ill conceived."

"Well, most certainly a difficult endeavour," said Arúthíen. "Our good High Lord does not take well to foreigners integrating into our society."

"True, but now Yosef is gone. The boy is lost to the forest now, along with Ninthalas."

Arúthíen shook her head. "It cannot be."

"Indeed, it cannot be."

A pause fell between them.

"Have you told mother and father?"

"Not yet. They do not even know I am home."

"Let it rest for a day without them worrying," Arúthíen suggested. "It is like you always say: Ninthalas is the blessed of Yahlírin. And he most assuredly will come home alive. That much I believe to be true, even though the story you tell me is a hard one to grasp. He will bring home with him the boy you spoke of. Yosef Mathíus. In my dealings with foreign folk, I have never heard such a name. How unique."

"Indeed." He didn't bother telling her that Yosef was a half breed. "I just feel as if I have done him a disservice by abandoning him."

She kissed him.

"Oh, Kai-Tsú. You are always so unsure of things. What does your heart tell you? What does the still, small voice whisper to you?"

Kai-Tsúthlen listened. It wasn't long before he had his answer. "Ninthalas is alive."

"Then it is so. Your brother is alive."

She was right. Ninthalas was a son of Yahlírin. And Yahlírin protected his children. Ninthalas would come home.

Tormented did not begin to describe Tahlen's mood. His heart raced. His soul sat like a brick in the pit of his gut. He had failed his Company, his friend Lamnek, and now Ninthalas. What good was he? Child prodigy? The most he could do was slay skohls and taunt malshorthath raiding parties to chase him over the plains.

But that didn't compare to the guilt he experienced when he saw his parents' reactions the night he returned home. The farmers who had helped him each took an arm and practically dragged him to the front door. When Tahlen opened it, he found his parents across the hall at the dining table. They both stood at the sight of him. His father wore an expression of utter fury. His mother, a look of distress.

"Tahlen Dían!" his father roared. Too infuriated for words, he let the name hang on the air.

The man on Tahlen's left spoke softly in his ear. "I suppose we must leave you to your own business. Are you able to stand by yourself?"

Tahlen stood on wobbly legs. "Yes, good sir. My deepest gratitude for your assistance."

The men withdrew from the scene, leaving Tahlen to fend for himself. He almost wished they had stayed to protect him from the verbal onslaught he knew was coming.

His father stepped forward. "Why did you not return with your Company?" he demanded. "And what in all A'thería have you been doing? Look at you, a wreck of a man who has seen little rest or meal."

"I have my reasons—"

"They had better be satisfactory," his father boomed.

Tahlen's mother cut in. "Dúrlen, dear, do not distress the boy more. Can we not be at peace that he has returned home safely?"

"That does not exempt him from abandoning his duties," Dúrlen stated.

He picked up some scrolls that lay at the table, walked over and put them in Tahlen's arms.

"Read these and be ready to explain them once I have finished in the bath."

With that, he stormed off, his footsteps loud and solid. Tahlen heard the bath room door slide shut with a clang.

"I will try to calm him," Tahlen's mother said. "Though it will take some coaxing to ease his nerves. The country has been in an uproar since your Company returned, and we were worried you had suffered the same fate as your late sister."

Tahlen's eyes fell. Why did his mother have to bring *that* up?

"You look dreadful."

"I will be fine, mother," he replied.

"Well, you should review those in any case, and try to rest," his mother said before leaving to join Dúrlen. "You know your father. He will want a full report later."

Tahlen stood for a moment in the doorway, then slowly—sluggishly—made his way down the same hallway they had taken to his room.

Other than the ornate carvings of his bed frame, Tahlen's room was simple. The bed was low like all beds in Serenestí, as was his desk. A single square pillow allowed for a seat. A lamp on the corner of his desk emanated a soft glow, giving the room a warm light that would have been comforting if Tahlen wasn't stricken with remorse. Who had lit it Tahlen had no idea, though his mother often entered without his permission. It could have been her. On one side of the desk were a line of narrow vases yielding rolls of parchment. Several books, his own personal collection of writings to assist in the formal descriptions of accounts, lay in various piles in front of a sliding closet door. To the other side of the desk, racks for his swords lay bare.

Tahlen unstrapped his weaponry and let it drop to the side. They upset a pile of books, making a clump of a sound that grated on his ears because it was otherwise quiet. The scrolls and parchment he'd received from his father he put on his desk. Then he collapsed on the floor, exhausted.

He eyed the shadows dancing in the corners of the room. He wanted to fade into them, to disappear into nothingness so he didn't have to face his responsibilities. Such a pain, responsibility was. There was no getting out of confronting his father about his choice to leave his Company. He'd much rather have a bath and slide into bed, but the pecking order in his family demanded that parents bathe before their children. And speaking with his father meant that he wouldn't get to sleep until late. He would have to give his account of the battle.

The battle at Luthrey. It was like a nightmare Tahlen didn't want to remember. He had lost so many good men, and Lamnek... He choked on his breath, tears flooding his eyes. Lamnek, his close friend and second in command, was gone. He and Tahlen had been the best team growing up, and when their superior was absent, they would run their band of Denedrúath warriors flawlessly. Nothing ever went wrong when they worked together. Yet something *had* gone wrong thanks to Ninthalas' recurring dream. Tahlen didn't blame Ninthalas for the raid, or even going to Luthrey. Lamnek was—had been—the twins' cousin, after all. Ninthalas had wept all through the night when the Captain had told him the news. Even for Ninthalas, a crier through and through, staying up the entire night was an incredible feat.

Tahlen could hardly believe that his friend didn't make it out of *Lotah 'an Morkh*. The reality tore Tahlen's soul in two. How could so much tragedy happen in his lifetime? First his sister, then Lamnek and half the Denedrúath in his Company, and now Ninthalas. The sorrow was too much for Tahlen to bear.

He thought of Kai-Tsúthlen's reaction when they had escaped the forest. His friend had shown more emotion than Tahlen had seen in the entirety of his life. Under normal circumstances Kai-Tsúthlen was an immovable force, the kind of man Tahlen wanted to be: strong-willed, disciplined, righteous, a just man and a good father. Kai-Tsúthlen was like Tahlen's greatest hero, Namthúl Shadai.

Tahlen glanced at his copy of the Fehlthan sitting on the corner of his desk. What would Namthúl do in his situation?

Pushing the scrolls and parchment onto the floor, he grabbed the book and turned to the history section, reading aloud one of his favourite passages:

"At that time, Namthúl Shadai, son of Sinthúl, who was High Lord of the True Faithen people, was greatly troubled. And behold, oppression was readily upon him! And when he looked and saw that his enemies were at hand, he cried out unto Yahlírin the Provider, Creator of all that is:
'Yahlírin 'an Hathlen, kahlú síprola! Tí koslekath síprola shíkan!' (That is, 'Yahlírin of Hathlen, save us! Please save your servants!')

And Yahl fell upon A'thírin like thunder. Like a storm he came upon the enemy. He sent before Him His heavenly host. And His host of the Halloneth drove back every malshorth, back into the crevice of the quaking earth where there is no return. Thus Namthúl Shadai overcame the malshorthath, the evil host led by Dethshaiken the Third.

Thereafter did Namthúl call Yahlírin Yahl'Norkúrlaf, *God the Provider."*

The passage was an abridged version of one of many battles Namthúl led. More detailed records were still kept among the historical accounts in the Great Library of Serenestí. But Tahlen was more concerned with the prayer than the details of war. It was said that no other person was as righteous or steadfast as Namthúl Shadai, and his righteousness reflected his prayer life. Tahlen did not believe righteousness was something that could be measured, but Namthúl's prayers were a guideline for others, reflecting his devout commitment to his relationship with his Creator. Most often, Namthúl would cry out to Yahlírin in times of distress.

Tahlen always mimicked that prayer, believing that if he did, he would attain the same steadfast nature as Namthúl and Kai-Tsúthlen. And now was certainly a time to pray. His distress could not be more excruciating.

Closing the book, he clapped his hands flat together in front of his face, and, shutting his eyes, tilted his head upwards in customary prayer.

"*Yahlírin 'an Hathlen, kahlú síprola. Tí koslekath síprola shíkan,*" he prayed. "I mourn for my friend, Lamnek, those who fell in my Company, Ninthalas, and...Athlaya..."

He paused, opening his eyes. He hadn't thought about his older sister in years. Since meeting the Shadai twins in Port Shai, memories resurfaced, images recalled through the lens of an eight-year-old boy. No matter how hard he tried to push the vision aside, it remained, constant and fixed like an infectious disease.

Thoughts spiralled into the torment he had witnessed in *Lotah 'an Morkh.* Voices had scorned him. Most of them he did not understand, but the ravaging tones suggested mocking. Those he did comprehend questioned the Captain's ability as a soldier. They ridiculed his failure to be a leader. How had Kai-Tsúthlen not heard them?

Tahlen pulled his knees up and buried his face. Silently, he wept.

Just then, the door to his room creaked open. He spun, quickly wiping the tears from his eyes.

In the doorway stood his younger sister, staring at him with an expression depicting a combination of sympathy and shock. Tahlen had never cried in front of her.

"Kírinfay." He cleared his throat. "It is late, sister. Why are you awake?"

"I heard you," she replied. "I heard you reading the Fehlthan out loud, so I came to listen. Welcome home!"

Tahlen motioned for her to come forward. She trotted over and plopped herself into his lap.

"Why are you sad?" she asked.

"Ah," said Tahlen, still recovering. He rubbed his eyes. "Some bad things happened, and they made me upset. It is nothing for you to worry about."

Kírinfay wasn't convinced, her brow furrowing. The frown made her look cuter than she already was, and despite his overwhelming sense of remorse, Tahlen chuckled. Kírinfay was a beacon of joy to all around her.

"What is so funny?"

"You are," he said.

"I am not!"

"Does mother know you are awake?"

"No," Kírinfay replied, her frown turning into a smug grin.

"She will be angry if she finds you here. You should go back to bed."

The girl scowled, flopping her arms to her sides. "But I want to hear your stories! Why did you not return with your Company? I heard there was a battle."

"My stories can wait for tomorrow," said Tahlen. "Come now, I will tuck you in."

Reluctantly, she got up. Hand in hand, they went a little ways down the hall. Unlike Tahlen's plain room, Kírinfay had decorated her bedroom walls with colourful fabrics, small pieces of projects her mother had taught her how to weave. They foreshadowed her eventual integration into the trade business, a legacy her mother would pass down to her when she came of age.

Tahlen looked at the smidgens of tapestries, noting each one to make sure he hadn't missed any new ones since he had left Serenestí on errand. His eyes turned to the patched blanket draped over her low bed.

"Is that new?" he asked as she crawled under the covers.

"No, those were here last time. Don't you remember?"

"It must have slipped my mind."

"You always forget stuff like that. Now can you tell me a story?"

"Hmm…" Tahlen thought, trying to grasp at least one good thing about his journey. Sadly, there were none. "I rode south to Port Shai to meet Kai-Tsúthlen and Ninthalas. You remember them, do you not?"

"You always visit them," Kírinfay retorted.

"Yes, but this time was a little different. I was fatigued from the battle at Luthrey. I wished to tell the Shadais about my trials, but they had news of their own. In Shalom, they had discovered a boy who is not much older than you, I think. He was separated from his parents—"

"—That is sad."

"Yes, it was quite sad. Yet Ninthalas loves this boy, so he took him along."

Kírinfay yawned. "Brother, you are not so good at telling stories."

"Is that so?" He said, sitting up tall and folding his arms. "Well, my tale is not yet finished. We rode over the Balkai Mountains and came to the infamous *Lotah 'an Morkh*."

Kírinfay gasped. She was well acquainted with the frightening stories surrounding the Dead Forest.

"Why would you go there? Is that forest not dangerous?"

"Yes, it is," said Tahlen. "Yet if you wish to pass through that place, you had better take Ninthalas Líran with you. He is the blessed of Yahlírin, after all. Or that is what Kai-Tsúthlen says. He bravely led us into that dreadful forest where we suffered horrors that would haunt your dreams. We travelled even into the night, but at a cost, for we were all three separated. Kai-Tsúthlen and I escaped…" He trailed off.

Kírinfay gaped, gazing up at him.

"What happened next?" she asked when he didn't continue. "Did Ninthalas escape as well? And what about the boy?"

Tahlen's countenance diminished. "That will wait for another night."

"But you did not finish your story!" Kírinfay protested.

"That *is* the end of the story. There is nothing more I can tell you. If you wish to hear the rest of the tale, then you will have to wait until you next see Ninthalas. He is the bearer of great tales, not I."

Tahlen hoped he wasn't giving any non-verbal hints of the chaotic river of mourning surging through his veins. He had little hope that his friend would come back home alive.

"You should sleep now lest mother comes and gets angry at both of us," he said.

Kírinfay pouted, but nodded. Tahlen kissed her forehead and stood to leave.

"Goodnight, Tahlen," she said to him as he neared the door.

"Goodnight."

He shut the door behind him. Just as he left the room, he saw his father come out of the bath room from the other end of the hall.

"Is your sister well?" Dúrlen asked.

"She was having trouble sleeping, so I tucked her in again," Tahlen answered. He spun on his heels and began walking away.

He didn't get far before a firm hand clasped his shoulder.

"My son," Dúrlen said in his usual stern voice, the kind of voice he used when addressing matters of business.

"What is it, father? Can you not let me grieve?"

"What has come over you? Control yourself and tell me plainly."

"Luthrey is gone—"

"That much I know already. I have read the accounts brought back by your Company thoroughly. You were supposed to be with them."

"I had to tell the Shadais—"

"And abandon your command?"

"You do not understand!" He shook off the grip.

"What can I not understand? You withdrew from your duties as Captain for the sake of seeing your friends."

"Ninthalas is gone, father!"

Dúrlen hesitated. "What do you mean?"

"Honestly, you men," Tahlen's mother scowled, storming down the hall toward them. "You will wake Kírinfay. To the table with you if you are going to talk in such a manner, or better yet outside where such raised voices are permitted."

She grabbed both of them by the arms and dragged them into the dining room. The men sat down at the table while she prepared some tea. Eventually, she returned carrying a tray of three teacups and a fresh pot of a herbal brew.

"Now tell me, son," said Dúrlen, taking a sip after she had poured him a cup. "What do you mean gone?"

"Yes, even I overheard," said Tahlen's mother. "How is Ninthalas gone?"

Tahlen breathed in deeply, taking the time to formulate his account before he told his parents the story. When he spoke, the words came shaky and unsure.

"You said yourself, father, that you have heard from my men concerning the battle at Luthrey. I will thus begin with our arrival in Lepsin on the return journey."

"Ninthalas and Kai-Tsúthlen Shadai happened to be passing through town on their errand to the south. Ninthalas claimed he had had a dream wherein Luthrey was engulfed in flames. He said that he had been having the same dream for several nights, and he begged of us to travel there. We went of course, though many of us were sceptical of his musings. Yet it was as he described. We arrived just in time to protect our allies. The details of the attack have probably already been well-explained in Atheil Feiren's account."

"Atheil Feiren has been promoted to 2nd Command for his detailed report, as well as from supportive acknowledgement from his Company," Dúrlen cut in.

"Dear, let him finish," Tahlen's mother said.

Tahlen breathed in again. "The short of it is we were outnumbered, and though we drove back the malshorthath, many of our men, and the city's army, were killed, including Lamnek, the Shadais' cousin. The malshorthath eventually retreated somewhere, but not without taking some of the women and children. We did not pursue them because of our own losses—Ah! I forgot to add that even before we engaged in battle, the Shadais had left Lepsin before us while we were yet making the decision to go to Luthrey. They were not at the battle when we arrived. I apologize for the ill execution of my account." He shifted in his seat. "I gave specific instructions concerning the Denedrúath's return to Serenestí before I followed the twins' trail south to Kislanía. I thought it reasonable to notify them of Lamnek's death, you see."

"And following that, you returned home, I gather?" Dúrlen interjected. "What of Ninthalas then?"

"We...we lost him, for we were driven into *Lotah 'an Morkh*, and there we were separated."

He told his parents of the souls he and his friends had seen floating down the River of Plenty and the Black Assailant who had led the invasion on Mor'Lûn, and who had also driven them into the mountains.

"You fled to the mountains because of one malshorth?" Dúrlen asked, incredulous.

"This was no ordinary malshorth, father. Both Yosef and Ninthalas fainted before we saw him. When Kai-Tsúthlen and I rushed to help, we saw the figure racing towards us from the direction of Mepdokh."

"Yosef?"

"A refugee boy whom Ninthalas was planning on bringing to Serenestí. Kai-Tsúthlen told me he would probably adopt the boy."

"Adopting a foreigner. *That* is a rash decision, as is Ninthalas Líran's way," Tahlen's mother remarked.

"It is not illegal, Kavathíen," said Dúrlen.

"It does not matter," Tahlen interjected. "We lost him to the rider in black, and when we passed through *Lotah 'an Morkh*, we lost Ninthalas as well. Kai-Tsúthlen and I made it out, but then we saw two groups of malshorthath heading in our direction, one to our left and another to our right. We lured them away from the forest in the case Ninthalas might escape."

"What troublesome news!" Kavathíen exclaimed. "First our beloved daughter, then poor Lamnek, and now Ninthalas is gone?"

"And there is this new malshorth leader," said Dúrlen. He paused before adding, "We must find out who he is and what his interest is in kidnapping children."

"From the effect he had on Ninthalas, I would not like to get near him," said Tahlen, shuddering. "I got a strange feeling from looking at him, an old sorrow threatening to overcome my heart. And I—yes, even I—succumbed to fear, such as I have not felt for years. It was truly horrible."

"You sound like your friend, Ninthalas Líran," Dúrlen said. There was no touch of sympathy in his tone. "Never mind feelings, son. They come and go."

Tahlen nodded.

"Well, I am off to bed," said Kavathíen, standing up.

Without another word, she left the men alone. Tahlen could never read his mother, never knew if she took to heart what she heard or let it fly to the wind. His father was much the same. Unlike his mother, though, Dúrlen saw conversation through to the end, and he always had the last word.

Both father and son sat still at the table, the silence widening the space between them.

"Tahlen."

Tahlen didn't answer. His eyes blurred with tears.

"Tahlen, look at me."

He looked up.

"I know," Dúrlen said. "I know it is hard for you and for me. We are both in positions we do not wholly understand, and by law we must abide by higher standards with the responsibility given to us. I have witnessed death, so I understand what you are going through. I understand that your sorrow is great. Mine was as well. Yet in my position, regardless of how I felt, I had to persevere. My rank of High Councillor demands it. You know that High Lord Tothran favours—more tolerates—me because of my name."

"Why did you even accept that title if it is so hard?" Tahlen demanded.

"I did not accept it. I was appointed, just as you were appointed to Captain. There was no disputing, and you and I did what we had to as was our duty. That is what it means to carry the name of Lothlúrin."

"Duty," Tahlen scoffed. "Sometimes I wish I had never been born Lothlúrin so that I could have at least grown up like a normal child. I wish I were no prodigy of this family."

Dúrlen stiffened. "Do not be quick to despise your name.

Consider it a blessing. Have confidence in it, for it is by Yahlírin's grace that you are of this family, of a high rank, and of exceptional skill in both battle and leadership. That is your charge. It is your gift."

Tahlen heaved a sigh. He and his father had had this type of conversation numerous times. He loved his job, but he couldn't meet his people's expectations.

"I know all seems hopeless now, and fear and uncertainty surrounds us. But we must press on with what hope we have."

Tahlen didn't have any hope left. He wanted to face whatever hardship came his way, but he couldn't grasp any motivation to overcome it. He was not like Kai-Tsúthlen or the courageous—yet slightly outrageous—Ninthalas. He might have had the ability to dispatch a band of malshorthath, but he had still failed. He had failed his Company, his friends…and Athlaya.

"It is good you returned when you did," said Dúrlen. "The High Lord is calling a mass meeting tomorrow, and you would do well to attend."

"A mass meeting?"

"Indeed, and it is imperative that you study those parchments I gave you. You must prepare your account tonight since you will be presenting it to the High Council and the congregation."

Tahlen slumped his shoulders. Just like his father to assign him a task when he least wanted to do anything. Sleep would have to wait.

"Yes, father."

Dúrlen stood and made for the hall. In the doorway, he turned. "Oh, and I request you bring Kai-Tsúthlen Okran with you. He should be there."

Tahlen cringed. Kai-Tsúthlen wouldn't be happy about being asked to attend a mass meeting. But Dúrlen's word was law in the Lothlúrin household. Tahlen would have to obey.

———◉———

CHAPTER TWELVE

The Mass Meeting

Kai-Tsúthlen awoke to find himself in his wife's arms. He didn't know how he had come to be on top of her because he distinctly recalled keeping well to his side of the bed the previous night. And as far as he knew, he was not prone to roll over in his sleep. Not that he had a problem with his predicament of course. Few things were more comforting than lying in the loving embrace of his wife.

Arúthíen ran her fingers through his long, black hair, humming softly to herself. Kai-Tsúthlen relaxed. Arúthíen's song lulled him into a half sleep.

"Good morning," she said in a soft voice.

"Good morning," he replied yawning.

"Did you sleep well?"

"Better than ever." He kissed her neck.

"Our children will be here soon," she said as he continued to caress her. "I need to prepare breakfast."

"Breakfast can wait."

"Our children cannot."

"*Ai*, Arúthíen, wait 'til they come, love."

"Stubborn man," she muttered. "Enough now. I hear footsteps."

Sure enough, the door to their room slid open a crack and a curious face peered in. Arúthíen shoved her husband off and hastily pulled up the comforter to compensate for the cold of the room.

"Come in, Ahnthalas," she said.

The boy opened the door wide and bounded over, wearing a grin that would rival Ninthalas'. He climbed onto the bed and collapsed on top of Kai-Tsúthlen.

"Good morning, father," he greeted cheerfully.

"Good morning, my son. Why are you awake so early?"

"It is not early. You slept in. Now is time to wake up."

"Ahnthalas, your father just returned from a long journey," Arúthíen said. "He needs his rest."

Ahnthalas wasn't listening. Instead, he decided to play the 'Let's Fall on Dad' game, a title which he had proudly come up with himself for an activity he exercised whenever Kai-Tsúthlen came home from a long trek. It primarily consisted of lifting himself up and falling like a breaching whale. Kai-Tsúthlen grabbed him and pinned him down. Arúthíen rolled her eyes at the boys' play and scooted closer to her edge of the bed.

Another patter of footsteps ran down the hall and in came Kai-Tsúthlen's daughter.

"Dada, dada!" she chanted as she trotted over to the bed. With a little help from Arúthíen, she climbed up and snuggled up to her mother.

"Good morning, Kírthíen, good morning," Kai-Tsúthlen greeted while trying to avoid several flying blows of small feet and fists. At last, he lay defeated on his back with his son sitting on top. Ahnthalas had won the struggle.

"We were waiting for you, father," the boy said.

"Were you now?" said Kai-Tsúthlen. "What did you do while I was gone?"

"We went to see grandpa and grandma."

This was the climax of the story, and Kai-Tsúthlen braced himself for the details to follow. His son loved to talk.

"Grandpa took me to the Selestorinth and we met High Councillor Dúrlen. He was very serious." Ahnthalas made an over-exaggerated frown. "He was pretty boring, though. There were guards and grown-ups and we saw a guy named General Konran who is very important, I think. And then we went to the glade together and played chase."

Kai-Tsúthlen had a bit of a hard time taking in the quick

speech. The fatigue from his journey still lingered and he rubbed his eyes, trying to focus. He understood the places and names his son spoke of, but he could only guess as to which glade his son had gone to. Serenestí had many.

"Oh! And we had sweet sticks, too!" Ahnthalas added. "Well, *I* had sweet sticks. Grandpa did not have any. Actually, I ate his."

"Indeed, it was definitely an enjoyable time," his mother summarized.

"I see," said Kai-Tsúthlen with a smile.

"Mother measured me, too! I am this much bigger than last time." He motioned with his thumb and finger a small space apart.

"*Bai*, you are growing so much," Kai-Tsúthlen said. "Someday you shall be taller than I am."

"And I will be stronger, too!"

Kai-Tsúthlen and Arúthíen glanced at each other. This was a frequent conversation, one they had actually started counting. So far, they were up to about fifty-two times whenever Kai-Tsúthlen had returned from an errand, whether it be for only a couple of days or an entire month. And that was only within the present year.

"I am sure you will," said Kai-Tsúthlen.

Arúthíen interrupted them. "Ahnthalas, your father is still tired and needs to rest. Take your sister to the kitchen."

"But mother," the boy whined.

"Go on."

Obediently, he took his sister and left the room, shutting the door behind.

"Such busy children we have," Arúthíen commented.

She got out of bed and hurriedly dressed for the day. Kai-Tsúthlen watched her with droopy eyes.

"I love you," he said to her.

She turned and smiled. With all the grace of a dove, she glided over to the bedside, knelt down and kissed him.

"I love you, too."

Then she rose and left, closing the door behind her.

Kai-Tsúthlen rolled onto his side. He would have slept more, but his son's eager voice could be heard from the kitchen, constantly inquiring when father would come out.

Indeed, what busy children he had. Rest would have to wait.

The day was bright and clear, the sky a brilliant blue without a single cloud. Kai-Tsúthlen breathed in the morning air. He would have soaked up the peace and remained gazing up at the sky if his son didn't demand his attention. He was teaching Ahnthalas basic sword techniques, what he thought was reasonable for a child, except that his son was picking up the skills a lot quicker than expected. The boy sported a *saiken*, a practice sword made of wood. It would be another eight years before Ahnthalas was allowed to own his own blade.

While he and his son were practicing, Arúthíen showed up at the back door with a visitor. Kai-Tsúthlen immediately stopped the lesson.

"Tahlen, my friend, 'tis good to see you," he greeted. "What brings you here so early?"

The captain bowed his head to Arúthíen and stepped forward.

"I apologize for my unwelcome intrusion, especially when you are in the midst of spending time with your family," he said.

Ever the rigid man, right down to his speech. Yet there was something off about the Captain. His eyes were tired, reddish, like he had spent the whole night awake.

"Think nothing of it, Tahlen. You are welcome here any time."

"Hello, Captain Dían," Ahnthalas greeted.

"Good morning, Ahnthalas. I see you are learning sword techniques. You have a good teacher."

"I think you would be better."

"Perhaps some other time. I have certain matters to discuss with your father. Would you allow me to converse with him?"

Ahnthalas slumped his shoulders. "I guess so."

"Many thanks to you," Tahlen said, rustling his fingers through the boy's hair.

Kai-Tsúthlen told his son to keep practicing and the two men went inside to talk privately. Arúthíen brought them tea, then led Kírthíen outside to join Ahnthalas. The men sat cross-legged on cushions on the floor with a clear view of Kai-Tsúthlen's family through the open sliding door.

"You have a wonderful family," Tahlen said at length.

"Am I supposed to understand that statement a certain way?"

Kai-Tsúthlen saw his friend's eyes glaze over.

"Tahlen, my friend, I see in you a man who is unsure of himself. Tell me, what troubles you?"

"Indeed, I am no leader—"

"But you are, and you must be."

"My father said roughly the same thing last night, though I am not so sure. My mind is clouded by the turn of events from our journey."

"Indeed, there has been much sorrow, and both of us have seen things that we should not have, perhaps even experienced more than we can handle," Kai-Tsúthlen agreed. "Yet we must hold strong, my friend, and not lose hope. This sorrow should not last forever."

"But Ninthalas—"

"Ninthalas is alive, Tahlen. I would know it if he was dead. We are twins born of the same womb; we know how the other fairs even when we are apart."

"Perhaps so," said Tahlen. He sat up straighter, his face more resolute. "I am to speak before the Council today at a mass meeting. My father knows of my account. He says that the Council and other authorities would want a firsthand report, especially since I forsook my Company and fled south."

"Forsook your Company? Was there a breach in order?"

"Apparently, or so my father tells me."

"I will have to check the records, though your father knows the law better than I do. This must be a worthy opportunity for you to speak before the council. I do not expect anything ill will come from it."

"I am considering whether or not to tell them of Yosef as well," Tahlen added.

"That…may not go well with the High Lord," he said. "Yosef is none of his business."

"We do not keep such matters secret in our society," said Tahlen. He stiffened. "I actually came here because I have a favour to ask. I want you to come with me to this mass meeting."

Kai-Tsúthlen's aspect grew stern. "And what would I benefit from going? No News Bearer has ever been present at a council. I would rather not speak of our journey, for it is yet near and troubles me."

"I do not request that you say anything, Kai-Tsúthlen, simply that you be there. No, you will not benefit anything by coming, but I ask this of you because I need a witness…and support." He hesitated. "I *need* you there, Kai-Tsúthlen. I would be more at ease if a trusted friend were present. Never before have I been tried with giving an account to the High Council."

Kai-Tsúthlen eyed him, trying to figure him out. Tahlen rarely exhibited such emotion in front of people. Yet he also had more societal pressure than any other eighteen-year-old in Serenestí. It was rare for a man so young to speak before the High Council, let alone be promoted to the rank of Captain. Tahlen may have had considerable skill with a sword, but he still lacked the maturity befitting a leader. He certainly ran his Company well, but there was something missing that Kai-Tsúthlen couldn't quite put his finger on. Tahlen was still the second born in his family, and he had no prospect of taking on the responsibilities of a firstborn.

"Alright. If you truly require my presence so badly, I will go with you."

Kai-Tsúthlen didn't know what he was getting into; it was like following Ninthalas on one of his odd quests. Yet he was a devoted friend, and if he was needed, then so be it. Besides, he was interested in the role of the High Council anyway and this opportunity would give him a glimpse of political affairs.

The friends made their way north, walking at a fast pace through their hometown of Selestía and into the thick of trees. Tahlen didn't speak to him the entire way, and Kai-Tsúthlen didn't bother to ask how last night went.

At High Sun, they reached their destination. The Selestorinth was a massive complex consisting of three buildings central to Serenestí's political and religious activity. It was built in the days of Namthúl Shadai in the largest glade in Serenestí. Though Kai-Tsúthlen had been there many times on his visit to the Great Library, he still marvelled at the Selestorinth's magnificence.

Upon passing under the wide gates, the friends followed the path through the central courtyard and branched right towards the west building, Selest'Hí, whose activity pertained strictly to the government. Kai-Tsúthlen had accompanied his father a few times on his visits to see High Councillor Dúrlen. After such a laborious errand to other nations, he had since forgotten its grandeur. Inside a spacious lobby soared two stories high, and a balcony from the second floor overlooked the circular lobby. Four enormous pillars held up the high ceiling, each one embroidered to resembled climbing vines. Unlike the other two buildings of the Selestorinth, Selest'Hí contained murals on the walls which depicted scenes of Namthúl Shadai and his accomplice, the nameless Lothlúrin, bestowing the law upon four slabs of stone to the people of the nation. Those same stones lay preserved in a tall glass casket at the centre of the lobby, a symbol of True Faithen religion.

Kai-Tsúthlen and Tahlen took the right wing to a set of double doors, large strong stone fastened with silver hinges and curled doorknobs. They were already open. The two walked inside, into the Great Hall. Kai-Tsúthlen gaped. He'd never been in the domed sanctuary before, but he'd heard that it was capable of holding hundreds of people. Those hearings were correct. The hall was filled with soldiers, Denedrúath Companies and Pellendrath Squadrons alike. Having grown up a News Bearer, Kai-Tsúthlen didn't know the difference between the two military groups.

"We are late," said Tahlen.

"It seems to me the meeting has not yet started," Kai-Tsúthlen noted.

"It is about to begin. Come now, we are to sit in the Authorities in Question."

Kai-Tsúthlen simply nodded and followed to the back of the front row of seats. Chairs. Few places in Serenestí had chairs. As soon as they sat down, the hall went quiet. Down the central aisle marched the High Lord and High Council, all eight members, shuffling in single file. They wore robes of white overlaid with sleeveless cloaks coloured a deep blue. Woven silver sashes were tied about their wastes, the corded ends falling down their gowns. Each member carried a single scroll.

Before reaching the seats of the Authorities in Question, the Councilmen turned right, circling to the outer wall where a stairway led to their high positions above the congregation. Kai-Tsúthlen spotted Dúrlen among them. Tahlen's father sat second from the right. His countenance was stern, unreadable, like the cold of winter unhindered by the promise of spring. It was that same expression Tahlen had inherited, a resolve that saw through change and never wavered. Though lately, Tahlen's stoic demeanour had changed.

Kai-Tsúthlen looked at his friend. The young captain stared straight ahead, his alert facade a mask that hid an exhausted adolescent. Red circles under his eyes were the only hint of his fatigue. The Captain was nervous. His hands fidgeted over folded papers in his lap.

Once the High Council was seated the High Lord rose. This was Kai-Tsúthlen's first time seeing him, an aged man of seventy-three who had ruled over Serenestí for more than thirty years. His face, more rigid than Dúrlen's, bore faint wrinkles but otherwise refused to age.

He spoke in a voice that demanded everyone's attention. "Greetings to those who have gathered for this mass meeting. We are here to witness the accounts of those who help govern our country, to take note and to judge what is right and wrong. In contrast to previous meetings, there are many accounts which have come to my attention as of late, and they require prompt addressing. In short, a breach in order has been undertaken."

He lifted up his scroll and read it aloud.

"'While on route to the city Melbé, it was noted that General Konran was not with us. We therefore inquired of 2nd Command Eflan Shadai, who in turn addressed the issue to our commanding officer, Captain Dían Lothlúrin. We were informed that General Konran had pressing matters to deal with, and he was not to accompany us.'"

He set down the scroll.

"Now, let us hear from this General who has not filed a single report regarding this matter. May we witness the reason he abandoned his post."

He sat down.

Konran Lothlúrin, a distant relative of Tahlen, stood up. He had served long in the Denedrúath, and through hard years had reached the title of General, a single rank above Tahlen and the highest capable in a Denedrúath Company. Kai-Tsúthlen had heard of the General's greatness from Tahlen. According to the Captain, it was not common for Konran Lothlúrin to dismiss any duty, so for him to 'breach his order', his reason must have been dire. It was a shame that one of his men had commented on the general's absence during the check-in. Understandable, but a shame. Kai-Tsúthlen had a good idea of whose account the High Lord had read.

General Konran Lothlúrin stood, bowed and spoke in a firm voice that demanded as much respect as the High Lord's. "It is true I have not filed a report, and for that I express my deepest apologies. My reasons for not embarking with my Company I had explained to Captain Dían, and they are as such: a member of my family is gravely ill, and I remained in Serenestí so as to provide aid. That is all I have to say with regards to this *abandoning* of my post. So ends my account."

"Captain Dían," the High Lord called.

Tahlen stood at the sound of his name and bowed low.

"Is this true? Do you attest to General Konran's excuse?"

"It is precisely as he stated it," Tahlen replied. "General Konran did indeed approach me and explained his situation. I accepted his dismissal and carried out the annual check-in as first commanding officer."

He sat down.

"As much as I sympathize with you concerning your relative, General Konran, I am displeased with your neglect of requesting permission to not accompany our woodsmen," said the High Lord. "I will further discuss this matter with the members of the High Council to determine your punishment.

"Now, there is yet another peculiarity that has been brought to my attention. This very Company was involved in a malshorth raid in a city off the route of its check in. I call upon the recently promoted 2nd Command Atheil Feiren to speak regarding the battle at Luthrey."

Kai-Tsúthlen glanced at Tahlen questioningly. The captains gave him the same confused look. Even with his limited knowledge of military ranks, Kai-Tsúthlen knew that 2nd Commands were never called upon to speak at mass meetings. Technically, a Company's general would speak first regarding a matter, and his captain and 2nd Command would attest to events as witnesses. This order of conduct was out of line. If only Ninthalas were here now. He probably would have enjoyed this misconduct.

2nd Command Atheil stood and walked up to the pulpit. Kai-

Tsúthlen knew him to be an eccentric man, even more so than Ninthalas. There was no question that his promotion was due to the sincerity of his account. Without bowing to the congregation, Atheil unfolded his written report and read it aloud, explaining everything from the Company's departure to its return. He explained how Ninthalas Líran Shadai, the News Bearer, had persuaded the Company to go to Luthrey, and the details regarding the attack from the malshorthath.

"We lost many of our own that day, and we still mourn for them. Many of those were young fathers, others betrothed or dear husbands. But, though the odds were against us, we drove the enemy back. They vanished over the hills without a trace. We stayed in Luthrey two days afterwards to mourn for our dead, then returned home. Captain Dían left me in charge while he went south to seek his friends, the News Bearers Kai-Tsúthlen Okran and Ninthalas Líran Shadai, to tell them of the loss of their cousin, Lamnek Eflan."

He folded up the paper and ended with, "So ends my account," then returned to his seat.

From the moment he finished speaking, the congregation was in an uproar. Malshorthath had seldom been seen, and most had never had the misfortune of meeting one, let alone a raiding party.

The High Lord raised his hand, silencing them.

"I was going to request Captain Dían to speak for his contrary actions as General Konran did, but need I hear more? We have a crisis to deal with and I am sure Captain Dían's betrayal of his Company can wait."

By this point, Kai-Tsúthlen was thoroughly unimpressed. The High Lord had breached his country's order of conduct by condemning a General in front of the entire mass of officials, as well as disregarding a Captain's report entirely. Tahlen had not acted unjustly by going to Luthrey, unless the High Lord had instated a new policy. Ninthalas was the one who had had the dream regarding the invasion, so it was only natural for Tahlen to inform his Company. His Company, in turn, had the choice not to go. As for his 'betrayal', Kai-Tsúthlen could not guess how that was a breach in order. If Tahlen hadn't joined the twins, Kai-Tsúthlen, Ninthalas and Yosef all would have died.

High Councillor Dúrlen spoke. "If I may plead with you, High

Lord Tothran, let my son speak. I have heard his story and believe it to be valuable information."

The High Lord eyed him dubiously. "Very well," he replied. His gaze fell on Tahlen. "Let us hear your reasoning, *young* Captain."

Tahlen stood up, walked to the podium, and bowed low. Then, resolutely, he recounted his tale. "I will begin from when I left my Company..."

He went into impeccable detail, his account even more impressive than Atheil's. He recounted how he had met the Shadai twins at Port Shai, journeyed with them to the old bridge where their path was diverted, and how they had been attacked by skohls. Less detail did he recall the passage through *Lotah 'an Morkh*, probably because he was embarrassed by his inability to stay sane. Though Kai-Tsúthlen was impressed. Not once did Tahlen mention the appearance of Yosef or the prospect of bringing the boy to Serenestí, and he finished on the assumption that Ninthalas had returned with them last night. The only oddity of his tale was the appearance of the mysterious Black Assailant.

The congregation listened silently, remaining quiet even after Tahlen had finished with the customary, "So ends my account". The High Council sat motionless, bewildered expressions drawn on their wise faces. Only Dúrlen appeared relaxed, having heard the tale before.

At last, one of the other Councilmen spoke.

"This news is indeed shocking to all of us, yet perhaps we have been living too prosperous in this time of peace. Have we not been expecting unrest? Captain Dían's tale is a difficult one to swallow, especially that which concerns this...new foe he claims to have seen. But we have witnessed one raid and it alone is a sign for precaution on our borders."

"I agree," said another High Council member. "Let us take up arms on the borders and be ready."

"And what of the devastated villages?" asked High Councillor Dúrlen. The rest of the High Council looked at him, and Kai-Tsúthlen could see distrust in a number of their faces.

Dúrlen ignored their odd looks and continued. "For centuries, our News Bearers have brought tidings from them. We have traded with them, and we have become their allies. Should we just give up on them and not provide aid?"

"Those villages to whom we so freely give have offered us little to nothing in return," stated the councilman to his right.

"And since when have we ever expected anything in return?" Dúrlen pressed. "I suggest we send what aid we can. The raid and the threat of further attacks concern every nation of A'thería."

"Do you mean to say that we should risk our men's lives?" said the first man. "Our provisions could be raided by bandits while they travel, or have you not heard from the very News Bearers you claim to support? You know as well as the whole congregation that we are not well-received in every part of A'thería. I say we look to our own borders. Let us not be too quick to forget the losses we have already sustained from the attack on Luthrey."

The High Lord interjected. "I am not so convinced of Captain Dían's account. Has he two witnesses to justify the mysterious events and his actions therein? For never before has word of a 'Black Assailant' come to light, even in the entirety of the accounts of recorded time."

Everyone looked at Tahlen as he stood to answer the indirect address. "I have but Kai-Tsúthlen Okran Shadai, who was with me during those events."

For the first time, the entire congregation realized that a News Bearer was in their midst and a murmur spread across them. The High Lord glared at Kai-Tsúthlen.

"News Bearer," spoke the councilman on the far left. "Do you attest to these things which Captain Dían has proclaimed?"

Kai-Tsúthlen stood and bowed. He held himself in firm resolve as he eyed the High Lord, knowing full well that the elderly man disapproved of his presence at the mass meeting. Yet he couldn't have cared less about what everyone thought. His frustration outweighed his anxiety. Too long had the general populous discriminated against his family's name and status. They would see now that Shadai held as much importance now as it did in Namthúl's time.

"I attest to them," he replied in a loud voice. "It is as Captain Dían said, and the Black Assailant he speaks of is real. That foe threatened us, and we fled to the mountains where we suffered attack from skohls. I have every reason to believe that we were pursued for the remainder of our journey."

"And you expect me to believe you?"

"I expect you to believe two things, my lord Councilman: one, that a raid has been wrought on a trade city with whom we do business; second, that a new threat has arisen and his intentions are undetermined. Whether you choose to believe the latter, though, is irrelevant because now you have an issue on your hands. An attack on a city means a potential attack on our country. The malshorthath have returned. The Three could follow, plunging us into another war."

He bowed low and sat down again.

"Where is this Ninthalas Líran who is apparently gifted with prophetic dreams?" the High Lord asked.

"He is not present, my lord," Tahlen replied. "The trials we faced were particularly hard on him."

"Captain Dían, I will only believe your fairytale if you can bring me a second witness. You must send this other News Bearer to me by tomorrow; that will seal the validity of your account. Until then, it is void."

He turned to the congregation. "Since we all agree that these matters must be taken to heart, we will set up watches on our borders. Every Squadron of the Pellendrath and Company of the Denedrúath will be on guard. Every man who is not part of the defence will watch over his own family and that of his neighbour, and no News Bearers are permitted to leave this country without government waiver. Furthermore, trade is to be closely monitored and anyone passing in or out of the country is to be strictly questioned about his business. I will delegate more specific duties as follows…"

The 'end' of the mass meeting went on much longer than the telling of accounts. Kai-Tsúthlen would have become bored had the matters of the meeting not given him a clear view of the workings of the government. Despite his interest in formalities and conduct, however, he was thankful when the High Council left, signifying the end of the mass meeting. By then he longed for a good night's sleep. He couldn't imagine how Tahlen was fairing.

He and Tahlen exited the Great Hall before anyone could inquire of them, retracing their steps down the wide hallway toward the lobby.

"That went on much longer than any other meeting I have been to," said Tahlen, yawning. "And it was far more tense than anything I have ever experienced."

"I found it amusing, long though it was," said Kai-Tsúthlen. "I have often wondered at the workings of higher classes."

"Higher classes? My friend, from the way you spoke, I would have considered you a nobleman."

"Tahlen, I said one thing, barely an opinion."

"But it was the way you carried yourself—unwavering."

"Well, my mother made no mistake when she named me Okran, meaning 'steadfast'. Yet you as one befitting his rank as well."

"Kai-Tsúthlen Okran."

He looked up and saw Dúrlen and another member of the High Council approaching them. Kai-Tsúthlen stiffened. The last thing he wanted was to speak to Dúrlen. Now he knew why Tahlen had invited him. It hadn't been because Tahlen needed him, but because Dúrlen wanted him to be there.

"That was a splendid performance," Dúrlen said.

Kai-Tsúthlen bowed. "I heard much the same praise from Tahlen Dían, sir."

"Your father tells me you would excel at a governing profession."

"Indeed, he is persistent on the matter even at home," said Kai-Tsúthlen. "Have you come to persuade me as well?"

"You are perceptive. I have a proposition for you. You may not answer now if you so choose, but it is something to ponder." He turned to his associate. "This is High Councillor Afren."

Kai-Tsúthlen bowed his head to the elderly man, who returned the courtesy.

"He is due to retire in five years and as such will need a replacement. What I propose is that you study under him until his retirement and succeed him."

Kai-Tsúthlen studied the councilman. This High Councillor Afren was the same man who had questioned him in the Great Hall.

"Well, this is…an unprecedented offer," he said, shifting his gaze between the older man and Dúrlen. "How did you come by this decision?"

"I have met your father on numerous occasions," Afren replied. "And I trust High Councillor Dúrlen's judgement. I have been greatly disturbed that since Namthúl Shadai the respected families of Lothlúrin and Shadai have not been represented in government. We had initially considered your father a worthy candidate, but after much discussion, including with your father, we decided upon you. You have the qualities of a leader; that much I saw from your presentation at the mass meeting."

"I would oblige, but have you not considered my age?" Kai-Tsúthlen questioned. "Even after five years, I will still not be of the proper age to assume that position. Or have you forgotten that I must be at least thirty-five for the masses to consider me eligible? And even that is young."

"I have considered it," said Dúrlen. "Yet do not neglect your skills, Okran Shadai. You are well-travelled, married to one of the mistresses of trade, and brother of the finest international negotiator A'thería has ever seen."

"I did not think you thought so highly of my brother based on his track record."

"The High Lord would have this nation become isolated when in reality we should be reaching out. We may have traders among us, but politically, we are isolated, even though we send the Denedrúath on check-ins every other year. We need strong allies, strong friends, and a News Bearer in high standing would aid that. You have sound knowledge of international ties."

"I will think it over."

"Take your time. You are in no hurry," said Dúrlen.

Kai-Tsúthlen bowed to the older men, turned and walked away with Tahlen. As they left, he heard the Councilmen speaking to each other loud enough for him to hear.

"How composed he is," Afren noted.

"That man has the potential to become High Lord someday," said Dúrlen. "I know it."

CHAPTER THIRTEEN

Ninthalas Returns

"What did Tahlen need with you that he had to pull you away?" Arúthíen asked.

Kai-Tsúthlen had just put his children to bed and joined his wife in the bath room. His trials hadn't ended when he returned home. His son had pestered him with questions and stories that could have rivalled Ninthalas' tales. Now, with the children in bed and the day finished, he could finally relax.

Almost. Dúrlen's proposition toyed with his mind.

"He invited me to a mass meeting," he replied.

She rolled her eyes. "A mass meeting, how fortunate. I have heard tales of such things, and never have they been described with much excitement."

"It was rather intriguing actually. I had the opportunity to speak before the High Lord."

"You lie!"

"It is true. They inquired whether I attested to Tahlen's account or not."

"And?"

"Naturally, I did, and defended myself when the High Council questioned me." He paused before adding, "High Councillor Dúrlen approached me afterward. I have a feeling he was the reason for my presence. Tahlen would not have invited me otherwise despite how sincere his request was. He had a most appalling proposition for me, actually."

"And that was?"

"One of the councilmen is to retire in five years. Dúrlen Lothlúrin suggested that I study under him and take his place."

"Are you serious? That is wonderful, Kai-Tsú!"

"I question whether or not to take it."

"And why not? This is the perfect opportunity. Have you not always wanted to study law?"

"Arúthíen, have you not seen how Dúrlen has become since he assumed office? He is more rigid than ever. He only resumes his old self when father goes to see him."

"But you would not become like that."

"How so?"

"You are a composed man, Kai-Tsú, yet you are not like Dúrlen Lothlúrin. And you have not endured loss like he has."

"It is easy for you to say. You were Kavathíen Lothlúrin's apprentice and have since attained your own trading booth when the merchants come. Your success rivals even hers."

"And who is to say that you cannot rise as well in your own field? Take heart, love. You are well able to do this."

Kai-Tsúthlen sighed. "I must think it over."

"How about you discuss it with mother and father? They may have better insight."

"Perhaps so." He stood. "I am off to bed early. I have much on my mind."

"I will be there shortly."

He dried, threw on a gown, and left.

Tap, tap, tap.

He paused. Was that the front door, or was he imagining things? He went to the door and listened. Three firm knocks rapped the wood. He grasped the handle and opened slid the door open…

And gasped. Then tears filled his eyes and he grasped the visitor in a warm embrace, laughing for sheer joy.

"I knew you would come back!" he exclaimed. "I knew it! Blessed of Yahlírin indeed!"

"Would I ever choose to remain parted from you?" Ninthalas said, lifting the atmosphere with laughter of his own.

"Yet…how? When did you arrive?"

"Just now. I went home first to drop Yosef off with mother

and father. You should have seen the looks on their faces when I came bounding through the door!"

"You found Yosef? You must tell me everything! I have been worried sick about you."

"My thoughts were on you as well," said Ninthalas. "How is Tahlen?"

"Oh, Tahlen, the poor man."

Ninthalas leaned forward. "What is wrong with him? Is he alright?"

"He is home and safe. Yet he was exhausted when I met with him today. He looked like he had been up all last night."

"Dúrlen Lothlúrin's doing?"

Kai-Tsúthlen nodded. "I believe so."

Arúthíen appeared from around the corner of the doorway. "My, it *is* you, Ninthalas!" She rushed forward and pulled him into an embrace.

"Fair greetings, sister," Ninthalas said with a chuckle.

"Kai-Tsúthlen told me everything."

"Did he now? Mother and father appear to be oblivious."

"We did not tell them," said Kai-Tsúthlen. "How could we when you did not return with me? We decided to wait for you to come back."

"Indeed," said Arúthíen. "Come in for some tea. Mother brought me herbs the other day—"

Ninthalas held up a hand. "Sadly, I must decline. I am yet troubled and weary, and Yosef needs tending to."

"I am sure father can care for him," said Kai-Tsúthlen. "Come, you must tell me about your escape and how you found Yosef."

"I…well, it is truly a trying story. Though really, I must return home. Would tomorrow suit you better? I honestly am fading. I need rest."

Kai-Tsúthlen eyed him quizzically. "I see." His brother never refused an invitation to dine. Something was different. His brother was hiding something, but Kai-Tsúthlen couldn't guess what.

"Very well, brother. I will see you tomorrow," he said at last. "Then you may tell me your story, and I will tell you mine. Tahlen and I attended a mass meeting this afternoon."

"A mass meeting!" Ninthalas exclaimed. "Then we both have

stories to tell! I look forward to yours in earnest."

"Indeed," Kai-Tsúthlen agreed. "Goodnight, brother."

Ninthalas returned the statement, turned and walked off into the night.

"There, you see? You had nothing to fear. He is back at last," Arúthíen said.

Kai-Tsúthlen didn't comment. He was stuck on Ninthalas' refusal of hospitality. How unlike him. Whatever had happened in *Lotah 'an Morkh*, Ninthalas had changed. Kai-Tsúthlen could see it, could sense it.

Before shutting the door, he looked out again. Ninthalas was barely a shape among the shadows of the stone path that wound away from his house. Kai-Tsúthlen squinted. His brother wasn't alone. Another shape walked beside him, a glowing figure with long, silver hair and white, clean robes.

But maybe it was just Kai-Tsúthlen's imagination.

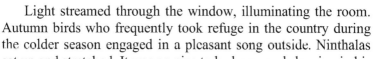

Light streamed through the window, illuminating the room. Autumn birds who frequently took refuge in the country during the colder season engaged in a pleasant song outside. Ninthalas sat up and stretched. It was so nice to be home and sleeping in his own bed again. He clapped his hands together in front of his face and turned his head upwards.

"Blessed Yahl, generous Provider, I thank you for this day. My deepest gratitude for getting us home safely."

Yet as soon as he spoke the prayer, a sinister chant rose in his mind. The words had plagued him since he escaped *Lotah 'an Morkh*, but it wasn't the chant itself that frightened him. It was the voice that spoke them, the sound of his own voice.

Run, run, Líran Shadai, flee if you will. Yet the shadow will find you in the night and swallow you whole. And you shall be mine, dear brother, and make me whole. Run, run, brother Shadai...

That wasn't the only peculiarity. Yosef had told Ninthalas that the Black Assailant was a woman. Shadai had confirmed it.

"Oh that my heart would not be in distress, Yahl," he prayed. "Yet truly it must be over. You delivered Yosef to me, and we are home safe."

He opened his eyes and looked down. Yosef was still asleep beside him, easily taking up what little space the single bed had to offer. He showed no sign of waking anytime soon. The poor boy had been through a trying dilemma, what with being kidnapped and dragged into *Lotah 'an Morkh*. The boy had suffered two bites from skohls, one on his arm and the other on his leg. Ninthalas had used up the rest of his ointments to treat them and last night his mother had set the wounds with fresh bandages. Yet they would still need to be looked at. Ninthalas would have to take him to the clinic to visit his grandmother, who specialized in medical care.

Not wanting to disturb the boy's sleep, Ninthalas quietly rose from the bed, got dressed, and slid the door shut on his way out of the bedroom. He followed the hall to the dining room where the table was adorned with plates, eating utensils and cups, as well as fresh bread from the bakery in town. A delicious aroma floated out of the neighbouring kitchen, which was only accessible from the dining room. The aroma mixed with the scent of herbs from a fresh pot of spiced tea, a standard morning brew for every True Faithen household.

Ninthalas entered the kitchen and found his mother, Lethría, cracking eggs into a square frying pan over the stove.

"Good morning, mother," he greeted.

Lethría turned and smiled. "Good morning, my son. You appear to be in a much better mood than the night before. I was quite worried, you know. How sour you were, too much like the way your brother broods in the morning."

He peered over her shoulder at the meal she was preparing. "Can I help you with anything?"

"Boy! You have just returned from a long journey, and here you are asking to serve me? No, you may not help! What you *can* do is go wash up for breakfast."

Ninthalas chuckled and did as he was told. A large basin of water sat in the far corner of the room filled to the brim from several trips to the local well that morning. Ninthalas drew from it using a small pitcher and diligently scrubbed even though he had removed any trace of dirt during his bath the previous night. When he was done, he took the pitcher to another deep bucket which was already half full of dirty water. Routine told him that he would have to empty it into the river later.

He went back to his mother's side and wrapped his arms around her.

"I missed you, mother."

"And I you, son. Now go relax while I get breakfast ready."

"Is there truly nothing I can help you with?"

She huffed. "If you are that desperate, the fruit can be chopped and put out."

He obeyed. In no time, he had a platter full of diced fruits ranging from apples to cranberries to peeled figs. Lethría brought out a plate of the sweet egg omelet she had been making and fresh greens from her garden.

When the table was set, they heard the front door open and close, and in walked Kai-Tsúthlen.

"And there is my other son, back from his journey!" Lethría exclaimed. She crossed the room and gave Kai-Tsúthlen a hug.

"Did you think I would pass up one of your meals, mother?" he said.

"You two have much explaining to do. How did you come across this boy?"

"You have not told her, brother?" said Ninthalas with a knowing grin.

"I did not want to worry her."

"'Twas probably for the best. Should we tell her now, though?"

"Enough talking over me. I will not tolerate such rudeness."

"Of course, mother," said Ninthalas.

He and Kai-Tsúthlen sat down on the square cushions at the table.

Before they could tell their tale, the door burst open and in strode the twins' father, Athestin. Ninthalas' grin vanished when he saw his father's sour expression. His father rarely got upset, but when he did, it frightened even the most well-meaning of people.

"What in all A'thería happened on your errand?" he demanded.

Ninthalas had never seen him so upset.

"I beg your pardon, father?"

"I was just over at the Lothlúrins'. They say Kai-Tsúthlen and

Tahlen returned the night before last while you, Ninthalas, came back last night."

Ninthalas glanced at his brother. "I suppose we have no choice now, do we?"

"Would you like to go first?"

"I do not care who goes first, only that I hear both stories."

Athestin went to sit by his wife, who was busy dishing up everyone's plates. She didn't seem too impressed with the news either.

"I guess I will start," Ninthalas offered.

He told his entire account like a famed story teller, from the morning the twins had set foot out the door on the News Bearer errand to their meeting Tahlen's Company in Lepsin. He wove an elaborate tale of his insanity from a recurring dream he had had and their fortunes in meeting with the king of Luthrey to deliver the news of invasion. Kai-Tsúthlen filled in the details during the time Ninthalas had gone insane in Luthrey. Then Ninthalas spoke of their arrival in Shalom.

"There is something eerie at work in the golden city," he said. "I know it has not been the same since I upset things years back, but the citizens seem more hostile. They would not even speak to us. There was but one woman who showed me favour."

"Indeed, they were more unkind than they have ever been," Kai-Tsúthlen agreed.

"Because of their ignorance toward us, we resolved to move on to Kislanía the next day. Yet that night at the usual inn, a young boy came came upon our dwelling. I thought I heard a knock on the door, but Kai-Tsúthlen assumed it was nothing. Lo and behold, the door creaked open and when we ventured downstairs, we found this boy asleep on one of the bags. He looked terrible. You probably saw why last night in the bath, father."

"I did. What is the story with him?" Athestin asked.

"We do not know," Kai-Tsúthlen replied. "Not much, that is. We did not find out until we went to Port Shai that his village was raided by malshorthath, and that he is the only child to escape from the enemy."

"And I heard Luthrey was invaded as well, which is several fathoms away."

"Exactly," said Ninthalas. "It does not add up. Furthermore,

Yosef ended up in Shalom with no memory of how he got there, what happened to his village—which is Mor'Lûn, by the way—nor of the refugees we found in Port Shai."

"Peculiar," Athestin mused.

"That is what I said. Now Tahlen met us in Port Shai and told us of Luthrey."

"We also know about Lamnek," Kai-Tsúthlen added.

"As do we," said Lethría solemnly.

"We asked Yosef if he would like to come with us to Serenestí and he obliged. I would not wish to leave him with those refugees. He is not entirely Kislanían."

"That much I could tell. What is his other half then?"

The twins glanced at each other.

"The refugees told me his father was a giant, though they did not know where he came from," Ninthalas explained. "They told me of the raid, how the malshorthath had borne their women and children away. Then when they had finished, they said it would be best if Yosef went with us. Of course, how could I refuse? Is he not adorable? I quite enjoy caring for him."

He smiled, recalling his journey from *Lotah 'an Morkh* to Serenestí with only Yosef for company.

"Are you still considering adoption then?" Kai-Tsúthlen asked.

"Indeed, I am."

"That I have some opinions about," Lethría stated.

"Let them finish," said Athestin.

"So we took Yosef with us. We stopped across the river from Fethlin for the night. That was when the first phenomenon occurred. From Mepdokh, a host of floating spirits drifted downriver."

"Spirits?"

"They were souls, drifting transparent bodies, mangled and deformed as if they had suffered some terrible fate."

"Massacred," Kai-Tsúthlen clarified.

"No doubt the remains of the villagers of Mepdokh."

"So Mepdokh is destroyed," said Athestin.

Ninthalas nodded.

"The next day, we stopped at the old bridge for Ninthalas' benefit," Kai-Tsúthlen went on. "That was when the real oddities began."

"As if the souls were not odd enough," said Ninthalas. "Yosef and I were on the bridge and about to turn back when he freaked. He was shouting, 'yellow eyes,' like he was being attacked by some unseen force. Then he fell unconscious."

"And that was when it *really* got strange," said Kai-Tsúthlen.

"Indeed. I began to hear shrill voices in my head and they drove me mad."

"Before Tahlen and I knew what was going on, he fainted, as did Yosef. Then we looked and saw a rider coming to meet us followed by a hazy darkness about the horizon, coming from the direction of Mepdokh. Tahlen and I took the others and fled across the bridge. On the second crest, we looked back and saw the rider turning to follow us. We panicked and fled."

"You fled knowing full well that there are skohls in those mountains?" said Athestin incredulously.

"What choice did we have?"

"Go the other direction," said Lethría.

"And lead that rider to Port Lenhan where she can wreak havoc?"

"She?!"

Both parents gaped. Kai-Tsúthlen looked at his brother as well.

"Yosef claims this new foe is a woman. She calls herself *Emkalaf Morlúrnan*, and she led the invasion on Mor'Lûn."

"So Yosef saw her. How?" Athestin asked.

"We were attacked by skohls, naturally," Kai-Tsúthlen replied matter-of-factly. "Yosef was kidnapped. Led by Tahlen, we pursued, tracking the skohls to their tribe. Yet when we arrived, we found the tribe slaughtered. Tahlen caught a glimpse of the Black Assailant leading Yosef away. Of course, we went after, heading north until we came upon *Lotah 'an Morkh* and went in. During the night, we were all three separated. I found Tahlen writhing and screaming in the midst of a circle of ghostly eyes. It was...horrifying, as if he was being whipped and he was crying out like a madman. When we were finally out of the forest, he was not the same. I refused to leave without Ninthalas, but he did not come. I strove to wait for Ninthalas to emerge, but two hosts of malshorthath flanked us. Tahlen and I thought to lure them away from the forest in the case that Ninthalas might come out."

"So that is why I did not see them," said Ninthalas. "I heard the malshorthath horn, yet when I came out of the forest, I saw no enemies waiting for me."

"How did you find your way out?" Kai-Tsúthlen asked. "We were led by a seemingly healed pair of eyes, but then the healing wore off and a horde of them chased us out of the forest. They prevented us from reentering."

"Allow me to start from the beginning," said Ninthalas. "Before we separated, I saw a greenish yellow light, which the others claimed they could not see. Quickly, I followed, but I did not realize that as I rushed forward, I lost Kai-Tsúthlen and Tahlen. What I found in that light were eyes, malicious and desiring to feast. More appeared so that they surrounded me, and they spooked Hallas, forcing us to flee. On and on for longer than I could imagine we raced, barely dodging trees and branches, thick shrubbery all around. Then Hallas halted so quickly I flew forward and landed in a thick of thorns."

He rolled up his arm sleeve, revealing faded scrapes.

"My word, Ninthalas," his mother gasped.

"When I thought I might die, I did not. I rose from the tangled mass to find Hallas was gone and in his place a pair of eyes floating in the air, and the other malicious eyes had vanished. These were different from the others, a bluish green like those of our kin. They spoke to me and led me out of the forest. Naturally, I asked questions, but the eyes would not answer me plainly. They kept telling of times long since past, of lush green and glades and crystal waters. Sometimes it went on and on about these things and then broke out into song in a language akin to True Faithen, though I did not know the words. The eyes led me out of the forest, but when I turned back, they had disappeared. Soon after, Hallas emerged bearing Yosef. I do not know how the horse found him, but I do know that he had escaped from *Emkalaf'Morlúrnan*, for I heard her voice raging from the trees. Once I had Yosef, I found the river Lothsháin and followed it home."

"So that is why you took so long," said Kai-Tsúthlen. "That and Tahlen and I travelled nearly non-stop day and night for fear of the malshorthath."

"I do not understand how Hallas found the boy," Athestin

said.

"Neither do I," said Lethría, taking a sip of tea. "Perhaps a *hallon* bore him away."

Ninthalas continued, ignoring their musings. "While I was fleeing across the plains, I heard a screeching cry and looked back toward the mountains. I thought I saw a most horrible malshorth in the sky."

"What kind?" asked Athestin.

"I am not sure, though it was a flying creature. Perhaps it was one of the creatures of old, a beast with wings the span of a few men. But I got a stronger feeling from the cry, much stronger, even at that distance. I wonder if it was one of the Three."

"Do not utter any of their names, Ninthalas," said Athestin. "Your speculations may be reasonable, and I am sure they have some truth in them, but we cannot be certain. This new foe with yellow eyes is our primary concern. Who or what is *Emkalaf Morlúrnan?*"

"Leave such trivialities to the High Lord and the High Council," said Lethría. "What I am more interested in is how you plan to adopt a child when you have no wife to aid you. Raising a child is no simple task, and you are frequently away for the News Bearer trade."

"There is more to Yosef Mathíus than just the result of a coincidental meeting, mother. I cannot possibly describe the desire in me to keep him as my own. He has nowhere to go. He is a foreigner in his own land. I could not just leave him with the other refugees in Port Shai, not when he has endured so much. I believe he wishes to stay with me as well."

"Have you asked him about adoption?" she said.

"Well...no."

"Then you should consider what you are thinking."

"You know I have wanted to adopt for a couple years now."

"Adopt, yes, but a foreigner who does not know our language or customs? Think about how this will affect him."

"I can teach him."

"Ninthalas, this is no easy task. That boy will face discrimination in this society. Just look at Belthosh."

Ninthalas knew of the blacksmith who had married a True Faithen woman. Even after having lived in Serenestí for twenty years, he was still an outcast. The only ones he really spoke to were his wife and daughter or merchants according to Lethría. And he rarely left the country because he was always back-logged with special orders.

"I will not go back on my word," he declared. "I have already made up my mind."

"There is a chance that the High Lord will not allow it."

"That does not matter. You think I have not lived a similar life of isolation? Look at me, mother. I am useless with a sword, constantly speak of my feelings, and search for origins religiously. And I know a woman's trade! Or have you forgotten that medicine is not masculine in any fashion? At least Yosef trusts me, and he will never be alone again."

They heard stumbling steps from down the hall. Yosef appeared from around the corner of the doorway. Through dreary eyes, he looked up at each of the Shadais in turn until his gaze landed on Ninthalas, and then went to Ninthalas' side, cuddling up to him.

"Good morning, Yosef," Ninthalas greeted in the Common speech, patting Yosef's head.

"Morning," he said with a yawn.

Ninthalas put a full plate in front of him. "Are you well?" he asked. "How are your arm and leg?"

Yosef took a bite of the bread and poked around at the food items on his plate with a fork Lethría had provided. The adults used finger picks for utensils.

"Still hurts, but I'm fine."

Kai-Tsúthlen rubbed the boy's back. "I am so relieved that you are alright."

"What happened to you?" Yosef asked. He tried a nibble of the sweet egg roll and, realizing he liked it, shoved the entire thing in his mouth.

"We were separated. I found Tahlen and fled from a group of malshorthath."

"Malshorthath?" Yosef said, his mouth full.

Lethría grimaced, a face Ninthalas noted with disdain.

"Yes, swallow before you speak, dear boy."

Yosef did so, then exclaimed, "I saw those in my dream just now!"

"In your dream?" Ninthalas repeated.

"*Aye*, they were fighting and killing and…" He stared into space. "…And the Black Assailant came."

The Shadais looked at one another.

"Yellow eyes. I can't get them out of my head."

"Neither can I," said Ninthalas.

"So it is true," Athestin mused, speaking in True Faithen. "Now we have heard it firsthand."

"Oh, I heard you talking, by the way," Yosef went on.

"We were discussing something," Ninthalas explained.

"It sounded more like arguing."

Ninthalas glanced at his mother. Her cheeks flushed red.

"You know, Ninthalas, I've been thinking," Yosef went on. "You know how you asked me to come with you here and how we've been travelling together and stuff?"

"Yes. What of it?"

"I was wondering…well, if it would be okay to stay with you forever."

"Forever?"

"Yeah, like…well, I dunno, like a father maybe. My parents are gone. I don't remember how exactly, but I just know. That's why I was thinking you could be my new da."

He looked up at Ninthalas with hopeful eyes. Ninthalas smiled back at him.

"My dear Yosef, I was going to ask you the same thing. I wish to arrange for you to stay with me for as long as I live. To adopt you, if that suits you."

"Really? I'd like that!" He resumed eating, staying well clear of the green things and questionable fruits.

"Well, there we have it," said Athestin, changing the conversation to True Faithen once more.

"How do you propose we go about this, father?" Ninthalas asked in the same language.

"High Lord Tothran does not take to foreigners in our midst very well, whether they are to stay or visit for a time. Yet we may be able to bypass him. There may be more information at Selest'Kath that can help us. The librarians are well-versed in True Faithen law, almost as much as the High Lord, I am sure. And you know how Kai-Tsúthlen ponders legal matters. They may be able to provide us with copies of the proper documentation or accounts to defend our adoption inquiry. Surely Dúrlen Lothlúrin may be able to help us as well. Let us go to the Selestorinth at once—"

"Or after finishing your meal, which has gone cold from all this discussion," Lethría suggested. "I suppose I had better brush up on my Common as well."

"You will need to take him to the clinic, mother. His wounds must be properly tended to. I admit my skills were not enough."

Lethría sighed. "Very well. I might as well see if I can inquire of Belthosh's wife. Her family runs medicine in this country. Their skills are renown in all A'thería."

"How is it that you know these kinds of people?"

Lethría smiled as if her son was yet a child and knew nothing of the world. "When you are a business woman, my son, and the wife of a Shadai no less, you know everything there is to know about everyone. That is how trade works and in this family, it is how you survive."

———◉———

CHAPTER FOURTEEN

The Foreigners of Serenesti

Tahlen sat quietly at the table with his family, nibbling at bits of food while Kírinfay chattered away about all the amazing things she had done while he was away. He was only half listening. No matter how hard he tried to focus on the day's duties, his mind kept returning to Lamnek and Ninthalas. If only fate played a more pleasant role in life. Did Yahlírin enjoy seeing him suffer like this? He had lost the three people closest to him, and that didn't include the bulk of his Company that fell in battle. He sighed. Clearly he had chosen the wrong profession—No, he'd been forced into this profession. Yet if he was being honest with himself, would he have had it any other way? Responsibilities aside, fighting was his life. It was as common to him as breathing.

"Tahlen, are you listening?"

He turned his attention to his sister.

"My apologies," he said. "What did you say?"

"I *said* mother is going to start teaching me how to weave silks today."

"Ah, that is wonderful."

"I am getting much better at stringing cottons and simpler material, but mother says I am ready to begin learning to use more expensive materials like silk."

"You sure are progressing quickly."

Their father interrupted. "Still no word from Ninthalas?"

"None at all."

"I fear the worst has come to pass," Dúrlen said, bowing his head.

"Father, do not be so quick to give up hope—" He cut himself short, marvelling at his own statement. Where did this hope come from?

"You do not believe he is gone?"

He had to go with it now. "Kai-Tsúthlen does not, so neither should I."

"You refuse to believe many things, son. Losing Ninthalas is not the first."

"Have you lost faith already, father?"

"Do not start, you two," Kavathíen interjected.

Kírinfay looked up at her brother. "Did something happen to Ninthalas?"

"It is alright, daughter," said Dúrlen, his face softening a little. "These things are not for you to fret about."

Kírinfay shrugged, resuming her invasion of the vegetables on her plate.

"There are more current affairs to deal with," said Dúrlen. "Tahlen has become part of the watch on our borders, a truly noble task, but one that will keep him away from home for an undeterminable amount of time."

"So I heard," said Kavathíen. "Where are you posted, son?"

"Along the eastern border north of the river," Tahlen replied indifferently. "I have thirty men under my command who will be patrolling the northeastern curve and further inland in groups of five. My young Company will have even younger rookies fresh from training, which should prove interesting…"

"How many?" Dúrlen asked.

"They count sixteen in addition to the fourteen still alive of my Company." He leaned back, stretching. "I imagine my posting will be uneventful unless a band of malshorthath decides to invade."

"Let us pray they do not!" his mother retorted.

"A worthy position, son," said Dúrlen.

"Atheil Feiren will be my second," Tahlen added.

"A just decision. You two work well together. Do you know who will be assigned as your general?"

"Not yet," Tahlen replied. "I guess I will find out at my post."

"I never cease to be amazed at your progress." His father leaned back against the wall, folding his arms. "Now that your occupation is secured, you can settle down and marry."

"Yes indeed!" his mother approved. "You are in need of a good wife, son. You have been of age for some time. Is there any girl left who has caught your eye?"

"Mother, please. It may be custom to marry young, but I have no will to settle down. Just look at Ninthalas! He is still without a wife, and I should not think it reasonable to marry before he does."

"Well, Ninthalas is special," his mother mused.

Tahlen quickly finished his meal and dismissed himself from the table.

"I must be going. I have much to prepare for my Company's leave."

In reality, he just wanted to get out of the conversation. The last thing he wanted was to hear his parents' nagging. And about a wife. Again. He left the house as his father rambled on about how a woman would be good for him.

A clear sky and slight breeze welcomed him outside. He strolled down the stone path from his house to a road that led to the northern town square. Though normally the centre of activity in that part of the city, right now the square was deserted. Open market didn't begin until mid-morning. Most families would be having breakfast at this time, or wives would be preparing the morning meal.

The square wasn't actually square at all, rather a circular clearing where the women gathered to pull water from the well and chat about the various happenings of Selestía. This was no place for a man, let alone a captain of woodsmen. If the square had been bustling with people, Tahlen would have received odd looks. In fact, he would have avoided it completely.

He saw someone walking in his direction and hid in the shadows. Athestin Kamesh Shadai strode by, probably on his way to see Tahlen's father. The two had been friends growing up, which had led to the close connection between their families. Tahlen wondered if Athestin knew about Ninthalas yet. If not, he'd probably find out from Tahlen's father. He began imagining a meeting of quarrelling and bickering, but immediately pushed those thoughts aside. He was already depressed enough and loathed having to attend to his duties. Perhaps he could delay himself a bit. He still had time.

Checking to make sure no women were about, he crossed the stone yard to the well's edge and sat down to ponder. His grief returned and long lost hurts resurfaced. If only he were a better man. If only he was strong enough to protect the ones he loved most. But he wasn't. Not yet. He had to find a way to become stronger. Perhaps the malshorthath would invade to give him a chance to test his skill.

A sound caught his ear and he turned to see a girl fastening a rope to a bucket. What should have been frustration changed to a strange sensation in his chest, a mixture of awe-struck wonder and shock.

"I am sorry to startle you," the girl said.

She couldn't have been much younger than him. Her eyes were a combination of blue and green, a rare hue that added an exotic hint to her delicate features. Her brown hair gave away her ethnicity. Or at least half of it. Only one foreigner lived in Serenestí, and he had married a True Faithen woman.

"Belthosh's daughter," he said.

"Ah…yes, truly," she said, fumbling with the rope. She kept her eyes down at her work.

He stood and went to her side. "Do you need some assistance?"

"No, don't trouble yourself—*do not* trouble yourself, I mean."

Tahlen smiled. "That knot will not hold."

She smacked the bucket handle and flopped her arms to her sides. "Oh goodness, fine! Help, if you must."

He took over and secured the rope, then lowered the pale into the well.

"Sir."

He glanced at her and her cheeks flushed red.

"Yes?"

"Well…if it is not patronizing on my behalf to note—"

"Why am I at the well," Tahlen finished.

"Indeed."

Tahlen pulled hard on the rope and hauled up the bucket, now full to the brim with water. He set the pale on the well's flat stone edge.

"Why am I at the well?" he repeated.

"You seem distressed," she said.

"My troubles are none for you to concern yourself with."

"I'm sorr—My apologies."

He glanced at her and noticed her looking him up and down, studying him. Interesting. This was no ordinary girl, and not just by her ethnicity—half her ethnicity, if he was thinking properly. Her flustered nature disappeared and an inquisitive expression drew upon her face.

"You are a soldier, if I am not mistaken."

He chuckled. "Are you going to guess my reasons for being here?"

Her lips pressed together before she answered. "I'm—*I am* perceptive."

"How often do you speak Common?"

"I will try not to be offended by that."

"By what?"

"You gawk at my unrefined speech, soldier."

He cleared his throat. "You come at a time unbefitting a woman. Should you not be having breakfast with your family?"

"My profession demands I make trips here frequently, whether there are women here or not."

"What is you profession?"

"You aim to quiz *me* now?"

He leaned against the pale. "If you are not inclined to answer, I will not answer you."

"I'll guess then," she resolved. "You are a soldier, although I cannot guess if you are Pellendran or Denedrúan."

"That much is correct. And you are Belthosh's daughter. If I, too, am not patronizing to note, you would not come to the well when other women are gathered here, even when you must make several trips."

Her face flustered. "Yet you as well came here when no one else was around. You are distressed, as I said. Not only distressed, but grieving."

"So what do you assume?"

"I do not assume. I know. You fought in the battle of Luthrey and are mourning the loss of your comrades."

Tahlen's jaw dropped. "How…?"

"Soldier, I have seen grief in all its forms, for I have seen illness to its unfortunate end and borne bad news to families. There is no doubt that you are grieving."

"Now that gives me some clue. You are a medic, are you not?"

"I am."

Her reply hung in the air between them. He looked down at the bucket, then back at her.

"Show me where you work. I will help you carry this water."

"Don't trouble yourself—"

"I am already a troubled man, fair lady. How could a simple task as this dismay me further?"

Her cheeks flushed red again. Tahlen froze. Did he just call her fair? Obviously he did because she wouldn't have given him that look. He didn't mean to say it, but his insides were tumbling in the pit of his gut and his heart was beating at a thousand beats in a moment. What was wrong with him? He had never felt this way in front of a woman. Then again, not all women were attractive half-breeds blessed with the genes of two ethnicities. This girl was fascinating. Unrefined speech aside, she could masterfully steer conversations. He risked a glance at her arm and noticed she wasn't wearing a wristring that signified marriage.

As if knowing what he was thinking, she rubbed her wrist and bit her lip. "I...suppose I could allow you to aid me. If it suits you."

"It does."

She took one end and Tahlen took the other, and they traced the western road towards the medical clinic. The silence between them became awkward the longer either of them refused to talk. Tahlen glanced over at her several times and noticed she was doing the same. Every time their eyes met, she hastily looked away, her complexion immediately turning pink.

"I heard the battle at Luthrey was hard," she said at last.

"I lost many good men."

"I am sorry."

Tahlen didn't know what else to say. How could he? His grief returned, but another glance at her suppressed his twisting emotions and added new ones.

"I didn't—did not know that our soldiers travelled to the other nations," she added.

"I am one of the Denedrúath," he said. "Unlike the Pellendrath, who are grounded in Serenestí, my woodsmen are charged with journeying on bi-annual errands to our trade partners. I must speak Common because of it."

"How convenient."

"How so?"

"Never mind."

He chuckled. "I cannot figure you out, my lady."

"Strange. I can read you forward and backward without even knowing your name."

They reached the clinic, a three story building that had the appearance of a wealthy man's house. Tahlen had little understanding of clinics and medicine except that this building was maintained by the most skilled medics in the country. Which meant this girl must be brilliant if she worked here.

"You need not assist me further," she said, stopping at the door. "You were kind enough to help a foreigner like me. That is more than I would ever expect from a high-esteemed man like yourself."

"Are you not of True Faithen blood?"

"I am *half* foreign. Can you not see that?"

"Indeed, yet the last time I checked, two halves make a whole."

"Why are you being so kind to me?"

"Why?" He started to laugh, but saw her expression melt, so he coughed instead. Replies swirled in his head. Should he confess or come up with something different? She was beautiful in her own exotic way, but she was also foreign. His parents constantly pestered him about finding a wife, but what would they say if he brought Belthosh's daughter to dine one day? His mother would have a heart attack. His father would rant about their second born tainting the blood of Lothlúrin. But this girl was so intriguing.

"My apologies. I did not mean to discriminate against you. It is just…" Where were the words? "I could search A'thería in its entirety, yet I would not find one so beautiful as you. Belthosh must be proud."

Her face flushed red. "It is not as if I have a line of suitors at my door requesting my audience."

"No? Why not?" Terrible answer. He knew why not.

"Again, you forget my heritage."

Now he had to go with it. "And again, is it not True Faithen?"

"It is not so simple, sir. Not everyone is as kind and understanding as you make yourself to be." She looked him up and down. "Or at least as you *try* to make yourself to be."

"Well, they should be. I will make it so. Everyone shall know that the lady, Belthosh's daughter, is the fairest in all A'thería, and they should pay her due respect."

Smooth, Tahlen. Even he could not match the eloquent speech of Ninthalas or the respectable nature of Kai-Tsúthlen. He sounded like a fool.

He looked to the sky.

"Ah, it is late!"

"I…suppose you must be off."

"Indeed. Thank you kindly for your company."

He bowed and turned to leave.

"Soldier."

He spun around on his heels.

"If I may ask—if it's not too much trouble—what is your name, lest I am blessed to meet you again?"

He straightened, chin turned high. "I am none other than Tahlen Dían Lothlúran, Captain of the Denedrúath, son of Dúrlen Lothlúrin of the High Council of Serenestí."

She gasped.

"A Lothlúrin! And the child prodigy Lothlúrin at that! I am most truly in your debt!" She bowed low.

"No, lady, I am in yours," he said, rushing back to her.

He took her hands in his, a gesture that made her cheeks turn redder. This was far from appropriate, but by this point he didn't care. If he was a fool, then let him be one, if only just this once. His parents didn't have to know.

"I am grateful that our paths crossed this morning. Truly. I do not kid you. Meeting you has banished most of what was weighing heavy on my mind. It is I who should thank you. You freed my soul."

He meant every word.

"…Indeed," she said.

"The time! Farewell, my lady."

He turned and raced down the road, leaving the girl in the

doorway of the clinic. As he retraced his steps to the town square, he stopped. He had forgotten to ask the girl for her name. No matter. He knew where she worked. He hoped he would be relieved from his post so he could meet her again.

Dían Lothlúrin. *Captain* Dían Lothlúrin. Elkeshlí's face grew hot. Her heart raced. She had heard stories about the Captain, about his excellence in the training of soldiers and progression through the Denedrúath ranks. He was far more handsome than rumour made him out to be. Young maidens swooned over him, every one of them wanting him to notice them, though he never turned an eye toward women. That very man had called her fair. Her, Elkeshlí, fair. A half breed, daughter of a foreigner.

Her upbringing had been one of discrimination. She had learned at a young age the consequences of going to the town square. Though it was inappropriate to stare in True Faithen culture, everyone did at her. They usually had the same reaction as Dían Lothlúrin's initial shock. Sure, he had been rude at first, but there was a sparkle in his eyes that had captured her. If only she hadn't succumbed to verbal blunders. She might not have seemed like such a fool.

Not like she had *meant* to sound like one. It was all thanks to that awkward feeling of liking a man at first meeting. She had succumbed to infatuation several times, but nothing like this. No man, no matter how much she liked him, had ever taken an interest in her. That was the price paid for being born a halfbreed. Yet this Dían Lothlúrin had noticed her, even went so far as to call her fair. Fair! Of all people to dote upon her.

"Elkeshlí."

She looked up and saw her mother at the foot of the stairwell. Alshanda Íren Hashlen was one of the chief medics in Serenestí after Elkeshlí's grandmother, a leader among women and demanding of respect despite her marriage to a foreigner. Medicine ran in the family. Elkeshlí's ancestors had founded the practice, honed their skills and become masters of the trade. That trade had passed down to Elkeshlí, and she was determined to become the greatest of her people like her mother and grandmother before her.

Silly infatuations with accomplished men had to be put aside.

"Who were you speaking to?"

"No one, mother," Elkeshlí lied. "Just a distressed soul in need of comfort."

"Apparently. Come now, I need that water. I must make another drink for Lathlí Lothlúrin."

"Yes, mother."

Elkeshlí followed her to the second floor. Their worst patient in their years of the medicine trade, Lathlí Lothlúrin, the wife of a Denedrúath soldier, lay on one of the six beds in the room. She had been moved to Selestía from the northern city of Leithen, the medics there having been unable to treat her illness. What a mystery her sickness was, like a common cold, only her fever was high, her skin cold and clammy, and her breath short and wheezing. Her skin wore raw in places, like her body was slowly eating itself from the outside in, and her complexion was deathly pale, even for a white-skinned True Faithen. She refused to eat anything, resulting in her growing weaker by the day. It was the strangest sickness Elkeshlí had ever seen. Her mother and grandmother, too, had been baffled. All they could do was treat it in the hopes that Lathlí Lothlúrin would recover.

"Pour half of the bucket in the basin," her mother told her. "The rest I will take down to the laboratory while you feed her."

Elkeshlí did as she was told. While her mother was gone, she took some of the water and mixed a softened gruel. Though easy to swallow, Elkeshlí had to practically shove it down her patient's throat. Lathlí flitted her eyes and moaned in a half-conscious state. She swallowed a few spoonfuls before refusing any more. Elkeshlí gave up, setting the bowl down, and instead made a sweetened drink that went down more smoothly, though Lathlí managed half the cup before choking.

She set the cup down and rechecked her vitals. No change from the previous night and her pupils were dilated. She sighed. Without a proper diagnosis of the illness, it was difficult to treat the poor woman. Her lack of recovery proved problematic when her husband came to check on her. Elkeshlí had been the bearer of ill news to families who had lost loved ones before. She knew death in all its forms and had seen every stage of grief in those who had faced loss. That was why she could read Dían Lothlúrin's remorse so easily.

Yet those families' grief motivated her to strive for perfection. She resolved years ago to surpass her mother and grandmother and become the medic who suffered no losses, to be able to cure any disease no matter how severe.

Her mother returned, carrying a tiny bottle of a red liquid.

"Another one? Did you not already give her half a dose earlier?" Elkeshlí asked.

"This is a little stronger," her mother said, crossing the room to the patient's bed. "It should suppress the fever."

"It should, but you know it will not," said Elkeshlí. "There must be something else we can do."

"Do you have any suggestions?"

Elkeshlí shook her head.

"How many times must I tell you, Elkeshlí, you cannot save everyone. It was so with the plague that ravaged your father's village. It is the same now."

"There must be a remedy."

"We have tried everything we know and everything we sought to know."

Elkeshlí stood. "I don't believe that. I'll find a cure."

She disappeared through the door, found the stairs, and took them to the third floor to her personal study. Stacks of books littered the shelves and floor. Tables of half full flasks and bottles of herbs and ointments lay sprawled out in an organized mess.

She went straight to her books, researching treatments to Lathlí's symptoms and possible diagnoses, searching for hours through pages that were worn from overuse and splattered with stains of concoctions. She perused her own notes written on parchment that lay in unkept stacks of paper or filled notebooks. There must be something—anything—that could help.

She began mixing her own remedies, altering the proportions of ingredients. Her mother always disapproved of her experiments, claiming they had the potential to kill a man. Some had done more harm than good in the past. Yet not once did Elkeshlí let those failures faze her. She would find a cure. She would save this woman's life.

After an unsurmountable amount of time, she still had no

solution. Heaving a deep sigh, she slumped back against the wall and flopped her arms to her sides.

"How, Yahlírin?" she prayed aloud. "How do I cure this? Please, tell me, lest I tell yet another person of his loss."

The poor General. Elkeshlí's mother had told her that he had been demoted to 3rd Command of a Squadron for refusing to attend to his duties. Elkeshlí had scoffed at the demotion. The General didn't deserve this kind of dishonour, the same way Elkeshlí's father didn't deserve to be discriminated against for being foreign. True Faithen society was unfair. Serenestí was a cage. There were days, more frequently now than ever, that she wanted to escape.

A knock disrupted her thoughts. She turned to see her mother in the doorway.

"We have some guests downstairs you may serve," she said. "It will help get your mind off of Lathlí Lothlúrin's case."

Elkeshlí sighed. "Yes, mother."

She rose, leaving behind the mess which had become much more disorganized thanks to her researching.

Visitors. Like that would ease her mind. Most people who came in had some minor ailment that could easily be treated. It was a good chance for young medics to practice their skills, but Elkeshlí found it distracting from the challenge of more serious cases. Illness was a puzzle to put together, and the reward for curing a patient of disease was much more so than treating abrasions and mending broken limbs. Although as she thought about it, broken limbs often had better stories attached to them.

She reached the bottom floor and circled around the corner of the hallway to the main lobby. When she saw the visitors, she skidded to a stop. One was a foreign boy of an ethnicity Elkeshlí had never seen before. The other was a woman renowned for not only her astounding beauty, but also her connection with just about every citizen in Selestía: Lethría Temesh Shadai. Elkeshlí's mother often went to her for the vast assortment of herbs she grew in her garden, most of which, in addition to making good tea, had medicinal properties.

"To what do I owe the honour of meeting you, Temesh Shadai?" Elkeshlí asked. She looked at the boy, who stared at her with particular interest.

"Kindest greetings, Belthosh's daughter," Lethría said. "My son brought this boy home from his rounds in southern A'thería. Unfortunately, he has seen injury from skohls in the Balkai Mountains. My son dealt with his wounds as best he could, but they require a professional. Your mother said you could treat them."

"Indeed I can, my lady," Elkeshlí replied. "Come this way."

She led them down the hall to a room containing nine beds and an equal number of overhanging curtains that provided privacy for patients. Each bed was coupled with a station set with tools used for treating physical wounds. Rarely did the clinic receive a large influx of patients, but the odd time it did, such as the return of soldiers from the battle at Luthrey, those ready stations proved their worth.

"If you do not mind my asking, why would your son bring a foreigner to Serenestí?" Elkeshlí asked.

"I am afraid I cannot provide a direct answer," Lethría replied.

"Well, let us see what the damage is, shall we?" Elkeshlí said, smiling at the boy. She switched to the Common speech. "Have a seat on the bed, young sir."

The boy continued to stare at her. "You can speak my language?" he asked.

His face lit up. How adorable.

"Of course. I have known it my whole life."

She unwrapped the bandage on his arm, noting how formidable the dressing had been put on. When she saw the bite marks, she gasped.

"I almost thought you were joking when you said he was injured by skohls," she said to Lethría in True Faithen. "Yet whoever treated these is no amateur. Has no one else tended to these other than your son?"

"No one," Lethría replied. "My son is no professional, but he learned from his grandmother who is stationed at the southern clinic."

"Interesting."

"Ah, I imagine the tailors should be done by now," Lethría said. "Can I leave him in your care while I go to the shops? I will not be long."

"Certainly."

"I know your mother's name, but I do not know yours. Should I need to call upon you when I return…"

"You know me already as Belthosh's daughter. Anyone would know of my heritage. And this place is all but empty. It is with no effort that you would be able to find me again."

"Yes, but your name, dear girl," Lethría persisted. "You are one of my people, and I make a habit of knowing peoples' names."

"You are the second person to tell me I am True Faithen," she said, blushing slightly as she remembered Captain Dían. "I am Elkeshlí Sen Hashlen, if you really must know."

"Well, Elkeshlí Sen, I will return soon."

Without another word, she kissed the boy's forehead and exited the room.

"That was a little awkward," said Elkeshlí, switching again to Common. She began to work at the scabs.

"Are you foreign like me?" Yosef asked.

She hesitated. "Yes…and no."

"What's that supposed to mean?"

"It means I have a True Faithen mother and a foreign father."

She dabbed at the wound and he winced.

"I'm surprised there's nothing more than bruising and scabs. Sure, there is sign of infection, but it appears to be on the mend. Did the skohls do anything more to harm you?"

The boy lifted his leg. "They bit my leg, too."

Elkeshlí unwrapped the bandage and treated the wound.

"You don't sing when you work," the boy noted.

"Why would I sing?"

"Ninthalas—or I guess Líran Shadai said that singing eases the patient's soul."

"Well, I'm sorry but I do not sing." She finished bandaging his leg.

"They hit me on the head really hard."

She smiled, shaking her head, and proceeded to rustle through his hair. On the posterior of his head, she found a swollen egg-sized lump surrounded by a blue and purple ring of internal bleeding. She grimaced. That would take much time to heal. How in all A'thería did these people encounter skohls?

She gently touched the swollen area.

"Ow!"

"Sorry. It is a wonder you survived those skohls. I've heard terrible things about them."

"Are there more people like you in Serenestí?"

That was one way to change a conversation. "Not that I know of."

Taking a cloth, she dipped it in cold water and placed it on his head.

"Hold this," she said.

He did as he was told and she went back to work cleaning his injured arm, applying ointment and re-bandaging it.

"I'm glad there's another foreigner here," he said.

"Why is that?"

"Everyone looks the same here and speaks True Faithen. Today we were walking around town buying clothes and I got some nasty stares from people, all awkward-like."

Elkeshlí smiled. "That is normal. Most True Faithens are not used to seeing anyone who isn't like them."

"Why's that?"

"Foreigners don't come to Serenestí."

"Huh. Well, True Faithens don't come to Mor'Lûn either. I think Ninthalas is strange-ish and not just the way he looks. He's gonna be my new da, you know."

"Is he the one who treated your arm?"

"Yeah, that's right." He yawned.

"Why don't you have a lie down and sleep? Listening to another language and being in a place where everything is new can be tiring. I know from experience."

The boy obeyed. Not long after his head hit the pillow, he fell asleep. Elkeshlí watched him curiously. She wanted to meet this Ninthalas Shadai, to find out why he had brought a foreigner to Serenestí. No True Faithen would think of taking in a foreign orphan. No *normal* True Faithen anyway. That abnormality and his knowledge of a woman's trade made him intriguing. Perhaps she would pay the Shadai household a visit and inquire of him tomorrow. She would have to check the boy's wounds anyway, and it would give her a break from her duties at the clinic.

CHAPTER FIFTEEN

Quest for Adoption

"Who do you suppose we should talk to for the adoption process, father?" Ninthalas asked as he, his brother and father entered the east building of the Selestorinth.

"You leave the inquiring to me," his father replied. "You and your brother go to the Great Library and see if you can find any accounts of adoption."

"There are some familial law periodicals there. Perhaps I can peruse them," Kai-Tsúthlen offered.

"We already know adoption is legal, son," said Athestin. "Yet if you find anything that would hinder adoption of a foreigner, then yes, that is a good idea."

"Delving into historical records will take time," said Ninthalas. "It would take me a week to peruse five shelves."

"Anything from Namthúl is greatly revered. You can begin there. Seek the accounts of other high lords. That should narrow your search."

"Very well."

Athestin turned right while the brothers went left to the Great Library. The Hall of Records it was called, a circular, two-story library that contained the accounts of recorded time approved by the revered Accounts Sifters. Rows upon rows of books filled shelves lining the walls, and a number of low shelves arranged in half circles surrounded a spiral staircase that led to the second floor. Elegantly encrypted signs that either dangled from the ceiling or were secured to the walls labeled the various sections. Tall pillars, arranged in a circular pattern, held up the upper floor whose ceiling curved into an enormous dome.

Ninthalas gazed at the collection of books, noting the writing of section headings and carefully carved designs on the walls. The structure of the Hall of Records reflected a tranquil location where people could sit and read at their leisure. Ninthalas had spent hours studying the elaborate carvings and embroidery of the pillars and shelving trim alone, and even more time searching the annals of history for inconsistencies. Despite having visited several times, he always stopped at the library's entrance to soak in his surroundings. He breathed deep, letting the smell of books young and old tease his olfactory. The Great Library was home.

Kai-Tsúthlen diverted paths and purposefully went to the law periodicals and decrees while Ninthalas found himself wandering toward the spiral staircase. He took to the stairs, winding upwards to the second floor.

The library fell quiet. If there was anyone reading up here, Ninthalas couldn't see or hear them.

Now, where to begin?

His feet knew better than his head. His steps led him down an aisle between two shelves of the accounts of Namthúl Shadai. At the end of the aisle by the far wall, a circular carpet with a seating arrangement of cushions and a long table offered whoever had time to spare to ponder the historical accounts. Ninthalas turned left at the end, following the back wall to an older section of books. The accounts here were very old, telling of the First Age of the world around the time of the Great War. A thin layer of dust upon the tops of books indicated that this was a section seldom visited. Ninthalas had read these before, but it had been a while. He scanned the dark leather bindings until he reached the far end, a wedge that sandwiched him between the bookcase and the wall.

"*Prophecies of the First Age,*" he read aloud. "*Visions of the Elder Ones, Revelation of Lothlúrin, The End of the Age*...fascinating, yet not what I seek. Where might I find a text to aid me?"

A sound caught his ear, coming from the second bottom shelf. Two of the books wiggled apart. Curious, Ninthalas crouched low. A thinner one slipped in between the moving books. It was about the size of a journal and bound in some green material. Ninthalas grabbed it and peered through the cracks in the bookcase. A blur of blue and purple darted away, quick footfalls pattering on the floor. Ninthalas rose.

"Who is there?"

Whoever it was didn't answer.

He started toward the end of the bookcase.

Ninthalas.

He jumped and spun. The green book fell from his hands and landed on the floor with a noise that shattered the silence.

Where he had been perusing the book spines, the silver-haired man named Shadai stood wearing an expression Ninthalas couldn't read.

"You startled me," he said. "Who was that just now? I thought I saw—"

What did you find? Shadai asked. *Some new trinket to add to your wealth of knowledge?* Though his lips moved, Ninthalas didn't hear the words. The questions resonated in his heart. Just like the dream.

Ninthalas knelt and picked up the book. The binding had the appearance of layered leaves, but when he ran his hand over the cover, the texture was more like leather.

"What is this?"

I told her you were not yet ready for it, but she is persistent and a chief meddler of sorts.

"Who is she?"

Why not read and find out?

Ninthalas did just that. He opened to the first page. Worn golden letters glistened: *Personal Notes of Namthúl Shadai.* He turned to the first entry and read aloud:

"'Herein lies the account of Namthúl Shadai, son of Sinthúl, first High Lord of the True Faithen people. This is script written by my own hand, in my old age, that I may fill in the gaps of time as I see fit, bypassing an oath I once took with him whom I shall not name. May this journal be held as proof that there are things that came before.'

"An oath once taken? Things that came before?" Ninthalas questioned. "I never knew Namthúl Shadai had a father. The records clearly state he was the first called out of chaos."

Keep reading.

"'For at the time I was called to light, I came to know of Shadai's sister, who is named Endahlúmin, fairest of those who came before, who had bestowed upon me the task of adopting one of the northern folk of the native believers. Ever will I speak of this adopted with gladness, for he was like I was, a man come out of chaos. Thus he came into our country and became one of my people. And it shall be noted that I took him as my own. Indeed, Ethron Lothlúrin and I both cared for him. He shall evermore be a Shadai, adopted as I am in the family of Yahlírin. And we dwelt in our home that is beyond the North Kingdom.'"

Endahlúmin, Shadai said.

"So that is your sister? Why do you call her chief meddler?"

In time you may meet her and see for yourself, but I will not speak more of her here. What is done is done and now you have Namthúl's journal. Many of the answers you seek are there. What is most important is you now know that you are not the first to have compassion on a foreigner. It is in your blood to do as brother Namthúl did.

"I must tell my brother—"

No!

The force of the command sent a tremor through the building. Ninthalas shrank under the awesome power.

"Why not? I…keep little from my brother."

That book is meant for you and you alone. It is a gift from my sister to you, a legacy you shall pass on to your first begotten.

Ninthalas chuckled. "First begotten? I am quite certain you need a wife for one of those."

Never mind. You have what you need. Go now.

Ninthalas closed the book and slipped it into the folds of his tunic, then made his way back down the aisle and descended the stairs. About halfway down, he stopped. There was some void in his gut like something was missing. Spinning on his heels, he sped back up. Sure enough, there was the one whose existence he had sworn an oath to keep secret. Shadai was sitting on one of the cushions holding a thick old book in hands.

So, the righteous man had a confident mouth, he said, his wise face pulled into a deep frown.

Ninthalas came to his side, peering at the pages the silver-haired man was reading. Before he could see the book's contents,

Shadai snapped it shut and laid it back on the table.
I thought I told you to go.
"Are you not coming with me?"
Why should I? Yahlírin is already with you.
"But you are Yahlírin's sent, and since I left *Lotah 'an Morkh*, you have ever stayed by my side."
When will children learn to sprout wings? Very well, let us go.
He stood and followed as Ninthalas descended the stairs again.

Ninthalas found his brother in a mix of half-walls musing over strict doctrine.
"What are you snickering at, brother?"
"Do you know, Ninthalas," Kai-Tsúthlen said, grinning, "that according to this account, it is not lawful for us to mix race? But this was written by a man of regulation by the name of Ehroshlan Lethava Oren-Fohlaf. Apparently, he was a traditionalist thinker of the early Second Age and he created a plethora of new laws to protect True Faithen isolation."
"Are his musings as hard to digest as his complex name?"
Kai-Tsúthlen burst into laughter, catching odd looks from others nearby who were trying to read.
"Honestly, Ninthalas, you are going to get me in trouble."
"I am not the one raising my voice," Ninthalas replied with a smirk. "I wonder if our High Lord knows of this…whatever-his-name-is, or if he believes this doctrine to be sound. It would hinder Yosef's integration."
"It would if this Lethava Oren-Fohlaf's laws were proper doctrine. Just look at the section we are in: 'Debatable Proclamations of the Second Age'. Even if the High Lord approved of these, he could not pass them as valid because they were imposed by a man who may or may not have been led by Yahlírin."
Those are ill sounding musings of an unfaithful man.
Kai-Tsúthlen frowned. "Did you hear that, brother?"
"Hear what?"
"There was a voice just now. I could hear it clearly as I can hear yours and mine."
"A voice now, that is peculiar."

"You pathetic lier. You *did* hear it, did you not?" Kai-Tsúthlen pressed.

Ninthalas clasped his twin's shoulder and leaned in close to whisper. "Perhaps I heard something, perhaps I did not. I cannot tell, brother. I swore an oath I would not say, and that oath is my word."

"Secrets from your own brother," Kai-Tsúthlen retorted, leaning away. "What is that book you carry in your tunic?"

"I am told that our trusted ancestor, Namthúl, had a rather talkative nature and this is proof of it."

"And who told you of this?"

"A divine source."

"An unmentionability of sorts?"

"What?"

"Never mind. It was something—or someone—I saw. With you, actually, rather recently."

That was a strong hint. Kai-Tsúthlen had seen the silver-haired man. He smiled and Kai-Tsúthlen smirked back.

"The voices, dear brother," Ninthalas said.

"Voices in the forest," Kai-Tsúthlen added. "One of them is with you, yet he is a divine being, and he brought you out."

Ninthalas' smile broadened.

It appears I cannot keep much hidden between the likes of twin brothers, said the voice. *This one has discovered me before his appointed time, it seems.*

"Is he trying to stay hidden from me?"

"He is remaining hidden from everyone but me."

"Blessed man, you are. I am almost jealous."

The twins reunited with their father.

"I have good news," Athestin said, holding up some sheets of paper. "It is possible to bypass the High Lord and request adoption from a member of the High Council."

Ninthalas beamed. "Such as Dúrlen Lothlúrin!"

"Indeed."

"Then let us be off at once. I want to finish this quickly."

They headed towards the government building.

"Did you two find anything in the library?" Athestin asked.

"I did not find anything save for some accounts from the

'Debatable Proclamations' section, yet that is no leverage for the High Lord to disapprove of the adoption."

"Good. Ninthalas?"

"I found some things, but nothing of value to the High Lord," he said.

Athestin gave him a queer look, but Ninthalas didn't expand on his findings, and his father didn't press him further.

They entered Selest'Hí and took a wide staircase to the second floor. At the end of the north wing, two large doors marked the entrance to the High Lord's office. Just the left of it, a small door led to a series of smaller offices where members of the High Council carried out their work. Inside, Ninthalas followed his father down a narrow hall to the last sliding door on the righthand side.

Athestin knocked.

"You may enter," came Dúrlen's voice from the other side.

Athestin slid open the door and went in, his sons close behind. Dúrlen's office was about the size of a man's personal study, containing a single desk, a bookshelf stacked with law books to the left and a mural to the right. A lonely window above his desk let in natural light and gave a stunning view of the Selestorinth's courtyard. Dozens of reports lay scattered on his desk. Another he held in his hand. When he saw his guests, he put down the paper and stood.

"Two days in a row, my friend. Is this to become regular?"

Athestin chuckled. "You have all the answers."

Dúrlen gestured to the two empty cushions at his desk.

"How is your family?"

"Very well, thank you," Athestin replied, taking a seat.

"Kai-Tsúthlen. I thank you for coming to the mass meeting yesterday and on such short notice. I am truly grateful that you could be my son's witness."

Kai-Tsúthlen bowed his head.

"And...Ninthalas." He paused and the smile faded. "By Yahl's blessing, you are alive! I heard everything from Tahlen—I imagine you have not been to see him yet. He has been charged with patrolling the northeastern border with thirty men under his command. So relieved am I to see you, though!"

Ninthalas bowed and sat on the other available cushion. Kai-

Tsúthlen went over to the bookshelf to peruse the law periodicals.

"My friend Dúrlen," said Athestin. "My apologies for cutting you off in your surprise, but we have a matter to discuss with you, if you will."

"By all means."

"When Ninthalas returned last night, he came bearing a Kislanían child named Yosef Mathíus."

"Indeed, Tahlen has told me of him," said Dúrlen, temporarily shifting his gaze to Ninthalas.

"Just as well, my son would like to adopt him. We have confirmed that all we need are these documents and the seal of a High Council member."

He showed Dúrlen the papers he had acquired. High Councillor Dúrlen skimmed through them.

"You realize that normally such matters are brought to a Town Representative first before coming to the High Council. Although you are not necessarily wrong in bringing these directly to me. I see you have taken into consideration our High Lord's distaste for integration. Quite clever, my friend, and well played."

"So can you apply your seal and validate the adoption?" Ninthalas asked.

Dúrlen placed the documents on the desk, his face expressionless.

"Indeed, I can."

Ninthalas breathed out a sigh of relief.

"However, I must also file a report in addition to these documents stating my reasons for agreeing to the adoption proposal."

"Which means the High Lord must actually see it," Ninthalas guessed.

"That is correct. But once my seal is upon these, the adoption cannot be revoked, even by the High Lord himself. Yet there is a risk in me doing this, Líran Shadai. My report may come under fire when it has been read, even if that is weeks after being signed and sealed."

"You have a request for me then…in return for this favour."

"I do," said Dúrlen. "My son gave his account yesterday at the mass meeting, but he only had one witness. That was Kai-Tsúthlen. I would like you to meet High Lord Tothran and attest to Tahlen's words, to be a second witness."

He handed Ninthalas some neatly folded papers. "This is his report. Regardless of whether or not you do this for me, I will seal these adoption papers for you. But I truly would appreciate my son's *fairytale* to be believed and his name cleared from fallacy. Keep in mind that in so doing, your name will become known to the High Lord, and for a Shadai, that may not be a good thing, especially since you are also a News Bearer. I have already stated that this adoption will not go unnoticed and the High Lord will become aware of the neglected portions of Tahlen's account. No doubt this will bring distrust to our names."

"I understand," he said.

"Good. You must report to the High Lord at once."

"At once?"

"He is expecting you today and no later. If you are so put off, then you can take Kai-Tsúthlen with you."

Dúrlen waved his hand in a dismissive gesture. Athestin's subsequent nod told Ninthalas to obey. Ninthalas and Kai-Tsúthlen left and went to linger by the double doors to the High Lord's quarters.

"Is there anything you can fill me in on before I meet him?" Ninthalas asked.

"I suggest you read Tahlen's account. It is not too long. I will answer any other questions you have."

Ninthalas opened the report and began reading. He frowned. "Say brother, this report mentions nothing of Yosef."

"Nor did Tahlen say anything concerning him at the mass meeting. You see, my dear brother, you are believed to have arrived at the same time as Tahlen and I even though you did not."

"No details, no questions."

"Indeed. Tahlen protected a tale from becoming more outrageous than it already was, thereby protecting our family's name."

"Tahlen Dían, that genius! I owe him my thanks."

"We should visit him once we are finished here. He would appreciate knowing you are alive—"

The double doors at the end of the hall slid open and out strode the High Lord. The twins stood aside and bowed low as he strode forward. High Lord Tothran wore the long wrap-around robe of a noble, a wide red-and-gold embroidered sash holding it in place. Another robe of scarlet with gold trim draped over his shoulders, the sleeves wide and billowing. He wore his long black hair in a thick braid that spanned the length of his back.

When he saw the Ninthalas and Kai-Tsúthlen, he stopped, a hint of recognition washing over his face.

"Twins! I had no knowledge of twins being born of our people," he said. "Yet one of you is the News Bearer Okran Shadai, if I am correct."

"Indeed, my lord. It is me," Kai-Tsúthlen replied, bowing again.

"And who is your brother?"

"This is Ninthalas Líran Shadai, who was with Dían Lothlúrin and I on our journey in the south."

Ninthalas, too, bowed once more, a full ninety-degree bend which he held for a few seconds. "Kindest greetings, good High Lord," he said.

"So this is the dreamer Captain Dían Lothlúrin spoke of, the one who foresaw the attack on Luthrey."

"Indeed, my lord. It was I who persuaded the Denedrúath to journey south. I also understand that I am to confirm Dían Lothlúrin's account. I attest to its validity."

High Lord Tothran turned up his nose.

"Very well."

Without another word, he strode down the hall, his robes billowing behind him.

"That was awkward," Ninthalas said when the High Lord had left.

"You should have seen him at the mass meeting," said Kai-Tsúthlen. "He was reluctant to even hear Tahlen's account, and he gave me the same ignorant expression when I spoke before the High Council."

"*You* spoke before the Council?"

"I did not say much."

"I would have liked to hear it all the same. You have a certain countenance that demands people's attention."

"If it were an international meeting, you would have faired better."

Ninthalas dismissed the comment. "Let us visit Tahlen. I am

anxious to see him. Where is he again?"

"Dúrlen said he is stationed at the northeastern border."

CHAPTER SIXTEEN

Reunion

The twins raced through the forest, twigs crunching underfoot. Golden yellow and red leaves shimmered overhead, flashing patches of light on the forest floor below. Beside them, the eastern arm of the Lothshaín River wound up out of the forest. Ninthalas would have wished to relish in the forest's beauty, a year-round brilliance that somehow repelled winter's advance of snow, but his brother maintained a quick pace that would stop for nothing and no one. Thick brush often forced them to veer sideways in a weaving path that would have been easier to tread had there been a road. Yet there was no reason to build one. Beyond the northeastern border lay a vast expanse of rolling grassland void of civilization. That begged the question as to why Tahlen's Company was keeping watch there. Ideally, a malshorth raid would come from the south.

A whistle sounded, followed by a wave of shouts. Overhead, Ninthalas saw flat, sturdy disks like reefs jutting out amidst the tree branches of the canopy. The feature spread the entire border of Serenestí where the Denedrúath set up their encampments.

A rope dropped a few feet ahead and down shimmied a young man the twins recognized.

"Kai-Tsúthlen! Ninthalas! So good it is to see you," 2nd Command Atheil Feiren greeted in his usual chipper manner.

"Likewise to you, friend Atheil Feiren," said Kai-Tsúthlen.

"What brings you here to the border?"

"We wish to speak to Captain Dían if you will let us," Ninthalas replied. "There is much we must tell him."

"I hope you bring better tidings than our last meeting," said Atheil, grinning.

Ninthalas smiled back. "No, my friend, I bear no dreams this time, but I have a story to tell that even you would find entertaining."

"What new news can you tell me?" asked Atheil. "I have heard everything from the mass meeting."

"Oh, dear Atheil Feiren, do you really rely on mass meetings to supply you with stories? It is I who tells the best ones, and I guarantee you will find this one in particular intriguing."

"Let us speak with Captain Dían, and perhaps you will learn something of his wily adventures," said Kai-Tsúthlen.

Atheil nodded and led them up the rope. He reached the top while Ninthalas and Kai-Tsúthlen were yet halfway up.

"Shall I throw you a ladder, or is this a fine challenge to suit your tastes?" he joked.

Kai-Tsúthlen looked down at Ninthalas.

"That man takes every opportunity to kid. I find it hard to tolerate him."

"Indeed," Ninthalas said. "Yet he means well, I am sure. If you approve of the ladder, then ask for it. I would not mind an easier climb, either. Give me a day and even then I would not make it to the top."

Kai-Tsúthlen requested the ladder. Eventually, they made it to the first platform where two disks from neighbouring trees met. Though having comfortably exerted his strength during the climb up the tall tree, Ninthalas grimaced when he heard they still had to climb to the third disk, then jump and swing six trees over. He was panting by the time they reached Tahlen. The Captain sat on a smaller shelf near the forest border with a clear view of the plain beyond. He immediately dropped what he was doing and shot to his feet when he saw them, his mouth agape.

Ninthalas was the first to swing himself across. Tahlen barely let him land before grasping him in a warm embrace, practically lifting Ninthalas off his feet.

"Greatest blessings, you are alive!" the Captain exclaimed.

Ninthalas laughed.

"How…when?"

"I arrived last night," said Ninthalas. "And in the company of Yosef, if you must know. He and I are safe, but oh the story I have to tell, Tahlen!"

"I want to hear everything. I thought you were lost, Ninthalas. I thought you were gone like Ath—I felt like I did that day, back when I saw…"

"'Tis alright, my friend," Ninthalas said, clasping his friend's shoulders. "May you suffer loss no more. Here is one friend you will not lose."

Atheil's voice called to them. "Do you suppose you could let us cross and partake in your jolly meeting? I have yet to hear this gripping tale of yours, Ninthalas."

Ninthalas looked over to where he and Kai-Tsúthlen were waiting. Kai-Tsúthlen stood stoic like a statue, patient and steadfast. Atheil was the exact opposite.

"How does he know you have a story?" Tahlen asked, a hint of irritation in his voice.

"I told him."

"Ninthalas, he will spread word of your late arrival around the entire country. People will talk—"

"People always talk, my friend. I have learned not to heed their opinions."

Ninthalas motioned for them to cross. Kai-Tsúthlen swung over first, followed by Atheil. Somehow, the 2nd Command had managed to salvage a bottle of wine and four glasses in a hefty shoulder bag. All four sat down and Atheil immediately saw to supplying each of them with a glass.

Ninthalas raised his glass in a toast. "To our good health and friendship. May it last until our final days."

They clinked glasses and drank.

"Well, Tahlen, you must tell me. Is there a reason for why you are posted here?"

"The High Lord fears an invasion after hearing what has happened at Luthrey as well as my account."

"So I heard from my brother." He pulled the report from his belt-sash and held it up for Tahlen to see. "I read it. Smart words, my friend. Very clever."

"I thought you would approve," Tahlen said with a grin.

Ninthalas raised an eyebrow and glanced at his brother. Tahlen rarely showed emotion, let alone smiling.

"Yet why here?"

"He is paranoid, I believe," said Tahlen. "The malshorthath attacked a village and a city that are in entirely different places. He assumes an attack may come at all fronts."

"True, but did they not attack from predictable locations?" said Kai-Tsúthlen. "Luthrey is in the middle of the hills between *Lotah 'an Lí* and *Lotah 'an Morkh* and Mor'Lûn is right next to the Wall of Separation. The most feasible invasion on Serenestí would come from the south."

"Who knows what the High Lord is planning? I simply do what is expected of me."

"What of the other nations?" asked Ninthalas. "Will they be warned?"

"High Lord Tothran sent out News Bearers to warn them before the mass meeting was held. Other than that, all News Bearers are to remain in the country."

"I wonder if the other nations will take action, if we will bind together," said Atheil.

"We shall see," said Kai-Tsúthlen.

"Now do tell me, friend Ninthalas," Atheil went on. "What is this tale you have for us?"

Tahlen interjected. "That actually requires you to be filled in on some more detailed information regarding our journey."

The Captain gave a brief summary, including finding Yosef, the boy's kidnapping, and their pursuit of the Black Assailant.

"That is where your story comes in, my friend," he said, nodding to Ninthalas.

"Indeed." Ninthalas took a sip of wine.

He then recited the same account he had told his parents that morning, but left out that the Black Assailant was a woman. In fact, he rarely mentioned her at all. He wove his story around fleeing from the souls, the pair of eyes that had led him out of the forest and the flying malshorth he had seen in the sky from a distance.

"I fail to understand how a horse found the boy and not you," Atheil said when Ninthalas had finished.

"Indeed," said Tahlen. "Peculiar as always, Ninthalas. Yet

what is most important is that you and Yosef are safe. What of the boy now that you have brought him here?"

"If all goes well, I aim to adopt him thanks to the seal of your father."

"That will not go well here," Atheil commented. His cheeks had turned pink from the three and a half glasses of wine he had managed to consume during the conversation. The bottle he had brought over was nearly empty.

"No, it is good news," said Tahlen. He raised his glass. "Let us toast to it! To Ninthalas' return and his adoption of Yosef Mathíus."

"And to Tahlen's fated encounter," Atheil added.

The others paused.

"What encounter?" Kai-Tsúthlen asked.

Tahlen glowered, but Atheil ignored him. "Our dear Captain Dían has met a woman, and a beautiful one at that."

"Is this true?" Kai-Tsúthlen asked Tahlen.

Tahlen's cheeks turned pink. "I did. Yet it is nothing to gawk over."

"Who is she?" Ninthalas asked. "I shall arrange a meeting."

"No. I will see her in due time."

"And suffer should she find another man? I should think not, Tahlen. I have never seen you enraptured by a woman, which leads me to believe this to be an important affair."

"Ninthalas, enough."

"You might as well accept it, Tahlen," Kai-Tsúthlen said. "There is no stopping him now. He will not rest until he ensures you have had significant time to speak with her. He did the same for Arúthíen and I, though I found her lovely after having spoken with her but once."

"I mean no harm in suggesting you two meet again, Tahlen," Ninthalas explained. "Do you like her?"

"I found her...captivating."

"Then that is reason enough. Tell me who she is and I guarantee you two shall meet again."

"I...cannot say."

Ninthalas withdrew the account he kept in the folds of his tunic, as well as a wrapped piece of charcoal. "Will you write it down then?"

Tahlen took the paper, scribbled on it, and handed it back. Ninthalas quickly returned it to his tunic without looking at it.

"What does it say?" asked Atheil.

"Never mind," Tahlen stated.

Kai-Tsúthlen stood. "It is best we get going. I must return to my family and I am sure Yosef is eager to see Ninthalas. Such is the duty of a father."

"Indeed, let us go," Ninthalas agreed.

With a disappointed scowl, Atheil rose, empty bottle and glass in hand, and he and Kai-Tsúthlen swung back over the expanse separating their shelf from the direction they had come.

Ninthalas was about to cross when Tahlen grasped his arm.

"Tell no one of that name," the Captain said under his breath. "No one save Kai-Tsúthlen. I do not want word to get out that I have feelings for her."

"Your secret is safe with me, my friend," Ninthalas reassured.

He grasped Tahlen's arm, held it firm. Then he left to catch up to his brother.

While the twins were making the trek back to Selestía, Ninthalas withdrew the parchment to read the name.

"How interesting."

"Who is it?" Kai-Tsúthlen asked.

"Belthosh's daughter."

"No wonder Tahlen wishes for us to keep it secret."

"Constructing a meeting will prove much more difficult than I thought."

"It is a good thing you are an expert in these sorts of things then."

"What? Romance?"

"Indeed, romance."

"Brother, I have not had the desire to court a lady since I was thirteen."

"Yet I remember you were quite good at it, young though you were. And you superbly arranged countless encounters for me and Arúthíen despite her father's disapproval of our family."

"Perhaps so."

"You miss those days, I see."

Ninthalas sighed. "I do."

"There are other women, Ninthalas. Athlaya was not the only maiden in Serenestí."

"Yet there was no maiden like her, no maiden like myself, a fellow oddity. She was my equal, Kai-Tsúthlen."

"I will not argue with you, but consider my words, lest you waste your life away as an unhopeful man."

Ninthalas nodded, but didn't say a word. He tried to focus on how he would comprise a meeting between the foreigner's daughter and the well-esteemed Captain, but his thoughts kept drifting to the loss of Tahlen's sister long ago. His parents had told him countless times that he should let go and move on, but Ninthalas never seemed to be able to. He had prayed for freedom from that sorrow. Yahlírin, however, never answered his prayer.

"But I have Yosef now. I can hope again. I will raise the boy well as my son."

"Of course you will," Kai-Tsúthlen agreed.

"I just hope the High Lord does not take heed to the adoption."

CHAPTER SEVENTEEN

The High Lord's Command

A firm knock sounded upon the front door. Ninthalas poked his head through the doorway of the dining room and watched his father go and open it. On the other side, a young man clad in the attire of the servant of the Selestorinth bowed low.

"Kindest greetings to you this fine morning," the man said. "I presume you are Kamesh Shadai?"

"Indeed I am," Athestin replied. "I am afraid you come while my family is partaking in the morning meal."

"My sincere apologies for the disturbance, but I have been bourn in urgency. The High Lord requests your presence today, you and your immediate household. You are to present yourselves before him by high sun and no later."

"Summoned? The High Lord has no direct dealings with News Bearers. For what reason would he wish to speak with one, let alone his whole family?"

"Forgive me, but I do not know the nature of the summoning," the young man said. "I was merely told to relay this message to you: that you are to see the High Lord at his own office by high sun."

"Very well," he said. "We will fulfill the wishes of our good High Lord."

The servant bowed, turned and left.

Ninthalas withdrew from the doorway and returned to his cushion. A meeting with the High Lord. This could only mean that

High Lord Tothran had seen the adoption papers.

He watched his father enter the dining room again and return to his seat. All eyes were on him, waiting expectantly.

"We are to meet with the High Lord," Athestin said sombrely.

"He has learned of my adoption of Yosef!" Ninthalas exclaimed.

"Relax, my son."

Ninthalas breathed in deep and let it out slowly, but his heart still beat furiously. "Why else would he summon us? This may go ill, father."

"You may be right. We all must go with our family, which means our children with us unless we can find someone to sit. The High Lord will see Yosef and pose questions and the validity of anything we account for thereafter will be deemed void."

Another knock at the door interrupted the conversation.

"Who could that be now?" asked Lethría.

"I will get it," said Ninthalas, already on his feet and making for the door.

When he opened it, he found a young girl on the other side. Brown hair. This was Belthosh's daughter.

"Fair greetings, sir," she said, bowing. "I am a medic from the northern clinic. Two days prior, I tended to Yosef's wounds. If I have not come at an ill time, I would like to check on them."

"Please, come in." He led her to the dining room.

"Elkeshlí Sen!" Lethría exclaimed.

"My apologies for interrupting your meal, Temesh Shadai," the girl said with another bow. "Is it alright if I assess Yosef's injuries?"

"By all means. He is in the living room there with the other children."

Elkeshlí bowed and disappeared in the direction Lethría gestured. Yosef's excited voice burst from the other room.

"You're here! I need your help. Ahnthalas keeps speaking in True Faithen. What's he saying?"

Ninthalas smiled as Ahnthalas rattled off several sentences and Elkeshlí roughly translating in Common.

"I believe she wants to speak with you, Ninthalas," Lethría said.

"How so?"

"I told her how you treated Yosef's wounds."

Ninthalas frowned. "Well, another one to mock my skills. I think we should be more concerned with how this summoning will play out."

"Indeed," Athestin agreed. "We may have no choice but to bring the children with us."

"Father, High Lord Tothran will most likely revoke the adoption."

"No, he cannot," Kai-Tsúthlen interjected. "He has no power to do so according to not only High Councillor Dúrlen's words, but also the familial statutes I found in his office."

"When did you get the chance to read those?" Athestin asked.

"While you were talking at our last visit, of course," Kai-Tsúthlen replied. "I have delved into those books before on our other visits as well thanks to Ninthalas' constant pestering about adoption."

"So we know that he cannot revoke the documents," said Athestin. "Yet we still do not know how this summoning will pan out."

"Excuse me…"

They turned to see Elkeshlí in the doorway. Kai-Tsúthlen's daughter clung to the medic's garments.

"Kírthíen, what are you doing?" said Arúthíen.

"Oh, it is alright, my lady. I do not mind in the least," said Elkeshlí. "Actually, I overheard you talking. Do not tell me the High Lord disapproves of Yosef. My father faced such hardship trying to integrate into True Faithen society, and he still does. This poor boy needs none of that."

"You need not concern yourself with the affairs of our family," said Lethría.

"My apologies, Temesh Shadai, but I understand this situation perfectly well. I face discrimination every day, yet it was you and a man of the Lothlúrin family who spoke of me as one of your own. If the oldest family lines in True Faithen history have such a positive opinion of people like me and my father, then I will do what I can to support you."

"Can you babysit?" Ninthalas asked.

"Of course."

Ninthalas looked hopefully at his father.

"You do realize that you are dragging yourself into the affairs of Shadai, Sen Hashlen," Lethría said.

"No, my lady. This is an affair of foreigners."

"It is settled then," Athestin declared. "Let us leave at once."

The sun barely reached its zenith in the sky when the Shadais arrived at Selest'Hí. Ninthalas walked behind his family, occasionally glancing up at the pair of couples. Butterflies fluttered in his stomach as wild imaginings of worst case scenarios played out vividly in his mind.

Peace, peace, brother Líran, he heard the silver-haired man's voice say to him.

The words failed to calm him. His thoughts tormented him all the way to the front doors of the High Lord's office. His father knocked and the door slid open, revealing the same servant who had come to the Shadai home.

"Kindest greetings to the family Shadai," he announced, stepping aside to let them in.

The family entered and gawked when they saw the interior. Ninthalas gazed up and around. The High Lord's office was a massive room fit for a king. The walls held murals of beautiful tapestries. Columns holding up the ceiling were engraved with swirling designs and the floor was smoothly polished marble. A series of giant polygon-shaped windows on the far wall allowed sunlight to stream in, lighting up the entire room. On either side of the office, single doors probably led to High Lord Tothran's personal quarters.

High Lord Tothran himself was standing sock-footed at his personal library, a towering bookshelf filled with his own collection of law periodicals, statutes, and by-laws. About the foot of the library a red velvet carpet stretched out in a half circle. Beside the carpet his jewel-adorned sandals glinted under the light that filtered through the windows.

The High Lord looked up to see the family and, after putting the book away, slipped his shoes on. He beckoned them to sit as he went to take his place in his padded chair at the other end of a table, a seat so finely ordained with gold, silver and jewels that it could have passed for a throne. On his desk lay neat stacks of books and parchment.

As the family sat down on the chairs that seemed so unbefitting Serenestí, he studied each of them in turn.

"Welcome," he said, though his tone was dry and business-like. "I express my appreciation to you for coming on such short notice. There is a certain matter that I wish to discuss with you. But first, where are your children? Did I not request your entire immediate household?"

"We made arrangements for them to remain at home," Athestin replied.

"A shame, for one of them concerns me."

He held up the adoption papers, which were duly signed and sealed by Dúrlen Lothlúrin. Ninthalas sank into his seat. His worst imaginings were true.

"I was hoping you would explain this to me," the High Lord said.

"What is there to explain?" Athestin asked. "It is as the documents say."

"Then you mean to tell me that you allowed a foreigner to cross our borders? How come I heard nothing of this boy in Captain Dían Lothlúrin's account?"

"Captain Dían was mostly concerned with the battle at Luthrey. Do you not know that he suffered the loss of half his Company? Though the time of mourning is passed, he is probably still overcome by grief."

"That is no excuse to provide a flawed account."

Kai-Tsúthlen cut in. "Yet you have two witnesses, and the law states that two witnesses are needed for an account to be valid. And this is no serious matter since it is just one boy, no threat to our country's customs."

High Lord Tothran glared at him, a look so furious that if it were a weapon, it would kill a man. "Kamesh Shadai, I would have hoped that you raised your sons well, to not speak when it is not their place."

"As much as you distrust my son, I ask that you pardon his outburst," Athestin said sternly. "Kai-Tsúthlen is a respectable man and well-versed in the law."

"News Bearer, believe me when I say that it takes years to become *well-versed* in the law."

"What is your verdict, then?"

"I have spoken with the members of the High Council. We have decided that the boy must be evicted."

Ninthalas shot to his feet. "No! He is my son now. You cannot revoke that."

"I may not be able to revoke it, but I can make decrees."

"You cannot do this!"

"Sit down, my son," said Athestin calmly while keeping his gaze fixed on the High Lord.

"Again, petty outbursts," said the High Lord. "You should have raised him better."

"I raised him in the way he ought to go. Who are you to speak of rearing children since you have none? If you are finished shaming my family, then I request our leave."

"I am not finished." He looked at Ninthalas. "My dealings with your family have yet to be stated."

"Dealings?"

"Indeed. I understand that one of your sons is a promising negotiator. I am aware of our position on an international scale, and I cannot ignore our policy of informing other nations of these raids."

"You would have them bear witness though they have only just returned from their last journey?" Athestin asked. "They have been away from family for much too long as it is."

"I am sending only one of them." He paused, letting the statement sink in before continuing. "Allow me to explain. When we learned of Luthrey's fall, five News Bearers set out to bring word of the attack to the authorities of the other nations. Specifically, they were tried with going to Hémon to meet with the four kings, for the cities of that country are central to international trade. We have had no word from them since their departure. If Hémon falls, the capital power of A'thería dies."

"To Hémon!" Athestin exclaimed. "That is folly, 'tis suicide! Surely you do not expect either of my sons to go there."

"What I request of one of your sons is that he find out what has become of those five men."

"Does that include entering that dreadful City?" Lethría asked. "I would not have my sons go there, not even within a day's travel of that place. No True Faithen has ever breeched the walls and come out alive for many a century."

High Lord Tothran's face grew sour. Whether it was some sort of disvalue for women or simply that she spoke out of turn was a mystery.

"It is true that Hémon is a dangerous city to breech, yet should we leave our brethren to die forgotten?"

"We do not know for sure whether or not they are even there," said Athestin. "Perhaps they bypassed Hémon and travelled to Tírithor first, then reconsidered their oath upon their return to the City. I do not imagine any True Faithen would want to breech the walls for fear of his own life."

"This is the task that is appointed to you," High Lord Tothran declared.

"Which of my sons would you have go?"

"The one named Líran Shadai."

Lethría and Arúthíen gasped. Athestin and Kai-Tsúthlen stared agape at Tothran. Ninthalas went livid.

"You cannot do this to us," Athestin argued. "It is unjust."

"I did not say he had to go into Hémon, only that he find out what has become of the other News Bearers. I also demand that he travel to the other common cities: to Melbé, Pehneppé, Súnlin and Celodía. The other nations must be warned."

"To the desert?" Ninthalas asked. "I...have not the skill for desert travel, nor the tanned skin of a farmer to survive. The sun would burn me."

"This is your task. You have a week to prepare."

The Shadais remained frozen in their chairs.

"Let me go with him," Athestin pleaded. "The travel would be safer with two—"

"I am granting one pardon to leave this country and one pardon only. And that is for Líran Shadai." He waved his hand in a dismissive gesture. "That is all I have to tell you. You may return to your home now."

One by one, they rose and walked away, single file.

"Do you have something to tell me, Okran Shadai?" High Lord Tothran asked.

Ninthalas glanced over his shoulder. Kai-Tsúthlen stood up straight and turned his nose in the air.

"I know this is unjust, to send my brother when he has just returned and to send him alone. I know it is against the laws of our people. And when I find proof in our records and gather what evidence I can against you, be ready because you will loathe the day I face you in trial. This breech in order will be made known to all."

Dúrlen Lothlúrin paced the width of the wide hall, listening to the raised voices through the door. His longtime friend, Athestin, rarely became agitated. Dúrlen didn't know he'd become so upset over a simple adoption.

"That does not sound like a pleasant meeting," Afren said. He leaned against the wall, arms crossed.

"If I were to receive such news for myself, I would not be thrilled either," Dúrlen replied.

Just then, the doors burst open. Out walked Athestin, his expression so frightening, Dúrlen hesitated to approach him.

"I am sorry, Athestin," he said. "We were outvoted six to two."

"Let me be," Athestin fumed, storming past.

Trailing behind him were the women and Ninthalas. Ninthalas' complexion was paler than usual. Whatever had come to pass in the High Lord's office hadn't ended well.

"I have never seen him so cross," Dúrlen whispered to Afren. "Ninthalas Líran is ever the joyful fellow. I have not seen him in such despair since I lost my daughter."

"When such an injustice has been done to your family, I would not be too happy either," Afren said.

"I signed and sealed those papers myself. They cannot be revoked. Yet I had no idea the High Council would take it so badly."

Lastly, Kai-Tsúthlen came out. Normally stoic, his aspect showed the same fury as his father's.

Instead of joining his family, he marched right over to the Councilmen.

"High Councillor Afren, Dúrlen," he said with a bow of his head. "I wish to tell you that I accept your offer. I will study under High Councillor Afren and succeed him when he retires."

"That is good to hear," said Dúrlen. How was the young man

staying so calm?

"I also request to meet with you as early as *Jímen'Yahl*. There is a matter of great importance that I must discuss with you."

"About the adoption?" Afren asked. "We already lost that vote, and there is nothing more we can do about it."

"No. It is about something else entirely."

"What exactly?"

"I will tell you when my blood has cooled." He bowed. "I take my leave."

He stormed off in much the same manner as his father and disappear down the stairwell.

"I pray, what has the High Lord done now?" Afren asked.

"I do not know, but something tells me Tothran has crossed the line, and I have a feeling it has to do with Ninthalas Líran."

"What can we do about it?"

"Let me catch up to Athestin. I will find out what has happened and report back to you. In the meantime, you had best prepare how you plan to teach Okran Shadai."

"I shall await your report then."

Ninthalas walked several steps behind his mother and sister-in-law. Dúrlen had pulled his father away, probably to speak to him about the High Lord's command. His brother walked several paces behind him, eyes cast to the ground and his face so furious Ninthalas knew better than to speak to him.

He could barely believe what was being asked of him. To go to the other nations *alone* to bear news? And to Hémon and the Athsúmek Desert? Every News Bearer was assigned routes that they maintained throughout their whole lives. That way, villagers would come to trust them. Ninthalas had an easier time relating to other ethnicities than his own. Perhaps that was because those people expected him to be different and didn't judge him. At least not to his face.

Yet to Hémon? And alone? News Bearers almost always travelled in groups of three or more, and they never embarked on an errand solo.

He picked up bits of conversation between the women ahead

of him. His mother spoke of her worry while Arúthíen tried to comfort her. Periodically, they glanced back at him, pitiful looks on their faces. Ninthalas met their gaze every time. He shared their shock and remorse, though his reasons were different. He didn't want Yosef to be sent away. After all he and the boy had been through and the ordeal of filing for adoption, Ninthalas was set on keeping Yosef as his own. Why the High Lord was so against integration? The Fehlthan and statutes didn't forbid it. Not to his knowledge anyway. The only nation that had ever given True Faithens trouble was Hémon.

Ninthalas shuddered. He had no desire to come remotely close to that country. They'd surely kill him, torture him like they did in the missionary days of the second age.

They crossed the bridge over the Lothshaiín River. The road branched off and two directions and Ninthalas diverted paths with his family, letting his feet guide him without his mind following. The buildings of northern Selestía became more numerous as he entered northern Selestía. At the town square, chattering women gathered around the well like they did every mid-morning, the second social gathering of the day. As he strode into the square and through the scattered groups of people, it didn't take long before the topics of conversation revolved around him.

"Is that not one of the Shadai boys?" said a middle-aged woman. She huddled with several others near where he was walking.

"One of the twins? No."

"It is. I recognize him. He is the unmarried one," another said.

"How can you tell? They both look the same."

"Yes, but who else would go to the square where only the women meet? You know, I heard he knows medicine."

The younger women leaned closer. "No, really?"

"Indeed, I heard as well," the middle-aged woman said. "Temesh Shadai is not shy about it, though I wonder if she realizes it is a woman's trade?"

"Did you see her not two days past? She had a foreign boy in tow."

"Tainting the blood of our people, that one," an elderly lady cut in. "That woman has always been headstrong."

"Oh, nothing like the Lothlúrins, I assure you."

"But a woman's trade though! Do you suppose he will start dressing like one of us now?"

"That would explain why he is unmarried. Queer fellow."

They laughed, but immediately hushed when they noticed him looking at them. Scores of snarky comments crossed Ninthalas' mind as he charged past. He hated the gossiping, hated the discrimination against him just because he was different *and* a Shadai. If he hadn't taken on his father's trade and become a medic instead, the High Lord might consider evicting him as well.

Poor Yosef. Realization dawned on Ninthalas. The boy would face discrimination his whole life if he lived in Serenestí. What had Ninthalas been thinking, dragging him north and asking him to become his son? Yosef would have been better off in the hands of those Mor'Lûn refugees.

Or would he? They had seemed as taken aback by Yosef's ethnicity as any True Faithen.

A lump formed in Ninthalas' throat and tears blurred his vision. He loved Yosef, loved him like a son. He *was* his son, he reminded himself. Ninthalas didn't know what he had gotten himself into by adopting him, but he was willing to endure with the boy. He never wanted to leave Yosef's side.

He shook his head. Don't cry. Just don't cry. Not here.

He left the town square down the western road. Trees that had been less numerous in the town square enveloped the scenery, pocketed by residential houses that were connected by hard dirt paths. They became less numerous as his feet took him out of town.

He sighed. "I should go back. This brooding is getting me nowhere and I should be comforting my family."

He was about to turn back when his ears caught the sound of metal clanging on metal. The sound played on Ninthalas' memory, bringing forth a similar time when he had felt downcast and upset. The smithy, and not just any smithy. This was the best one in all of Serenestí. He had helped Ninthalas then. Ninthalas had gleaned from his mother's garden the best herbs he could find so he could bargain the smithy for a sword.

He took to a dirt path that dove into the thick of vegetation, following the sound of the clanging. The smithy's small cottage lay almost completely concealed by foliage. Next to it, a large dome-shaped building made for his shop.

Ninthalas walked up to the front door and turned the knob, one of the only doors in Serenestí that didn't slide. The scent of a stoked fire and hot metal overwhelmed him as he pushed the door open. He breathed it in, welcomed it. The metallic scent gave him an exotic, unreal sensation. The fires of bellows obliterated any hint of the autumn cool outside. An L-shaped half wall separated customers from the workspace. Several clips of paper lining the far right wall marked a backorder of customer requests.

The smithy pounded, sparks flying with every hit on the hot steel of his most urgent order. Dirt smothered his face and bald head. His beard was a short stubble that gave him a gruff appearance, his shirt sleeves rolled up to reveal large muscles as thick as Ninthalas' thighs. On his feet, he wore thick boots that looked unbearable for the room's temperature. This was Belthosh Hashlen who had married a True Faithen medic, the only foreigner in Serenestí.

Belthosh looked up and stopped pounded.

"Something I can do for you lad?" he asked in a northern accent.

"Perhaps, perhaps not," Ninthalas replied.

"Well, you'd best be specific and make it snappy. I'm booked solid and can't spare much at the moment, but something tells me you're needing something special." His accent was thick, his words choppy and unrefined.

Ninthalas sighed. "I am sorry, sir. I am upset, unsure of myself."

"Ah, I know who you are." Belthosh grinned, taking a sip of water from a nearby jug. "The boy with the heavy heart who had me fashion a fine blade. That sour face of yours has always been etched in my memory. How'd the sword turn out for you?"

"It was not for me, good sir. It was for a lady valiant and true. Yet she is long since gone, or have you not heard of the loss of Kírin Lothlúrin?"

"I did. Shame, that was. You still have the sword, though, or her family does?"

"No, sir. It went with her."

"Well, no good I am telling you what to hope for and what not. I lost my whole village to the plague, you know."

"I am sorry, sir."

"Don't be. What's done is done. Yahlírin gives and takes away, though the taking away be grievous and heart-wrenching. That is the way of the world."

Ninthalas nodded.

"Well, sir, there is one thing you may be able to help me with. I actually came here because you might have some knowledge on how to handle my situation."

"Have at 'er."

"I returned from a trip to the south some days ago, and I brought home an orphan boy whom I wish to adopt."

Belthosh put down his anvil and came over to the half wall, wiping his hands with a cloth. A keen interest twinkled in his eyes.

"Adopt a foreign boy? That's wonderful!"

"It would be if he was not ordered to be evicted," Ninthalas said.

"Ah, I see. That *drat* High Lord wanted me away as well until I showed him I could make finer material than any other smithy in this country. When will he learn that the world's out there, not cooped up in a cage?"

"I can neither agree nor disagree with you, sir. The High Lord is our leader."

"Fair that. So what're you going to do about it?"

"Do? There is nothing I can do! I am ordered to leave next week on another errand."

"Take the lad with you then."

Ninthalas opened his mouth to speak, then shut it. It hadn't occurred to him that he could do that, but it made sense. Yosef was to be evicted and he was to go on errand, so there was nothing stopping Ninthalas from taking his new son with him. There was only one problem.

"My path takes me to the borders of Hémon."

Belthosh's expression turned hard. "You'll be at risk if you go there. The boy should be fine, but you...Oh no, lad, don't go to that wretched land. They're some fierce people when a True Faithen crosses their path. Just ask my wife and daughter. When they go to Tírithor, they bypass the City altogether."

"Yet I must. It is only to the border. I can leave after I find out what happened to the five messengers who were sent before me."

Belthosh continued to stare at him, brows furrowed. After a while, he shrugged and resumed his work.

"Looks like you have your answer then. There's nothing more I can help you with. Just be on your guard, and don't get yourself killed."

"Indeed. Thank you for your thoughts, Belthosh Hashlen."

Belthosh lifted a hand and dropped it just as quickly, a strange gesture Ninthalas took as meaning "you're welcome".

Ninthalas left the smithy with firm resolve. He would bring Yosef on his quest to the other lands. He needed a companion anyway, and since Kai-Tsúthlen couldn't go, Yosef would have to fill the spot. At least Ninthalas wouldn't have to be alone.

CHAPTER EIGHTEEN

An Earlier Departure

A sharp kick jerked the Black Assailant awake.

"Get up," her master said.

His deep voice echoed like thunder off the secret cave's walls. The unwelcome bellowing killed the silence she had fallen asleep to.

She slowly sat up and rubbed her shoulder. Two nights of barely any sleep and too much activity left her weary, stiff and sore. She'd hoped for a little more rest.

Rest. She chuckled. When did she begin to require rest? She had her answer while the question was still forming in her mind. Shadai. The *hallon* was in the company of Ninthalas, who had unfortunately taken it upon himself to keep Yosef by his side. Everything that could have gone against her wishes had.

The Third kicked her again.

"What!?" she spat. Her two-part voice reverberated through the tunnel like a serpent's hiss.

"It's time."

"Time for what, fool? You do realize that the entire border is under heavy watch, do you not? Or have you forgotten what I told you earlier? I have been searching for a way to breech that accursed country for two days and a night. There is no way in without being spotted, not when the borders are on high alert."

"I can get you in."

"You?" She couldn't help but laugh. "May I remind you that

218

when you change the earth, the ground shakes enough for everything and everyone within half a day's travel to feel it."

Dethshaiken crossed his arms. "They won't feel a thing."

She shook her head. This idiot's mind was a hollow chasm of stupidity. "You also forget that there is a boy among them who can sense my presence, so even if you could get me in undetected, he would raise the alarm before I have a chance to wreak havoc. Oh, and did I mention Shadai?"

"Shadai is long gone, woman. Nothing but a myth."

"That is where you are wrong. You have never met him, having spent your miserable days of the First Age dealing with common people. But my possessor knows. He remembers that *hallon* all too well. Shadai has returned, and he bears the goodwill of the Enemy. If I go topside, he will most certainly find me."

"Are you refusing your task?"

She pressed her lips together in a sneer.

"You know your orders regardless of how you feel or what you fear. You will do as the First commands."

"So you are using *his* words against me? Funny since you hate him as much as I do."

"I'm here to make sure your job gets done. So do it."

She scowled. The last thing she wanted was to disobey the First. She hated Dethshaiken, but a world of torment awaited her if she every went against the First's command, and that frightened her more than a rough beating from the Third.

"When do we leave?"

"At sundown."

Light faded as the day came to a close and still Ninthalas had not returned. Yosef was beginning to worry. Arúthíen and Lethría had told him that he had diverted paths with them at some point during the walk home from the Selestorinth. But with night closing in, Yosef wondered if something bad had happened, especially since his sense was on overdrive. The sense had paid him frequent visits since he'd gone to the medical clinic and met Elkeshlí. That grating chill tingling on the back of his neck remained constant. It almost disappeared at one point, but was quick to return, biting at the base of his neck like hungry flies. But then it faded once again just after half sun as if it had sunk into the earth.

He knew what it belonged to. A few times during the day, he had sat down, closed his eyes and focused. She was quick. Dreadfully quick. She'd circled the forest border in only two days and a night. When she had been furthest away, the sense felt different. He'd woken from the trance with a splitting headache and blurred vision.

Consequence, the silence whispered to him.

What could that mean?

Poking and prodding from an ever-energetic Ahnthalas diverted his thoughts. Yosef's tanned skin contrasted with the True Faithen boy's pale complexion, and the four-year-old frequently poked and pinched throughout the day just to make sure Yosef's skin was real and not some paste that could be scraped off. Yosef didn't mind, really. It took his mind off of Ninthalas and the loud silence.

Words sprung out of the younger boy's mouth. When Elkeshlí babysat them, she had translated as much of Ahnthalas' quick speech as she could, making for a fun afternoon playtime. Yet when she had left to go back to the northern medical clinic upon the return of Arúthícn and Lethría, Yosef was stuck with enduring the incomprehensible speech. He often spaced out while the younger boy went on and on as if Yosef could understand him. It was during one of those zoned out moments that the poking disrupted him, calling him back to reality.

Arúthíen spoke to her son, what Yosef assumed was some rebuke because Ahnthalas immediately stopped poking and whined in response.

"How come he's not back yet?" he asked.

"Again, Yosef, I am not sure," Arúthíen replied.

"You sure he's okay?"

"Oh, I am quite sure. He often escapes into the forest to ponder things."

"How do you know?"

"I have known him for five years, Yosef. He is a brother to me, and the Shadais are closer to me than my own family."

"I wish he'd come back now."

"He will in time. You must be patient."

She resumed speaking to Lethría, whom Yosef learned couldn't speak Common as well as the others in the family. That was a shame because Lethría was not only the most beautiful woman Yosef had ever seen, but she also had an enchanting voice that held his attention even when she spoke in broken Common.

Yosef drooped his head. He stood, left the dining area, and puttered down the hall to his new room. It had once belonged to Kai-Tsúthlen before he had married and had since been transformed into a common study. The Shadais outfitted it with a temporary cot before they could obtain a permanent sleeping arrangement for Yosef. He sat down on it, cringing as the springs in the mattress creaked under the strain.

All around the room were things not his own: a filled bookshelf which seemed a staple of every bedroom besides a bed, a circular window, a low table, and a closet with a sliding door. The things that did belong to him now were his new clothes, both common and ceremonial wear, which lay draped over the table. A wooden sword which he learned was called a *saiken* lay on the floor. Kai-Tsúthlen—now Uncle Kai-Tsúthlen—promised to teach Yosef the way of the sword known to every True Faithen man. Why Ninthalas couldn't teach Yosef was unclear, but he assumed it was because his new father couldn't actually use one properly. Ninthalas was a peaceful man, Kai-Tsúthlen had told him.

Just then, the bed rattled. Startled, Yosef looked up. A slight tremor shook the bookshelf. That couldn't be the silence. He hopped to his feet, grabbed his *saiken* and ran down the hall to the dining room. When he reached the doorway, he stopped. That dreadful sensation washed over him.

"What is it, Yosef?" Arúthíen asked.

"No," he whispered, then rushed to the living room.

He flipped the latch unlocked and slid the door open a crack, just wide enough for him to peer outside. The light from inside flooded out, casting a rectangular glow on the deck and a sliver on the backyard grass. Faint rays of light illuminated the dark shapes of Lethría's garden and the bushes and trees surrounding.

Nothing stirred, but she was out there. Yosef knew it. And in her company was another ginormous force.

"Yosef, close the door," Arúthíen said.

She pried his fingers from the doorframe and slid the door shut again.

"What are you thinking?"

"We have to find Ninthalas!" Yosef exclaimed. "We have to find him now!"

"Why? What is wrong?"

"She's here, Auntie Arúthíen. Ninthalas is in trouble! He'll die if we don't save him!"

"Who is here? Who is she?"

"The Black Assailant."

"Nonsense. Guards patrol the border. Nothing can enter Serenestí."

"I know she's here!"

He ran to the front door, quickly slipped on his shoes and dashed outside. Arúthíen and Lethría called after him. He ignored them and ran, his sense guiding the way. The same sense told him the Black Assailant was close behind, but he couldn't tell if she was following him or not. His fear suppressed the silence.

"Ninthalas! Ninthalas, where are you?"

He found the main road and took it north. Clustered buildings lined the streets, homes and stores alike, the lamps by their windows providing him with just enough light to see where he was going.

"Ninthalas!" he called out again.

"Yosef?"

He turned to see a man coming towards him.

"Yosef, is that you?"

Yosef ran into the man's arms. "Ninthalas! Is it really you?"

"'Tis me, my son. What in all A'thería are you doing out in the cold? You will fall ill dressed like that."

"She's here, Ninthalas! She's come to get me!" Yosef exclaimed.

He looked up into the True Faithen's eyes and gasped. Ninthalas' eyes were glowing, just like the ones that had led Yosef in the Dead Forest.

"Da, your eyes!"

"*Aran*? Ah, yes, of course. Do not worry, my son. It is normal for some True Faithens' eyes to glow in the dark every now and then. Mind you, we do not know why or in what circumstance, except that it is easier to spot people if you are searching for them."

Yosef stared, mesmerized. Then he came to and whipped around, searching the darkness.

"What? What is it?"

"She...stopped."

"What do you mean?"

"I mean she's not moving anymore."

"Why not?"

"I dunno."

Both of them looked out into the night. Through the trees, Yosef could make out a faint glow, but he couldn't tell what it belonged to.

"Come, my son. We should go. If *Emkalaf'Morlúrnan* is prowling in the night, then we should be indoors."

They took each other's hands and walked away. As they went, Yosef felt the evil sensation fade, and a new, bright one take its place. What could it mean? Did the white light defeat the Black Assailant? That hardly seemed possible. The one thing Yosef could be certain of was that the Black Assailant had returned for him. And he was sure Ninthalas wouldn't be able to protect him.

"By the way," said Ninthalas, "would you be interested in going on another adventure with me?"

Yosef stopped. "Again? I thought we'd be staying here for a while."

"Well...I thought so as well. But I have recently been charged with another task, and I am afraid my adopting you did not go over too well with this country's leaders."

"Does that mean you can't be my da?"

Yosef sure hoped not. He was looking forward to having a new father.

"Oh no, the papers went through. You are legally my son."

Yosef breathed out a sigh of relief.

"It is just that...well, they do not want you living here in Serenestí. They want you to leave."

"Why?"

"It is complicated. However, since I have been charged with a new mission, we can go together. I will not leave your side if you will not leave mine."

"Good. I don't wanna leave you either." He paused before adding, "What're we gonna do about that Black Assailant lady person?"

"We shall have to leave sooner than expected. Tomorrow is the holy day, which by law requires us to rest. The day after I must prepare for the journey and gather what goods I can to trade and enough food for the road. We will leave the day after that—two days from now—on *Jímen'Thírin*, the second day of the week."

"Sounds good to me."

"Curses, Shadai!" the Black Assailant raged.

She had been so close. The boy had led her right to her target. She could just barely see Ninthalas through the trees, had her sword drawn, ready to kill.

Timeless Shadai stood behind her, clutching her shoulders. The touch had sent her possessor cowering into the deepest recesses of her soul, cursing every step of the way. As a result, she almost felt free. Yet it came at a cost. Burning pain seared through her limbs, climbing around her skin in sore, twisting veins. Her possessor couldn't stop it from spreading.

Again, you trifle with the ones I am meant to guide. What a troublesome woman you are, Emkalaf'Morlúrnan.

"And what a meddlesome fool you make yourself out to be!" she returned. "I have a hard enough time righting the wrongs of that sister of yours. It is thanks to her that the boy escaped."

Shadai ignored her. *What is your story, woman? Why do you want this man dead and possession of the boy?*

"Can you not see for yourself? What has become of your Eyes of the Ages? Or did you lose the power when you became a *hallon*?"

Answer my question. Why do you wish to end him?

"You think it is me who wishes him dead?"

So this is my brother's doing? It was a statement more than a question.

"Every act is your brother's doing. You should know that. It was with me; it is with that man. Damn you elders and your torment of the common folk!"

Still, what does he want with the boy?

"That is my own business, and I am not about to tell you," she spat. "Now let me go! It burns!"

He did, and she fell to her hands and knees, gasping. Her possessor returned in full force, suppressing the veins of sore pain that had wrought her limbs.

What is the matter with you?

"It is none of your concern. Go away, Shadai!"

I will not. I am that man's guide by the command of Yahlírin. It is you who must turn and go your own way. Return to your master.

That meant a beating, but she found herself obeying.

"*Curses, the foul.*"

After a few steps she stopped. Shadai's glow still illuminated the surrounding trunks and shrubbery. The Watcher, her possessor had called him. The one who sees what was, what is and what ought to be. Yet for some reason he could not fathom her.

"*Your brother yearns for you, you know,*" her possessor spoke through her. "*It is buried deep, an almost unseen thing in the pit of his heart. He would never admit it, though.*" Then she added with her own voice, "He satiates his grief by turning it on me by the very touch of his hand."

So that is why you spoke to me out of pain. Not many can withstand his touch. I see why he chose you. You are more fearsome than most men, a woman tried and true, raised by malice and through hardship. Even so, leave the one Yahl calls blessed be.

"That I cannot promise you," she stated. She continued walking away.

How are you able to leave when the borders are so heavily guarded? It is impossible.

"Not so when the Third is your ally. Again, where are your famed Eyes of the Ages?"

He didn't answer. She disappeared into the night, loathing to have to meet her master with an ill account. Dethshaiken would reward her failure with a good thrashing.

"No, no, absolutely not."

"Why not, mother? You heard as well as I did that *Emkalaf'Morlúrnan* is here. Yosef attests to that."

"That is exactly it, is it not? How is it that Yosef knows she is here?"

"He feels it, like he said. A sensation like the tingling of the hairs on his neck."

"And how is it that no one else can sense her like he can? I do not believe him."

"Oh come now, mother. Yosef is special. He can feel things that others cannot."

"Oh? And how come you cannot feel those things as well since you also are special?"

"Lethría, let him speak," Athestin interjected.

She ignored him. "I just cannot believe that some boy from the south can sense things that we, Yahlírin's chosen, cannot. There is no way that evil woman—*Emkalaf'Morlúrnan*, or whatever she calls herself—has breeched the border. It is too well-guarded."

"Mother, please, trust me on this," Ninthalas pleaded.

She scowled. Clearly, this was an unfortunate way to end the holy day. Everyone was dressed in ceremonial garb: smooth silks woven into fine fabric that fitted as wraps with long, wide sleeves. Broad sashes, purple and scarlet for the women and blue and green for the men, bound their wastes. The sashes tied at the back in bows and rounded knots, the ends flowing out onto the floor. The women's hair was tied up in a single bun, the rest of the long locks falling down the base of their necks. The men each had three braids: one down the back of their heads and two at the sides, the rest of their hair left to flow about their shoulders. The True Faithen attire was designed to restrict movement yet be comfortable enough for them to be at rest.

Yet their conversation at the dinner table was anything but restful.

"Um..." Yosef interrupted in Common, breaking up the argument. He was the only different one among them thanks to his ethnicity. His hair was done the same as the men, but the braids were much shorter and his natural, dirty blonde curls contrasted with their straight locks. He wore billowing pants like Ahnthalas instead of a flowing gown.

The rest of the family turned to him.

"I just wanted to say…you know…I wasn't lying when I said I can sense the Black Assailant lady. I know she's here. I know it sounds crazy, but she's here. That's the truth."

"Can you tell *where* she is exactly?" Athestin asked.

Yosef looked nervously at Ninthalas.

"'Tis alright, my son. You are a member of this family now, and your word is considered valid."

"I dunno *exactly*," he said, thinking. "It's as if she's underground outside the country somewhere. You know, last night I felt the bed shake, and the bookcase in my room was shaking, too. After that came the tingling feeling."

"*Joldashlí*," Kai-Tsúthlen mused.

"Indeed. I wonder what it could mean," Ninthalas agreed.

"You don't believe me?" Yosef asked.

"Oh, I believe you, Yosef. I believe you wholeheartedly. I have just never heard of such a tremor shaking these parts."

"Even so, we may as well conclude that *Emkalaf'Morlúrnan* is in Serenestí, or remotely close. And if so, she apparently wants me dead and possession of Yosef. That is reason enough for us to leave early."

"Ninthalas," Lethría began. She hesitated, noting a warning glance from Athestin.

"I can agree that you must leave soon," said Athestin, switching the conversation again into True Faithen. "On *Jímen'Thírin*, as you suggested. What I am most concerned about is what happens when that woman catches you."

"Indeed, she will slaughter you, brother," Kai-Tsúthlen said.

They were right. If Ninthalas met her, he would surely meet his end. He didn't want to die. He didn't want Yosef to be taken away, either. But he had to stay true to his courage, the same courage he clung to when he looked into the gloom of *Lotah 'an Morkh*. Surely, Yahlírin would protect him. Surely Yahlírin would deliver him from her hand.

"Hémon," he said at last.

"What?" they all exclaimed at once.

"If I go to Hémon, she will be at risk as well as me."

"Yet they persecute us, Ninthalas!" Lethría exclaimed.

"Then they will persecute her."

His mother shook her head.

"No," she said. "No. You cannot go."

Ninthalas stood, commanding their attention. "Are we not people of the Faith?" He let the question sink in. "Are we not Yahlírin's hand-picked vessels? What have I to fear when Yahlírin is so much greater?"

Kai-Tsúthlen answered. "Yet the rain falls on both those of the Faith and those who are not, as we saw from our cousin Lamnek's death. And let us not forget that half of Tahlen's Company fell by the sword. You could lose your life, Ninthalas. I nearly lost you once. I cannot bear to lose you again. And this time I will not be there to protect you."

"Then how am I supposed to evade her?"

As soon as he finished speaking, light flooded the room, shimmering like the morning star. Ninthalas shielded his eyes and crouched low until the light faded. When he opened his eyes, there at the foot of the table stood the silver-haired man. He glowed with the radiance of a heavenly being, yet as calm as a pleasant ghost. His white robes matched the style of True Faithen garb and had it not been for his silver-white hair, he could have passed as a member of their family.

Athestin and the women stared at him, mouths agape. They looked at Kai-Tsúthlen, wore a puzzled frown.

"*Bai*, I knew it! He *does* look like Kai-Tsúthlen." Ninthalas exclaimed.

Shadai smiled and knelt at the table. *Dear brethren of Shadai, what troubles you?* he asked.

"Timeless Shadai, thank Yahlírin above you have come to us!" Ninthalas exclaimed.

"Timeless Shadai?" Athestin repeated.

I am Shadai, the silver-haired man declared. *Sit, brother Líran, sit. Do not worry. Your family are distressed, I see, and that is precisely why I have appeared to them.*

"What are you?" asked Arúthien.

I am as you are, sister Lolekh, a child of Yahlírin, and I do His bidding. I come to you now, for you have questions and I may very well have answers should He who sent me permit me to answer.

"Is it true then?" Lethría demanded. "Is *Emkalaf'Morlúrnan* in Serenestí?"

It is as your grandson tells you.

"And she is here for Yosef," Kai-Tsúthlen stated. He still had that contemplative frown on his face.

Yes, though I am not sure why. Her motives are unclear, yet she has one devilish purpose. He turned to Ninthalas. *She is hunting you, brother Líran.*

"What? Hunting me? How...?"

It is as I have said, and you already know it to be true. She hunts you. Both you and Dían Lothlúrin are her targets.

"But why?"

That I am not sure, for Yahlírin has kept that information even from me.

"Then what is my son supposed to do?" Lethría asked. Tears flooded her eyes and began streaming down her cheeks. "I do not want my son to die!"

Die? No, sister Temesh, not die. I said merely that brother Líran is being hunted. Yet why is this a problem? You do know that he is under the protection of Yahlírin, do you not, and that his destiny must be fulfilled?

"But..."

You must have faith, dear sister.

"So what then?" she asked. "Is my son to go to Hémon and risk his safety and Yosef's well-being?"

Yosef? Shadai smiled at the boy. *Do you not know why this boy and brother Líran are together? Yosef Mathíus is strong, stronger than most. If anything, he will protect your son as long as they are together. Do not underestimate him, though he is but a boy.* He paused, as if to listen to the heavens above. *Indeed, his destiny is yet to be revealed, and we wait for it in great anticipation. As for brother Líran, he must heed the command of his High Lord.* He turned to Ninthalas. *I beseech you to leave as you planned. In two days, no later. For if you stay, then your entire family will be at risk.*

Then, just as suddenly as he had appeared, Shadai vanished, his last words echoing in their minds.

Do not let uncertainty frighten you, Temesh Shadai. Be not afraid. Hope in Yahl.

Lethría spoke softly, her voice barely above a whisper. "I...suppose it is decided then." She wept.

Ninthalas wrapped his arms around her. "I will come back to you, mother. I promise. I will return."

"Oh please, Yahl, keep my son safe," she cried.

The rest of the family gathered round, and laying their hands on Ninthalas, prayed.

Part 3

CHAPTER NINETEEN

The Leave Taking

Jímen'Thírin, the second day of the week, came quickly. Ninthalas rose just before daylight, dressed in his traveller's clothes and stepped outside. Low grey clouds brought a cool, light rain. His breath fogged as he exhaled, a reminder that winter would be on A'thería's doorstep in a month and a half or two. If all went well, he and Yosef might be able to make it back before the first snow fell. Yet somehow Ninthalas doubted they would make it back before then. This was going to be a long journey.

A grunt caught his ears. Hallas, his faithful steed, lingered not too far away tied to a tree. Ninthalas had retrieved the horse the day before after he had got his permit to leave the country. He brushed the horse's hair. Hallas, in turn, pounded the earth with its hoof.

"Are you eager for another trek, my friend?"

The horse whinnied and Ninthalas smiled. He'd been worried that his faithful travel companion would be too tired for another journey. But seeing the horse's energy this morning brought a cheery start to his day.

By the time daylight crept over the forest, Ninthalas had Hallas saddled up and laden with provisions. Kai-Tsúthlen dropped by, bringing with him extra food for Ninthalas' journey and some of Arúthíen's prized fabrics wrapped in tightly-woven twine-cloth that would keep out the rain.

"My wife spent long hours fashioning these," he said.

He strapped them where Ninthalas had put some of their mother's spices and his and Yosef's bags.

"There are these also." He withdrew a small wool cloak and an extra twine-cloth poncho. "For Yosef. His name is woven into the fabric in both True Faithen and Common."

"Thank you," Ninthalas said.

"It may be slow going with the extra weight," Kai-Tsúthlen noted.

"Not so for dear Hallas. He is bred for these long treks, to haul what he needs to where he needs to. There is no finer steed in A'thería."

"Of course, of course."

"I do have my concerns about the desert."

"You should find a guide in Sûnlin."

"Indeed—Oh, before I forget, brother, would you be so kind as to bring our new friend Elkeshlí to visit Tahlen while I am away?"

Kai-Tsúthlen chuckled. "Oh what a matchmaker you are, Ninthalas."

"Hardly so. I only encourage young love when it seems well."

"Indeed," Kai-Tsúthlen mused, shaking his head.

"Tahlen is so enraptured by her. I should only think it necessary to orchestrate an opportunity for them to meet. Of course, if I were to stay here, I would have brought her to him myself…"

"Alright. I will take her."

"Poor Tahlen needs some encouragement anyway since he has been so depressed lately. A kind young woman would do him some good, I think."

"Even more so would one do *you* good."

"Have we not discussed this already, Kai-Tsúthlen? The only woman for me has long since departed from my life."

He looked up to the sky as if to chart the progress of the sun. It was far from a convincing gesture, but he had to change the topic somehow.

Kai-Tsúthlen clasped his shoulder. "The morning is already underway. You should wake Yosef."

"Ah, yes. Indeed."

He hurried into the house. Yosef woke fast to the touch on his shoulder, but he wasn't so quick to get dressed. He seemed haggard, weary as if he did not get enough sleep.

"Are you alright, my son?"

"…Tired," Yosef murmured with a yawn.

"Was it the nightmare again?"

"Yeah. It's always the same. Creepy-like room, cold floor, screaming and whatever."

Ninthalas stroked the boy's hair. Since leaving *Lotah 'an Morkh,* Yosef had been having the same nightmare from when they stopped in Port Shai. It didn't plague him every night, but when it did, Yosef woke, then struggled to go back to sleep. Ninthalas had told the boy to tell him when the dream woke him in the night, but Yosef never did. He probably wanted to suffer on his own, to deal with the Black Assailant alone.

Yet the truth was Yosef's dream had become a reality for Ninthalas as well. He had almost forgotten about *Emkalaf'Morlúrnan* at home where woes had faded and the quest for adoption had occupied his time. He never imagined she would pursue them north. And now she was hunting him. Who was she? Why did she want him dead? Now that he thought about it, who was Yosef's father? So many questions. So many riddles! Yet despite his curiosity, he wasn't so sure he wanted answers. He got the feeling they'd make him more miserable than not knowing.

After dressing Yosef in a plain tunic and the new wool cloak from Arúthíen, Ninthalas and his son went to the kitchen. Lethría was already making breakfast, her aspect grim and brooding. Since the holy day, she had hardly spoken. Ninthalas had heard her pray aloud at the dining room table every night and morning. He didn't know if she had accepted Timeless Shadai's words or not. He couldn't tell what she was thinking sometimes. All he saw in her was sorrow.

He and Yosef sat down at the table. Not long after, Athestin entered the dining room, one arm flinging wide, the other cradling several rolled parchments.

"Good morning, my son!" he bellowed. "And good morning to my grandson!"

"Good morning, father," Ninthalas greeted in a far less cheery manner.

"'Morning," Yosef mumbled.

Athestin plunked the scrolls down on the wood. Lethría glared at him, but didn't say a word. No belongings were allowed at the table during a meal. Yet she wasn't prone to speaking against her husband.

Athestin ignored her look of disapproval and handed Ninthalas one of the parchments. Ninthalas unravelled it. It was an old map of Hémon.

"Where did you get this?" Ninthalas asked.

"Dúrlen managed to find me one. We do not keep many. You are holding one of the only maps of Hémon this country has."

"He is too kind."

"That country is the first stop on your list," Athestin explained. "Melbé and Lillié should be easy places to seek council with the elders and tell them the news of Luthrey and Mor'Lûn. So say other News Bearers I have conversed with."

"I suppose it would be best to get it over and done with," said Ninthalas with a sigh.

His father unfolded another map.

"Celodía," said Ninthalas. If he was being honest with himself, he was more nervous about traversing the desert than going to Hémon.

"I spoke with the Elrindon family who care for Hallas. They know the two desert traveller messengers who were part of the five. Should you find them on your journey, you should seek their aid. I have also heard of thieves roaming the desert between Sûnlin and Celodía. When you go there, make sure you get a guide, and preferably one who can fend off offenders."

"And that is not including the gangs of Pehneppé."

"You must take care on the roads. The days grow shorter, so do not travel more than is necessary by night. That is when thieves strike. If you can, reside at an inn, and if you find other News Bearers on the road, seek their company for safety."

"I will be careful."

Their dining was short. Ninthalas wanted to get an early start to the trip, and Yosef was just as restless to embark on a new adventure. The family stepped outside for one final farewell before the departure, the atmosphere about them bitter and the ill weather adding to their sorrow. Kai-Tsúthlen's family joined them, their faces just as melancholic.

Ninthalas lifted Yosef onto Hallas. The boy loved his new cloak and poncho, noting how he stayed dry under his netted hood. His *saiken* was strapped to his side. Ninthalas strapped his own weaponry to the horse's saddle. The only weapon he carried on him was a dagger wrapped in cloth.

"You still carry that thing with you?" Kai-Tsúthlen asked.

"Always," Ninthalas replied. "Every time I gaze upon it, I am reminded of what courage I need, the bravery she once held in abundance."

Kai-Tsúthlen shook his head.

Ninthalas mounted. He was about to take off when he saw the pained expressions in his family's faces.

"Do not despair, nor worry for our departure," he reassured them in a confident tone. "We will return before late, I assure you."

"Uncle Ninthalas," Ahnthalas piped up. "I will miss you, and Yosef, too."

"And I will miss you, nephew," Ninthalas responded warmly.

"Da, tell Ahnthalas we'll be back before he knows it," Yosef chirped, his face beaming with a smile.

Ninthalas relayed the message, brightening the younger boy's mood. He then looked to his mother. Lethría's gaze was downcast, her hands clasped modestly in front of her.

"Mother, I tell you, I will return," he said.

"Do not fall to that brash woman, Ninthalas," she answered, her tone firm.

"I will not. I assure you."

Lastly, he turned to Kai-Tsúthlen.

"Goodbye, brother. I wish you well in your new intern position."

"Likewise to you on your journey. While you are gone, I aim to bring the High Lord's injustice before the council. This wrongdoing against you will not go unnoticed. I will fight also for the right of foreigners to live in our country. When you return, Yosef may be free to roam here as he pleases."

"I will trust your word then. But for ill or not, this may very well be the will of Yahlírin. For if the threat of *Emkalaf'Morlúrnan* follows me, then you shall be safe."

"Apparently, from Timeless Shadai's words."

Ninthalas smiled. "I wish you farewell. Take care, all of you." They lifted their right hands in the air in response, a gesture for safe travel and fair speed. Ninthalas gave a great "Yish!" and Hallas jerked forward, breaking into a gallop.

Emkalaf'Morlúrnan jerked awake from another firm kick to her side. She twisted, painfully sat up. Her back screamed with the sores of her master's whip, a beating she had received because she failed her mission. Again. She could handle mocking laughter from her subordinates and bruises from squabbles with malshorthath in the caves south of Kislanía, but there were two pains she couldn't stand. One came from her master's steel-studded whip.

"Get dressed," came Dethshaiken's voice through her pulsing, aching head.

"Is there something wrong?" she asked as she pulled on her undershirt and over-wrap.

Her back had been in so much pain the past few nights that she slept wearing only her chest wrapping, and that wasn't modest in the least. She'd abandoned modesty years ago. She slipped on her hard-leather chest plate, bracers and shinguards, and strapped on her weaponry. Her short sword she handled with extra care.

"Yes, there's something wrong," Dethshaiken scoffed. "The vibration of hoofs galloping caught my senses. They ride from the Shadai dwelling north."

"How do you know that they indeed ride from the Shadai dwelling?"

"I am the Third, wench. I can feel anything that walks upon the earth, whether it be beast, creeping insect, or human being. It's like a sixth sense."

"Yet you cannot tell if it is Ninthalas, can you?" the Black Assailant said with a sly grin.

"There were two riders, a man and a boy. I knew their footfalls before they mounted. And no other horse rides to and from the country."

"So it *is* him. Intriguing. I wonder where he is going, what his quest is."

"Regardless, we will follow him. You had best end him before taking on that child prodigy. For that man, you will need your strength."

"You are not worried about Shadai?" she asked. "He did intervene with my last attempt to kill Ninthalas."

Dethshaiken scowled. "Shadai? I can't believe that fool stopped you. He's weak, not even a fighter."

"Some powers do not come from physical strength, Dethshaiken. You should know that well thanks to Morkhen."

He ignored her as he often did when she mentioned the First's name. Closing his eyes, he tilted his chin upwards, breathing in deeply. She knew he was listening to what he called the 'voice of the earth.' Only when he did this or shaped the land was he open for attack. She almost wanted to kill him while his defences were down. It was tempting. Even her possessor hated him, had wanted the brute dead for years. But the Black Assailant had a certain respect for the four-armed giant. She understood his lust for fighting, his desire to take down the next best challenger. For her, that challenger was him.

After a while, he opened his eyes. "We leave now. I'll punch a hole and we'll pursue topside."

"Understood, master."

CHAPTER TWENTY

Bellim's Request

What began as a light drizzle turned to a solid downpour that drenched Ninthalas and Yosef the moment they left Serenestí's forest border and embarked onto the open plain. In a day they reached Melbé, a social hub for News Bearers leaving and returning on errand. The city was a crossroads. To the north lay Hémon and further the mountain city of Tírithor. To the west lay Central A'thería and eventually the Athsúmek Desert.

"Young Shadai, where is your brother," asked the inn keeper. Avaron Toklan. He knew Ninthalas and Kai-Tsúthlen by name and birth year.

The older man looked curiously at Yosef. Yosef, in turn, stared right back at him.

"Strange times have come upon us, Avaron Toklan," Ninthalas replied. "And they are about as peculiar as my travelling alone without my family."

The inn keeper handed him a key. "Twenty-three down the west wing."

Ninthalas bowed his head as he accepted the key with both hands, then led Yosef to the spare room.

"You know him?" Yosef asked when they had found their room.

"Indeed. My brother, father and I stop here on our bi-annual errand south."

"You sure know a lot of people."

"Yes, but it will not help me where we are going. I have never been to Hémon."

The conversation ended there. Ninthalas hung their wet clothes and they rested for the night.

In the morning, they ate a mighty meal served by Avaron Toklan himself. The inn keeper didn't ask any questions. Neither did others in the common area who were partaking in the morning meal. They only stared, more so at Ninthalas' companion. Ninthalas, however, acted as if such company was commonplace.

After informing Melbé's mayor of the news, they took to the northern road and reached the next city well into the night, settling at a comfortable inn near the south-side outskirts. In the morning, they set out again.

"So what's this city called?" Yosef asked.

Ninthalas had been so lost in his thoughts, the sudden question caught him off guard. Normally, he would have dazzled Yosef with stories, but this time…this time his quest didn't lead him into certain danger.

"The city? This is Lillíé, town of the conjoining rivers."

He pointed up ahead. In the heart of town a massive bridge crossed a wide expanse of water with soaring banks. On each bank a fence spanned east and west as far as the eye could see. A clean, carved sign to the left of the bridge bore the words 'The Crossing.' Another sign stuck up on the right.

"*Corralléa'Den'Kúl* and Muddy South River," Ninthalas read. "*Corralléa'Den* is the True Faithen name and Muddy South is the Common. The north, which converges with this one at this point, is called *Corralléa'Tahleth* and Muddy North."

"Why do they have two names? Why not just stick with one?"

"I suppose it is because the locals cannot speak True Faithen," Ninthalas replied.

"Does it have giant fish people?"

"Giant fish people? I have never heard of such a thing."

"In Shalom that one night, well…"

Ninthalas waited, listening. Yosef had only told him that he stumbled upon the inn the twins had been staying at. Now that he thought about it, the boy must have wandered for hours before coming across it. The shabby inn wasn't anywhere near the bridge that crossed the Great River of Plenty.

"There were voices," said Yosef. "They kept whispering to me and told me to jump into the river. I didn't want to, but then the wind pushed me and I fell down and down. But then this fish monster person saved me and scared the voices away."

Ninthalas was speechless. Where words almost never failed him, now his mind offered no response. He simply sat there, leading Hallas across the bridge and onto the other side of the river.

"Is that strange-ish?" Yosef asked.

"I...well..."

"It is, isn't it? Everything about me is strange-ish. I don't like being different."

"It is your oddness that draws me to you, my son," said Ninthalas. "I find your gift fascinating."

"Do you?" Yosef twisted in the saddle and looked up at him with sentimental eyes.

Ninthalas wrapped his arms around him. "Of course, Yosef. Of course."

The conversation gave him an aching heart. Had Yosef not been with him, he would have broken down, let the tears flow until they fell no more. He loved Yosef. No child was much like himself: different.

After speaking with Lillié's mayor and government officials, only one trading settlement stood in their way before their next destination. The road forked and they took the right path. On midday of the last day of the week, an enormous sign yielded a single word announcing the country they were about to enter. Though the letters were foreign, Ninthalas knew the name.

Hémon. The one place he never imagined he'd visit.

The landscape changed from dusty barren land to flourishing town of wide farmland patches darted with stone houses. As they neared the centre of the first city, the houses became larger and more numerous until they bunched together in condensed blocks separated by narrow cobble-stone streets. The town was bustling with people dressed in bland colours of brown, beige and tan, their skin tones ranging in the same shades as their clothing. Among them strutted white-skinned soldiers clad in chainmail who glared at Ninthalas as he rode by.

Ninthalas pulled his hood over his head, but the gesture probably made him seem more suspicious than he already was. Fear trickled down his spine; his stomach fluttered with the beating wings of an insect. The confidence he had chided his parents with in Serenestí was completely gone. He had the urge to turn back and abandon his quest, to leave it all behind.

Yet that was a foolish idea because Yosef couldn't go back with him.

"Where are we?" Yosef asked.

Ninthalas pulled out a folded map from one of the horse's packs and unfurled it in front of his son.

"This must be Hemnak," he stated, pointing to the southern point of a diamond shape. "The main of Hémon is up ahead, I presume, encompassed by a wall rivalling the greatness of the Wall of Separation in Kislanía."

"I don't like the looks of this place city," Yosef said. "Everyone's starin' us down straight."

"They most certainly are. I do not approve of it either."

He caught sight of three soldiers in his peripheral vision standing in the shadows of a side street. Two were young, about his own age. The other was older with a scalp of grey hair and squinty eyes darted with creases. A narrow scar cut from above his left brow down his cheek, his skin stretching away in a hideous disfigurement. He wore a yellow armband while the others sported none, probably as a sign of higher rank. Despite the goings on around him, Ninthalas managed to pick up a little of what they were saying. Naturally, it pertained to him.

"Looks lost, he does," one of the young ones said. "Think he knows he's in bad territory?"

"Ho yeah! Faithen scum don't belong here. We should arrest him."

"Shut it, both of ya. Can't arrest him unless he breeches the walls."

The younger two dropped their heads.

"But you know I'd give him a good beating to scare 'im off."

They're faces brightened again.

"True saying, sergeant," the first one agreed. "I'd give the scrawny man a wallop he'd never forget."

Ninthalas didn't disbelieve them. Even if they couldn't arrest him, he had no way of fending them off if they gave him trouble.

A commanding voice stole his attention.

"Hémon's no place for a Faithen."

He turned to see a lean man taller than any True Faithen standing in front of him. His hair was dark brown, beginning to grey in areas; a short stubble covered his chin, stretching the length of his jaw. His eyes, fixed in sockets lined with a few wrinkles, were dark but friendly. He was clad the same as the soldiers except that he wore a blue armband. Whether he had a higher rank than the yellow-arm-banded man Ninthalas didn't know.

"Good day to you, sir," Ninthalas greeted.

He thought to say something more, but hesitated. Saying too much might mean trouble. In this country, he had to be careful.

"What brings you here?" the soldier asked. He walked casually up to the horse, grabbing the reigns. Hallas flinched, but didn't jerk free.

"I…well, that is…I seek news of certain News Bearers who supposedly came this way," Ninthalas replied.

"What's a News Bearer?"

"Ah, perhaps I should say men like me. Have you seen anyone of my complexion from the country of Serenestí within the past week or so? I have reason to believe they passed this way."

"You mean Faithens? None here. You'd be arrested."

"Is that so? I mean, of course I would never doubt the validity of your words. Yet I overheard those men over there say that I could not be arrested outside the City walls."

He nodded towards the three soldiers who were muttering amongst themselves, watching the scene play out between Ninthalas and the blue-banded soldier. The big man stuck up his chin towards them. Frowning, they disbanded, the two younger ones turning quickly down the side street and the other heading to Hémon's outer wall.

"Don't need to be arrested. Underlings are always looking for a fight."

"I see you are a leader among men."

"Sure am. I'm better company than most."

"So you would mean me no harm?"

"Depends what kind of harm you're thinking about."

An awkward pause fell between them as Ninthalas pondered a proper reply. Before he could speak, the soldier cut in.

"Why don't you come over to my place for a rest? Your beast looks haggard and I bet you two could use a good meal."

Ninthalas eyed him suspiciously. "And who are you that you should offer me such kindness?" he asked. "I do recall your people's treatment of mine, and the accounts of survivors speak none too kindly of it."

"Why, I'm Bellim Farthorn," the man said as if the answer should be obvious. "Chief General Trades Captain in Hemnak. If you don't know what that is, it's chief administrator of goods and people passing in and out of the City."

"Do you live around here, Bellim Farthorn?"

"No, too busy 'round these parts for my liking. I live in Fíthera. Come on, you're no good staying at an inn here. None of 'em would accept you. Come to think of it, they're probably all full what with Hémon's Day being tomorrow. Join my family for dinner."

"I am not so sure…"

"I guarantee your safety."

Ninthalas didn't know if he could trust this man, but the soldier's supposed sincerity made him nod anyway.

Bellim Farthorn hauled on the reigns, leading them off onto a narrow side street. The street broadened, taking them out of the city. Soon, Ninthalas spotted a bridge in the distance. Looking at his map again, he saw that it crossed a river that passed right through the middle of Hémon.

"I believe my map is incomplete," he said. "What is the name of that river?"

"Doesn't have a name," the trades captain replied. "We just call it the river."

"Then how do you not confuse it with other rivers like the *Coralléa* twins and *Lothshaín*?"

Bellim glanced over his shoulder at him, a perturbed expression on his face. "What the mad rambles is that?"

Ninthalas flustered. "Never mind. So this is Fíthera, is it? That sounds much more True Faithen than Hémonian."

Indeed, the town had a comforting feel to it. Pockets of forest dotted the riverbank and rolling plains yielded farmland and livestock, a sight that reminded Ninthalas of the farmland south of Serenestí's tree line border. Aside from the stone and brick homes, it was a glimpse of home.

"Apparently, a Faithen founded it back in the Missionary Devil Days," Bellim explained.

"The mission what?"

"Best you don't know about that one. It'd ruffle your feathers."

Before they reached the bridge in the centre of town, Bellim veered off road towards Hémon's wall, taking a narrow riverside path through a comfortable setting of oaks, maple trees and tangled hedges. Away from the thick of town a two-storey stone house stood tall with a pointed roof. Further into the trees, Ninthalas could make out another larger building. The smell of livestock caught his nose, allowing him to assume that the other building was a stable.

"Nasty," Yosef said, pinching his nose.

Bellim called toward the nearly concealed building. "Fehnan! Fehnan, son, where are you?—Confounded boy is always off lazying around somewhere."

A young teen poked his head out from the other side of the house. He was a scrawny boy, not older than fourteen from what Ninthalas could guess. He lacked the breadth and height of Bellim, but was sure to have a few more growing years left in him. When he saw Bellim, he ran over to meet them. Ninthalas noticed a book in his hand, silver letters etched on the front in a script far more elegant than what the True Faithen would expect to come out of Hémon.

"Take this man's horse to the stable. He and the other lad here will be staying with us tonight," Bellim ordered.

Ninthalas dismounted, lifted Yosef off and untied the packs. Without a word, Bellim grabbed the bags in his giant arms, including the trading goods Ninthalas had brought from Serenestí, and began marching toward the house. The teenager, Fehnan, looked curiously at Ninthalas and Yosef before leading the horse away. The travellers hurried after their host, struggling to keep up to the man's brisk stride.

"Come on in," Bellim boomed, opening the front door. "Don't worry. You'll be safe here. No one thinks twice about questioning me and the soldiers never bother coming. Not unless they want a mad ramble thrown at them."

He laughed in spite of himself.

"Come put up your feet. Félia? Félia—oh, there you are. This here's my wife."

He dropped the luggage on the floor and gestured to a woman sitting on a sofa in an open living room, knitting. When she saw the visitors, her eyes glazed over.

"Félia?" Bellim said again, calling life back into her.

"Why, yes!" she exclaimed, standing up to curtsy. "Fine day to you, sirs."

"Kindest greetings, my lady," Ninthalas replied with a bow.

Yosef clumsily mimicked his father. "Hullo."

Félia quickly gathered her knitting into a bunched mess, skittered across the floor and shoved it into an already-full chest.

"I'll go fetch you some tea then," she said, then disappeared into the kitchen.

Bellim motioned to the sofa. "Go have a seat. I'll get your things upstairs."

He, too, disappeared, along with the travellers' belongings.

"What a flitty couple they are," Ninthalas commented.

Yosef only nodded.

They took a seat where Félia had been knitting. The cushion was hard, stiff.

"These big cushion thingers sure are different than sitting on the floor at your place," Yosef said.

"Indeed. I am not so used to them, though I have travelled to places that use seating arrangements such as these. Serenestí is one of the only countries I know of that does not."

"Why's that?"

"I am not sure."

Before long, Bellim returned to the living room carrying a silver tray laden with delicate pottery teacups, silver spoons, sugar, and a white teapot bearing an image of lilies.

"You know, you came at a good time," he said as he set the tray down on a glass-topped table and sat across from them. "My wife just had the kettle boiled for a good brew not too long ago— Oh, you can remove your hood. Like I said, you're safe here, friend."

Cautiously, Ninthalas took the suggestion and let his features show. He felt barren, exposed.

"You came all the way here and didn't even think about using a disguise? Any Hémonian could tell you're a Faithen," Bellim said as he poured some tea for the three of them. "What brings a True Faithen to the City? Missionary work?"

"I am afraid not. My quest is quite different," Ninthalas replied. He took the teacup and sipped the hot brew. The tea was far more bitter than what he was used to, enhanced by a strange taste no doubt from the water.

Yosef tried the drink and his face turned sour. He quickly set the cup back down and squirmed as close to Ninthalas, and as far from the cup, as he could.

"Right. The five Faithens. Is that all? Not going into the City?" Bellim gulped his brew, downing the entire cup in a swig like he was drinking ale.

"I was not planning on it for fear of my life. My task is merely to discover the fate of the other News Bearers. Nothing more."

Bellim sat back in his chair, stroking his stubble as if in contemplation. During the pause, Ninthalas felt a tug on his shirt.

"Da, can I go play with those toys over there?" Yosef asked.

Ninthalas looked over at the toys, then at Bellim.

"Go ahead, my boy," Bellim replied.

Yosef trotted off and the soldier turned his attention back to Ninthalas. "'Da,' huh?"

"Yosef is adopted as of a week and two days ago."

"Interesting." Another pause. "You still haven't told me your name."

"Ah, forgive me, sir. I am Ninthalas Líran Shadai of Selestía in Serenestí. I often travel with my father and brother, but unfortunately was required to embark on this quest on my own."

Bellim's expression changed from friendly to stern. In a loud voice, he called to the kitchen, "Ya hear that, Félia? We have a Shadai here of all people!"

Félia shuffled in, wearing the same aspect of shock she had worn from when she had first seen the newcomers. "It can't be. You're a Shadai?"

"I see you have some familiarity with my family's name. How is that when you are so isolated?"

The couple glanced at each other.

"You have to meet with the kings," Bellim said.

"What? How so? Do you not know that they persecute my people? Come now, I asked you how you knew my name, and I request an answer."

"You said you were looking for the five messengers. I can tell you what happened to them. In return, you have to meet with the kings and tell them what you know."

"What I know about what?"

"The battle at Luthrey."

Ninthalas hesitated. "You know about Luthrey?"

"Yes."

"And how would my account benefit the kings?"

"Because the five messengers told us that the battle started with the dream of a Shadai."

"I do not understand."

"Look, I know your family's name. And Lothlúrin, too. Not many do, but I've heard it time and time again from Faithen passersby. Always some respect when they talk about you, but some sort of superstition, too. Never understood it."

"Sir, whether or not you truly understand the honour or curse of my name, I do not believe you know what it is you are asking of me. I told you that I will not go into the City for fear of my life. I do not know what the messengers told you, but I simply cannot risk my life and that of my son. Do you not know how devastated my family will be if news returns that I am dead? And what of my son?"

"You won't die and your son can stay with me until you get back."

"Yet I imagine you cannot assure me that. I have heard horrific tales of the torture methods of Hémon. Their hatred of my people runs deep."

"True, there's torture, but it's not a public display like it used to be. Once they got the point across those years back, the beatings and such got moved to the underground prisons."

Ninthalas couldn't tell if he was trying to be reassuring or not. He stared long and hard at the trades captain. Both he and Félia looked frantic, desperate even.

"I cannot understand you, Bellim Farthorn," he said at length.

"I cannot tell if you are a truth sayer or a liar. First you say that I do not belong here, that I would be arrested outside the wall of Hémon even though you knew it was against your law. Then you say I should visit these four kings of the country on account of my name. What is this game you play with me? If you do not answer, I am afraid I will find someone else to tell me what I must know about the messengers of my people."

He waited. When they didn't answer, he stood up and called Yosef to him. Yosef trotted over.

"I request my belongings, then—"

"They were here!"

The door slammed shut. Fehnan stood feet planted in the doorway.

Bellim shot up. "Fehnan, you—"

"Nah, pops, I gotta tell 'im. He deserves to know." He turned to Ninthalas. "They were here in Fíthera. All five of 'em. We housed 'em for a night and then my pops helped 'em into the City. Last I heard, four of the five escaped, but their message got through. Something about a battle at Luthrey? Anyway, one of 'em's still in prison, but don't think they're torturing him or anything."

Ninthalas turned to Bellim and Félia.

"Is this true, Bellim Farthorn?" the True Faithen asked.

Bellim's chin dropped. "Yes. It is."

"Then I suppose you have some explaining to do."

"Look, Faithen. We're just as at risk as you are. If word gets out that we helped the Faithens breech the wall, then we'll be done for. I'll be stripped of my rank."

"Why did you help them if it was such a risk?"

"Because it was my responsibility. We're converts."

Ninthalas' eyes widened. "Converts? Are you serious?"

"Look. There's a reason I want you to see the kings. It's not just because you're a Shadai. The kings didn't like your messengers' tale. But I believe them and I don't want to see this City go down in flames. I've heard the scriptures, Faithen. I know about the First War. I can imagine how terrible those demons are. If the kings won't listen to the messengers, then maybe they'll listen to you."

"And what makes you believe they will indeed listen to me?"

"You're a Shadai, aren't you?"

"That means nothing here, Bellim Farthorn."

"It *has* to mean something. You're a descendent of Namthúl Shadai. The five messengers spoke of a Shadai who predicted a war through dreams. When one of those Faithens was imprisoned, he said that he would prepare the way for Shadai."

"Is this imprisoned News Bearer still alive?"

"I don't know."

"What will I benefit from heeding your case? What good will it do me to perform this enormous task on your behalf?"

"I'll do everything in my power to make sure you don't suffer. I'll see to it myself that you get in and out alright."

Ninthalas felt a tug on his cloak.

"Yes, my son?"

"She's here," Yosef said.

Ninthalas shuddered. *Emkalaf'Morlúrnan* had followed him to Hémon just as he expected. Now he was at a crossroads. Fear gripped him like a vice. No matter which way he fled, the Black Assailant would find him, kill him, and kidnap Yosef. He didn't want that, didn't want anything to do with this quest.

But this task had been appointed to him. He had been chosen.

'Yahlírin, what should I do?' he prayed.

Then a thought occurred to him. Perhaps he could throw off her perception. If he and Yosef split up, she would be forced to follow one of them, and Ninthalas had a feeling it would be him. At least that way, even if Ninthalas did not survive, Yosef would have a chance to escape. And if Ninthalas was in the City, there was also a chance she would be captured because she looked so different.

"Alright, Bellim Farthorn," he resolved with a sigh. "I shall see the kings, but you absolutely must keep my son safe at all costs."

"I'll guard him with my life," Bellim declared.

CHAPTER TWENTY-ONE

Plans and Prayers

"Reckless, Ninthalas, even for you," the Black Assailant hissed.

The sun beat down on her, her black attire absorbing every ray. Despite the warmth, she still felt the chill of autumn on a northbound cross breeze. Sitting atop the crest of a steep hill that overlooked the vast City, she watched billowing columns of smoke rose from the nearest factory behind the wall. She could smell the fumes from the hill crest and grimaced. She'd never wanted to visit this country in the first place, and the stench of its factories made her loath it even more.

"I cannot believe he would even dare go near that City."

"What's he to fear?" Dethshaiken asked. He sat cross-legged next to her, wrinkling his nose. Apparently he didn't like the smell either.

"Have you no knowledge of the City, master?"

"I thought you said it was four cities."

"It is actually eight. The ones outside the walls are referred to by their names, but the enclosed four are collectively known as the City."

"Whatever. Why do you call him reckless?"

"Really, Dethshaiken? You truly are pathetic."

"Answer me."

She scowled. Conversing with the Third was like trying to reason with a rock.

"I know of its history thanks to Líran Shadai. The four walled cities, Helfohr, Feilan, Aerthkûn and Dalfin, were founded by four brothers of the same names centuries before the Age of Missions. They settled here, thereafter calling the land Hémon, which was their family name. Aerthkûn, the eldest of the brothers, thought it a grand idea to build a great hall atop the lone mountain on the island which split the river's path. They called it the Hall of the Four Lords and the mountain they called Mount Hémon."

"How original."

"History tells that the brothers established themselves as kings and later as god-like entities—"

"This tale is getting very boring very fast."

"Well, how else are we going to pass time?"

"How about a pounding to your sassy mouth?"

"How about you shut your own trap and listen, you blithering fool?"

He grumbled. "You could at least make it more interesting."

"Alright. I shall speak of the torture."

"Torture? That sounds much better. What kind?"

"I will tell you only if you listen to how it came about."

Dethshaiken grumbled, muttering some profanity or other too soft to hear. "I'll never understand your people's love of history."

"I never said I liked history. And they are not my people."

"Is it because of *him*, then, that you trail on and on?"

She gazed down at the small town darted with pockets of forest and farmland. "Do you want to hear my tale or not?"

"Fine. But hurry it up."

"At the dawn of the Age of Missions, Serenestí sent missionaries to Hémon. At first, they were well-received, but then the higher powers feared a corruption of their culture and an end to their power. That was when the persecution began. The things they did to True Faithens would make even you giggle like a child, master."

"Specifics, woman. You're dragging this on far too long."

She rolled her eyes. "Some they would drown in the river, others burn at the stake. But the worst were the pulleys and compressors that caused disfigurement. At the height of the public torture displays, they resorted to more…creative means. They would place a man in a small chest and one by one, drop in poisonous creatures that would draw out a slow, painful death. Other times, they would hang a man upside down and spear him in the sides until loss of blood claimed his life. Yet the most dreadful were the fast-growing barrel shoots. They would stretch a man out over the young shootlets, and during the height of the wet season in spring, those shoots would spring up through his body in a matter of days."

"No use of ravenous beasts?"

"There are none unless you consider livestock threatening."

"A shame. Those are interesting methods, but too slow and drawn out for my liking. Screaming and suffering only go so far. And they're loud. I'd prefer a fight to the death. Much more exciting."

"Just like you to enjoy the thrill of combat."

"So there is a chance that this Líran Shadai will suffer such a fate. Doesn't sound like he has too many options, and he already let himself get dragged into some stranger's house. Not the brightest fellow."

"His expertise is certainly not in fighting practice and military tactics."

"Some man he is."

"I beg to differ. Regardless, I do not think Ninthalas will enter the City, even though he knows I aim to kill him. I have reason to believe Shadai told him of my intentions."

"If he breeches the City, we'll take him there."

She shot him a perturbed look. "Are you mad, Dethshaiken?"

"No." He folded two of his four arms in front of his chest.

"The fool and his terrible ideas," she muttered, shaking her head.

"What did you say?"

"Oh yes, break into the City when I am so similar to a True Faithen and you are a four-armed giant brute! *That* would be discreet. Even you cannot defeat the entire army of Hémon."

"Honestly, woman. I am the Third and a shapeshifter—*the* Shapeshifter. I can shift shapes, bend the land at will. And I have the transcendent sense of the shapeshifters of old."

"Your point?"

"There's a cave network that extends under the mountain. And there are people in there."

"Is there now? And how do you suppose I conceal myself should you get me inside?"

"I'll make you a mask. Steal a soldier's garb. I'll fill in the gaps in the armour."

"We do not even know if he will breech the City, you dolt."

"But if he does, we will strike."

"Should we not just wait for them to kill him?"

"Stop questioning me, woman!"

"What are you to do if I die?"

"You're expendable! You're nothing!"

"Expendable? You *need* me, Dethshaiken. You spent the better part of a decade teaching me, molding me into your perfect apprentice. None of your other generals can lead legions like I can. This silly quest does not matter in the greater scheme of things."

He backhanded her across the face, sending her crashing to the ground. Her head throbbed with a dull ache that left her mind cloudy. Out of the mist came his booming voice.

"This is *your* kill, Kírin. Not some filthy malshorth's, not even Hémon's. It's yours. If you don't do this, your fate won't be sealed. Morkhen will have to get himself a new Second and Third who will actually get things done right. And you and I both know no one else exists that can take our places. My reputation's on the line just as much as yours. So is that bloody Second's."

She sat up, her eye already swelling up. "Fine. So be it. I just hope Shadai is not down there guarding that man."

"Just kill him. He's nothing."

She scoffed at him, the sinister voice taking hold. "You cannot kill Yahlírin's anointed."

"You can if you stab him enough."

"Idiot. Trying to kill Shadai is like trying to kill the former Lothlúrin. It cannot be done."

"Then leave him to me."

The day went by faster than Yosef would have liked. What made it more dislikable was that Ninthalas was preoccupied with preparations the entire time. First, there was Bellim telling the True Faithen his plan. Then, a scholarly fellow, whose round, thick glasses made him look like a bug, dropped by to give Ninthalas accent reduction lessons. Then Bellim was back, introducing Ninthalas to nobleman's clothes and coaching him on how to smear on a tanned paste and dust his hair to make him look Hémonian.

The disguise looked ridiculous. Ninthalas didn't look at all like himself, and he didn't look comfortable, either.

It wasn't like Yosef was oblivious to the risks. He knew the City people killed True Faithens, even tortured them. Fehnan Farthorn spared no details on some of the beatings centuries ago. Gruesome, terrible ways to die. And Ninthalas was about to go into that very place. That frightened Yosef, and he could see that same fear in Ninthalas' expression. His father was scared, scared to be caught and die. No disguise could mask that.

The fear didn't just come from Hémon. The Black Assailant and the other giant malshorth weren't far away, over on a hill northeast of Fíthera. They were waiting for the chance to strike, a time Yosef imagined would be in the dead of night in a dark, damp prison cell. When they had killed Ninthalas, they would come for Yosef.

Why would Ninthalas risk going into the City when their enemies were so near? Hémon sounded as lifeless as the Dead Forest, a place from which no one returned. It seemed to Yosef that they should just leave now.

But then again, if he could sense the malshorthath, perhaps they could sense him as well. And if they could sense him, they would follow him wherever he went. There was no escaping them. What little hope he could have possibly had was gone.

Tired of waiting around, Yosef went upstairs to the spare bedroom on the second floor. It was a large room with very little in it. In fact, there was only a bed, the one he and Ninthalas were supposed to share. Only Ninthalas was to go into the City, so Yosef would have it all to himself.

Alone. In the dark.

He sat down on the end of the soft mattress. The bags and trading goods Bellim had hauled up earlier that day lay sprawled out on the floor. Yosef had rummaged through them just before supper, admiring the fine fabric and opening the little cloth bags to smell Lethría's fragrant teas. The result was a mess of unravelled cloth and tea leaves on the floor. He wouldn't have cared about the mess if he didn't fear a scolding from Ninthalas. Out of all Yosef had learned about Ninthalas thus far, one of the more prominent things was that the man was very particular. That alone prompted Yosef to begin tidying up as best he could before the True Faithen came upstairs.

As he cleaned, he brought to memory his recurring nightmare. He wasn't afraid of the dream in his waking moments. He could stare down the Black Assailant's yellow eyes straight. The green strands in her irises grew and faded. Occasionally they overpowered the yellow, but when that happened, some distraction would pull Yosef back to reality, such as Ninthalas showing up at the doorway.

Yosef froze. Ninthalas was standing in the doorway now.

"Yosef, what are you doing?" the True Faithen asked. "Do not tell me you tampered with the goods."

"I was just looking," Yosef replied.

Ninthalas came over and took over the boy's job. "You would do well to ask next time. These goods are meant to be traded for food and shelter. If they are spoiled, there is no use in trading them, is there?"

"...Okay."

He watched as Ninthalas neatly folded the fabrics and stacked them by the bags, then scooped up the rest of the straggling leaves, wrapped them in a cloth and set it by the fabrics.

"Ninthalas, are you okay?"

"Why do you ask?"

"You sound angry."

Ninthalas stopped what he was doing and slowly sat back on his knees, hands clenched and resting on his thighs.

"Yes," he said. "I am extremely agitated."

"Is it because of me? Because of my strangeness?"

"It is not."

"Is it because *she's* here?"

Ninthalas heaved a sigh. "It is many things, Yosef. A great many things. And my brother is not here that I may lay my burdens on him, nor my father that I might ask him for advice. I am very much alone without them and so very lost. I cannot do this by myself."

"But *I'm* here. Doesn't that mean anything to you?"

"Yosef, I did not mean—"

Yosef jumped to his feet, fists clenched by his sides. "You know what it's like to be alone? It's awful! Like sitting in a cage by yourself and no one's coming to save you. That's all I remember before meeting you, Ninthalas. I don't wanna go back to that. Not never! You can't just leave me here by myself. I thought you were my new father."

"I do not want them to hurt you."

"I don't want them to hurt you, either!"

Ninthalas cast his sight to the ground.

"What happened when you were happy?" Yosef went on. "When we came out of the Dead Forest and I hurt my arm and leg, you helped me. It was just you and me then. You didn't have Kai-Tsúthlen around or Tahlen. Not your father nothin' neither. Just you and me. You weren't mad then. You wanted to save me when no one else did, didn't you?"

"I did."

"You always made it better by telling stories and smiling."

Tears were in Ninthalas' eyes.

"I didn't mean to make you cry—"

"No, Yosef, it is not you." He chuckled to himself, wiping away the tears. "You are much stronger than I. You are fearless and bold."

"But so are you. You weren't afraid on the bridge or in the Dead Forest."

"Perhaps not. But you, Yosef, you can sense what others cannot."

"I don't want to be special like that."

"Yosef, gifts are a good thing, and we are all gifted in some way. My own is often wrought in dreams, for by a vision Yahlírin showed me the destruction of Luthrey before it happened. By the vision, many people were saved."

"Did Yahlírin tell you to see the kings in a dream?"

"Well…no. But I feel as though I must. It is more of a strategy, actually. And if Yahlírin is on my side, then who can be against me?"

"What exactly can Yahlírin do?"

Ninthalas thought for a moment, then stood, went over to his bag and withdrew a brown leather-bound book. Yosef had seen him read it many times. That was the holy book and when Ninthalas went to get it, that meant story time. The holy book was filled with heroes, men of renown who Yosef admired.

"Change into your nightclothes. I will read to you before I have to leave."

Yosef did as he was told. It wasn't long before they were both sitting in bed, the book open on Ninthalas' lap.

The True Faithen flipped through a few chapters and began to read:

"'In the first ruling of High Lord Dolavar, during the third month of the year 534 of the First Age, the Third broke war upon the Wall of Separation. Thereupon, Lavareth Kanron Trúthar of the Fourth Squadron Pellendrath died by the sword of the malshorthath.

"'And his son, Kai-Drathlen Fon, was full of grief. And he fell to his knees and worshipped Yahlírin, saying "Holy is Yahl, who gives and takes away! May He do unto me as to my father. Yet if such fate does not take me, then hear the cry of Your servant! Cast stones of Your wrath upon my enemies!"

"'And when they waited forty days, a great quake shook the earth, and the heavens opened. Yahlírin rained hailstones upon the malshorthath host and drove them back beyond the Wall. Thus Yahlírin heard the cry of his people and delivered them from the raid of the malshorthath.

"'Thereafter those of True Faith fell and worshipped Yahlírin, for He had delivered them from the plight of the malshorthath. And we celebrate to this day on the fifth day of the third month, for it was commanded us so, that on this day Yahlírin remembered His people and had mercy on them'"

Yosef listened intently. Like previous story tellings, there was much he didn't understand because of words such as 'thereupon' and 'worship' and 'deliver' and the names were difficult to grasp.

"Well, that sounds nice. What's it mean?"

"The man Kai-Drathlen Fon prayed for Yahlírin to save them from the malshorthath," Ninthalas explained. "Yahl heard his prayer and sent a rain of hailstones to crush the malshorthath."

"So that's what Yahlírin does? He sends hailstones? What's a hailstone?"

"What Yahlírin *does* is protect those who believe in Him and trust Him. He answers their prayers."

"Okay, but what's a hailstone?"

Ninthalas smiled, a glimpse of the joyful man Yosef had come to know.

"Perhaps you will yet see one with winter coming, my son." He kissed Yosef's forehead and rose from the bed. "Just remember: Yahlírin protects His people. I am His; you can be His. Yet you must believe. And pray, son. Never cease to pray. For by prayer do we become closer to Yahl."

"I wanna know what a hailstone is."

Ninthalas chuckled, bent down and gave him a warm hug. "You will someday. Goodnight, my son. I will see you when I return."

"'Night, da."

When Ninthalas left, Yosef rolled over onto his side. "Yahlírin, I hope you're there and you can hear me. If you can make hailstones fall on malshorthath, then you'd better save my da, too. I lost one. I don't wanta lose another."

CHAPTER TWENTY-TWO

The City's Breech

Yahlírin protects His people. Ninthalas didn't know where his newfound hope came from, but he whispered a prayer of thanks anyway. He would take any encouragement he could get even if it was just a statement. And speaking to Yosef always left him feeling refreshed and energized. Yosef was a source of life, a glimmer of the life of Yahlírin.

"Ninthalas?"

He jumped and spun.

"Goodness, Fehnan. You startled me."

"Sorry, sir," Fehnan said. "It's just I heard that story just now. Was that from the holy book?"

"Indeed, it was," Ninthalas replied.

"I've never heard it read before."

"Do you not have a copy translated into Common? Most converts have one—"

"No, sir, not here. Not since the book burnings decades back. Most stories are spread by word of mouth nowadays."

"That is truly a shame."

"You know, I've always wanted to say this, but I'm jealous of you. You True Faithens, that is. You live in a place where you can be who you are, believe what you believe without getting a mad flogging."

"Oh, believe me, dear Fehnan, I am an oddity even in my own country."

"But you can go wherever you want and people know who you are, what you stand for. And they respect that. Not so here." Ninthalas placed a hand on his shoulder. "Let us hope that if this disguise fails, I can be who I am here as well."

"What happens if you can't?"

"Then I have a request if it suits you."

"Anything, sir."

"You must keep Yosef safe, to watch over him in my absence and guard him should the townsfolk rise against him."

"I'll take care of him, no question. You can count on me."

"Good man."

He turned and descended the stairs, Fehnan's heavy steps close behind.

"I've another question, sir. Yosef said 'she's here.' Who's 'she'? Friend o' yours?"

Ninthalas stopped at the foot of the stairs. "Not a friend. If you ever have the misfortune of seeing a woman in the likeness of myself whose eyes shine golden yellow, turn and flee. Do not engage her. She is dangerous and will surely take your life."

"Fair that, sir."

They found Bellim at the doorway holding a velvet shoulder bag that contained Ninthalas' disguise, as well as a canteen filled with water. He handed it to the True Faithen. His face carried no expression that would offer support, nor a grimace for the danger ahead.

"I ain't seeing you off," he said, opening the door. "Watch change is almost afoot, so you'd best be going."

"I take my leave then," said Ninthalas. He extended a hand to the soldier. "I wish you well, Bellim Farthorn, and thank you for your hospitality."

Bellime took the hand, shook it hard. "Don't get yourself killed."

Without turning back, Ninthalas departed out the door.

The blackness of night was complete, the chilly air sinking into Ninthalas' clothes like a sponge. Ninthalas crept to the shadow of the wall, sticking to the concealment of the trees. His heart beat like the wings of an enormous hummingbird. His body yielded a cold sweat despite the cool night. This was the hour that would test his limits, his meagre skill of speed and cunning. And he loathed it.

Hémon's outer wall towered above, a black mass lit by torchlight. The wall broke where the river came gushing out, its banks rising high and dry. At the tunnel under the wall, an overhanging lamp lit the entrance. Two guards stood watch atop the wall, peering down and out over Fíthera. Just like Bellim had told him. The watch was extra strict thanks to Hémon's Day being tomorrow, making the risk of getting caught that much more nerve-wrecking.

A bell rang in the distance and the guards disbanded. The change of the watch. Quickly and quietly, Ninthalas darted from the trees and raced along the riverbank. He dove under cover, pressed his back against the damp side of the tunnel. Struggling not to pant from his thumping heart, he listened. No shouts, no raise of alarm. They hadn't noticed him.

Taking a deep breath, he began side-stepping along the narrow embankment. Up ahead in the middle of the tunnel a grate blocked the way, extending into the river. The bars had been cut, the twisted ends so rusty that whoever had pried them open had done so years ago. Once through the small opening, he took another deep breath and continued to the other side.

A second bell sounded, the signal of the next watch. Ninthalas had to hurry before the replacements took over. Cautiously, he peaked his head out from under the tunnel. No one above. No one nearby. He dashed into the open and into the cover of thick bushes.

Shouts rang. Running footsteps beat upon a cobble stone road. Someone was approaching fast. Ninthalas' breath caught short in his throat, a million worst case scenarios tumbling in his mind. He had to escape. Fortunately, he found a narrow tunnel that burrowed through the bushes and beyond. He squirmed through on his belly before the guard reached the area where he was hiding. Watchmen atop the wall shouted and the guard yelled a slough of profanities back.

Ninthalas left them behind, shuffling along until he was out of earshot. The bushes ended abruptly and opened up to grassland darted with patches of tough dirt. Seeing no one, Ninthalas crawled out, finding himself behind a stone building yielding dark windows. Up ahead, he could just make out the outline of a bridge.

He was supposed to take it, according to Bellim. His next host's dwelling was on the other side of the river.

Halfway there.

He made his way among the shadows behind homes whose windows were dark. He would have assume that families were asleep, except for one building in particular from which he heard moaning he'd rather not hear. He cringed and hurried by, the last before the bridge.

The bridge itself was lit be a single lantern, shattering Ninthalas' hopes of concealment. To make matters worse, a man stood in the middle smoking a pipe and leaning against the far railing.

Ninthalas considered his options. He couldn't go under the bridge thanks to the river. He couldn't go back because of the patrolmen. According to Bellim's map, this was the nearest bridge to the right bank by a long shot, so the only option was to go across.

He tucked his hair into the back of his shirt, threw up his hood and cautiously crept forward. The bridge was solid stone and with Ninthalas' soft-soled footwear, he didn't make a sound as he tiptoed across. He was almost on the other side when an updraft caught the Hémonian's pipe smoke.

Ninthalas caught a whiff and coughed.

"*Spizzaz* dolls!" the man exclaimed, whirling around. "*Bajeez*, fella! Where'd you come up from? Scared me senseless."

"My apo—sorry," Ninthalas said.

He kept his back turned, so frightened, he couldn't move.

"You're dressed something funny there, kid."

Ninthalas thought fast. "Dressed to impress. It is for a lady."

He cringed. He was a pathetic liar, and to do so when he wasn't jesting to his brother felt wrong.

"With that?" the man scoffed. "Pfft! You got some weird lady if she likes that dud-look."

"Whatever. Goodbye."

He'd never been so rude in his life.

He started walking.

"Hey, wait!"

The man caught up to him and slapped a hand on his shoulder.

"Didn't mean nothing by it, sir. Your lady's secret's safe with me."

"Thanks. Better be off."

"No hold on. I'll make it up to ya. Got some good pipe weed. On me, no cost."

"No thank you."

"No really. Come on."

He pulled on Ninthalas' sleeve, dragging him toward the bridge's lantern. Ninthalas kept his head down.

"You'd like the weed, sir. Best in Hémon, it is. Grow it myself out back. Wife there, she throws the fits at me every day for it—"

The ground rumbled and the bridge shook, cutting the man off. He toppled over while Ninthalas managed to keep balance as the bridge creaked and swayed.

Peculiar. Did earthquakes occur often in this country? The shaking stopped just as suddenly as it had started. Just like in Serenestí. He remembered feeling that slight tremor, barely noticeable, but strong enough that he knew it couldn't be right. That was when Yosef had looked for him and claimed that the Black Assailant had breached the country. And that meant...

"*Emkalaf Morlúrnan.*"

The Hémonian sat up, rubbing the back of his neck. "What the mad ramble—"

Ninthalas looked down at him, and the man's eyes widened.

"What the...? Wha-what are you?"

"A human just like you," Ninthalas replied.

"You're no person! You're some kind of...apparition or somethin'!"

Ninthalas didn't think to answer. He dashed across the bridge. The man cried out after him, but he paid it no heed. If someone else saw him...

A mask of haze covered his trail as he veered right, taking a street that led to the group of houses lining the riverbank. The air smelled of rank fumes, wretched, sickening. He coughed again. And again. Soon, his throat was running dry.

"Who's there?" a voice called.

Ninthalas darted between two houses, his coughing uncontrollable. Quickly, he withdrew the canteen from his bag and took a drink. The cold water soothed his throat slightly, but it tasted bitter.

A misty light shined into the darkness.

"Who's there, I say?"

The light grew brighter. Ninthalas watched helplessly as the light found him, unmasking his identity. He shielded his face.

"...Shadai?"

Ninthalas looked up to see a man holding a lantern.

"Yes...it is me," Ninthalas answered, his voice raspy.

The man knelt beside him. "Your eyes are glowing. How...?"

Ninthalas couldn't reply, his throat gone sore.

"Come on. My place isn't far. Keep your head down in case someone sees you. Don't want any glowing eyes freaking them out."

"Someone...saw me."

"*Spizzaz* dolls!" the man cursed. "Well, just keep your head down."

Ninthalas followed him down the street. He stopped at a house that looked identical to the others: stone walls, pointed, thatched roof. A glowing window told them people were still awake inside. The man turned the knob, opened the door and shoved Ninthalas forward. He lingered in the doorway for a while, then closed the door and latched the lock.

When Ninthalas could control his coughing, he found himself in a cozy living room. Two sofas sat opposite each other, one on the far wall and one under the near window. Between them lay a brown rug and a low table set with teacups whose design was similar to those of the Farthorns. A woman sat on the far sofa, her two children on either side of her. They stared at Ninthalas, wearing curious expressions.

The man peered out the window, then pulled down the blinds. He went to sit with the woman and children.

"Your eyes aren't glowing anymore," he said, his eyes as wide as his family's.

"It is sporadic," Ninthalas replied. "I suppose I should thank you for assisting me."

"I'm your host, aren't I? That's what I signed up for."

"So you are Mallon, Bellim's friend?"

"In the flesh. And you're the one called Shadai. Mighty honour, sir."

"You need not thank me, friend Mallon. I have put your

family at great risk."

He broke into another coughing fit.

"Sit and have a drink. It's a fresh pot."

"Thank you." He knelt at the table and poured himself a cup.

"Guess you're not used to factory air, are ya?" Mallon said.

"Not in the least," Ninthalas replied, taking a sip of the tea. The drink was far milder than the bitter brew he had drunk at the Farthorns', but the taste was strange.

"Suppose the tea's not quite to your liking, either."

"I apologize for my ill expression. It is just not the same."

"It's the water. Came from the well, but thanks to the factory, it's tainted. Mind you, we don't really notice it all that much."

Ninthalas looked up at him. The man seemed amiable with his amazed yet friendly eyes. He appeared strong, his angular body a solid force not easily uprooted. His clothes were simple, the apparel of a labour man. A matted beard swallowed up his square jaw line, dark like his curly mop of hair. His children looked just like him, curly locks and dark eyes. Mallon's wife, simple and plain, had seen years of cooped up service in some business with her matted hair and tough hands. They seemed too poor a family to be living in a house outfitted with furniture, but perhaps their jobs paid well.

"Speaking of tea…" Ninthalas rummaged through his pack and pulled out a small cloth bag drawn closed by a tight silver string. "I brought this gift for your family. It is not much, but I hope you appreciate it. It is a token of my gratitude."

"What is it?"

Ninthalas smiled. "Open and see."

Mallon untied the string. The fragrance caught his nose almost as soon as he opened the bag, and he breathed in. He smiled and handed the bag to his wife. The children, too, leaned over to sniff.

"My, that is lovely," Mallon's wife said. "What is it?"

"They are tea herbs from my mother's garden, the finest in all of Serenestí. This particular blend is one of her favourites."

"Serenestí. It's like another world," she said, dreamlike. "Isn't this lovely dear?"

"Best try some tomorrow for breakfast," Mallon replied.

"Truly lovely."

"Can I offer you anything, Faithen? Dinner? I've got a bottle of ale—"

Ninthalas held up a hand. "No, thank you. If you do not mind, friend Mallon, I would very much like to retire for the night. I am truly weary from travelling, having not rested well since Serenestí."

"Of course. We've got a room all ready for ya."

Ninthalas stood, bowed to the wife and children, and followed Mallon down the hall. He could hear the kids whispering to each other excitedly as he left. It must be strange for them to see a True Faithen, just as strange as it would be for a foreigner to walk around in Serenestí.

Mallon showed him the spare windowless room. The room was none too inviting, containing only a small bed in the corner, the air stuffy and stale from the lack of air circulation.

"Well, have a good night then," Mallon said.

He left Ninthalas alone and returned to the living room where his children were now talking instead of whispering about how Ninthalas looked like an angel and if he actually was one.

"He is rather becoming for a foreigner," Mallon's wife commented.

"I'll be listening to none of that, woman," Mallon barked.

Ninthalas breathed a sigh. The weight of the day's activities and the new setting crushed him with fatigue. He missed home already, the forest where the trees grew tall and majestic and the air was fresh and clean. He missed his family, especially his brother. And even though he had just left Bellim's home, he missed Yosef.

Exhausted, he crawled into bed and drifted off to sleep.

———◉———

CHAPTER TWENTY-THREE

Case Before the Kings

Ninthalas' own coughing woke him up, the floating dust particles tickling his throat. The room was so dark he had no sense of time. Rolling out of bed, he went over and opened the door. Daylight flooded the spare room; it must be late morning.

"Mallon?" he called.

No one answered. The house was quiet except for the muffled sounds of activity going on outside.

He took a deep breath. This was it. This was the day he would speak before the kings. The task seemed so daunting now that he was within the walls. What was he thinking? Was it merely because of sympathy that he had taken up this quest? No, it was *Emkalaf'Morlúrnan* and the High Lord who had brought such travesty upon his life. Yet who was he to blame? Blame, in his experience, never solved a problem.

He pushed the door half closed and went about putting on his disguise. The clothes fit, but the material felt tough and restricted his movement. He then smeared the paste over his hands and face and dusted his hair. When he was finished, he opened the door wide and checked his disguise in the hallway mirror. His reflection revealed a completely different person, though he couldn't hide his beardless face and sky blue eyes. He had no idea if Hémonians shaved. How convincing did he really look?

Returning to the room, he folded his True Faithen garb, put it neatly in his bag, and slung the strap over his shoulder. He then traced his way back to the living room. A breakfast of bread and cheese lay on the table, along with a note written in Hémon script, characters that were unfamiliar to Ninthalas. He figured the family had gone somewhere or other and that they would be back later. After gobbling down the meagre meal, he stepped outside. The day was bright and clear, though smog from the nearby factory gave the sky a dusty hew. It still wreaked of the same stench he had smelt the night before, yet a slight breeze made the atmosphere more pleasant.

He began heading north. The cobblestone street led him back to the bridge he had crossed the night before. Several people crossed it, some carrying large bags or packs, others empty-handed. Ninthalas, nervous to the core, wove his way into the crowd, following the flow of bodies along the right side. No one noticed him, everyone minding to their own affairs. His disguise appeared to be working and it gave him a boost of confidence as he stepped off the bridge and swerved right.

The road cut north along the outskirts of the main of Helfohr's city proper. Horse-drawn carts replaced the throngs of people, and when he neared the next bridge, carriages joined them. Most were headed for the centre island where the lone mountain rose up from the ground with its hall sitting on top like a beacon. Pretty soon, Ninthalas realized he was the only one on that road walking, and the drivers passing stared at him oddly as they rode by.

"*Oi*, sir!"

Ninthalas spotted a teenage boy waving at him, leaning casually on the railing at the foot of some steps that lead to a dressed up tavern. Ninthalas stopped. Had his disguise failed?

"No nobleman should be walking anywhere," the boy told him. "That's for the peasants."

Ninthalas breathed out, muscles relaxing. "You offering a ride?" he asked, mimicking the same harsh tone and dialect.

"Gonna cost ya."

"How much?"

"Five silvers flat."

Ninthalas checked his pockets. Of all things distraught! He hadn't brought any money with him. The last thing he wanted was to make it obvious he didn't belong in the City.

"Seems I left it at home."

"At home? Ha! You're a funny one. Guess that gets pickpockets off your back. Afraid I can't give ya a ride since ya can't pay."

As soon as he finished speaking, the door to the tavern swung open and out came a ravishing woman wearing a white, tight-fitting gown. A fir coat draped over her shoulders. Her long, dark hair tumbled over her coat in small ringlets. Though she probably had Ninthalas by at least fifteen years, her skin was devoid of any sign of age, mostly thanks to a thin cover of makeup.

She took one look at Ninthalas and turned up her nose.

"What's this? A nobleman standing in the street?"

The teen was instantly at her side.

"Good day, ma'am," he said with a bow. "Where can I take you today?"

She ignored him, instead speaking to Ninthalas. "Tell me. Where's your ride?"

"I have none, lady," Ninthalas replied.

She smiled a coy grin that could capture any man's attention. "Ride with me." She handed the teen three silver coins.

The boy ran off to retrieve his coach.

"Where are you headed?" Ninthalas asked.

"The Hall of the Four Lords, of course."

"For three coins? The boy charged me five."

"Get over here and help me inside before I restrain my offer."

Forward woman. He sped over just as the carriage pulled up. The teen got down, opened the door, and Ninthalas offered the woman a hand.

"Such a gentleman," she commented.

"Does courtesy not suit you, my lady?" he asked.

"You jest." She shuffled to the other side. "Get in."

He did. The carriage rolled forward, bumping along the street. Ninthalas looked out the window, watching other coaches and carts drive by. He had never ridden in a carriage before. He neither liked nor disliked the experience. It certainly made getting to places a lot quicker, but if he was being honest with himself, he preferred to walk.

"Tell me, nobleman, what's your business?" the woman asked.

Ninthalas turned to her. She let her fur coat slip, revealing slight, delicate shoulders and a low neckline. His eyes wandered, but he quickly averted them. He must have blushed because her smile widened.

"I seek an audience with the kings," Ninthalas replied.

"You're quite handsome. How come I've never seen you before?"

"You could say I lead a sheltered life, my lady."

"Obviously. No one says 'my lady' here."

Ninthalas didn't answer. He turned back to the window, watching as the lone mountain grew closer. Having seen the Balkai Mountains that bordered the country of Suíten down south, Mount Hémon seemed small in comparison, barely larger than a steep hill. On its summit stood the Hall of the Four Lords, a huge building rivalling the height and breadth of one of the Selestorinth's buildings.

"You never seen the Hall before?" the woman asked.

Ninthalas caught himself gaping and snapped his mouth shut. "What? No—I mean, yes." He shifted. "You have not yet told me your name."

"Meldesha, High Cleric to King Dellon."

"I suppose I should be courteous, then."

She laughed, a guffaw that carried a mocking edge. "You really are a funny man. You should pop by the central temple tonight. I'll fit you with a fine cleric."

"A...cleric?"

"Of course. In fact, I know a maiden who would suit you for tonight. Sweet girl, gentle but strong."

Ninthalas could only imagine what she was talking about. He cleared his throat. "You say you are cleric to King Dellon—"

"*High* Cleric."

"Yes, of course. High Cleric. And it being Hémon's Day means you can go in to meet him? Would I be permitted entrance since you are in my company?"

"Where have you been living your whole life? *All* nobles are permitted to see the kings on Hémon's Day. That's why you're going, isn't it?"

"Indeed, it is. Though I have never been. Politics bore me."

"Indeed."

She said the word with a strong emphasis that teased his

speech. Ninthalas realized he had let his accent slip, but to his relief, she didn't comment further. Hopefully it hadn't been enough to give himself away.

At last, the carriage reared to a halt. Meldesha was out the door in a heartbeat, gone up the steps to the Hall's landing. Ninthalas jumped out, watched as she entered the building.

High Cleric. What a dominant, controlling presence.

"*Oi*, out of the way, nobleman!"

Ninthalas hopped to the side as the carriage scooted by. He didn't know whether or not he should yell something back, but the carriage fled so quickly he didn't get the chance. He shrugged. It wasn't in his nature to speak disrespectfully anyway.

Weaving through throngs of well-dressed noblemen and ladies, he crossed the landing to the front gate—two large doors embroidered in silver and gold. They stood wide open, held in place by wooden pegs sticking out of holes in the stone landing. Four stone pillars, each carved in the image of the four kings of old, held up the Hall's overhanging roof. Ninthalas gazed upwards as he walked in, awe-struck at the incredible size of the building.

Inside, the Hall opened up into a spacious lobby, its ceiling rising high above the floor in a wide arch and held up by smooth, cylindrical pillars. Colourful murals depicting the foundation of Hémon and the Hall's construction adorned the ceiling. Long beams that connected the pillars broke the paintings into sequential frames. The colours contrasted with the plain white walls, clean and pristine, but their whiteness couldn't be fully appreciated because of booths of expensive merchandise lining them. Sellers taunted the nobles with materials or offerings that only the rich could afford to buy.

Ninthalas stopped in the entranceway, overwhelmed by the onslaught of people. Even in Shalom or the markets of Central A'thería's cities, he had never seen so many rich people gathered in one place, not even on the fifth and sixth levels Luthrey's spiral mountain frame which were known for their splendour.

He barely had a moment to observe before he was bumped and pushed into the mix of colourfully dressed bodies, shuffled along until he drifted toward the other side of the lobby. Two guards stood at attention in front of big double doors. Beyond was the throne room.

Before he knew it, Ninthalas was standing right in front of the soldiers. The guard on the right glared at him. He was clad head to toe in polished, plated armour, a halberd held tight in one hand. He stood at least a head taller than Ninthalas, a man of such breadth, the True Faithen shrank under his stature.

"State your business," he said.

"News…" Ninthalas cleared his throat. "News from Bellim Farthorn, Chief General Trades Captain in Hemnak."

"General Farthorn never calls on the kings on Hémon's Day," the guard said.

"It's urgent."

The guards glanced at each other with single raised eyebrows, then back at him.

"How urgent?" asked the interrogating guard.

Ninthalas leaned forward, causing both soldiers to bend over in order to hear.

"Some trouble with the traders," he said softly, glancing side to side as if to ensure no one else was listening. "Their Majesties should know about it, those foreign traders coming in, meddling with things."

Of course, he was referring to himself as the meddler, though he may have slightly stretched the truth. And stretching it was awkward enough.

The guards glanced at each other again, this time wearing confused looks.

"Alright. You can go in," the one guard relented. "But be brief. The Lords are extra busy today what with the feast tonight."

They pushed open the doors. Ninthalas faked confidence as he strode by, but when the doors closed behind him, the mask disappeared. Nobles, young men and old, filled the throne room and every one of them were engaged in a heated discussion of loud outbursts and boisterous claims. He had expected a calmer atmosphere of sophisticated diplomats taking turns to pronounce their requests or concerns. This, however, was a tumultuous verbal brawl akin to peasants quarrelling at a tavern. Speaking before the kings would be much more difficult than he'd anticipated.

Quietly, he slid into the back of the left-hand side of the crowd and observed the scene. Aside from the nobles and four kings, guards clad in chainmail and helms lined each side of the wide room. Like the ones guarding the throne room, they were much taller than Ninthalas—

Except for one. Ninthalas frowned. One of the guards was different. His armour swallowed him up, too big for his small body, the metal scratched in places like he had recently endured a struggle. Quite the odd one out compared to the others who towered above him in gleaming armour. Had he not stood in the far corner away from the general public's view, someone would have definitely noticed him.

Ninthalas shook his head. He had to focus. Right now, his primary concern was somehow getting his story before the kings in such a way that sounded convincing. But where to start?

He stood on his tippy toes and peered over the shouting bodies to the middle of the room. A curtain of scarlet covered almost the entire length of the back wall behind an elevated platform. Upon the dais, the kings sat on glamorous thrones fashioned in gold and silver plating. Each monarch was dressed in a colour that might have represented his own city: red, blue, violet, and green, in order from left to right. The three kings closest to Ninthalas grew beards, while the one furthest was clean-shaven. This green king seemed the most up-kept of the four based on his appearance, though his aspect suggested a fierce, passive-aggressive approach to discussion.

The most distinct of the four was the one closest to Ninthalas. His hair and beard were as red as his clothing, his crown silver instead of gold like the other monarchs. He listened in a way that depicted contemplation, like he considered every side of an argument. This would be the king to speak to. That was, if he got the opportunity. How was a soft-spoken True Faithen supposed to interrupt this?

As he studied the kings, he spotted Meldesha sitting at the foot of one of them, the second from the right. This was probably Dellon. She sat opposite another beautiful woman, this one younger and fairer. Each of them leaned against Dellon's legs in a fashion that was obviously for show rather than comfort. The other kings also had women at their sides, perhaps as a statement of wealth or position. The only one who didn't sport a woman was the red king.

Voices rose and the argument heated. The loudest came from

a man directly in front of the thrones who was decorated in lavish colours and half a dozen rings and necklaces.

"They're a nuisance!" he proclaimed in a strong, baritone voice. "Too many get in to see the festival just for sightseeing. They deter the traditions because they know nothing."

Another man from the far side of the room countered the argument. "But they pay tribute at the temples. That's good for city business."

"Those *people* will destroy our culture," the first man spat.

"What? For one day of the year? Preposterous! We forget them when they leave, barely an imprint on the entire year."

"Foreigners! Aliens! Outsiders!"

How these words justified the man's case was a mystery to Ninthalas. Surprisingly though, the man's followers barked similar words in agreement.

"Tax payers!" the second man protested. "*Our* tax payers!"

More protests for and against.

"Suppose they decide to live here!"

"Suppose they don't!"

"Suppose they do and start killing our culture!"

"Killing our culture? What's a few more people?"

"More and more come here. Next thing you know, another Faithen problem—"

"Ah, the Faithen problem." The far man broke into a mocking chuckle.

"Don't laugh! It was a catastrophe!"

"That was centuries ago."

"We have laws. They must be kept."

During the entire argument, other nobles were voicing their own opinions, some using vile profanities Ninthalas wished he hadn't had the opportunity to hear. It seemed to him that each man simply wanted to hear his own voice rise above the noise regardless of the problem at hand.

The two middle kings joined in the wild jest, uttering their agreements with the centre man. The far king argued against them, instead siding with the far man. The red king, however, remained quiet, leaning on the arm of his chair and rolling his eyes as if the issue were meaningless.

Just then, a nobleman standing in front of Ninthalas spoke

louder than the rest. "The newcomers increase every year. We should be more careful!"

The red-headed king glanced at him and immediately noticed Ninthalas, the one spectator not adding verbal monstrosities to the mix. He stared long at the True Faithen, his aspect calculating.

Then, when Ninthalas thought he had been found out, the king's eyes shifted. The True Faithen followed the gaze, turning around. He gasped. The short guard was gone.

"You there! What do you have to say about this?"

Ninthalas spun back around and a wave of shock shot through his body. The red king was standing and pointing right at him.

"I beg your pardon?" Ninthalas asked, a response that got peculiar looks from those close enough to hear.

"What do you say about this? The trade. The foreigners entering the City on Hémon's Day."

The nobles hushed down, one by one turning their attention to the standing king and the obvious newcomer.

"It does not matter," said Ninthalas.

"Why not?"

"Only the kings can make decrees, whether or not I agree with them."

"Maybe your opinion matters now."

"*My* opinion? How does my opinion reign over noblemen here richer than me? Your majesty, you and the other lords have all the information you need and more. What matters now is your decision."

The room fell silent. Ninthalas shifted his feet under the weight of their stares.

"Who are you, nobleman?" the red king asked.

"I'll tell you who he is. He's a foreigner."

All eyes turned as Meldesha stood. King Dellon grumbled and pulled her down to sit again.

"How do you know?" the red king asked her.

"I rode with him on the way up here. He was on his feet in the street and he spoke to me in an accent. Can't you hear it? He's not bad at masking it, but it's still there."

"Is this true?" King Dellon asked Ninthalas.

"Come to think of it, he *does* look different. Look at those eyes," the other king in the middle said.

Ninthalas remained silent, wondering what to say. He could either deny Meldesha's claim or go with it. Yet apparently they didn't know he was True Faithen, so he could at least admit to his foreignness without having to lie.

"Alright, Your Majesty. By way of your cleric, you have caught me."

Meldesha glared at him. Right, she was a *High* Cleric, not just a cleric.

"I am from outside the wall, but I only come by the urgency of my message."

"I'll listen," the red king declared. He sat back down on his throne. "Speak."

For the first time since entering the room, the entire congregation of nobles fell silent. Ninthalas had got his wish: to speak to the red king. Only he wasn't quite sure if this was a good thing. Mind you, this was Hémon. Nothing about this trip would be natural.

"I have journeyed to distant lands, and I bear news from the south: Luthrey is no more."

"Why does this concern us?" asked the king sitting next to the red-haired one.

"And what's Luthrey?" muttered King Dellon.

"They are one of your trading partners in the south."

"We can trade with others," King Dellon said. "You're wasting our time, foreigner."

"Luthrey traded grain and wool."

"So?"

"That is food and clothing, oh king."

"It's still only one little city," the blue king scoffed. "Not even a city. And we have our own farms."

"Should we dismiss him?" asked Dellon. "His message isn't urgent."

"He's still a foreigner," the blue king said, standing up. "He shouldn't be here anyway. Guards!"

The soldiers marched forward and grabbed hold of Ninthalas' shoulders.

"Wait!"

The red king stood up. "Young man. There's more, isn't there? Much, much more. You haven't told us everything."

"Indeed, I have not," Ninthalas replied, his accent rolling off his tongue.

"There it is!" the king exclaimed. "You're not just a foreigner. You're Faithen!"

The crowd gasped. The soldiers released him and stepped back.

Ninthalas looked around at their shocked faces. So this was how it was going to be. His identity had been found out. Very well. If he was to negotiate, he would do it his way regardless of the disguise. He would be himself.

He stepped around to the centre of the platform and bowed low before the monarchs.

"Indeed, I thought that I could outwit you with this disguise, oh king. My respect to you since you have the wisdom to see the truth."

The blue king shot to his feet. "Who are you?!"

Ninthalas rose. "I am that which you dislike most, Your Excellency, a True Faithen from the country of Serenestí. My name is Ninthalas Líran Shadai and I am borne by the urgency of my message. For I am a News Bearer and though I came here against my own will to a country that persecutes my people, it was a task I had no choice but to undertake."

The red king patted his colleague's shoulder, moving to the front of the dais so he was standing directly in front of Ninthalas. "Why would you risk your life in coming here? Don't you know what we do to your people?"

"I have need to believe that five messengers were sent before me to speak with you, and as yet they have not reported back to my country."

"So they sent one man?"

"I am no ordinary man, my lord. I am of the family Shadai, one of the oldest and most respected names of my people. And if you bring me to harm, then may a curse fall upon you and your country, for I am chosen by Yahlírin himself."

"We don't believe in your god."

"Whether or not you do, you should at least heed my words. Luthrey was destroyed and you have every reason to be concerned. Your kingdom is at risk."

"One town's destruction doesn't put us at risk."

"That one 'town' is only the first part of my tale, and a very small part. I am an eye witness to more strange tales further south than the hill country, tales of foes that sought my life, of perils that would frighten even you, oh king."

"We don't care for outside—"

"Yet you should. As isolated as you believe yourselves to be, the entirety of Hémon is upheld by trade. It is the same with my country, as well as the other nations of A'thería. Even if you refuse to believe it, some of your imports come indirectly from our land."

"From your land? I highly doubt that."

Ninthalas sighed. "I did not come here to argue with you about the details of trade. Nor have I come to convert you to the Faith as my ancestors did centuries ago. I come merely to bring you this news. For I am a News Bearer as I have said, and not a government official or a soldier. And my news is this: two villages and one city were attacked and destroyed by *malshorthath*—demons as you would call them—creatures that have not been sighted for an age."

"If these demon things haven't been seen for so long, then how do you know it was them?"

"My lord, my people have been recording events since the dawn of time, including the happenings of other cultures such as the foundation of Hémon. The accounts of history are sifted through and validated by the elders of Serenestí and maintained only by the most trustworthy of scribes, so there is slim chance of alterations to the original texts. Therefore, if you wish to denounce the existence of *malshorthath* in this world, you reject truth, for I know those who fought with them, and have heard their first-hand accounts."

The red king stared long and hard at Ninthalas, studying, calculating. After brooding for much time, he straightened and returned to his seat.

"You may go," he said with a wave of his hand.

Ninthalas bowed low. "I take my leave then."

The crowd parted as he walked away, and the doors slammed shut behind him.

Ninthalas hurried through the lobby, his mind in a frenzy. In a flurry of emotion, he had let loose a buildup of tension from his soul in front of the kings. He had revealed his identity, rendered the congregation speechless. It was like he had transcended outside of himself, been lifted out of his normal body into more than just a man. He was filled, and that cup overflowed. Despite the fear, despite the uncertainty, the apprehension, he had succeeded. And now he was free. Yahlírin had delivered him. He whispered a prayer of thanks.

Now that his task was complete, he wanted out. He thought of Yosef waiting for him to return and them continuing on their journey, one giant hurdle over and done with.

Yet Bellim Farthorn's plan only accounted for getting Ninthalas into the City. The trades captain hadn't said anything about how to get him out. Should he march through the front gate? Or should he return to the grate during the night? Perhaps Mallon would have an idea.

He retraced his steps to his host's house and knocked lightly on the door. Mallon answered it.

"Greetings, friend Mallon," Ninthalas said.

"Shadai?"

"Yes, it is me."

Mallon stepped aside and Ninthalas went in. As soon as he stepped in the doorway, he got an odd sense about his host. The man smiled, but unspoken gestures suggested he was agitated. His fidgeting hands were one, and he didn't bother to check for threats outside. His eyes frequently shifted to the hall.

"How did the inquiring go?" he asked.

"My message got across in part, but my identity was found out. The red king is a smart one. He saw through the disguise, and I had little choice but to heed his questioning."

"But they didn't arrest you," said Mallon.

"They did not and I am grateful for it."

He heard noises from the hall.

"What was that? It sounds unnatural."

"Kids playin'."

"How can children make such strained commotion?"

"It's Hémon play. You probably wouldn't get it."

"I suppose so."

They remained in the doorway. Ninthalas felt the air around him grow stiff as if the pollution from the factory choked the very room they were in. He cleared his itchy throat. The fumes and stuffy atmosphere reminded him how much he wanted to leave.

"I suppose I should not keep you, yet I have some trouble I must speak to you about."

"Yes?" Mallon blurted.

"I am not so sure how I am to get out of this City. Do you suppose I would be arrested if I marched through the front gate?"

"Don't think so."

He was lying. Ninthalas could see it. Something was definitely wrong.

"Then I must be going—"

"You sure you got everything?"

He hesitated. "All I brought with me was this bag."

"Coulda sworn you left something in the room." He started walking to the hall. "Got something to show you, too. You know, for the nice tea and all."

"I cannot accept anything from you."

"Come on. It'll only take a minute."

Ninthalas followed. He barely reached the corner of the hallway when a blow to the face knocked him to the ground. Rough hands grabbed him and tied his hands behind his back.

Ninthalas winced, his eye burning, perception cloudy. With his good eye, he made out two soldiers on either side of him. Another stood in the hallway, holding a knife to Mallon's wife's neck. Two others clasped their hands over his kids' mouths, holding their squirming bodies fast.

The soldiers hauled him to his feet.

"I'm sorry, Shadai," said Mallon. "I had no choice."

Ninthalas looked at him, then at his family. Just as well. It had been too easy, his passing into the City and seeing the kings far simpler than he imagined. His one mistake had been giving himself away when he should have hidden under the broad term of 'foreigner' and escaped. His folly had been his demise and now he would meet his end. A gruesome, torturous end.

"They said it was either us or you," Mallon went on. "I...I couldn't let them hurt my family—"

"'Tis alright, Mallon," Ninthalas said. "I hold no grudge

against you. May you and your family live well."

He allowed the soldiers to lead him outside. He wouldn't struggle. He would accept his fate, whatever it might be.

The soldiers pushed him outside and up the street. Halfway to the nearest bridge, Mallon called after them.

"He's a good man, I tell you! He's done nothing wrong!"

Ninthalas glanced back. The poor man had sunk to his knees, weeping. That was the last Ninthalas saw of him.

CHAPTER TWENTY-FOUR

Imprisoned

The arrest sparked outrage from passersby. Passengers from carriages barked out protests as they passed by.

"*Shnerkin'* bigots! You can't arrest a noble!"

"This one's a foreigner," one of the soldiers spat back.

"It's Hémon's day! No law against him there."

"General's orders."

Similar conversations went back and forth until the soldiers got fed up and veered off the main road. They took Ninthalas across the second bridge on the east bank of the river towards Mount Hémon and led him around the base of the mountain. A sheer cliff rose up to the rear of the Hall of the Four Lords.

"You there!"

Ninthalas jumped. Two soldiers approached them from behind and shoved the other two off. Ninthalas stood his ground, dumbfounded. These were guards from the throne room, or similar ones anyway, their armour clean and polished.

"What're you—?" the others started, but clamped their mouths shut.

"That's right. Just back away. We've got special orders for this one."

Without a word, the others walked away. Ninthalas frowned. What was going on? These soldiers in shining armour weren't taking him back to the kings, were they? Ninthalas had no trouble speaking before an audience again, but it made no sense as to why they would request him.

He found out quickly that that wasn't the case. The throne room guards continued to lead him to base of the mountain. Yet this only raised more questions. Why would the kings arrest him only to change hands midway to prison?

At the floor of the cliff punctured into the solid rock was a large steel door guarded by two strong sentries. No words were exchanged as the sentries moved aside to let the soldiers and their prisoner past and into a long corridor burrowing into the mountain. Dim torches gave little more than a flicker, hardly penetrating the hollow, black tunnel. The rugged walls allowed for a narrow passage that made Ninthalas slightly claustrophobic.

Down the passage they went, stairs and hallways turning this way and that until the tunnel flattened out into a long, straight passageway. Openings to other tunnels lined the walls on either side, each marked with a symbol over the entranceway that Ninthalas couldn't read. He lost count of how many openings they passed before they took a sharp left into a passage opened up into a chamber containing five jail cells. A fire blazed in the middle, illuminating the cavern but offering no clue as to the contents of the barred cells. Beside the fire, a man sat on a stump, rubbing his hands together to keep warm in the dank cold. A hefty pile of firewood lay within an arm's reach from him.

The jail keeper eyed them quizzically. He wasn't much of a soldier; more like a shabby peasant. His tattered clothes coupled with his long grey beard and wrinkled face made it seem like he had been cooped up underground since the foundation of Hémon.

"You fellas get lost?" he said, his voice a screeching tone. "This ain't the place for land folk. Just fish food. You'd best take him down to the lower level where the prisoners are kept."

Ninthalas raised an eyebrow. Fish food? It certainly smelled fishy. But why would a prison function as a pantry?

"We were told to bring him here," one of the soldiers replied in a gruff tone. "Orders straight from King Amon. He said the man would need to 'freshen up'. Don't know what he meant, but it doesn't matter. This place used to be a prison anyway."

"For fish," the jail keeper muttered. "Still is. Always has been." He fumbled for the keys hanging from his belt and walked over to one of the cells. "Well, we change the water every week—

every Orlam. You're in luck, kiddo."

He grinned and winked. Ninthalas cringed at his incomplete rows of chipped, yellow teeth. He didn't know the Hémon calendar, but he assumed Orlam must have been recently.

His captors unbound his wrists, shoved him into the cell, and locked the gate.

"Not gonna take his things?"

"Don't need to. He's harmless."

They turned and left.

Ninthalas rubbed his wrists, happy to be rid of the bindings. He used his free arms to hug himself. The fire did little to compensate for the cold of the cell's rocky wall, cut shallow so the jail keeper had a clear view of him.

The prison guard sat back down on his stump by the fire. He stared at Ninthalas, wearing a puzzled expression.

"So, whatcha in for, lad?" he asked. "Must've done something terrible if you're here. Get caught killing somebody?"

"I am not so sure," Ninthalas replied.

He didn't feel like talking. The heated events of the day were finally catching up with him, and he wanted to take the time to sort through them while they were yet boiling under his skin.

"Strange that," the man went on. "You any idea what's about this 'freshening up' business?"

Ninthalas shook his head, trying to ignore him.

"Didn't you run trial?"

After getting no answer, the jail man shrugged. "You don't wanna talk. Fair that. I just thought you'd be more interesting than the fish. Quiet, unexciting bunch they are."

Ninthalas leaned forward. "Fish in a prison. Now that I find peculiar. Why, I pray, do you keep fish in a place such as this?"

"You willing to talk now? Answer my question first."

"Very well. I did not stand trial, though I do not expect to because they know who I really am and what I am about."

"You talk awful strange for a noble."

"Indeed, I would. I am not of Hémon."

The guard's eyes widened. "That accent. That speech." He rose from his seat. "You—you're Faithen, aren't you?"

"Indeed, I am," Ninthalas replied.

"Not another one of you!" He made for the entranceway.

"Wait, good sir! What do you mean 'another one of you'?"
He was gone.

Ninthalas looked on, dumbfounded. What an odd reaction. He was used to being either welcomed or ignored for his ethnicity. Deserted was something new. But the prison guard had most likely seen the other True Faithen. The messenger could still be somewhere in the prison. Ninthalas had to find him. He had to break free somehow.

He clutched the jail bars, searching the room with what little light the fire gave. In his haste, the guard had left his keys by the fire, but there was no way Ninthalas could reach them.

"*Bai*! What am I to do?" he said, slumping to his knees.

He flopped his arms to his sides. His left hand splashed into water, and he immediately lifted it, startled to find his sleeve soaking wet. Water for fish food. Right.

He remembered the soldier's comment about 'freshening up'. A bath would do him well. It'd been some time since he had properly bathed.

The pool was frigid, but it was nice to remove the paste and dust, and though he shivered and smelled slightly of seafood, he was thankful to be clean. His wet hair he wrung out and wrapped in the noble's clothing, and he dressed in his much more comfortable News Bearer's clothes. When he was done, he curled his knees up and sighed.

"Now to wait, I suppose."

Footsteps caught his ears and he sat up straight, straining his ears to listen. Three soldiers appeared from around the corner, each carrying nets, ropes with hooks and other objects such as a spiked club. Their aspects were sombre, focussed. They retrieved the keys from the floor and went over to one of the cells, unlocking the gate with no gentle grace.

Water splashed. A shrill cry screeched like an off-strung key. Ninthalas covered his ears. He knew of no creature that made *that* sound.

The men yelled back and forth at each other.

"Watch out for its fin!"

"Keep it down! Keep it down!"

"Knock it out!"

The chamber fell silent. When the men appeared again, they

were hauling a blue, scaly creature out of the cell.

What a creature it was! Ninthalas had never heard of or seen anything like it. It almost had the appearance of a man, yet it bore fins—a dorsal and others jutting out from its joints. Its hands and feet were webbed like an amphibian's. Its head, having fins for ears and a pointed nose, was bruised and bloodied. The hooks dug deep into its body, the ropes wrapped round tight. It was dead. How cruel! Did these men have no understanding of the brutality of their actions?

Just as quickly as they had come, they were gone. Again Ninthalas was left alone in the chamber. He slumped back against the wall.

"Fish people."

It was as Yosef had described, what had leapt from Great River of Plenty and saved the boy's life.

"So he was right. They do indeed exist. Yet where do they come from and how have we not come to know of them? My people's records contain everyth—"

No, they didn't. There were several holes in the historical records, mysteries he had spent years trying to piece together.

A painful sound penetrated the chamber, coming from the direction of the cell that had contained the fish person. Ninthalas leaned forward, jaw dropping as he saw a small arm reach out between the bars. It appeared to belong to a child, and its voice was like a marine animal's lament echoing throughout the chamber.

"A child? What atrocity is this?" Here, they were eating children! The cannibals!

The sound tug at Ninthalas' heart, twisting it in agonizing pain. What a remorseful song. It reminded him of a song he had made dedicated to a dear friend he had lost long ago, a song that had long burned in his heart, the words etched in his mind for eternity.

Slowly, he began to sing:

At first I saw her fair as snow
the daughter of Yahlirin.
Her hair fell long about her waist,
her eyes an emerald green.

I sought her fast across the square,
and asked her for her name.
Athlaya Kirin Lothlúrin
like music she did speak.

Oh Athlaya fair, dearest child,
how I cried and mourned to hear
when you upped from sweet Selestia,
laid to rest within the earth.

I strove to ever be with her
whenever we did meet.
She was so strong and valiant
as I had never seen.
Upon her brow was valiance,
and courage in her will.
Compassion dwelt within her heart,
her hands fashioned for skill.

Oh Athlaya fair, my dearest one,
why did you have to go?
Winter freezes my aching heart,
my soul laden with snow.

It came upon a fateful day
that I went out to find
the young maiden fair, the warrior child
who ever consumed my mind.
Yet when I came to yonder square
she was not there as planned.
Her brother told me remorsefully
that she had parted from this land.

Oh Athlaya fair, Yahlirin's blessed,
wherever are you found?
You left me bare, have gone astray
to lay within the ground.

His voice caught short. There were several more verses, words he had written himself, but he couldn't bring himself to sing them. *Ninthalas.*

Ninthalas looked up. "Shadai?"

Dear brother Líran, what troubles you so?

"What troubles me? What troubles me! Do you not see where I am, Shadai? They have found me out, and I am to rot in this cell until I breathe my last. *Emkalaf'Morlúrnan* will find Yosef and bear him away. Tell me, Shadai, what hope is there left for me? Does Yahlírin take pleasure in seeing me suffer like this?"

Oh brother Líran, how can you be so distressed? Hope in Yahl! For who made the heavens of Hathlen and the world, A'thírin? Who spoke into existence the birds, the beasts, and every living thing and to this day provides for them? Was it not Yahlírin? And He has also called you, that you may do good in His sight. Though the storm lasts for the night, a clear dawn follows.

Ninthalas couldn't answer. He rolled onto his knees, bowed low, and wept. Shadai placed a hand on his shoulder.

Take courage, Líran Shadai. For as the wind stirs water so that it tumbles into waves, so an injustice is being wrought in this country and you shall be the spark of its demise.

"An injustice? How so, my lord Shadai?"

Choose your friends well, brother Líran, and flee from immorality. Remember, Yahlírin is with you. He hears you.

The silver-haired man disappeared.

"Wait, Timeless Shadai. Do not leave me alone…"

Loud footsteps reverberated in the cavern. A splash of water told Ninthalas that the young 'fish' sought the safety of its pool. From around the corner of the entranceway a man appeared, hooded to conceal his features. He walked over to Ninthalas' cell.

"Shadai. Now that I see you, you really *are* one of them."

"Who are you?" Ninthalas asked.

The man withdrew his hood and Ninthalas' eyes widened. It was the red king.

"My lord." Ninthalas bowed.

"No need for pleasantries, Faithen," the king said. "As far as anyone knows, I'm not here. You can call me Amon. I'm the king of Feilan. That's the western city."

Ninthalas rose. "There is a stump by the fire. Take it and sit with me."

The king took the small stump and brought it over to the cell. "It may come as a surprise to you," he said, sitting down, "but I didn't order your arrest. Nor did any of my colleagues."

Ninthalas frowned. "How so? Do generals have the authority to make such an order?"

"Anyone outside the throne room wouldn't have known who you were. Your disguise was that convincing." He paused. "Were you crying?"

Ninthalas straightened. "I am ill at ease."

"No matter. I didn't come here to mock you."

"You wish to know of my tale," Ninthalas guessed.

"Yes."

"Yet why now? I am honoured by your presence, but should you not be feasting with you people, let alone your family? I understand that it is Hémon's Day—"

"There've been Hémon's Days since the dawn of Hémon. Every year's the same. If I don't want to take part, I don't have to."

His gaze fell. Ninthalas got the impression that there was another reason why the king wasn't participating, but the uncomfortable silence between them hinted that he wasn't willing to disclose it.

"Before I begin," Ninthalas said, "may I ask the names of the other monarchs and their cities? I make a habit of knowing the names of esteemed men."

"From left to right on the thrones, they are Morin of Aerthkûn, Dellon of Helfohr, and Levin of Dahlfin. Morin's the lead according to law. Any decree he makes we cannot revoke." He shifted in his seat. "Now tell me what you know."

Ninthalas told him of the events that had unfolded since first leaving Serenestí until the High Lord's command to leave on errand. Amon listened without once interrupting, a quietness that seemed strange compared to the rash outcries Ninthalas had witnessed from the other monarchs. Of the several events Ninthalas spoke of, the king seemed most interested in the Black Assailant. His brows furrowed and widened at every detail concerning her, the most exaggerated gesture being when he heard that she was a woman.

When Ninthalas finished, the king pondered before speaking.

"You weren't lying when you said your story was strange. Do all News Bearers bring bad news?"

"They do not so long as I have known the profession. This situation is unique. Nothing remotely similar has happened for at least an age according to the record books. And it is equally rare to send messengers to Hémon since you are notorious for persecuting my people."

He paused. When Amon didn't respond, he continued.

"Yet I knew the risk when I left my home, and it was my choice to breech the City to meet you. You see, there were others sent before me who had made it into the City without incident, but we do not know what has happened to them, nor have we received any word of their trials. Yet I heard recently that one still remains in this prison."

King Amon's expression was contemplative. "Your intel is correct," he said after some time. "The Faithens did see us. There were five of them. The others wanted to kill them right then and there, but I fought to keep them alive. We threw them in prison until...well, they were meant to die here. Then they slipped past us, escaped from the City. All but one. I heard he sacrificed his safety so the others could get away. That was how he put it at least, only he sounded more humble than proud."

"How long ago was that?" Ninthalas asked.

"It doesn't matter. Your my primary concern."

"Why is that?"

"That messenger—News Bearer or whatever you call yourselves—he said you would come. He said that you'd bring disaster with you and great change, something that would alter Hémon's future."

"What does that mean? Clearly you see that I am of no formidable physique and I have shown no struggle that you should fear me."

"I was hoping you would tell me."

The king breathed in deeply, let it out slow. Ninthalas saw in him a conflicted soul. Indeed, a far greater pressure rested upon the king's shoulders and Ninthalas was certain it not only pertained to himself, but also would determine his fate. And that gave the conversation a sharp edge that could lead to either a positive or negative outcome. He had to be cautious. Somehow.

"If you died here and your family came to know of it, would your people attack us?" Amon asked.

"I should think not," Ninthalas replied. This couldn't be the reason behind the king's unease. "They would merely mourn for years and years to come. Do you truly wish to kill me?"

"No. I'm not like Morin or Dellon. I'm not so foolish and blind to the outside like they are either. And luckily, I have Levin on my side, so I can keep you alive as long as I want."

"Yet can Morin not have me executed? You said yourself that no one can revoke his decrees."

"True, but he can't order against a two way tie, either. That's how the kingdom hasn't fallen apart yet. Standstill arguments prevent unrest. But in case you were wondering, Morin can't stand me. You won't believe how annoying it is listening to him run off his mouth every day. The man's a *shnerkin'* bigot."

"I fail to understand how a kingdom built upon distrust can stand."

Amon's face grew hard. "Look. I didn't come here to argue with you. I really can't stand all the shouting going on upstairs."

Ninthalas bowed. "My apologies, Your Majesty. I did not mean to upset you so, nor should I speak so rashly of your country or its customs—"

"I just want answers," Amon interrupted. "Like who that guard was standing in the throne room today."

Ninthalas sat up. So he *had* seen the one different guard. "I presume you are referring to the shorter one who was standing almost unnoticeable in the corner of the throne room?"

"Who else? He's not a real soldier. Anyone could see that, but those rambling nobles don't care for anything but themselves. That soldier though. I think he ordered your arrest."

"How did you come to know of my arrest then?"

"A messenger boy told us. He broke into the throne room, marched right up to the throne level he was so angry. Said the soldiers were looking for a nobleman that fit your description."

"And how did that spark such outrage that he would tell you?"

"You can't just arrest a noble and throw him in prison."

"I heard that much from the jail guard. Yet once he found out who I was, he fled."

"You had us worried when you said you were Shadai."

"It is as I told you, King Amon. I am none to be feared. In fact, there is another who you must fear and that is the Black Assailant. It is quite possible that soldier was twisted to do her bidding. Do you have spies in your court?"

"Not that I know of, but there's always some backstabbing fool among the noblemen," Amon replied.

"He was gone when I looked back before you addressed me before the court."

"I thought you were in league with him."

"Yet now you see that I am not."

"True. But here's the thing: I don't know where he could've gone. There's only one door and that's at the entrance."

"Are you sure? Perhaps there is a passage of which you are unaware."

"Impossible."

"Then what do you guess, that he hid behind the back curtain and waited until you left before exiting through the front door? Or did he vanish into nothing, which you and I both know is not possible? I should think neither. Whoever this man is, he escaped from that room while people were yet present, and that is all we know."

Then it occurred to Ninthalas. Perhaps the soldier was not of Hémon. Perhaps it was *Emkalaf'Morlúrnan* in disguise. What a relief, yet how terrifying! The former because his hunter had come after him just as he expected. The latter because he was in much more danger thanks to being imprisoned. Rotting in a dungeon sounded much more pleasing than suffering from the sting of *Emkalaf'Morlúrnan*'s blade.

"Are you on to something, Faithen? You look like you've figured this mystery out," said the king.

"It is hard for me to say what is true and what is not."

"Then let's go."

"What?" Ninthalas said. "Do you not distrust me?"

"Do I have a reason to distrust you?"

"I should think not."

"Then let's figure this thing out. Tonight's a good night for sneaking around. Hémon's Day leaves the men drunk with wine and the women serve them all night. That's plenty of time to find answers."

He got up, grabbed the keys, and unlocked Ninthalas' cell. The True Faithen remained where he was, unmoving. Was the king trustworthy or was he toying with him so he could humiliate him before killing him? If the latter, then King Amon was a brilliant actor. He had Ninthalas right where he wanted him. Yet a part of Ninthalas refused to believe that the king was a cold-hearted schemer.

The silver-haired man's words echoed in Ninthalas' mind.

Choose your friends well...Hope in Yahl.

He would choose, and he would hope.

He stood, slung his bag over his shoulder and followed the king. At the entrance to the chamber, he snuck a glance behind. In the faint firelight, half a head with two small black eyes peered out at him from one of the cell's pools. It sank back down into the water out of sight.

CHAPTER TWENTY-FIVE

The Search

King Amon was right about the soldiers being preoccupied. There were no guards in sight, not even the ones at the entrance to the prison, which was strange because the City wall had been so heavily guarded the night before. Ninthalas would have thought the City would put up a far stricter guard.

"I would have thought you would put up a higher guard," he said as they slipped out into the night.

They crept among the shadows and circled around the mountain in the opposite direction Ninthalas had come when he was captured. The full moon gave off a musty glow that provided just enough light to outline the silhouettes of trees and the restless current of the river.

"Are you not worried about prisoners breaking free on account of their comrades?" Ninthalas asked.

Amon simply shrugged. "No one would think of that on Hémon's Day."

'Other nations could attack,' Ninthalas wanted to say, but he kept it to himself. The only nation Hemon would ever expect an invasion from was Serenesti from what he could tell. If Ninthalas was an ill meaning man, he could escape and inform his country.

If he was an ill meaning man, which he knew he was not.

Partying was alive across the water, the sound of laughter echoing in the air from the western city of Feilan and the Hall above. Amon led the way at a pace that prevented Ninthalas from sufficiently taking in his surroundings. And that kept him on edge. What in all A'theria could the king be planning? Was this really an excursion to find out answers? He didn't muse for very long before he spotted an irregularity in the mountain. It was faint, but he could just make out a zigzag patter that wove up the side of the mountain.

"Look!" he said, clasping the king's shoulder.

The king spun. From the pale night, Ninthalas could see his face contorted into fury. He quickly withdrew his hand and pointed.

"There is a stair embedded in the rock. Do you see it?"

"I don't see anything," said Amon.

"Perhaps you could if we were closer. Come, I will lead."

It was a forceful statement, but the king didn't object. Ninthalas went to the cliff of the mountain's north end abruptly changed into a steep slope. There, its clear cut edges of uneven steps illuminated by the pale moonlight climbed up.

"I don't remember this ever being here," said Amon.

"You do ride a carriage to the Hall, do you not?"

The king considered. "True. Let's climb it and see where it leads."

They snaked up the rocky slope clambering up on hands and feet because the steps were so steep. They were wet as if they had succumbed to rain. Yet it had been sunny and dry all day.

Ninthalas was panting a quarter of the way up, his mental capacity waning thanks to the fatigue of a long day and intense concentration on what he was doing so that he didn't slip. He glanced down a few times. The king was having an equally difficult time. Apparently, he was just as useless when it came to physical strain as Ninthalas.

Eventually, they reached the top and collapsed, their backs leaning against one of the great pillars that held up the overhanging roof of the Hall.

"I already hope this ends soon," King Amon confessed between gasps of air. "What kind of wild chase have you led me on?"

"I believe you were the one who set me free and that we must see this through."

"Do you trust me, Faithen?"

The question nearly caught Ninthalas off guard. Was this a trick question? "I would not dare fail you, oh king."

"Then let's go."

They felt along the wall to the back of the huge building. A narrow ledge at the rear ended in a long drop. The Hall cut off the moonlight, casting a dark shadow that obscured any form.

"There's nothing here," said Amon.

"Just because we cannot see anything does not mean that nothing is there. Those stairs up the mountain wound in such a way that whoever took them would head around the back of the Hall like we did."

"But why? There's nothing but a sheer drop."

Ninthalas inched across. He reached halfway when his foot slipped through air. It took all his dexterity to keep from falling. He pressed himself against the wall, fear paralyzingly his body. When regained his composure, he crouched and felt the ground. There was definitely a break in the ledge. He sat down and swung his legs over the side, reaching one foot out to test what was ahead. His foot struck a wall. He slid his foot down and it caught in a small footing.

"Ah!"

"What?" Amon asked. "What did you find.

Ninthalas tested his weight on the notch, then slid his other foot down to find another similar pocket in the side closest to him.

"Are you mad, Shadai?" Amon asked. "You'll fall!"

"I most certainly will not," said Ninthalas.

He found another notch, then another and another. In no time, he was several feet down.

"There is a bottom. It is some platform, I think."

"How do you expect me to get down there?" said Amon. He had inched his way to the gap in the ledge, nervously looking down.

"If you are unsure, then wait until I have asserted its safety."

Ninthalas descended inch by inch down the crevice, until his foot struck the bottom, a platform still several stories up from the ground below. A glow emanated from cracks in the crevice, barely enough light to penetrate the black of night outside. He pushed hard. A stone slab easily opened inward on creaking hinges, revealing an opening. There hanging just inside like a gift was a torch. The light revealed a deep shaft with crude, stone steps spiralling up and down into darkness.

"What did you find?" the king asked from above.

"Come down and see."

"There's no way I can make it down there."

Ninthalas took the torch and held it up.

"How about now?"

Amon scowled. "If I fall, I'm blaming you!"

Ninthalas chuckled. "If you fall, you will surely die, oh king, and would have no need of blaming."

"Are you mocking me?"

"Simple jesting, my lord. That is all."

Amon took time getting down. Ninthalas waited patiently, though he was eager to discover where the shaft led. He had no idea he'd come across an adventure like this. It was almost as exciting as plunging into the heart of *Lotah 'an Morkh*.

"A door?" said Amon, his eyes wide.

"Indeed, and I can make a decent guess as to where it leads."

"You're far too happy about this."

"My dear lord Amon. Can you not appreciate this grand adventure."

"You're too eager, too," he added.

"You do not know me well enough then."

They went inside and up a short ways until they reached a hole closed off with loose tiles. Muffled voices from the festivities of Hémon's Day echoed loudly from above.

"The throne room," said Amon.

Ninthalas felt his fingers along the tile edges. "These tiles appear to have been moved recently."

He popped one up and peeked through. A wave of loud laughter and jeers flooded the shaft.

"Ah!" he exclaimed and lowered the tile.

"What did you see?"

"This door lies behind the large curtain that backdrops the thrones."

"So that is how the guard got away. I wonder how long this has been here without us knowing about it," the king mused.

"The walls are dry, the steps powdery. Those are signs of a recent excavation, I would presume, though I am no expert in such things."

"That soldier?"

"I should think not. *Emkalaf Morlúrnan* arrived as recently as I did. If she orchestrated this excavation, then that soldier would not have started until today."

"And one man couldn't have done this. Not even a group in that amount of time."

"Precisely."

"So what could've done it?"

Ninthalas had no idea, but if the Black Assailant used the shaft to gather intel from the throne room, she could very well be waiting at the bottom. Ready to take his life. Giving up this quest seemed the better option, but there was a tug of curiosity in Ninthalas' chest that wanted to discover her identity. At least he could die knowing the answer to one of his plethora of questions.

"Well, let's go down and see where this leads," Amon declared.

Ninthalas hesitated, then nodded. They descended into the dark abyss below, a seemingly endless spiral. The stairs were crude, uneven steps with a layer of dirt that offered little traction. Dust particles flew into the air with every step, adding to the already stuffy air. Yet the deeper they went, the shaft grew increasingly damp and the air staler. Eventually they reached the bottom.

Ninthalas rubbed his knees, gone sore from the descent, then started forward again through a narrow passage that cut through the rock. It wound a short ways before ending at a fork.

"Now which way should we take?" Amon asked.

Ninthalas looked to each opening. He'd rather not take either in case one way led to the Black Assailant.

"Well, Shadai?"

"I am not sure. Let us choose one and see."

He went right. The tunnel curved, then dropped in a sharp decline before straightening again. Ninthalas caught a decaying scent in the air. That was a bad omen.

"What is that smell?" he asked. "I am not so certain I wish to continue."

"Just keep going. We gotta see this thing through."

Ninthalas gulped. He got the sense that whatever lay at the

end of the passage, he didn't want to see it.

"There is a light up ahead," he said.

Embedded in the left wall was a wooden door, barred by a thick wooden beam. The tunnel closed off in a dead end. There was nowhere else to go. Tiny slits in the door frame allowed for a little light. Ninthalas reached for the beam, but hesitated. He knew he wasn't going to like what was behind the door, stench aside.

"Well, open it, Shadai," Amon ordered. "This is the answer to our questions."

Ninthalas heaved on the bar and laid it aside. He pushed open the door. The hinges creaked and strained. An overwhelming wave of stench rushed out in a billowing gust. Ninthalas had never smelled anything so putrid, yet he could guess the scent's source before he stepped through the doorway. His stomach churned as his eyes confirmed his speculation.

Bodies. Hordes of them. They littered a wide cavern, illuminated by blazing torches that lined the cavern's walls. Heaps of disfigured corpses of varying degrees of decay formed mounds. The largest pile lay on the opposite side of the chamber near a massive gate. Half decayed victims of suffering died with clawing hands reaching between the bars, griping, pleading for deliverance, only to receive none. All dead. The only signs of life were enormous rats feeding off the carcasses.

Ninthalas expected to hear screams from beyond the gate. Yet he heard none. The chamber held an eerie silence that gnawed at his nerves.

"The Death Chamber," said Amon.

Ninthalas threw up over the landing they were standing on which overlooked the scene. This was worse than the slaughtered skohls in the Balkai Mountains. How disgusting! How could any of the kings live on their high thrones and allow such a terrible prison to exist? This was savage! Ninthalas' blood both boiled and simmered in a mix of anger and hopelessness. He didn't have a very high opinion of Hémon, but after seeing this, his opinion plummeted.

He looked at Amon. The king turned up his nose, looking at the scene with a distasteful expression.

"This is where they dispose of the dead," he said. "I've never been down here. We kings don't like to get our hands dirty. But we know about it."

"This place is horrid!" Ninthalas exclaimed. "These people endured so much pain. How could you know of this place and do nothing? How can you sit back with the knowledge that people are disfigured and tortured and left to die here in such despair?"

"It's the law, Shadai, and the law rules," Amon answered indifferently.

"Yet these are people..." Ninthalas said remorsefully. He turned back to the chamber. "People with lives. Every face you see is an individual. Every body has a soul and spirit. People are worth more than this."

"Like I said, it's the law."

Ninthalas shook his head. The king wouldn't understand. Amon had no concern for human life. Perhaps Ninthalas had chosen his friends unwisely.

"I cannot bear this."

"Wait, look," Amon said, pointing.

Ninthalas looked up and let out a sharp cry. He dashed down into the mess of bodies, nearly tripping over them as he scrambled to the left wall. There sat a recently killed man, propped up facing the heaping pile of corpses, green eyes staring open in death.

Ninthalas couldn't hold back the tears. All the stresses of the past week came pouring out of his eyes and tumbled down his cheeks in torrents. His sobs penetrated the silence.

"I cannot..." he started. Where were the words? They'd left him to his misery, unable to translate the overflowing sorrow of his heart. Try, try to speak. Anything that might ease the excruciating remorse. "Alas for this day, that I may see this place, for it has taken one of my own!"

That was it. Nothing more could be said. He cried until his tears ran dry and the silence again swallowed up the chamber. Though his heart carried a weight of sorrow, his emotions gradually died down. He sat staring at the man who had been sent before him, the one messenger who had risked his life for the safety of others. Ninthalas would write about him with high respect, bestow upon him the greatest honour for choosing to protect his comrades. A melody was already forming in his mind and words befitting a hero. Indeed, he would write a song for this man. If only he had known the messenger's name.

He brushed the man's eyes closed and kissed his forehead.

"Be at peace, my brother, my friend," he sang. "Serenestí will remember your valour in the years ahead."

He sat back on his knees. That was when he noticed the book. The messenger clutched the hard leather bound pages to his chest. Gently, Ninthalas pried it loose. As soon as he removed it, his eyes widened. The book had been hiding a wound on the man's chest, still fresh. This man was killed recently. Carefully, he widened the rip in the man's tunic. Black, charred veins stretched from the torn tissue across his chest like poison seeping into the blood stream. This was no ordinary wound.

"*Emkalaf'Morlúrnan,*" he whispered. "Is this a *malthna* wound?"

He turned, frowned. The messenger faced the direction of the platform where King Amon still stood. But it wasn't the door to freedom he had been looking at. Below it was a gaping crack, one that was beginning to close. Ninthalas watched as new rock grew on the sides, closing up the hole. His jaw dropped. Was he seeing things?

King Amon's voice stole his attention.

"Shadai, let's go! We've found our answer. There's nothing more to do here."

Ninthalas turned back to the messenger and said one last prayer. Then he kissed the man's brow one last time and rose to his feet, book in hand.

"Very well. I am coming."

He rejoined the king and the two left the room and shut the door. He left the beam where it was. Perhaps the next unfortunate soul could escape and find new life.

Retracing their steps, they found their way back to the fork and took the left path. Sure enough, the tunnel led to a main corridor. Whining and murmuring could be heard, which soon turned to wailing. They must be in the main of the prison, the 'lower level' as the jail guard of Ninthalas' cell had put it.

"Terrible," Ninthalas commented, shaking his head. He wanted to free them, no matter how terrible their transgression against the law.

"The severity of the torture reflects the severity of the crime committed," Amon explained, grabbing another torch from the wall as they walked through a maze of passages.

"Truly horrible."

"Only if you get caught," said Amon. "I'll tell you a little something, Shadai. The City isn't rid of crime, and the best masterminds behind heinous acts are often nobles."

"So that is why the jail guard asked if I got 'caught' killing somebody."

"I have assassins under my command. They're the reason I've taken the throne."

"You mean you were not born into royalty?" Ninthalas asked.

"No. It's…complicated."

"I can see that."

Amon turned up a flight of stairs, Ninthalas trailing behind. It led to an upper level, a straight corridor lined with the ends of several diverting passages.

"I ordered my servants to kill that fake soldier. After hearing your story, I'll have him look for the Black Assailant as well. What did you call it in your language again? Emkala'mor-something-or-other?"

"That is *Emkalaf'Morlúrnan*. I mean no offence, my lord Amon, but this is no wily noble or devilish assistant. This is one who has sneaked into Hémon unnoticed and manipulated your guard. Not to mention she led the destruction of a village and slaughtered an entire tribe of skohls."

"She's here?"

"If I am here, then she is also."

Amon stopped in front of a particular entrance.

"This is your stop. I won't put you in your cell. What you do from now on is your choice, whether you try to escape or not. I don't care."

With that, he turned, continuing down the corridor. Ninthalas watched him go. The king was a mystery if he ever saw one. Their quest to the Death Chamber seemed worthwhile, but Amon had given up just as quickly. Perhaps he wanted to sort through what they had discovered alone. Or perhaps not. Once they had reached the main of the prison, Amon knew exactly where they were. He had extensive knowledge of the prison's passageways. That meant the king came down here frequently to see prisoners, maybe even orchestrate their torture. He could have visited the True Faithen messenger as well.

Ninthalas.

Ninthalas turned to see the silver-haired man in the centre of the chamber stoking the fire. He wore a slight smile that spoke of peace, completely opposite of the confusion rattling Ninthalas' mind.

What did you find there? the spirit asked.

Ninthalas looked down at the book in his hands. The blood on the cover had rubbed on his tunic.

"My lord Timeless Shadai, how can you be so calm? You would not believe the atrocity I saw!"

I see it as clearly as you see it, brother Líran, said Shadai with a smile.

"You see? How?"

Am I not with you? Come now, what did you discover?

"King Amon called it the Death Chamber," said Ninthalas. "I found one of the missing messengers there, dead from a recent wound. But the wound, it was covered in black decay like charcoal."

A malthna wound, Shadai stated.

"Was it? I figured so from what descriptions my grandmother told me."

And you found that book.

"Yes," Ninthalas said. He opened the cover and flipped through the pages. "Grace abound! It is a Fehlthan."

Ah, that is a good sign. You left your other one at Bellim Farthorn's, did you not? What else did you see?

"There was a shaft in the mountain, and a crack under the stair. The crack closed up…" He paused, thinking. "I have never seen such a phenomenon, nor read of anything similar. My eyes were not cheated, were they?"

You should have brought the green book my sister gave you, Shadai said. *If you had known its contents, you would have understood that phenomenon well.*

Shadai nodded to one of the prison cells. Ninthalas saw two eyes peering out of the water at them. The head plopped back into the water. Retrieving the keys, Ninthalas went over and opened the cell door. He tapped the water. No movement, but he wasn't surprised. To the child, humans hunted his kind.

"An atrocity indeed," he muttered, returning to the fire.

He sat down on the empty stump and flipped through his new book, reading some of his favourite scriptures and smiling as he pondered their meanings. Some of the pages were stained with blood, the blotches becoming more numerous as he flipped to the back of the book. At the very end, he found extra pages that had been written on—a journal of some kind. Most of the writing was illegible and smeared, but he could make out some:

> *Alas they have put me here for my judgement; here they lay me. I am to rot...*
> *...darkness undying...I will perish...*
> *...deliver me unto You, Yahl. Save me...*
> *Have I not found favour in your eyes?*

Most of those words repeated several times, a final prayer before the messenger's final breath. But then the writing came to a startling, hastily written section.

> *Darkness there like smoke*
> *A human I see?*
> *...and in it eyes...*
> *...eyes like fire...*
> *Eyes like death...*
> *...Alas...*

More blood smeared the rest of the scribble, and Ninthalas turned to the last page, the inside of the back cover. In clear True Faithen print, he read in horror a familiar, haunting chant:

> *Run, run, Líran Shadai, flee if you will. Yet the shadow will find you in the night and swallow you whole. And you shall be mine, dear brother, and make me whole. Run, run, brother Shadai...*

He dropped the book and gasped. His lungs constricted, catching his breath, and he clutched his chest. An image of yellow eyes flashed in his mind. It was like that time on the old bridge with Yosef.

"*Mí Yahl! Mí Yahl, mahlú síprola!*" he exclaimed.

He felt a touch on his shoulder and spun around. The aquatic boy stared at him with wide, focused eyes, dark like the deep, having pupils of obsidian enclosed by thin irises of jade.

Horror and shock turned to curiosity as Ninthalas observed the creature. His emotion repurposed, Ninthalas held out his hand. The child took it, its own skin scaly like the skin of any fish. The rest of its body ran silvery blue in shimmering scales. The hand that had grasped him was four-fingered and webbed in greenish-turquoise fins. Other fins like sharp-edged wings protruded from its elbows. The skin on its face was distinctly smoother and lighter compared to that on its arms.

Despite the marine features, though, this child looked as much like a human as it did a creature of the sea. How sickening that these creatures, as aware and human like as himself, were shipped in from the coast to be killed for their meat. This child was doomed to be served to the nobles of the City.

"*Veidna'mar ja?*" it said to him.

Ninthalas' jaw dropped and he laughed. Though some of the sounds were voiced, the child was speaking in True Faithen.

"Yes, I am Faithen," he replied. "I am *True* Faithen."

"How nod Valze Vaithen?" the fish asked.

"False Faithen? I have heard that term before, but from something else. What in all A'theria is a False a Faithen?"

Again, slight details from brother Namthúl's journal.

Timeless Shadai stepped forward and crouched down to the boy's height.

"Are you really Jadai?" the boy said, a smile beaming on his face. "Jadai dza wadger."

Indeed, I am, young one. Tell me, what is your name?

"Eera."

Friend Eera, this is Ninthalas Líran of the sons of Shadai. He is the descendant of Namthúl who was once of the False Faithens, but has since been restored.

"Again, what are False Faithens?" Ninthalas asked.

Read my sister's book and you will come to know of them.

Ninthalas sighed. There was so much beyond common understanding—beyond A'thería—that he didn't know. He thought of the journal, sitting in one of his packs in Bellim Farthorn's house. He regretted not bringing it.

"I must free him," he said. "I must return him to his people."

Indeed, you must, Shadai agreed.

"What am I to do? I must return to Yosef, and now I have this one under my care. And I imagine there are many others trapped here who must be freed."

That is well thought, yet stay in this chamber for now. Your son must come to you, and if you leave now, Emkalaf'Morlúrnan will find you. As long as you are not in the main of the prison, she and the Third are oblivious to your location.

"The Third? Here?"

Ninthalas went livid. How could he stand against a foe as great as Dethshaiken, a giant known to fend off as many as ten men?

Now you understand how Emkalaf'Morlúrnan broke into the City, and how the shaft was formed and the crevice closed. For the Third can shape the land at will using the ancient power of the shapeshifters.

"I…I cannot…"

Shadai put a hand on his shoulder. *Peace, peace, brother Liran. Be patient and wait. Yahlirin is with you.*

CHAPTER TWENTY-SIX

The Black Assailant's Demand

Amon strode up the steady incline of the tunnel, heading towards the exit. So much was on his mind. Levin had given him a task and he'd failed. He'd had to. How could he betray the Faithen when the man was so genuine it seemed a crime to do him wrong? Shadai had followed him freely without struggle. He had trusted the king even if it meant going to his death. Amon had never met a man so loyal, and he had only known the Faithen a day.

But had he been right? He feared a scolding from Levin, the only one of the monarchs who had supported his rise to power. Without Levin, he was nothing. Morin and Dellon despised Amon and had wanted him off the throne since he took it. Yet Levin had seen a certain wisdom in Amon, or so Amon assumed, and that was the main reason he had sent Amon to inquire of the Faithen. That much Levin made clear. It wasn't just about the Faithen's presence in Hémon. It was because of the trouble that had come upon Levin's household.

He reached the door, opened it, and was startled to find the green-clad king of Dahlfin on the other side.

"Well?" Levin asked. His face was a placid mask, but Amon could detect the severity of the question just by his tone.

Amon shook his head. "I discovered a few things, but I don't think this man orchestrated the kidnapping."

"This is serious, Amon. I want answers—"

"I might have them. Shadai spoke of an enemy he calls the Black Assailant. He believes *she* came here. I don't know why, but the two are linked somehow. But that doesn't mean Shadai's the one causing trouble."

"So what's the deal with this assailant person? You said it was a *she*. How could a woman best a man?"

"I don't know. When Shadai spoke of her, it was out of fear. But, then again, he's not what I would call a tough fellow. More like a scholar."

Levin heaved a sigh, slumping his shoulders. "So what do we do? We've got this false soldier running around arresting people he shouldn't, and he probably abducted Karvene."

"Maybe we should tell the Faithen," Amon suggested.

"Don't you dare! I don't want this getting out and raising alarm."

Amon shrugged. "Levin, he's a prisoner and a Faithen. I don't see how he could spread anything."

"Just keep your mouth shut about it."

"Fine."

They started walking around the mountain. Amon looked up to see the secret stair Shadai had discovered. He still couldn't believe it was there, as well as the recently excavated hollow that delved into the mountain. He knew the Hall and prison inside and out.

Levin followed his line of sight. "That wasn't there before," he said, brows furrowing.

"No, it wasn't. Shadai and I climbed it. There's a deep shaft behind the Hall that leads to the Death Chamber."

"Did you do as I asked?"

Amon hesitated. "Yes."

"You're lying."

"What did you expect? The man's done nothing wrong and I don't see him as a threat."

"He might know about the kidnapping, Amon!"

"You could go ask him if you want."

"What's wrong with you? I helped you ascend to the throne. I demanded that you return the favour someday."

"So?"

"This is someday, Amon!"

"Putting him in the Death Chamber doesn't solve anything. Actually, I'm not pleased you put the other one in there, either."

"That was Morin's idea."

"Of course it was."

If there were two men Amon hated reasoning with, they were Morin and Dellon. The two of them were a hot-tempered duo. Both had superiority over Amon because they had been monarchs for much longer. Levin was the only other sensible one of the kings. Amon could maintain a real conversation with him without resorting to rash arguments. Levin was a leeway between Amon and the other two. Somehow they could have a conversation when Levin was present. Without the king of Dahlfin, though, communication was lost to mockery about Amon's appearance.

It'd been that way his whole life, really. Thanks to his mixed roots, including Faithen somewhere in the line, Amon was always stuck with an appearance that hindered his ability to fit in. But he had played the nobleman's game and managed through heinous acts to get to the top. It was a wicked game of treachery finding your way to the throne. Backstabbing, mistrust and having people killed were commonplace. Amon had both loved and hated it.

Perhaps that was why he had a certain respect for Ninthalas. The True Faithen may be scrawny and hardly worth the description of a man, but he was who he was. The five messengers before him were much the same. Amon admired their bravery in walking into certain danger just to deliver a simple message. Nothing about his position as a monarch required courage or trustworthiness in any form.

"So what do we do now?" Levin asked.

They stopped in front of the first bridge.

"I need time to think. Maybe talk it over with Amelí."

"I still can't believe you only settled for one wife. And she bore you children of all things."

"I don't see what this has to do with your situation."

"That's just it. I at least have a cleric to spare. Doesn't change the fact that I'm upset with you, though."

"I'm sorry, alright? Look, we'll talk in the morning."

"We should both go see the Faithen," said Levin, crossing his arms.

"Without Morin and Dellon."

"Fair that. I'll see you tomorrow."

They parted ways. Amon crossed the bridge into Feilan. He would have taken a carriage, but this was the one day everyone was off celebrating.

Another Hémon's Day come and gone. Truth be told, he was getting tired of the celebrating and drunkenness that wrought the City year after year. It had been fun when he was younger, but now that he'd reached his mid-thirties, there was something artificial about it, as if that fun and celebrating didn't amount to anything. He suddenly became curious about other countries in— what was it called—the Common World? He was terrible at geography. How did other cultures celebrate? Was it more fulfilling than Hémon's drinking and sleeping with the temple whores?

The hour was late, but the temple was still alive, the last signs of the festival day. The clerics and some 'devout' men would be up through the night. Those same men would be kicked out at first light so the clerics could enter their cleansing period. Seeing the temple reminded Amon of his wife, Amelí, and the many nights he had spent in her arms before he married her. It was because of her that he began to have these feelings of artificiality. He had conversations with her. Eventually, his 'service' to the temple became something else. He grew fond of Amelí. She used to tell him of being free from temple life, made him believe that there was more to a woman than just her body. And there *was* more to Amelí. She may have seemed delicate, but she was strong-willed. He wanted to invest in her, take her as his own. So he did. And as if by a miracle, she gave birth to two children, unheard of for clerics who were supposed to be sterile.

He came to his dwelling, a rich mansion bordered by a high wall. Normally, guards patrolled the grounds, but Hémon's Day allowed his servants to forsake their duties for one night of the year. Even assassins had the day off, a law that protected the lives of citizens and kings. They would be whoring at the temple or home sleeping off the ale.

But something was wrong. Amon paused at the entrance. The gates were wide open, swinging on their hinges in a breeze that had picked up into a stronger wind. They should have been locked.

Amon stepped forward, circled around the courtyard and

ascended the steps to the massive building. He grabbed one of the wall torches and used its dying flame to provide enough light to find his way. The halls were clean, not a trace of dirt or dust. The mansion seemed alright, but the air was stiff, biting, like a predator clawing at his clothes, weakening him with every step.

"Amelí?" he called, but he received no answer.

Two stairwells took him to the third floor. He turned down the left wing and followed it to a dead end where double doors marked his bedroom. One of the doors was cracked open. A light streamed out, casting a rectangular shape on the hall floor.

"Amelí?" he said again.

He pushed the door open. Inside he found another woman waiting for him. An attractive young woman. She wore a black dress with a high neckline, gold trim, and laced sleeves. Her hair flowed straight, draped over one shoulder. Her skin gleamed white, smooth, her legs crossed, feet bare. A slit in her dress taunted his eyes and he followed the cut to just above the knee. She would have made for a tempting night had Amon not noticed her eyes. They were the only unnatural thing about her, glowing golden yellow.

"Who are you?" he asked.

"You should already know, king. I imagine Líran Shadai would not keep my identity secret," the figure replied in a twisted voice. Her accent sounded like Shadai's, but her voice was twofold, one a woman's, the other a raspy croak.

"The Black Assailant," he said through a sneer. "What are you doing here? Where are my wife and children?"

"Does it matter? I was going to offer you a splendid night, king. That red hair of yours is a compliment to your green eyes. Quite alluring. Exotic, to say the least. Yet alas for you, for I had other more pressing matters to attend to."

"*Schnerkin* woman! What did you do with my wife?"

Amon looked around for a weapon. The room was stripped bare.

"What did I do?" she replied with a coy grin.

She stood, stepped over to the window and withdrew the long drapes. On the deep windowsill, a woman sat bound and gagged. At the sight of Amon, she slid off the windowsill, but the Black Assailant caught her, held her fast.

"Amelí!"

He stepped forward, but the ground rumbled and the floor gave way. He twisted and grasped the ledge as a sinkhole formed in the middle of the bedroom. He clung to the doorframe, struggling to haul himself up. Muscles strained. Behind him, the Black Assailant's laughter mocked his struggle. Amelí's muffled screams rang in an undertone.

Amon swung a leg up and held onto the doorframe to pull himself up. He took one look at the hole and grit his teeth. Then he looked at her, poor Amelí struggling in her grasp. The Black Assailant continued to wear that toying grin.

"How dare you!" he yelled.

"How dare I," she repeated, drawing out the words. "A proud king bent to submission."

"What do you want with her?"

"That is none of your concern."

"You took Levin's wife, too, didn't you?"

"Of course. Yet unfortunately for me, I misjudged which king's affairs to meddle in. I hear you were the one who interfered with my plans to trap Líran Shadai."

"So it's the Faithen you want."

"Precisely, which is why I am making you an offer."

"Try me."

"You must throw that True Faithen in the Death Chamber."

"We already put a Faithen in there."

"You imprisoned *a* True Faithen, not *the* True Faithen," the woman said.

"What difference does it make?"

All the difference, fool!

Amon shuddered. The raspy voice filled the room and reached into his soul at the same time.

"You cannot outwit me, king. I know you met Líran Shadai tonight. My request is simple."

"And what do I get?"

"I will return your wife to you."

"What if you don't?"

She laughed again, this time a beautiful melody rid of the raspy undertone. "Oh king, we Faithens tend not to lie, whether False or True."

313

The ground rumbled again. Amon crouched to keep from falling. A staircase jutted out opposite him, leading down into the abyss of the sinkhole. The Black Assailant stood unfazed by the shaking, as if the sudden appearance of sinkholes and structures was commonplace.

"How…?" Amon breathed.

"Do I have your word, king? Will you do this for me?"

Amon nodded.

"Good." She dragged Ameli to the stairs. "You have four days to lock the True Faithen in the Death Chamber. That is more than enough time. If by morning of the fourth day I do not find what I seek to be there, it will go ill for you. Consider that a friendly warning. I am seldom this lenient."

"What do you want with him anyway?" Amon asked.

She didn't answer. She descended into the hole, a wailing Ameli in tow. The hole closed up around them and they were gone.

Amon stood alone at the doorway. He was torn. How could he do the True Faithen wrong? Shadai was a genuine man, young and thin, but good natured and respectful. He hadn't known the man for very long, but he could already sense that Shadai was the type of person who could mend broken ties, maybe even bridge the gap between nations. An alliance with Serenesti would be a strong one, especially is the True Faithen's tale was true.

But Ameli, the pride of his life. Gone.

What was he to do?

"Four days? Four *days*?!"

"Yes, four," the Black Assailant replied.

She pushed her captive down the tunnel Dethshaiken had excavated. She wasn't quite sure how he'd managed to without the ceiling collapsing and the river flooding the chamber. She had to admit, the Third was brilliant at what he did.

Yet he was terrible at plotting and scheming.

"That's way too much time—!"

"No, it is not. I cannot persuade the kings over a single day. They need time to think it over."

"They need a time *limit*, wretch! That forces them to make hasty decisions in our favour."

She considered. "Perhaps."

"You're stalling."

"I am not stalling. Give poison time and it will cripple its victim. We have the wives of two kings, four more clerics and two children. How do you expect to take them all south with only four arms?"

"Chains, woman."

"Perhaps, but your pathetic malshorthath will be here in five days to take them off our hands anyway. I would rather wait for them than have to deal with squirming prizes."

Dethshaiken glared at her, then looked at her prisoner. The Black Assailant watched as he looked the king's wife over, a grimace on his face. He wasn't one to gawk over women. Fighting and shaping the earth. Those were the two things Dethshaiken loved more than himself.

"You'd better know what you're doing," he said after some time.

"Trust me. This orchestration of mine will succeed."

He looked her up and down and his grimace changed to consideration. "You'd better not let Morkhen see you in that dress. If he did, not even Ehnthatúlen or that prized sword of yours could stop him from advancing on you."

"I cannot believe you had me wear this! Do not tell me you have taken a liking to me."

"You do have an attractive figure."

"Dethshaiken! Really!"

"Just because I said you have a nice figure doesn't mean anything more. Don't think for a moment I would try my hand at you."

She shook her head. "For a *korme'khím* malshorth perhaps I might seem pleasant to look at, yet my scars are none to gawk at. My people prefer a lithe, delicate woman, not a lean soldier. Someone who can keep a house, not a leader of legions."

"I thought you said they weren't your people."

She didn't answer.

The tunnel ran more or less in a straight line and deeper, then rose slightly and stretched on until they reached a small cavern.

An odour of decay wafted towards them from tunnel on the other side. Though Dethshaiken had covered up the hole to the Death Chamber, the smell had seeped in, tainting his new excavations.

The Black Assailant veered toward a crude wooden door that led to her temporary living quarters. The other captives were held in another one of Dethshaiken's caves.

"I hope you don't expect me to sit around for four days," the Third said.

"You are more than welcome to cause mischief, master. In the meantime, I have some prisoners to attend to, and I hope you will not disturb me."

Dethshaiken's face went sour. "What exactly are you doing with them?"

"I am sure Ehnthatúlen would love to tell you."

I would not.

"That settles that," said Dethshaiken. "Probably something perverse." He disappeared down the far tunnel.

The Black Assailant smiled. She turned, opened the door and pushed the woman through. Her room was small, just a simple cave with a small cot for a bed. It was already occupied. Her previous prisoner, a woman fifteen years her senior, stood at their entrance. Out of the captives, this one had shown strict obedience to the Black Assailant's commands. But it wasn't only her obedience that the Black Assailant kept her close. The cleric had an unwavering demeanour and the way she looked at the Black Assailant depicted a calculating, studying nature.

"Kaw-veeng?!" the younger cleric exclaimed. Her eyes glistened with tears. Given the chance, they would probably join the dry streams that had fallen when she was first captured.

"Amelí," the other woman answered.

"Sit down, cleric," the Black Assailant ordered.

Without a word, Karvene obeyed. The Black Assailant brought Amelí over, sat her down, and untied the cloth around her mouth.

"Unzip this for me," the Black Assailant told the older cleric, turning around.

Karvene obliged.

"What have you done with my children?" Amelí asked. "You said I could see them."

"It's no use, Amelí," Karvene intervened. "I tried asking her the same thing about a a few of the clerics."

The women watched as their captor undressed, her white skin marked with black scars.

Amelí gasped. "What happened to you?"

"Again, she won't tell me," Karvene replied.

"And I would be grateful if you avoided speaking," the Black Assailant spat.

The clerics held onto each other for comfort and didn't say another word.

These prizes of yours are annoying, said Ehnthatúlen. *You are wasting your time with them. Put them with the others. And for the love of all things distraught, get some clothes on!*

"How many times have I changed over the years and you have not uttered a single word?" the Black Assailant said in the same foreign language.

I am saying it for their sake.

"So you care about these women?"

Shut it, wretch! Just get rid of these people.

"Oh Ehnthatúlen, you would not deprive me of feminine company, would you? I have been in the audience of you wretched Three for far too long. It gets tiresome."

You are plotting something. I know that tone, that one that claims to hold truth if only to flip it into deception.

"Oh come now, even you would enjoy what I have planned. Would you disapprove of thwarting the First's passions? You have many times before."

Her ears caught the sound of her prisoners whispering behind her.

"Is she mad?" the younger cleric asked.

"Probably. She speaks to that voice whenever the giant isn't around. If only I could understand them. From the tone of her voice, I think she's coaxing him."

"So she has a bit of feminine charm in her."

The Black Assailant turned to face them and immediately they went quiet.

"You have no idea how useful that feminine charm has aided me over the past decade," she said to them in Common.

"Aren't you going to tell us anything about you and why

you're here?" Amelí asked. She continued to hold hands with the more reserved Karvene.

The Black Assailant smiled, a grin that visibly put the younger prisoner at ill ease. "I would rather keep you guessing, cleric."

"Definitely feminine charm," said Karvene.

The Black Assailant chuckled. "You I like. Tell me, my dear. How would you like to be free?"

"You want to free us?"

The Black Assailant walked towards them, smiling the whole time. "I have something special for you. You are prime subjects of reproduction, and since you seem so used to men penetrating you, a life in service to my master's call should be of no real concern."

"Just because we're temple prostitutes doesn't mean we enjoy it," Karvene said.

"Is that so?"

"No one chooses to be a cleric. We were appointed."

"Besides, we can't give birth anyway," Amelí added.

"Then how did you beget two children?" the Black Assailant asked.

Amelí opened her mouth to speak, but clamped it shut again.

"You're wasting your time with us," Karvene intervened. "We have no idea how Amelí had children, but the rest of us can't."

The Black Assailant reached out and stroked Karvene's cheek, brushing her thumb on her lips. Both women were gorgeous, beauties that would please even Morkhen. A shame their beauty would go to waste among the malshorthath. But they couldn't give birth. Were they telling the truth or was this the cleric's way of toying with her? Regardless, the Black Assailant loved the conversation.

"How fortunate," she said after a while. "Well, if you truly must know what I am saying to my possessor, it is that I am bargaining for your life. Nothing I do goes unnoticed, and it is only by his approval that I can carry out my own desires."

"What desires?"

"To set you free, as I said."

There is no way I will allow that, Ehnthatúlen cut in.

The Black Assailant chuckled and switched to the foreign language. "Oh, I think you will, my dear possessor. Nothing would make you happier. Was it not Morkhen who defiled your wife so long ago? How angry you must be for him to have his way with any woman he pleases. Just think. Do this and he will become terribly angry. Think of your wife and how much you wished you could have saved her. You can save her twicefold now."

Ehnthatúlen grumbled, a tremor that made her twitch in discomfort. Her cuts and bruises flared in searing pain, reminding her of the curse on her body. But she had her answer. Thanks to her manipulation, her possessor would have to comply.

Fine. I hate the First more than I hate these women.

"My deepest gratitude to you, Ehnthatúlen."

She switched to Common. "Come, ladies. Help me dress."

Part 4

CHAPTER TWENTY-SEVEN

The Missing Horse

To say Yosef was bored would be an understatement. He had exhausted his playing opportunities by mid-morning of Hémon's Day. Fehnan Farthorn was lazying around reading his book outside, which Yosef discovered was pretty much the only thing the teen ever did. He had also satisfied his curiosity by conducting a full examination of Ninthalas' belongings.

That left Yosef with one option: visiting Hallas. He hadn't had the chance to properly thank the horse for saving his life in *Lotah 'an Morkh*, and he figured it was about time he paid the poor beast a visit. Besides, it probably wasn't that fun being cooped up in a stall all day.

The barn, located a fair distance from the house, stood tall and red, a sorry sight amongst the beautiful trees of colourful foliage. And it wasn't really a place Yosef would put a barn. Weren't these animal building things supposed to go in fields?

His feet crunched on a carpet of dying leaves, diverting his attention to the ground. Here was a wonder he had never seen before. Why did the leaves fall? Why did they die? Was it because the air was so cold, it seemed to blow right through him? He shivered as a particularly large gust blew against him. He didn't like this northern land. He could wear layers upon layers and still it would be freezing.

He pushed open one of the double doors to the barn, a wave of manure-saturated stench escaping as he did. He pinched his nose. How Hallas could stand such a place was beyond him. He went in, finding the last stall where Fehnan said he had put the horse...

Only Hallas wasn't there.

"Hey, Yosef, what're you up to?" a voice called behind him.

He turned to see Fehnan entering the barn. The scraggly teen had a half-eaten apple in his hand, which he chomped on so loudly Yosef wondered how he didn't hear him come in.

"I came to see Hallas, but he's not here."

"Not here?" Fehnan repeated. He took one look at the empty stall and cursed. "*Spizzaz* dolls! My dad's gonna throw a mad ramble at me if he sees this! Come on, *souther*. Help me find 'im!"

Then teen darted out of the barn and raced toward town, Yosef not far behind. He asked everyone he saw: men, women, children, fellow teens and the elderly. Most shook their heads and went their own way. The old men met them with frowns that made their wrinkled foreheads even wrinklier, then proceeded to ramble on about the weather or their good old childhood. Yosef marvelled at how their faces didn't get swallowed up in their wrinkles. For some, their eyes seemed to disappear altogether.

"Thank you," Fehnan said time and time again, often cutting an old man off before he rambled too much.

As the sun crept to its zenith, the teen's list of inquirees turned to pretty young ladies whose pleasant complexions and playful giggling caused him to grin and blush. Yosef pouted every time Fehnan struck up a conversation with one of them. It would take them all day to find a lead, especially where attractive young girls were involved.

"Where do ya suppose he could've gone?" Fehnan asked.

His eyes drifted to a group of girls he had just spoken to. They giggled amongst themselves and waved to him. He shoved his hands in his pockets and nodded back, sporting a wide grin.

Yosef rolled his eyes. "I dunno." He was already tired from following the teen around town like a shadow.

Fehnan scanned town centre. "Let's climb Watcher's Hill over there," he said, pointing to a lone hill outside of town. "We might be able to spot 'im high up."

"No way, Fehnan. I can't even breathe nothin'."

"Fair that. I guess we could rest a bit. Gotta find that horse soon though."

"Yeah, if you wouldn't keep talking to those girl people."

"Whatcha on about, *souther*?"

"Let's just climb the hill already."

Watcher's Hill wasn't that big, really. Nothing compared to the mountains Yosef remembered crossing with Ninthalas, Kai-Tsúthlen and Tahlen…and the Black Assailant. He shuddered. He wished the 'she' who could take memories away would take the ones about *her*. Those memories he could do without. Maybe he could work out a trade.

"There's no grey thinger skohls up there, is there?" he asked.

"What? No! What the mad rambles you talking about, *souther*?"

"Never mind."

They approached the base and began the climb. Yosef struggled to keep up with the bigger, stronger teen. Fehnan easily beat him to the top. When he finally caught up and reached the crest, he plopped himself down.

The view was worth it. They could see out over the whole town of Fíthera, even beyond the top of the City's outer wall.

"Quite a sight, ain't it?" Fehnan said. "Sometimes I come here to get away from the fam. Pops is always going on about 'responsibility this' and 'grow up that'. Never paid a mind to it and don't mean to."

Yosef had no idea what he was talking about, but he did agree that the view was amazing.

"What's that big building on the mountain over there?"

"Oh, that's the Hall of the Four Lords. My pops goes there a bit to see King Amon. Only king worth talkin' to, he says. You could say they're somethin' close."

"Like friends?"

"More like acquaintances."

Yosef didn't know the difference. He stared ahead, watching billowing shoots of smoke rise into the air, creating a haze over the horizon that melted the sky into a dull light brown. He could smell the workings of the factories from the hilltop. It wasn't pleasant. Even more unpleasant was the tingling sensation on the back of his neck. The previous day, Yosef had pinpointed it to the very hilltop he was sitting on. Now, however, the sense came from the direction of the City.

Let's explore!

The silence reached out its hand to him. Closing his eyes, Yosef focussed, allowing it to lead him into the ground, around the river and under the towering walls of the City. He felt the footfalls of people walking between buildings on the cobblestone road and the rolling, rattling wheels of what he imagined were carts. Then he dove into Mount Hémon and there, tapped the existence of a network of caves.

A bellow rumbled deep within the mountain. It was another presence, a huge monstrous form. And it had found him.

Who are you, boy?

Panicking, Yosef withdrew. The sense began to change form, gnawing at him like a sharp-toothed skohl. The silence joined the presence of the giant, extending its limbs out to grab him. Yosef scurried back. The giant groped and clawed. It was searching for him!

Reality smacked him like a hand slapping his face and his eyes flickered open. A dull ache rattled under his skull.

Consequence, the silence whispered.

Consequence of what? Finding a freakish beast man thing with the same sense as his?

When his head cleared, he found himself sitting on the hilltop again, Hémon stretched out before him. The sun had long begun its descent, but it still shown strong, bathing him in its warmth which was frequently disrupted by a brisk wind. Fehnan, he noticed, lay beside him napping.

How long had he been in a trance? For him, it seemed only a moment. But when he looked up at the position of the sun, it was indeed early evening.

An animal's grunt caught his attention and he spun around. Fehnan woke from his nap with a start and sat up. Rising to the crest of the hill was an enormous horse, black like charcoal, its eyes flaming red. It cried out, more a roar than a horse's whinny.

"What is that?!" Fehnan exclaimed.

Recollection dawned on Yosef. He recognized the beast, remembered how terror-stricken he had been when he had first laid eyes on it.

"That...that's the Black Assailant's horse," he said.

"The Black Assailant? You mean the one from Shadai's story? I didn't think it was true."

"It *was* true!"

The beast charged.

"Look out!" Fehnan yelled.

Before Yosef knew what was happening, the teen shoved him aside. Fehnan dashed the other way in the nick of time and the beast sped past. It wailed, skidded to a stop, then charged again, this time heading straight for Yosef.

"Yosef!" Fehnan cried.

Sharp neighing cut through the air. A blur of tanned hide obscured Yosef's view. The black beast screeched to a halt, blocked by a new enemy. The tanned horse reared, stomped its hooves and stood like a protective shield in front of Yosef.

"Hallas!" Yosef exclaimed.

The black beast bellowed and shot forward, and Hallas charged back. The horses galloped around the mounded hilltop and zigzagged in a fast-paced duel. Each tried to get the better of the other. Teeth bit. Legs kicked. Yosef scrambled out of the way to avoid getting trampled. He eventually crawled to the middle of the mound where Fehnan was watching the battle play out, mouth agape.

"Unbelievable," the teen breathed.

Yosef clung to him.

The battle went on and on in a never-ending cycle until the black beast found an opening. It roared and rushed at the boys. Hallas dashed beside it, nipping its hide and pushing against it. The animals veered off-path and over the edge. Yosef let go of Fehnan and ran to the edge of the hill. The black beast stumbled and rolled down the far side of the hill to the bottom. Hallas skidded to a stop and stood triumphantly above. It let out a braying challenge to its rival. The black beast slowly rose. It had met its match. Growling, the beast turned and walked away with a limp.

Yosef gasped for air that had somehow been lost in the chaos of the battle.

"Wow," he breathed. "Wow, Hallas, you're amazing."

He ran to the horse's side and immediately his joy vanished. The horse had succumbed to bruising and the nips of his enemy had left bloodied marks in its hide. It was breathing heavily, eyes fixed in the direction the black beast had gone.

"Fehnan, he's hurt!"

Fehnan came to the horse's side.

"This ain't good. We have to get him back home. I gotta tell my pops."

Yosef nodded.

Hallas followed the boys back to the house, but refused to be led into the barn.

"Oh, come on, horse," Fehnan said, pushing the beast's rear end.

Hallas grunted and stood its ground.

"He doesn't like the smell," said Yosef. "I don't either. It's dirty in there."

"Fine," the teen grumbled, crossing his arms. "But I ain't getting a mad ramble from the pops when he's found the beast's escaped."

As if on cue, they saw Bellim storm down the riverbank path to the house, his face red with fury.

"Uh-oh. Looks like he might throw one," said Fehnan.

"What's wrong?"

"Dunno. Let's find out."

They hurried inside. Bellim's voice boomed from the kitchen. Fehnan pulled Yosef behind the corner of the open door to listen.

"I had a feeling he'd be caught," Mr. Farthorn said, his tone grim.

"They'll probably execute him like the others," said Félía.

"No!" Bellim declared. "No one's going to get killed!"

"There's no helping it, dear. He was a nice man and all, but we have to consider the worst here. What should we do with the *souther*?"

Yosef's cheeks grew hot and he clenched his fists. He didn't like being called a *souther*.

"I think I might send him back with a cart of exports," Bellim said.

"Will he be okay like that? I mean, all alone as young as he is."

"Do you know how worried that *souther* would be if he found out Ninthalas is in prison?"

A lump grew in Yosef's throat.

"It's better than not telling him," Félía returned. "He has a right to know. We shouldn't be sending him off either."

Yosef had had enough. He ran up the stairs to the spare room and slammed the door shut. He couldn't believe what he'd just heard. Ninthalas in prison? His father did nothing wrong! And he wasn't a bad person either. He was kind, gentle and loving, and that wasn't a reason to put him behind bars. And now the Farthorns were going to make him go back to Serenestí alone? No way! Yosef was going to find his father, and they were going to go home together and live happily in the forest country. And no one was going to stop them.

A knock tapped the door and Fehnan entered. Yosef turned toward the sunlit window, sitting on the bed with his back to the door.

"I'm sorry, *souther—*"

"Don't call me that!" Yosef yelled. "I hate that word! Call me Yosef. My name is Yosef, okay?"

"Sorry," Fehnan apologized. "Is it...okay if I sit with you?"

Yosef nodded. Fehnan sat down beside him.

"Just spoke with my pops. Says he wants to send you back to Serenestí. Says it's the only way to keep you safe."

Yosef didn't respond. He tried his best to hold back tears, but they filled his eyes anyway. A dribble tickled his nose and he used his sleeve to wipe it away.

"I think you should stay," Fehnan went on. "But my pops, well, he just wants you to be safe, I guess. Can't really go against his word, you know?"

"I don't wanta go home alone," Yosef choked.

"Alone? No, kid, I'll go with you," Fehnan reassured. "I'll tell my pops simple, and my mom's sure to back me up. She couldn't see a kid like you travelling all by your lonesome. Besides, I promised Ninthalas I'd take care of you, and I will. A promise is a promise. I've always wanted to learn about True Faithen culture anyway. Maybe we could learn together—"

"I want to go with Ninthalas."

"...Oh" Fehnan muttered. "Right."

"Fehnan?"

"Yeah?"

"Ninthalas told me that Yahlírin would protect him, but he was captured anyway."

"Huh," said Fehnan. "Well, if Ninthalas said that, then it must be true."

"Why?"

"'Cause True Faithens don't lie, at least that's what I've heard of 'em. Just because he's in prison, doesn't mean they hurt him."

"Really?" Yosef wiped away his tears and looked up at the teen.

"Yeah, sure!" Fehnan exclaimed. "I mean, he's a True Faithen. Nobody'd ever hurt a True Faithen because everyone loves 'em!"

'Except for Hémon people,' Yosef wanted to say, but Mrs. Farthorn's voice calling from downstairs cut him off.

"Boys, it's time for dinner! Fehnan, I thought I told you to bring Yosef down!"

Fehnan stood. "Come on, my mom's going to get mad at us if we don't go now."

"Like throwing a mad ramble?" Yosef asked.

Fehnan chuckled. "No. My dad's the one who throws the rambles. My mom just tosses the fits."

Yosef shrugged. Hémon culture was confusing and not the kind he'd like to invest in. Not never.

———◉———

CHAPTER TWENTY-EIGHT

A Change of Course

The dinner table was a mix of solemn, dry moods and terrible eating habits. Yosef looked to each of the Farthorns in turn, who were slurping and chomping so loudly, he cringed. Such unrefined table manners compared to the Shadais, whose mannerisms border-lined perfection.

Mr. Farthorn had told him everything. Ninthalas was indeed in prison and to avoid risk the trades captain was sending Yosef back to Serenestí. Thankfully, Fehnan managed to persuade his parents to go along as well. But it did little to lift Yosef's mood. He just wanted his father back. Of course, he had protested. But Bellim wouldn't have any of it. It was too dangerous. Yosef was to live on, Bellim had said, and that was where the conversation ended.

Yosef quickly finished his meal and returned upstairs. There wasn't that much to prepare for leaving. He'd only brought one bag with him. His wooden *saiken* sat propped up against the side of the bed. He took it and swung it a few times, a clumsy effort at combat. He wished he knew how to fight. Then he could march into Hémon and free his father, and he and Ninthalas could go back to Serenestí. Yet that was impossible, he remembered. Going back was futile. Yosef had been banished from the forest country.

He put down the *saiken*.

"It's hopeless."

If only he knew how to use a real sword. His eyes drifted to

Ninthalas' weaponry. The True Faithen carried no shield. He had two swords—one shorter and one longer—a quiver of arrows and a bow. Yosef picked up each one in turn, then placed it carefully back down again. He sure wished he was strong. Strong like the giant his real father used to be. A real fighter.

He turned to packing, trying to fold Ninthalas' extra set of clothes as best he could. When he opened the bag to put the clothes back, he noticed a glint. Curious, he reached in and pulled out a dagger. The hilt gleamed silver, the blade itself wrapped in cloth. He unsheathed it. Inscriptions were etched on both sides. One side bore True Faithen lettering and the other had a symbol, a tree whose roots frayed. The two end roots curved inward, intertwined, then ended facing each other, one an outline, the other solid engraving. Likewise, the tree was half engraved, half embossed. He turned the blade over to the inscription, unable to read it. What did it mean? For Ninthalas, many things had a history: the land, the Fehlthan, the forests, cities…this dagger too, most likely. Perhaps, when his father wasn't agitated, Yosef could ask him about it.

He sheathed the dagger, wrapped the cloth around it, and put it in his own bag. He had a feeling it might come in handy at some point. Maybe to be used against the Black Assailant.

Like the previous night, Yosef tossed and turned in his sleep as nightmares plagued his dreams. Worse, he continued to remember them when he woke up in the morning, and a splitting headache accompanied them. He would have lied in bed all morning had not Mrs. Farthorn's stern voice belted out from the lower floor. Fearing her 'fits', he heeded her command and stumbled down to the kitchen.

He was halfway through a meal of oatmeal when stumbling footsteps echoed from the stairs. In walked Fehnan, just as groggy as Yosef. The teen took one look at the mushy gruel and grimaced.

"You'll eat that if you know what's good for you," his mother spat.

Reluctantly, Fehnan sat and ate. When he finished, he went back upstairs.

"Don't you go falling back to sleep, boy!" Félía called up.

"Ain't sleeping for a shnerkin' fool!" Fehnan answered.

"Don't you yap at me! Now get your things together." She turned to Yosef. "You'd best hurry as well. Need a good start if you're to make it to the Fork."

Yosef had no idea what the 'Fork' was, but he gobbled down his meal anyway. In no time, he and Fehnan were out the door with packs strapped to their backs. Fehnan gave one last hug to his mother, then walked off, Yosef trotting by his side. All along the way, the teen excitedly told Yosef of the things he would do in Serenestí, things he would learn, people he would talk to.

"As soon as I learn Faithen, I'm gonna march right up to that High Lord and give him a good ramble about sending Shadai here. You think there're pretty girls in Serenestí?"

Yosef didn't answer. He walked with his head bowed. The last thing he wanted to think about was Serenestí where people stared him down straight and didn't welcome him. At least the Shadais were nice people. But they couldn't revoke the law, the law that had sent him away.

Buildings popped up around them and soon they were in the main of Hemnak. It was as busy as Yosef remembered it when he and Ninthalas first came to Hémon. People darted to and fro. Soldiers strutted down streets, broad swords at their hips. Conversations buzzed all around him.

"Pretty upbeat for the aftermath of Hémon's Day," Fehnan said.

"Is it always this busy?" Yosef asked.

"Hémon never sleeps."

What in A'thería did that mean?

"So what do we do now?"

Fehnan scanned the premises. Carts of goods were either parked in alleyways awaiting inspection or passing to and from the south gate.

"We climb into one of those carriages," he said at length. "Follow me."

He crossed the square and went up to three carriages with domed tops stationed by a tavern. Their drivers were probably inside having one last drink before departure. The boys went up behind one. When they were sure no one was looking, they jumped in the back. Crates of wheat and bags of spices lay stacked on top of one another other. Fehnan crept up to one straggling crate in particular. He lifted the lid off. It was filled to the brim with bags. A strong aroma tickled their noses.

"Spices," said Fehnan. "Lucky pick."

He proceeded to remove some of the bags, then picked Yosef up by the armpits and put him inside.

"Hide here until I come get you again, alright? Whatever you do, don't move. Stay quiet. And if you hear my pops, don't you dare speak."

"But I thought—"

"Shush. I'll come get you. Don't worry."

Yosef nodded and crouched as Fehnan lifted the lid overtop, leaving the boy trapped inside. He waited. He heard Fehnan speaking with a man outside, muffled voices he could barely make out.

"Ya sure?" the man asked. "The guard's been up since some Faithen broke into the City yesterday."

"Positively, sir," came Fehnan's confident voice.

"Fair that. My boy and I can get ya through."

"Honest work with you, sir."

After that, the carriage started moving, rattling upon the cobblestone road. Curled up uncomfortably in the crate, Yosef tried to think about good things to ease his mind. But the more he thought about going back, the more he thought about leaving Ninthalas behind. What happened when he and Fehnan got to Serenestí's border and found out they couldn't get in? They'd have to turn around and go back to who knows where and find a place to call home. Tears flooded Yosef's eyes. Nowhere was truly home without Ninthalas.

The carriage jolted, and he bumped his bad arm, the one that had been bitten by the skohl. His leg had healed up well, but his arm still had bruising that wouldn't go away. He winced from the pain. How long was he going to have to stay cooped up? He remembered the days it took just to get to Hémon. Hopefully he wouldn't have to stay huddled in a ball that long.

The carriage stopped and Yosef heard voices again. One was Bellim's, interrogating the carriage driver about what sort of exports he was bringing into the City.

Wait, into the City? But that would mean—

"Proceed," said Mr. Farthorn in his monstrous voice.

So Fehnan was getting him into the City. That meant they were going to rescue Ninthalas!

The carriage rolled on. Not much longer, it stopped again and he heard more commotion, loud thuds and scrapes. Then his crate shifted.

"*Krikes*, this one's heavy!" a man cursed. "What kind of goods they rollin' in this time? Feels like those water beasties."

"Who knows?" said another indifferently.

"I thought this whole lot was spices, not heavy goods."

Yosef tumbled and turned as the men struggled to move it. The crate dropped and landed with a hard thud, banging his bad arm in the process. He squeaked. The few bags of spices left in the crate didn't offer much of a soft landing.

"You hear something?"

Yosef clamped a hand over his mouth.

"Nope."

"I thought I heard something from the crate."

"Ah, shush it man. You've been doing nothing but grumbling since we started this morning. Come on. There's two more of these carriages to unload."

Their voices faded into a backdrop of other muffled sounds.

Yosef cradled his injured arm. He hoped it wasn't bleeding. The box lid moved, flipped off and Fehnan's head poked in.

"Have a nice trip?" he asked, a smug grin on his face.

"No," Yosef groaned.

"Something wrong with your arm?"

"No," Yosef declared.

Fehnan helped him out of the box. When he had rubbed his backside and stretched his stiff limbs, Yosef saw that they stood in a narrow side street enclosed by tall buildings. The crate he had been one of several stacked next to the wall of a shop, and three carriages lined up in a row blocked one end of the street. These were being unloaded by a number of peasants, big burly men who had scruffy beards and dirty clothes.

"Is this the City?"Yosef asked.

"True talkin'. This is Helfohr, Dellon's city."

"Who's he?"

"A terrible king. C'mon. You up for a new adventure? We're going to find Ninthalas."

"Really?" Yosef beamed.

"Yes," Fehnan continued. He dropped his voice to a murmur. "But we have to be careful. If anyone finds out we're from outside, we might get caught and thrown back out or worse."

"Okay," Yosef whispered back.

He slung his bag on his shoulder and followed Fehnan through the crowd, careful not to get lost in the long skinny roads that twisted and turned between the tall buildings.

They didn't have to ask about Ninthalas. News about the True Faithen's imprisonment had already spread through town like an epidemic. Everyone was voicing their approval or disapproval—mostly the latter. Yosef heard some very distasteful language that he didn't like at all. He tried his best not to protest against some of the children in town who had adopted the coarse slang words of adults. Every one of them had an opinion, and arguments were loud yelling matches that grated on Yosef's ears. The most he could do was frown and trail behind Fehnan, who paid no mind to the noisy banter.

Eventually, they came to a second town square, and beyond a few houses to their left rose a large, square building.

"What's that?" Yosef asked, pointing.

"A temple," the teen replied indifferently.

"For what?"

"To pay tribute to the god of the city."

"I thought Yahlírin was the only god."

Fehnan stopped, spun and cupped a hand over his mouth.

"Don't *ever* say that word here. Ya hear me? Those guards'll snatch you up and you won't be seeing the light of day for the rest of your life."

Yosef nodded.

"But don't go thinking there're other gods either. They don't exist, sure as my pops says. Just old kings who worshipped themselves."

They continued on. Everywhere they went, Yosef gaped at the new sights around them. He had never seen so many buildings clustered in one place. Near town centre, they piled on top of one another and some were so skinny, they looked like they would get swallowed up by the bigger ones sandwiching them. Yosef asked Fehnan question after question, like why there were so many people, why some people wore tanned clothes while others wore colourful ones, and why children hitched rides on the backs of carts and carriages without so much as a nod from drivers. Fehnan answered them without much mind. The more Yosef talked to him, the more he noticed the teen's disinterest in Hémon.

"Don't you like your home?"

"I do and I don't," he replied, eyes focusing on where they were going.

"Why not?"

"It's just so…restricting. Backstabbing, crime, the rich getting richer and the poor getting poorer. I'd much rather go someplace else."

"Like Serenestí?"

A twinkle glinted in Fehnan's eyes, bringing him to life.

"Exactly. True Faithens are so well known, but so mysterious at the same time. They're kind of like Hémonians in a way. No one knows exactly how they live."

"It's kind of nice," said Yosef.

"Really?"

"Yeah, but I was only there like a week or something. Ninthalas brought me back from my home country. True Faithens have a different language, different way of doing things. It's kinda weird sometimes, but I like it a lot more than Hémon."

"When we get back, you should show me around."

Yosef's chin dropped. "That won't happen."

"Why not?"

"'Cause I was kicked out."

Fehnan shot him a distraught look. "Why?!"

"Because I'm a foreigner. That's why Ninthalas and I came here. I was kicked out of Serenestí and he was sent to deliver messages. He could've stayed, but he chose to adopt me and take me anywhere he goes. Except into the City, that is."

"Sounds like a fair new dad you got, Yosef."

"Yeah, he really is. I hope we can save him."

"Don't you go worrying yourself dead. We'll get him back. All we gotta do is find the prison. Pretty sure it's around the back of the mountain over there, but getting there without being caught is easier said than done. Need a plan."

That mountain didn't get any closer the more they walked.

Fehnan and Yosef took to a main trafficking road that led them from one busy city to another. Well, Fehnan said they were two cities, but Yosef had no idea where which one ended and the other started. By then, Yosef was having trouble keeping up.

"Let's rest for a bit," Fehnan offered.

The boys found a bench beside a high class tavern and sat down. Fehnan reached into his bag and pulled out two buns his mother had packed for them. He handed one to Yosef.

"It's too bad we didn't bring Hallas with us," said Yosef.

"It's too bad I don't have money for a ride. You could probably hitch one, but I'm too old. Once you get to a certain age, people start kicking you off."

"And throwing mad rambles?" Yosef guessed.

"Exactly! Now you're getting it."

They watched townspeople hurry by. When they were done eating, Fehnan stood.

"Ready to go looking again?"

"No," said Yosef. "My legs hurt like there ain't no hurtin'."

"C'mon, Yosef. We've gotta find Ninthalas and be outta the City before nightfall. We can't be wandering about past curfew here or there'll be trouble. Lots of mad rambles and tossing fits. Maybe even get arrested. We don't want none o' that."

Fehnan pulled him to his feet and tugged him along until he began to walk on his own accord. The interconnecting pathways were like a maze. Yosef's pace started to slow, and Fehnan was soon well ahead of him.

"You! I've never seen you before!"

Yosef darted behind piled crates. Peering around the corner, he spotted Fehnan out in the open square. A massive soldier had him by the arm.

"A lot of different faces in this town, sir," the teen said.

He shook himself free from the soldier's grasp.

"I know every face in this city," the man went on. "Yours is new."

"I live near the south gate," Fehnan stated.

The soldier's face turned sour. "You mean Helfohr Gate."

Fehnan's eyes widened. Before the soldier could say anything more, he bolted.

"Come back here!" yelled the guard. He sped after the teen.

Yosef had every inclination to stay where he was, but a fire burned inside him. Fehnan needed help, and there was no way Yosef was going to see another person thrown in jail.

He raced after despite his protesting legs and dashed across the square. Commotion from the chase let him know where Fehnan was going. The soldier barked out obscene words and orders, urging others to stop the teen. Then Fehnan's voice yelled back. Yosef spotted them and skidded to a stop. Fehnan struggled in the clutches of two massive soldiers. The one who had been chasing him hit the teen across the face, then bound his wrists behind his back.

"You can't do this to me! Don't you know who I am? I'm the son of—"

"Don't care, kid. No visitors outside of Hémon's Day," the guard retorted.

They pushed him away through the throngs of people.

Yosef watched helplessly from the shadows of a side street. So much for not getting caught. Now what was he to do?

CHAPTER TWENTY-NINE

The Clerics' Aid

"Just you wait. My pops'll find out what you've done—"

"Shut it, kid! We don't care!" one of the soldiers exclaimed.

That didn't stop Fehnan from yelling and causing a commotion. Every head within earshot turned in their direction. This offered Yosef concealment. His tanned skin and foreign clothes might have stood out had Fehnan not provided a distraction. As long as the teen kept yelling and struggling, Yosef didn't exist.

The soldiers marched Fehnan across a bridge to the central island and circled around the mountain. Mount Hémon towered above. Yosef could barely make out the roof outline of the Hall of the Four Lords sitting on the very top. Ninthalas probably would have gone there to see the kings. He would have been arrested and taken to where Yosef was going now: behind the mountain. The soldiers and Fehnan led Yosef right where he needed to go.

The men dragged the teen to a steel door guarded by two sentries. Moments later, the door shut behind them. Yosef couldn't go after them, not with those sentries standing watch. He needed a place to focus, ask the silence to tell him where Fehnan was being taken by their reverberating footsteps.

He looked around and spotted another building nearby, a secluded cube in the same shape as the building Fehnan had described as being a temple. He probably wasn't allowed inside, but if he could find a secluded spot to focus...

"Hey, boy!"

He spun and saw a man clad in velvet green. Fear shot through him like a current and he ran to the temple.

"Stop!" the man yelled.

Yosef dashed inside and raced down a corridor, skidding around several corners before diving into a room. Unfortunately, it was occupied. Sitting on a stool in front of a mirror, a woman spun and gasped.

"What are you—?"

Yosef didn't take the time to answer. He scanned the room, found an open wardrobe, and hid inside, shutting the door behind him. The green man's steps pounded down the hall and into the room.

"King Levin!" the woman exclaimed.

"Miral," the king replied. "Pardon my entry. Did you see a boy just now?"

"A boy? In the temple? I've never heard anything so absurd," the woman said. "Your spirits from yesterday haven't worn off yet, have they, my lord? Did you drink this morning as well? Or were you in for some mid-work laying?"

"What are you on about?" Levin spat.

"I meant no offence, my lord, but the young clerics are in cleansing. Even the kings aren't allowed to disturb us. We're protected by law."

King Levin grumbled. "I beg your pardon." He paused, then added, "I wasn't joking about the boy. I did see him run into the temple. I'll have Meldesha run a search."

"Of course, my lord."

The door slammed shut and the king's heavy footfalls gradually faded. Moments later, the doors of the wardrobe swung open. Yosef squirmed as far back as he could behind a row of hanging dresses.

"It's alright," she reassured. "He's gone now."

Yosef didn't move.

"Won't you come out?"

She held out her hand. Yosef looked at it a while, then took it and emerged from his hiding place. The woman was certainly beautiful, almost as beautiful as Ninthalas' mother. Her white dress glittered and it's gold trim shimmered, the cloth laden with fine jewels that glinted in an array of colours. Her hair was pulled back into a bun where a braid held it in place. She didn't look much older than Ninthalas.

"Thank you," he said, chin dropping.

"You know you shouldn't be here," she said. "Especially since you're from outside. You're a farmer's child, aren't you?"

"Why am I not allowed here?"

"Don't you know? No boy is permitted to enter the temples."

Yosef figured that already. "I'm sorry. I was just looking for a quiet place to think and focus."

"Think? What boy your age stops to think?"

He hesitated. Should he trust this woman? He really didn't have much of a choice. He needed to find his father and now he had to free Fehnan as well. Besides, she didn't *seem* like a bad person.

"Well, you see miss, my da and I are from far away."

"From Hemnak?"

Yosef shook his head. "No, from Serenestí. Not me, though. I'm from Mor'Lûn. Anyway, my da and I went on a long journey here because the High Lord told us to and then he—my da, that is—went into the City to talk to the kings. But they threw him in jail and Fehnan and I came here to look for him so we can go home together. But then Fehnan was captured, too, so I followed the soldiers." He paused, then added, "Do you know how to get inside the prison place?"

The woman blinked. "I assume 'da' means father?" she asked.

"*Aye*—or 'indeed', I guess they would say. He's my new father. He found me in Shalom and brought me to Serenestí— that's his home. And he adopted me."

The woman's eyes widened. "The Faithen," she said. "That Faithen is your adoptive father?"

"His name's Ninthalas," said Yosef. "Ninthalas Líran Shadai. Names are very important to True Faithens, you know. I have to find him so we can go away together. Do you know how to get inside the prison place?"

The woman slowly sat down on the stool. Yosef fidgeted, waiting for her reply.

"What's your name?" she asked.

"Yosef Mathíus Shadai, ma'am."

"Yosef Mathíus Shadai, do you know how dangerous it is for a foreigner like you to be here?"

"But my da's in trouble! He needs me, miss. We gotta leave together, me and him."

She smiled. "Alright, I'll help you. But you must stay here until it's safe. You actually came at a good time. There won't be any men in here for the cleansing period and that's a week long. In the meantime, I'll get you something to eat. Are you hungry?"

Yosef's tummy growled at the thought of food, and he remembered how famished he was.

"Yes, ma'am. And thank you."

She smiled. "You don't have to call me 'ma'am' or 'miss' anymore either. My name is Míral."

"Don't kill me! Don't kill me!" the teen screamed.

The Black Assailant shoved the slain soldier aside. The teen clutched his shoulder, a heavy gash in it thanks to her swift blade. Finished with her recent kill, she started toward him. The teen skittered back into the corner of the cell.

"*My hatred must be satiated,*" Ehnthatúlen spoke through her.

The teen whimpered, occasionally crying, "Please, please don't. Don't kill me."

She couldn't stop herself. Ehnthatúlen was getting restless, and when that happened, it meant blood must be spilt. The more the better. The last time the Second got antsy, she had slaughtered an entire skohl tribe. No tribe of scurrying grey folk lived here, so the Second had settled on the soldiers and prisoner. When he got this angry, all she could do was watch him work through her body and carry out his wrath.

She grabbed a handful of the teen's hair and yanked him off the wall and into submission. Her blade dangerously touched his neck.

"*Poor child you are,*" the spirit spoke through her. "*No one to save you, nor to hear your cries or witness your death. How terrible it must be to suffer me.*"

Her blade pushed against his skin, drawing a trickle of blood. The boy squeaked. "No…Please."

A light touch graced her arm, then firm hands clutched her shoulders. *Emkalaf'Morlúrnan* dropped her sword and screamed. Again, that wretched touch! Ehnthatúlen cowered into the deepest recesses of her soul. Old wounds resurfaced, those black veins of charred death coursing through her bloodstream. The touch of healing temporarily freed her from her possessor. But she didn't want it. All it brought was the pain of the curse.

A voice thundered throughout the cavern.

Calm your hatred, foul spirit! The power of Yahlírin silence you!

"Shadai!" she screamed. "Let me go! It burns!"

She struggled, but his grip was too tight and the pain from the curse too excruciating.

Did I not tell you to leave the blessed of Yahlírin alone? the hallon demanded.

"This boy is no blessed of Yahlírin, fool!"

He released her and she fell to the ground. Her lungs burned; her lacerations stung. For a moment she just laid there, unable to move from the shock of her agony. When she finally regained her strength and sat up, the teen was gone.

Shadai stood by her side, watchful, observing. She hated the way he looked at her.

"Ever do you prevent me from fulfilling my master's wishes," she said. She meant to sound threatening, but her voice came thin. "Where are you hiding him, Shadai? Where do you keep the one I hunt, the one I must end?"

You will lay no hand upon him while that spirit dwells within you, Shadai replied. *Yet do you not also wish to let him live? For at last I have come to understand who you are. Give up this task, woman. You know well that the path you walk leads to death.*

She looked up at him. As she gazed into his eyes, she grasped a fleeting sense of freedom long since forgotten. A freedom that brought hope. Ehnthatúlen crushed it as soon as it crossed her mind. His hold on her was strong, a spell woven with such care it could bend the strongest of wills. Though there was some remembrance of her former self deep inside her heart, it would never break free. Freedom brought pain. Pain brought death.

"If I do not take his life, I will be finished," she said. "Yet if I do, I will diminish also."

Shadai's expression melted into compassion. Or pity. She couldn't tell which one, but she didn't care. She didn't need his sympathy. She had chosen this path for herself.

Be strong, oh woman of valour. I will pray on your behalf that you may be free. You shall surely not die.

"Can you not see it?!" she exclaimed. "Again, where are those Eyes of the Ages, the legacy of your people? If not Ninthalas, then it will be me!"

You would take a life instead of give it?

She clenched her teeth. "I already gave my life."

Shadai turned. *Farewell, child. I will see you again, and let us pray that that meeting will not prove fatal for you.*

"When will it end?"

He faced her again.

"When will my suffering end?"

When the appointed time has come. Indeed the time is coming. It is coming quickly.

"You speak as your sister. Oft did she come to me to ease my suffering while I lay naked and broken in the pit of my condemnation. Oft did she put my soul to sleep while my body was still awake. He sent her, did He not? And He has burdened me to endure this trial. Yet I curse this affliction, and may I yet curse it until the day I finally lay to rest."

Whether he heard her words or not, she couldn't tell. He had disappeared, leaving her in the middle of the bodies slain by her own hand. Was there hope left for her? Yet Yahlírin had forgotten her!

Forget that fool of a Shadai, wretch, said Ehnthatúlen. *You shall be mine forever. All that is in you will be no more and you shall become the judgment that passes through this world. Like a consuming fire you will devour A'thírin.*

Yet deep inside her spirit that inkling of hope flickered into life like a dim candle. And it whispered to her softly as a still, small voice:

You are a woman of valour,
the called and chosen of Yahl.
For though your feet tread through darkness of night,
You shall walk with My strength in light.

If only those words were true.

A knock sounded upon the door. Yosef looked up from his meal as the cleric, Míral, went to open it. On the other side was a woman of the same attire and ravishing beauty, though her hair was near black as opposed to Míral's brown.

"Thank goodness you're here," Míral said. "I need your help."

She stepped aside to let the older woman in. The High Cleric Ailene, King Levin's second wife, took one look at Yosef and turned up her nose.

"You've got to be kidding me," she said. "Do you realize what you're doing, Míral?"

Míral shuffled—she didn't walk, she shuffled—to Yosef's side and put a protective arm around him. "Come on, Ailene. Isn't he the most adorable thing you've ever seen?"

"Adorable, yes, but this is wrong," the High Cleric scoffed. "We could get in a lot of trouble for helping him."

"Yes, but it's for a good cause. He's the Faithen's adopted son. Levin's got nothing against the Faithen. Didn't he go talk to him today?"

"Talked to him and came back out just as upset as he was when he went in. And I had to forsake my cleansing because of it. You know how the kings get."

"Please, Ailene."

Míral looked up at her with hopeful eyes. Yosef swallowed a mouthful of food and mimicked the same pleading face as best he could.

Ailene stared at them long and hard. Finally, she sighed. "Oh, alright. But first he needs a bath."

Next thing Yosef knew, he was scrubbed up and dressed in clean attire, a set of Hémonian duds he had to wear while his other clothes were being washed. They were stiff, not as easy to move around in as his other clothes, but High Cleric Ailene said they would do until his traveller's garb dried.

A few times both clerics had to hide him from the High Cleric called Meldesha. When he asked why, they said it was because she was King Dellon's cleric (whatever that meant), a high-strung woman who enjoyed thwarting people's affairs—or orchestrating affairs to thwart relationships. She was an evil woman, they said, and whenever he heard her conversing with Ailene while in the safety of the wardrobe, he believed it. She spoke in a conniving tone that demanded respect.

When Meldesha or any of her associates wasn't around, Yosef was introduced to several young clerics. Word had spread quickly that the boy was in the temple, and the clerics, mostly teenaged girls, all wanted to get a glimpse of him. Giggles and whispers fluttered around him, as well as comments ranging from 'cute' to 'adorable' to 'precious', none of which he particularly liked. There were lots of pokes and jeers and pinching of cheeks which he swatted at in distaste. Eventually, they became such a nuisance that Ailene had to shoo them away so Yosef could reside in peace. They may have been pretty girls, but they sure were pesky and altogether strange.

Finally night fell and Míral announced that it was time to sneak into the prison.

"This is so exciting!" the cleric exclaimed as she and Yosef tagged along behind Ailene.

"Shush," Ailene snapped in a tone that bellied her demeanour. Wherever the High Cleric went, she walked with her head held high, perfect posture, and a sway in her hips. It was the kind of walk that caught a man's attention, if not for her beauty. That was how Míral put it at least.

The younger cleric continued to whisper anyway. "I haven't been outside the temple since I was brought here. I was only fourteen years old. Two years of cleansing and studying the way of clerics before I assumed my duties."

"What're you duties?"

"Oh, well, let's just say I live a life of service. I don't like it, mind you. I'd rather be free."

"Wouldn't we all," Ailene commented.

They plunged into the darkness of night, veiled by the shadows of trees. The night was frigid and clouds obliterated the full moon. Yosef shivered despite the thick cloak provided for him. He clutched his bag—which he had refused to give up when Ailene confiscated his clothes—as if it compensated for the cold.

When they were near the entrance to the prison, yet not near enough to be seen, Ailene pulled him close.

"Listen closely," she said in a hushed tone. "Míral and I will distract the guards for a few minutes while you sneak inside. But be quick about it, alright?"

"I'll signal you," Míral added, making a flick of her wrist.

"Are you ready?" said Ailene.

He nodded, yet his knotting insides told him otherwise.

The women wrapped veils around their faces and strode up to the steel prison door. The two guards blocked their path and spoke harsh words that both clerics brushed aside. Yosef watched as the clerics touched and petted, diverting both men's attentions and drawing them skillfully away from the door. Then, when the men were well distracted, Míral flicked her wrist for the signal. Yosef hurried over, heaved on the door and snuck inside.

Two torches blazed in the entranceway, while everything else that the light missed was cast in shadow. He took one of the torches and walked slowly down the corridor, descending, down, down into the deep, dark cave. Passageways broke off to the left and right. They all looked the same. The silence roared, yet he dared not listen to it. The cave gave him an eerie chill and the sense pricked the back of his neck like needles. He felt like he was the only one there in that prison.

That prison...

Yosef had been in this situation before. The narrow rock walls, the blackness, the smell of stale, dank air. Yes, he'd done this before, walked a cavern just like this one. Another smell caught his nose, but it was more out of memory than what he sensed in reality. This prison...had he been here before? No, he couldn't have. Yet the deeper he delved into the maze, the more he found himself walking into a horrible memory. The walls echoed with his footfalls, the passageway narrowing. Voices bounced off the walls of his mind like beating drums. One rose up above the rest, a woman's cry calling out to him, calling his name, telling him to run. Yosef knew that voice.

"Ma...?" he spoke softly.

The torch fell from his hand, landing on the ground with a loud clang. He turned to run, to heed the woman's voice who urged him on.

But he hesitated. No, he couldn't go back.

Follow this road...

The girl who'd stolen his memories. She'd told him to go on, to stay along the path until he came to the safety of the golden city. Terrified, he crouched, pulling his knees up to his chest. Pain stung his back as the memory engulfed him. His arm and leg began to throb. The two yellow eyes burned in his mind.

You are korme'him, a mountain dweller.

What was a mountain dweller? Frustration overwhelmed him. He couldn't cry. He couldn't run. He couldn't do anything, but sit there in the dark. If only he could disappear.

Yosef.

Yosef looked up. A glowing figure stood in front of him, a man with silver hair, clothed in white, his skin gleaming, illuminating the tunnel. The man looked exactly like Kai-Tsúthlen...or Ninthalas. Both looked the same to him, and this man was no different. Was he...?

"Shadai?"

The man spoke to him softly in a language Yosef didn't understand and offered his hand. Yosef took it. Immediately the fear melted. He didn't have to be afraid. He trusted this man. The silver-haired man pulled him to stand and led him down the tunnel.

Not far away, Yosef heard a faint voice echoing through the tunnel singing a soothing melody in another language. Yosef recognized the voice. He looked up at his guide.

Ninthalas thúril, the man said.

Overjoyed, Yosef ran toward the singing. He made a sharp turn left through a short neck into a chamber. The singing stopped and there he was: his father, sitting comfortably by a crackling fire.

CHAPTER THIRTY

The Temple

"Da!" Yosef cried.

Ninthalas swept the boy up in his arms, crying for joy. At last, he and his son were reunited.

"How relieved I am to see you well, my son!"

"You're not mad at me for coming here?"

"I would be, but I was expecting you."

"How? Oh! Was it the silver-haired man?" Yosef looked around, but his guide had vanished. "Where'd he go?"

Ninthalas chuckled. "He comes and goes as he pleases. He calls himself Shadai."

"I know. I was there when he appeared to your family, remember?"

"Ah yes, I do remember now. I call him Timeless Shadai, for he is very old."

"He doesn't look old. He looks just like you."

"Is that so? I thought he looked more like Kai-Tsúthlen."

"You both look exactly the same!"

Ninthalas laughed. It truly was comforting to have his son by his side once more. How he had missed him.

"Now tell me, my son. How did you come into the City?"

Yosef told him about the horse fight, Bellim's idea to send him and Fehnan to Serenestí, and how they instead smuggled into the City. "Fehnan was arrested. Did you see him?"

"I did. They took him to the lower quarters. I thought to

intervene, but…well, you know how unaccustomed I am to fighting. I certainly hope they have not brought him to harm. Speaking of prisons, how did you manage to get in? The front door is guarded by two sentries."

"I found a temple and some lady women helped me get in here."

Right on cue, two women turned the corner into the chamber. Ninthalas stood. He had seen several pretty women in his life, but never the likes of these. He recognized one of them as the woman who had sat at King Levin's feet on Hémon's Day. Judging by the new face, there must be others in the king's service. Mind, the definition of 'service' might not be what he would consider proper.

He bowed low, a gesture that got odd looks from them.

"I imagine you are the ones who aided my son," he said. "My deepest gratitude to you for bringing him to me."

One of the girls giggled. The other held her head high, indifferent. She reminded Ninthalas of Meldesha, erect and confident.

"You are far more attractive without your disguise," said the older one. She looked him up and down as if in approval of his figure. "Even though you're foreign."

"I can say nothing of my features since no woman has told me such. Come, sit and speak with me. How can I repay the kindness you have shown me?"

"I can name a way," said the younger one.

Ninthalas went rigid. "You mean to lay with me? I have heard of the atrocities of the temple, and I tell you I will not adhere to them."

"Too bad," said the younger cleric. "He's a charmer. Not like those disgusting noblemen."

"Do you mean to tell me you enjoy such transgressions?"

"Transgressions?" the older one scoffed.

"That means breaking the rules," Yosef translated. "True Faithens have lots of rules. That's why they're perfect."

"In a manner of speaking," said Ninthalas. "We have laws to protect our hearts and bodies so that we may use them to serve our God."

"Doesn't concern us. What's your name, Faithen?" the older

lady asked.

"Ninthalas Líran Shadai, my lady. What is yours and that of your associate?"

"Ailene," she said.

"Míral," said the other.

Yosef cut in. "Da, these cleric ladies gave me dinner. A very *good* dinner!"

"Did they now?" Ninthalas mused, looking the two over and stroking his chin as if he had a beard. "Ailene and Míral. Those are splendid names, elegant but strong if I knew Hémon names well. Well, I may have to refuse your passions, but I can tell a tale or two that might interest you. I imagine you two have not ventured beyond the wall, have you?"

"Oh yes, please!" Míral said.

Ailene shot her a stern look that made her fluster. "We have to get back to the temple."

"Oh, please, Ailene! I've been cooped up in the temple so many years, I've forgotten what it's like to be outside. We can't leave the temple like you high clerics can."

"High Cleric," Ninthalas said. "So you are like Meldesha?"

"Don't compare me to that witch!" Ailene spat. Then, more softly, "Sorry. I just...I *hate* that woman."

"I will not condemn you," said Ninthalas. "Come, sit. Tell me what you know, and I will tell you stories you could only dream of knowing."

They did. Ninthalas enthralled them with his tales, captivated them with his words. The women would have listened forever had Ninthalas not cut himself off in the middle of a story.

"What is it?" Míral asked.

He held up a hand and listened. A sound caught his ears, the sound of heavy breathing.

"Stay here," he said

They nodded as he cautiously crept to the entrance of the cavern.

"Fehnan!" he exclaimed.

"Fehnan?" Yosef repeated, running to the entrance.

The teen was injured. Blood gushed from his shoulder. He collapsed to the ground, exhausted.

Ninthalas ran to his side.

"Fehnan Farthorn! Fehnan, what happened?"

The teen was in some kind of trance. He stared straight ahead, eyes glazed over as if caught in the horror of a nightmare.

"Don't kill me," he whispered. "Please. Please don't kill me."

"What devilry is this?" said Ninthalas.

"What's wrong with him, da?" Yosef asked. "Why's he acting like that?"

Ninthalas peeled away the torn fabric. The blood came thick, but he could detect charred skin underneath. The wound was like the one the fated messenger had suffered.

"Of all things distraught!" he cursed. "High Cleric Ailene! Míral!"

The clerics rushed to the scene and gasped.

"If you are willing, I need your help again," he told them. "You must get us out of here. Take us to the temple where I may properly treat this boy's wounds."

"The temple? We couldn't," said Ailene.

"The women are in cleansing," Míral added. "No men are permitted in—"

"It will make a better hiding place. The kings will not think to find me there, will they? Listen to me, dear clerics. There is more being wrought here than you can ever imagine, and I need your help."

Míral looked at Ailene with hopeful eyes.

"Alright," the High Cleric relented.

"Good." He turned to Yosef. "Yosef, grab my bag. It is over by the fire. And call for the boy named Eera. He must come with us."

"Eera?"

"Yes, Yosef. There is a tale I must tell you, one I think you will enjoy hearing. Let us make haste!"

At the temple, Ninthalas made a list of materials for Ailene to get him since his medical kit was still at Bellim Farthorn's house. Luckily, she returned with every one of the items or its equivalent and he immediately got to work treating the wound. And what a troublesome wound it was! He had heard of such an injury before, but he never imagined it to be so difficult to treat. A warning in his heart told him not to touch it. With the way it devoured most of the ointment he had conjured, he feared it might do the same to his skin. The best he could do was clean and wrap it using cloths Ailene provided him.

"I've never seen a wound like that," the High Cleric said. She and Míral stood idly by his side. "Mind you, I have seen very few in my life."

"*Maldna'goj,*" Eera said.

"*Bai! Malthna'kosh ka?*"

"What did he say, da?"

"That this is a *malthna* wound. *Malthna* means 'of hell' or 'demonic'. Wounds like these plagued the victims of the War of the First Age, and now they have returned to devour the living of the present. I do not know much more of them except that they are terribly difficult to cure."

When he had finished bandaging Fehnan's shoulder, he opened his Fehlthan to the section of psalms called the Songs of Healing. Whether or not the psalms actually healed a victim was up to question, but there was no doubt that singing eased the pain of the patient. Fehnan murmured the same inarticulate words of 'Don't kill me' and 'Please, don't kill me'. Despite Ninthalas' singing, the teen's mental condition didn't get any better.

He felt a tug on his sleeve.

"Yes, my son, what is it?"

"I'm hungry," said Yosef.

"Again?" Ailene exclaimed. "You just ate?"

"I imagine Eera is famished as well."

"I can get them something," Míral offered.

"That would be kind of you."

The cleric led Yosef and Eera away, leaving only Ailene, Ninthalas and Fehnan in the room. Had it not been the High Cleric's bed chamber, Ninthalas might have requested her to go as well. Yet surprisingly he felt the most comfortable around her. The way she carried herself almost reminded him of his mother. Almost.

"It's hard, isn't it?" she said.

He caught himself staring at her. "What do you mean?"

"The passion. It takes over you. Don't try to deny you feel

something when you look at us."

Well that shattered the similarities between the cleric and his mother.

"Do not be absurd! Those maidens are indeed lovely, yet I am a devout man. You cannot possibly understand my commitment to my God."

"I highly doubt that. I know a man's heart."

"You know a man's body. Keep in mind, cleric, that I am no ordinary man and I do not come from a promiscuous culture."

She didn't argue. Instead, she went to sit on the bed and stroked the teen's cheek.

"I'll tell you a secret," she said.

Ninthalas raised his eyebrows. "You will share your secrets with me?"

"You seem the trustworthy type."

"That I am, though I do not say it to boast."

She smiled at him. Perhaps he had misjudged her. Perhaps a woman lived underneath that mask and she hid much from the world.

"I always wanted to have children," she said.

"You have none?"

"None of us do. Except Amelí, that lucky girl. Don't know how *that* happened. And she's had two."

"How are you barren?"

"It's a terrible operation when we're admitted to the temple."

"I am sorry."

"Don't be. It's just the way things are. You get taken here and they rip open your…Well, I'll spare you the details."

She must have noticed him grimace. There were some things about a woman Ninthalas would never like to know, dreadful surgeries included. It must be a terrible thing to be assigned as a cleric. A life dependent on submission. That was no way to live, nor to treat a woman.

"You have a king for a husband," he offered, trying to see the bright side of her situation.

"Don't let his status fool you. Levin's a harsh king. They all are. Kind enough to men, maybe, but to women? Do you know that the kings and the highest of nobles are the only ones allowed to spoil themselves at this temple? But the High Clerics, they belong to the kings only. I'm Levin's."

"Yet by marriage."

"By decree. Technically, it's not a marriage contract. Just a verbal statement that says, 'Back off! She's mine!' It's illegal for everyone else, but the kings can do whatever they want. Amon did. Actually took that Amelí for himself right under the others' noses. I'm just happy I ended up with Levin and not Morin or Dellon. I've seen what they've done to Meldesha. Evil woman, but I do feel sorry for her."

There was such bitterness in her tone. Ninthalas had no idea such a promiscuous woman could be someone outside of what she was. For him, who you were reflected how you presented yourself to others. No lies. It was as Fehnan had said: Ninthalas could go wherever he wanted and people knew who he was and what he believed. It was the exact opposite in Hémon.

His eyes wandered across the room, and by chance he spotted a lyre sitting on a stand. He smiled. Yahlirin truly did bless him.

"What?"

He went over and picked up the instrument.

"Do you play this?"

"I'm terrible at it. It's more for decoration."

He returned to his seat. "Well, since we are both ill at ease, allow me to bless you with a merry song."

He began tuning the strings.

"You're kidding."

"I am not. When was the last time a man—" He held up a hand. "Though one to remain pure. Has anyone ever serenaded you?"

"Oh, please. You wouldn't."

"Indeed, I would and I shall."

He strummed the strings and began to sing in Common words that he made up off the top of his head.

> *Blessed me, High Cleric I see,*
> *You've been bound to the man in green,*
> *Yet he hurts you, hits you and you submit,*
> *To that man you call a git.*
> *But sweet lady Ailene*
> *Cleric of the man in green,*

You're meant for much more, more than this
For I'll bring you away
I'll bring you away
I'll carry you off to bliss.

Ailene first smiled, then broke into laughter. "Bliss? You'd give me bliss? I thought you were a devout man."
Ninthalas went on:

No, not bliss as his bliss,
That man you call git,
For he troubled you, hurt you and you subsided.
Oh, that in him you confided!
No, heed me now,
For here I vow
I solemnly swear in the pit of my breast
To carry you off
To carry you off
To bear you away...

He stopped singing, but kept on playing the lyre. "I cannot find a word to rhyme with 'breast,'" he said.
"Chest," Ailene offered, still laughing. "It rhymes with chest."
"Ah, yes!" he exclaimed.

To bear you away by the beat of my chest!

"What an atrocity that line is," he noted, and she laughed all the more.
"You really know how to woo a girl."
"Indeed, I have heard that many times, High Cleric Ailene," he said. Then his key turned minor and he changed the rhyme:

Indeed have I heard it often said
That I am a man of elegance,
For I bask in a woman's trade
Much to my people's dismay
And struggle to find acceptance.

Yet my dear Ailene, I too have a secret,
One that you may jest to hear.
For I once serenaded
A blessed, fair maiden,
A woman whom I thought fair.

"You were in love once?" she asked.

Oh love, that I loved,
I was but thirteen,
Thirteen, 'tis young I know!

"It's at thirteen that the boys are allowed to go to the temple."

"That is unfortunate."

"You would think that, wouldn't you?"

They were interrupted by the door flying open. In paraded Yosef, Eera close behind.

"Da!" Yosef exclaimed.

Ninthalas held a finger to his lips. "Speak softer, my son, lest you disturb Fehnan."

"Sorry," he whispered.

Ailene rose. "I'll leave you and your son alone," she said. At the doorway, she paused and added, "Thanks for the song."

Meanwhile, Yosef bounded over to his father.

"Da, what did you call the fish thinger?" the boy asked.

Ninthalas shook his head. He was still lingering on the song and laughter.

"Ah, yes," he said. "He is an Other."

"How do you say that in True Faithen?"

"*Nethi'ním.*"

"*Men'al Ndaljú dúr,*" Eera corrected.

"Yes, *Ndaljú*," said Ninthalas in Common so Yosef could understand. "That is what they call themselves. I do not know much about them, though I do know they are in as much danger here as we are."

At the word 'danger', Yosef went quiet and listened. Ninthalas guessed he was tapping into that gift of his. What a remarkable gift it was, too. Ninthalas almost wished he had it, to know *Emkalaf'Morlúrnan*'s whereabouts.

"She's in the prison, and the other malshorth, too," said Yosef. "I am glad we left. Can you sense anything else?"

"No. There's too many distractions. The silence was louder when I was sitting with Fehnan. But don't worry. I brought this just in case she finds us."

He reached into his bag and pulled out the dagger.

"*Aran*? Is that my knife?" Ninthalas said. "Why did you take it? You should have left it where it was with my other weapons."

Yosef's chin dropped sheepishly. "I thought you would need it," he said. "You said it was dangerous here, so I brought it."

Ninthalas took it from him and unsheathed it halfway, staring at the design with the words etched in the blade.

He sighed. "Think nothing of it, Yosef. You acted well, misguided though it was. This knife is not for fighting, if you could tell by the hilt. I had it made to remember."

"Remember what?"

Ninthalas hesitated. Should he tell his son the truth? Should he reveal the ache from long ago that had lain dormant in his heart? Those years, though behind him, began to gnaw at his soul, and he wondered why they had been unearthed after so long. Perhaps it was because of the song.

"The inscription here…says *onen'menan*," he said at length.

"*Onen'menan*? What does that mean?"

"It means 'only one' or 'dearest one' in True Faithen. A man would say it to the one he loved, his wife. Someday I may tell you why I carry this trinket, but for now, let us leave it to rest. And rest we must, for tomorrow shall prove a strenuous day."

"Why's that?"

"I am forming a plan to escape. Yet first, I must rid this City of the atrocity it has wrought upon the innocent. I must free Eera's people."

CHAPTER THIRTY-ONE

The Escape Plan

"Good lady Ailene."

Ninthalas had just finished breakfast with a handful of clerics and Yosef and Eera. What a meal it had been, and not in the way of enjoying meals. Aside from the bacon, he managed to consume an assortment of fruit and eggs. This, however, was not the reason for his unease. They had been served a platter of "fish", which Ninthalas could not be certain was the kind of fish he ate on normal occasions. Even Eera had a distaste for being offered a dish that could potentially be his own kind. The entire affair had been partaken in awkward silence and utter disgust as the clerics ate the aquatic meat. Ninthalas hadn't had the heart to tell them what it was, or could be.

He had caught Ailene halfway to her bedroom. The High Cleric had dismissed herself early. This was Ninthalas' chance to confront her about his plan. Since it was too much of a risk to venture out of the temple himself, Ailene could execute a portion of his plan. Hopefully his song the previous night had allowed her to drop a few walls.

"I need you to deliver a message for me."

"Another request?" the High Cleric exclaimed. "Is that why you sang to me last night?"

That wasn't exactly the response he was expecting.

"My apologies. You are the only one I can trust who is able to leave this temple, and you can enter the throne room with ease."

He paused, then added, "Unless of course you would permit me to ask High Cleric Meldesha."

"Only when Levin's there."

"Sorry?"

She rolled her eyes. "I can only enter the throne room when Levin is there. If he isn't, the guards don't let me in."

"Where is he?"

"Here."

"Here?"

"Where do you think I was last night? Not in my bed chamber, that's for sure."

That was awkward. She was a little too honest for his liking.

"I need you to deliver a message to King Amon though."

"Why him?"

"Because he is the only sensible one of the four."

She sighed. "I can't."

"Why not?"

"I can only visit Levin. I'm his cleric, remember? I can't just inquire of another king that hasn't claimed me."

Ninthalas bowed low. "Please, lady Ailene. My message must get to King Amon in all urgency."

She frowned at him for a long while before answering. "Oh fine. But I'm only doing this because you made me laugh last night. What's the message?"

"I need Amon to prepare a shipment of exports, barrels of water, nothing in them, to be shipped out on the morrow."

"On the morrow?"

"I mean tomorrow."

"Right. And what's it for?"

"Fish."

"Wait, what?"

"Just tell him that. If he needs clarification, he can speak to me directly. You may bring him to me if you need to."

Ailene shook her head. "Fine, fine. A letter would've sufficed."

"I do not know Hémon script."

She gave him an odd look. "Really. Well, if I hurry, Levin might not miss me. I'm his new favourite now that Karvene's gone."

Ninthalas cringed. Did she enjoy making him uncomfortable? He didn't bother to ask. Instead, he took the opportunity to go bathe and have his clothes washed. Yosef and Eera joined him in a humorous affair that consisted of splashing and giggling, hardly what Ninthalas considered relaxing. He was much more pleased to be finished and let the boys go off gallivanting in the many hallways of the temple. The clerics would entertain them, modestly he hoped.

That should have given Ninthalas some peace and quiet to think his plan through. But with Fehnan in the same room, muttering incoherent phrases, he was easily distracted. The teen's condition had worsened overnight and the gash sweltered into a hideous, blackening infection. Ninthalas feared for Fehnan's life. His own skills in medicine didn't suffice for such an injury. Unless the boy could be brought to Serenestí to receive proper treatment, he would probably die.

But he had a plan, and he couldn't back down, no matter his fear of the Black Assailant's pursuit.

"Don't kill me…please," Fehnan muttered.

Ninthalas felt his forehead. High fever. His plan may be elaborate and well-meant, but the odds were stacked against him.

"Come now, Fehnan Farthorn. You must pull through."

He clapped his hands in front of his face, tilted his head towards the heavens and prayed.

"Yahlírin above, please heal this boy. Bring him back to us. I beg of you, do not let him die."

He sang from the psalms and played the lyre to no avail. Fehnan showed no signs of improvement.

Eventually, Ailene returned. Her stern mask was on, proud and resolute.

"Well, how did you fair?" Ninthalas asked.

His eyes widened when he saw two men come in behind her. It wasn't just King Amon, but Bellim Farthorn as well. The trades captain took one look at his son and let out a sharp cry. He ran to the bedside.

"Fehnan!" he exclaimed. "Son, wake up!"

When the teen didn't respond, Bellim sunk to his knees, struggling to hold back tears.

"I must go check on Levin," Ailene announced and left the

men alone.

"Did she do this?" Amon asked Ninthalas, nodding toward the teen. "That Black Assailant?"

"I believe so."

"Why...? How?" Bellim cried. "What's wrong with him?"

"He has suffered the affliction of an evil weapon," Ninthalas explained. "Only the healing expertise of a True Faithen medic can save him now."

"You can't?"

"I have not the skill. True, I have some knowledge, but this wound requires the work of an expert."

"How long does he have?"

"I would say a week at most."

Amon cut in. "Will he make it in time?"

"I am not sure," Ninthalas replied. "I do have some healing herbs in my packs at Bellim's house. They would help."

Bellim nodded. "I can get them to you—"

"Why should we help him, Farthorn? Look what this man did."

"He didn't do anything and you know it, Amon."

"Levin's wife and a handful of clerics are gone, and now that drat *Emkala*-whatever-her-name-is nearly killed your son."

"I trust Shadai!" Bellim yelled, rising to his feet. "You don't know the holy people, Amon. They're not double crossers like us. I *had* to help him. He's a holy man!|"

Amon fumed. "So it was you're idea to bring him here! I've kept your secret safe for years and this is what I get? A Faithen lover who risked his country's safety?"

"It was for Hémon's good. We knew this was coming anyway. The last News Bearer told us Shadai would come and that he'd bring change. But you kings didn't believe him. Now look what's happened!"

"My lords, please, calm yourselves," Ninthalas interjected. "This is no time for accusations. What is done is done. What we must do now is find a solution to this problem and I have found one: Yosef and I must escape from the City. If we leave, *Emkalaf'Morlúrnan* will follow."

"Fine by me," Amon stated, crossing his arms. "But what's with the barrels of water?"

"I am bringing those whom you have captured along with me, the ones who call themselves *Ndaljú*."

"What are those?"

"Does it matter?" said Bellim. "The sooner we get out of here, the better. My son's life is at stake here."

"You may be Captain of Trade, but I'm the king of trade," said Amon. "Everything you do, I oversee."

"Must it be so?" asked Ninthalas. "It seems to me that the king is indifferent on the matter. So if it pleases the king, let my friend Bellim and I conspire without him."

"I make a habit of knowing what's going on."

"Yet for what purpose? I cannot understand you, my lord Amon, for you led me on a quest, then permitted me to free myself. Now you wish to know of my plans only to shut them down. What is your trial that you should act this way towards me? Have I done you wrong?"

"You wouldn't understand..."

"Then perhaps you should aid us."

"Don't flatter yourself!" He spun on his heals and made for the door. "You fools do what you want. I want no part in it."

He stormed out of the room.

"Don't think I've ever seen him cross," Bellim said once the king had left. "He's usually more calm, calculating. He'll soak up details before acting. But recently, he's been gathering knowledge and then cutting out."

"He is stressed, I should imagine. I wonder...no, it is not possible. I will say that he contradicts himself often."

"Something's eating him."

Ninthalas frowned.

"I mean bothering him. Something's bothering him."

"Ah, right. Of course."

"So what's the plan?"

"I thought you were the one with the brilliant ideas," Ninthalas said with a slight grin.

"Funny, kid. I wanna know what kind o' fish you're hauling."

"Oh, you would be surprised, I assure you. Let us take a tally tonight. Though we will have to evade the prison guards somehow."

"That can be arranged."

"Good. I will see you outside the prison then. Bring my packs and weapons when you return so I can tend to Fehnan properly."

"Fair that."

The trades captain knelt down and kissed Fehnan's brow, then left the room.

Ninthalas was about to check the teen's wound when Ailene entered.

"I thought you were tending to your master," he said.

"I lied. I was listening. I knew Amon wouldn't want me there. You're leaving?"

"Indeed, I am. My errand takes me to far off places, so I cannot stay in one city too long."

Her face was the same high-strung mask she always wore, yet Ninthalas could see a hint of sorrow in her eyes. He wanted to bring out the real Ailene somehow, to free her so she wouldn't have to hide behind the mask.

"If it is not too overbearing for me to ask—"

"What now?" she demanded, glaring at him.

"You can choose whether or not to accept."

She hesitated before answering. "Alright. Let's have it."

In a gesture that made her blush, he took her hands in his own and looked deep into her coal-coloured eyes. "Come with me."

"Wh—what? You cannot be serious!"

"I *am* serious. I want you to come and see new sights, to experience new things. You would not have to hide behind that mask with your nose turned high."

"I couldn't possibly!"

"Yosef and I must take a different path anyway. We are not returning to Serenestí, but must continue our journey to the far west. I need someone to accompany Fehnan to my home country. You could go with him."

"I...I don't know."

"You can find a life outside of this cage," Ninthalas went on. "I want to give that to you. You may adopt children of your own, find a husband who treats you well. You said yourself that the king only owns you by decree."

"True, it's just spoken word, but—well, I don't know. I just...I've never been outside Hémon."

"Think about it. We do not leave until tomorrow. That is

plenty of time to decide."

Just then, they heard a groan. Fehnan's eyes flickered open.

"Fehnan!" Ninthalas exclaimed.

He and Ailene rushed to the bed.

"Shadai?"Fehnan muttered. He squinted, eyes focussing. "Shadai? Is that you?"

"'Tis me, dear boy."

"Where am I?"

Ailene replied. "In the centre temple."

"Where? Who?"

"I'm High Cleric Ailene," she said. She glanced at Ninthalas.

"Ailene helped Yosef and I bring you to the temple," the True Faithen explained. "I took it upon myself to dress your shoulder, but I require more specialized ointments. Your father has gone to retrieve them for me. He was just here not long ago."

"My pops. In a temple," said Fehnan, chuckling a little. "What'd he say when he saw me?"

"He was worried as a father should be for his son," Ninthalas replied. He placed a hand on the teen's forehead. "I am quite relieved you are awake, my friend."

Fehnan stared at him a while, then his eyes widened.

Fear.

"Shadai, the Black Assailant..."

"Yes, I know. She attacked you, did she not?"

"How did Yosef survive when she kidnapped him? That woman's evil! And if she can get into the prison..."

"Do not worry, Fehnan. We will evade her."

Fehnan shook his head. "No way. The hatred in her eyes? Wanted to kill, no question. We heard wailing before she got to us. Soldiers thought it was just the torture machines at work."

Ninthalas stroked his chin"If she attacked you, then she could also attack...*great travesty abound!*"

"What is it?" Ailene asked.

"The *Nethi'ním*! I must hurry!"

Too late. When Ninthalas went to the prison, he found floating bodies in the pools of the prison's first level. Every one of them was *Ndaljú*, every one slain by *Emkalaf'Morlúrnan*'s hand. Ninthalas fell to his knees and wept. What would he tell Eera?

He felt a hand gently touch his shoulder. He didn't have to turn around to know who it was. The peace offered to enter his soul, but Ninthalas wasn't sure he wanted to let it in. Let him relish in his despair. No comfort could aid him.

I am sorry, brother Líran. I did not anticipate this, nor did I have the power to stop it.

"Who is she? What does she want with me and Yosef? And why does she want me dead? I do not understand. It is as if she knows me..." He trailed off.

Indeed, it would seem so, Shadai agreed.

"Yet I have not known anyone of such evil, nor have I wished to encounter a malshorth. Why does Yahlírin burden me with this sorrow? Have I done wrong?"

Do you suppose it is because you have done wrong or that you are a man whose faithfulness is proven through fire?

Ninthalas didn't know how to respond. He remained silent, soaking up the grief he felt for those he had wanted to save. "I do not like this uncertainty and these sudden mishaps. It is as it was back then. If only I could see what is to come."

Yet if you knew the future, would you still rely on your trust in Yahlírin? Shadai asked.

"At least I would know enough to save lives."

You cannot save everyone, brother Líran. Some die and others simply do not wish to be saved. I learned that long ago.

A tremor rattled the ground. Ninthalas stood and squinted, peering into the dark tunnel. "That rumbling again. It follows me wherever I go, and yet I do not know what causes it."

No? Did I not tell you who accompanies Emkalaf'Morlúrnan?

"It is Dethshaiken."

Indeed. He lurks near the Death Chamber. Never go there again, brother Líran, or you may very well meet your end.

"Does he seek to kill me as well?"

No, that is Emkalaf'Morlúrnan's task. The giant is here to see that it is done. Yet let us pray you do not come to die by his sword either. Should both strike at once, I will not be able to save you.

"What must I do?"

You already know what to do.

Of course. He had to get out of the City.

The time to go came later than Ninthalas would have liked. He fidgeted all day, wondering if the Black Assailant would find out his location and murder him. He had hardly slept, and when he did, he dreamed of the Death Chamber. Amon was there. The king dropped dead from the swiftness of a blade. The sword hovered, dripping blood, held by a hand whose white skin was paler than death itself. Ninthalas couldn't see anything of her features. Her body was a void shrouded in shadow except for two piercing yellow eyes. Ninthalas trembled before her as she chanted: *Run, run, Líran Shadai...*

Even in his waking moments, the chant echoed clearly in his mind.

"Are you alright, da?" Yosef asked, putting a gentle hand on his knee.

"I am ill at ease," was all he could say. He could not even bring himself to play the lyre.

At one point during the day, Ailene asked him the same thing. "You look dreadful," she added.

"I will be fine," he replied.

"Ninthalas."

He looked up at her. That was the first time she had used his first name.

"I've thought about what you said yesterday. About coming with you."

"And?"

"I've decided to stay here."

"...Very well."

"I'm sorry."

"No, it is I who should apologize. It was too much to ask of you when I do not even know you well."

She reached forward and pulled him into an embrace.

"Promise me you will come back," she said, her voice high and emotional. "Please?"

He wrapped his arms around her. "Of course, my friend."

As suddenly as she had embraced him, she let go and went

away.

When Bellim came that evening, he brought one carriage with a cloth tarp covering. Inside were a couple of crates, several blankets and fluffy pillows and one barrel of water. That was it. Ninthalas had shown him the bodies of Ndaljú the previous night.

"Much easier to save one," Bellim muttered.

Ninthalas couldn't tell if the trades captain felt any remorse or not.

Bellim picked Fehnan up in his strong arms and carried him out. All the while, Fehnan declared he had strength enough to walk. The teen was doing much better since Ninthalas had used his own ointments to dress the *malthna* wound.

"Shut your trapper, boy!" Bellim barked at him. "You ain't doing nothing but sit put 'til you get home."

Ninthalas and Yosef grinned at each other. As they walked behind the bickering duo, they bid farewell to the clerics. Poor Míral was in tears. Ailene stood at the door, her eyes downcast. She glanced once at Ninthalas, then let her gaze fall again. Yosef ran over and surprised her with a hug. She in turn wrapped her arms around him.

"Goodbye, miss Ailene," he said.

"Goodbye, Yosef."

He gave Míral a hug as well and then joined Ninthalas out the door. Bellim veered to the back of the carriage and opened the flap of the tarp covering. After setting Fehnan up in a nest of blankets and pillows from his own house, he jumped into the front. A hitched horse waited patiently to depart.

"Up into the back," he said. "The fish fellow can jump into that half full barrel there. Let's hope he has enough sense to not splash about. As for you two, keep hidden in the supplies. I have to keep the flap open to avoid suspicion. We shouldn't have too much trouble getting out, but best be wary."

The escapees obeyed and climbed up, taking residence among crates blanketed by brown sheets. Then they were off, bumping along down the road.

Bellim was right about having no trouble leaving the City. Ninthalas found it both surprising and disturbing. But then again, Bellim was a high-ranking officer. The guards saw him come and go frequently and answered him when he gave orders. They didn't even question him as they passed through the gate.

The carriage rolled down the road to the Farthorn dwelling and for the second time, Bellim welcomed the company into his home. After a late dinner, they showed Eera to the river, free to follow its long winding path south. Then everyone retired to their own beds and drifted off to sleep.

Everyone except Ninthalas. A tingling sensation of unease crept up his spine. Amon was on his mind. The king's his words and actions had been so irregular. Ninthalas wouldn't have thought too much about it had he not had a dream about the king. Was a prophecy like the dream he had of Luthrey? But that one he had had for several nights before warning the city of the malshorthath raid. This one had only occurred once.

Perhaps he shouldn't worry about it. Hémon was behind him now. When sleep finally pulled him under, he heard the voice of silver-haired man speak into the last bit of his waking consciousness.

He substituted himself for you, brother Líran.

Sleep prevented him from mulling those words over.

———◉———

CHAPTER THIRTY-TWO

To The King!

"Ninthalas!"

Ninthalas woke with a start. Sunlight streamed through the window, indicating it was already late morning. His dream had been the same as the night before, Amon on his knees as *Emkalaf'Morlúrnan* hovered over him. The dream vanished when he heard his name, drawing him back to the wakeful world. Yet he still remembered it. He could play it out vividly in his mind.

A firm hand shook him and he shot up with a start. Drowsiness still clung to his eyelids and he rubbed them to shake the last signs of sleep.

"Wake up, Faithen!"

That certainly wasn't Bellim Farthorn. When he could focus properly, Ninthalas was surprised to see Fehnan hovering over him. The strain of his wound showed in his eyes, but otherwise the teen appeared to be in a chipper mood. Quite the contrast compared to the previous night.

"Fehnan? What are you doing up and so well?"

Perhaps the ointments he'd dressed the teen's wound with had proven more helpful than he'd initially thought.

"Where is Yosef?" he added.

"Outside. We've found something. Come quick!"

Ninthalas swung his legs over the side of the bed and got up. He didn't bother with day clothes. He had to keep up with Fehnan who was already at the doorway and making for the stairs. When

369

he had stumbled down and outside, he spotted Yosef standing by the riverbank. Ninthalas hurried over. There by the water was Bellim and Eera and…

Ninthalas gasped.

"It's Mallon," said Bellim gravely. His eyes were swelling and red. "Looks like he's been dead for a while."

Ninthalas hopped down to the sandy bank where Bellim held his friend in his arms. Mallon's skin was light and water-logged, the flesh having been fed on in places by whatever creatures traversed the river. Yet a careful examination revealed something else.

"His shirt is torn." He spread apart the wet fabric, revealing a gaping hole in his chest. "This is no wound from an animal of the river. Mallon was killed by the sword."

"But who would have killed him?" Fehnan asked. "The guards?"

"No, son," said Bellim. "And what the mad rambles're you doing outside? Get back to bed and rest!"

Fehnan grumbled but reluctantly obeyed.

"Silly lad."

"He is doing remarkably well considering his injury. Yet now this has happened, and I fear it is my fault. The last I saw of friend Mallon was when I was arrested."

Bellim clasped his shoulder. "Don't blame yourself. Neither of us coulda known this was going to happen."

"You say that, but I know a part of you is dying within."

Bellim breathed in deep. "We converts know the risk of helping a Faithen. I've known people who've been killed for their faith. Family even."

"First Mallon, then the *Ndaljú*…Great travesty abound!"

"What?"

"The dream!" Ninthalas exclaimed. "*Emkalaf'Morlúrnan!* She aims to kill the king!"

"How do you know?" Bellim asked.

"Why else would his actions be so unconventional? At last, I finally see it! She threatened him to lock me in the Death Chamber. I am sure of it!"

"You can't just come to that conclusion."

"No, Bellim, it all makes sense now. Women and children

were kidnapped in the south. Levin told me that his wife was taken. Amon's must have been as well. I was warned to stay clear of the Death Chamber. Alas, for the king's life is in peril! I must help him!"

"Are you mad? You just escaped!" Bellim exclaimed. "We don't even know if you're right."

"Would I lie to you?"

Bellim opened his mouth to speak, but clamped it shut again. Ninthalas offered his hand. "Come with me."

"What?"

"You know the king better than I."

Bellim looked down at his fallen comrade. At length, he answered. "Fair that. But let me bury my friend first."

"Of course."

Ninthalas sprang up the bank.

"Come, Yosef."

The boy followed him back to the house.

"What do we do now?"

Ninthalas didn't answer. He had an idea, and his son would be able to help.

"Da?"

"Come."

They ascended the stairs and went to the bedroom. Ninthalas knelt down and put his hands on Yosef's shoulders.

"I need you to use the gift for me."

"Why?"

"Please, you must do this. Tell me where the Black Assailant is."

Yosef nodded, sitting down. Ninthalas dressed while he waited. What a truly remarkable ability the boy had. Where did it come from? His father? His curiosity flooded his mind as he began to imagine how big Yosef's father was, who his people were and where he could have come from. The Common world was just that. Common. There were regions unknown to Ninthalas, places he could only dream of exploring.

Yosef opened his eyes just as he finished dressing. That was quick. How often did the boy use his gift?

"Did you sense her?"

"She's in the prison place under the mountain," he said. "The big malshorth's outside the City."

"Close to us?"

"No, the other side."

Ninthalas considered for a moment. He couldn't face Dethshaiken. But with Bellim, he may be able to engage the Black Assailant. And if he could enlist the help of Levin…

"Listen carefully, Yosef. I need you to do two things for me. You must stay with Fehnan at all costs and know the locations of the malshorthath at all times. Do you understand me?"

"Wait, are you going back?"

"I must. But do not worry! I am taking Bellim with me and I will seek the aid of Hémon's kings."

"But da, she's too good for them. She's too good for you. If you go, you'll die!"

"Do you remember what I taught you before I entered the City?"

Yosef's gaze dropped to his feet. "That Yahlírin will protect us?"

"And did he protect us, even while we were in Hémon?"

Yosef nodded. "You said to never stop praying. But I don't know how to pray."

"Then let me show you the True Faithen way. Put your hands together and turn your face to the heavens. Now repeat after me. Divine Creator of the heavens…"

"Divine Creator of the heavens."

"Who is our Father."

"Who is our Father—He's a father?"

"Yes, He is. Now say 'you love us beyond imagination'."

"And you love us a lot."

"Please, protect us in the danger that is before us."

Yosef fumbled through that part and added, "and bring my da back to me because I love him and I don't wanta be alone ever. And make the Black Assailant a good lady, not a bad one. Make her stop hurting people."

Ninthalas took his son's hands in his own.

"Be strong, my son. I will return to you. That I promise."

He kissed Yosef's forehead, retrieved his weaponry and disappeared through the door.

Bellim was waiting for him outside. The trades captain had a sword strapped to his side and a large shield slung over his shoulder.

"Hope you're ready for some fightin'," he said.

Ninthalas just nodded. He really wasn't. A lump grew in his gut. His palms were sweaty. This was a moment he'd anticipated and a part of him loathed it. Now he would find out the truth: who the Black Assailant was and why she wanted him dead.

They marched to the front gate. Bellim roughly grabbed Ninthalas, unsheathed his sword and held the blade to his back. Ninthalas didn't struggle. This was a ploy to get them into the City.

"Open up!" the trades captain ordered.

"Yes, sir. Of course, sir," the sentries replied.

The gate creaked open. Bellim pushed Ninthalas through, receiving peculiar looks along the way from his subordinates. Once inside, Bellim waved down a carriage. Surprisingly, the driver happened to be the same teen who'd driven Ninthalas to the Hall of the Four Lords a few days ago.

"Five coppers," the boy demanded.

"Three if you know what's good for you, and I'll pay you when I get there. Now get moving!"

"No money's—"

"What'd I tell you?"

The teen cowered under Bellim's booming voice. He nodded and jumped in the driver's seat while Ninthalas and Bellim went inside. Soon, they were speeding to Mount Hémon and arrived at high sun.

Ninthalas and Bellim burst out of the carriage and ran to the front doors.

"My money, sir!" the teen called, but Bellim paid him no mind.

Ninthalas would have said something, but they were in a hurry. He'd inquire Bellim to pay the charges later.

They marched right up to the throne room sentries. The soldiers didn't give them so much as a nod. They simply opened the doors.

Inside, Morin, Dellon and Levin sat upon their thrones, their clerics at their sides. A handful of messengers stood at their beck and call. A scribe scribbled furiously on parchment. Soldiers lined the walls. Richly clad nobles stood in the monarchs' audience. All stopped what they were doing to see the visitors and every one of them gaped.

"Where is King Amon?" Ninthalas demanded.

"What is this?" declared Morin, rising from his throne. "How did you escape?"

"I have not the time for questions, oh king. Tell me where I can find my lord Amon. The king's life is in danger."

"It's true," said Bellim. "The Black Assailant's here and she means to kill him."

"He's not here," said Dellon. "Now leave before we call the guards. Guards!"

"Wait." Eyes turned as Levin rose from his seat.

"Stand down, Levin" Morin spat.

"No. I'm as much a king as you. I have the right to speak."

Morin grumbled and cursed. Levin went to stand in front of Ninthalas. He wore the same green velvet Ninthalas had always seen him in. His chin, once clean-shaven, now grew a light brown stubble. His eyes looked intense, focused, the kind of stare that unearthed a man's faults and left him barren in the wilderness.

"You wanted me dead," Ninthalas said.

"I wanted you thrown in the Death Chamber along with the other messenger. I told Amon to, but he refused. I bet he's gone to challenge her himself."

"He will not succeed."

Ninthalas circled around the dais to the back curtain.

"What the mad rambles, Shadai?" said Bellim.

"There are loose tiles and a shaft that lead to the Death Chamber behind this curtain. Amon and I found it on the night of Hémon's Day."

"Wait," Levin commanded.

"My lord Levin, I have not the time—"

"I'm coming with you."

"Are you mad, Levin?" Dellon exclaimed.

"No. Amon's the best of all of us. He deserves to live. Soldier! Lend me your sword."

One of the sideline guards stepped forward and handed him a blade. Levin took it and followed the others behind the dais. The thick curtain muffled the other monarchs' voices, but they spoke loud enough to hear.

"Looks like we might have to petition for a couple new kings," said Dellon.

"Good riddance," Morin scoffed. "I can't stand those two."

"Don't you think for a moment that I'm giving up my throne that easy, ya *shnerkin'* fools!" Levin barked.

"Then come back alive," said Dellin.

A loud *boom* interrupted them.The floor shook under the strain. The curtain swayed.

"What the *spizzaz* dolls was that?" Morin exclaimed.

"Beats me. That's the third one I've felt since Hémon's Day," Dellon answered.

Ninthalas paused before descending into the hole where he had loosed the tiles.

"Dethshaiken," he breathed.

"No way!" said Bellim. "Didn't think none of the Three were alive."

"Who?" asked Levin.

"I will tell you later. Let us hurry!"

They went down quickly but cautiously. The stairs weren't as stable as when Ninthalas had descended them with Amon. The tremor had loosened their hold on the shaft's walls, making every step a question of whether they would give way or hold strong. Ninthalas stepped down on light feet, but a step crumbled underneath him. It took Belim's quick reflexes to keep him from plunging into the abyss.

"Thank you."

"This is why I came with you," Bellim replied with a smirk. "Can't fight much, can ya?"

"And that is precisely why I brought you along."

The trades captain pinched his nose. "What's that awful stench?"

"The Death Chamber," Levin answered.

They reached the bottom and continued down the tunnel, turning right at the fork. The scent of rotting flesh suffocated the excavation.

A sharp cry reverberated against the walls.

"It's Amon!" Ninthalas exclaimed.

He ran ahead. He heard Bellim's voice calling for him, but he paid it no mind. As he neared the Death Chamber, a raspy voice spoke into his mind.

He is here. At last, he has come.

The door loomed ahead, swung wide open. Ninthalas burst inside.

For a scholarly built fellow, Ninthalas sure ran fast. Bellim could hardly keep up with him, Levin even less so. When the True Faithen shot forward, Bellim could only call out after him.

"Stop, Shadai!"

The True Faithen disappeared through the open door.

"Shnerkin fool!" he cursed. The Faithen was going to get himself killed.

He entered the Death Chamber and saw exactly what he expected to see. There was King Amon, brought to his knees. The Black Assailant stood above him, blood dripping from her blade. She held her sword high, ready to deal one final blow. Steel flashed as Ninthalas intercepted. But she didn't seem too surprised. Her blade pulled back, slicing his arm. In a jerk reaction, Ninthalas threw up his short sword to prevent it from cutting his limb clean off. He staggered back, clutching his wounded limb.

"Fool if I haven't seen one!" Bellim roared, jumping down onto the littered floor.

He'd never seen the Death Chamber, and now he never wanted to see it again. Grotesque bodies were everywhere. The stench of decay was bad enough.

He and Levin ran to Amon's aid. The king of Feilan was still alive, but he breathed heavily and was too weak to stand on his own. Blood gushed from lacerations on his legs, arms and side. The Black Assailant had been drawing out her kill, making the king suffer before she put an end to his life.

"Blithering idiot!" Bellim cursed. "What made you think you could take on this woman by yourself?"

"Fair talking," said Levin. "You're a fool, Amon."

They each took an arm, hauled the king to his feet, and started making for the door.

Ninthalas, however, didn't follow.

"Shadai!" Bellim called.

The True Faithen stood still, skin paler than his usual pale and eyes locked on the Black Assailant. The woman stared back, her intense yellow eyes sharp enough to pierce the soul. Neither one of them moved. Neither one of them spoke.

"Ninthalas, let's go!"

He and the kings were already at the door.

"What's wrong with him?" Levin asked.

"No idea."

"She was expecting him," Amon breathed. "She knew all along he'd figure it out and come save me..."

"Well, we can't just leave him here!" Bellim exclaimed

"You want to stay and face that woman?" Levin asked.

"I can't leave him behind. He's a Shadai! He's a holy man!"

"Then give me Amon. You stay here and see what happens."

Bellim looked at Levin. Amon had been his ally since the beginning of his career. Bellim had supported him in his rise to the throne. But he had an obligation to Shadai. That man was special. Bellim knew it from the first moment he heard the True Faithen's name.

"Go on. I can manage," Levin said. "Amon's light. Almost as small as that Faithen."

"Oh shut it!" Amon spat.

Bellim nodded. "Fair that. Speedy escape to you, Levin."

The kings left, each throwing curses and mad rambles at each other. Eventually, their voices died down and silence engulfed the chamber. Bellim turned his attention to the standoff between Ninthalas and the Black Assailant. What the mad rambles was going on?

CHAPTER THIRTY-THREE

Encounter

"It cannot be..." Ninthalas whispered.

He knew her face. He knew her from the way she stood, tall and proud, firm resolution in her stance and expression. The way she held her sword. Those eyes. Yellow, but he recognized the faint strands of emerald green.

His entire being shattered. He couldn't speak, couldn't move lest his body collapse dead. He heard the sound of his name, but it came muffled. The pain from the gash in his arm couldn't compare to the excruciating ache in his heart. All he had hoped for, all he had cried over. It all came crashing down at that moment as he stood looking at her, the woman he once loved.

"Athlaya..."

A few more strands of green twinkled in her golden eyes. Eyes that weren't hers. A spirit dwelt within her, some malshorth that had twisted her, brought her to ruin.

"It cannot be..." he said again. "I saw you die."

"You saw my grave," she answered.

Her voice was two-part, one her own, the other the voice of whatever spirit held her captive. Yet no spirit could possess a True Faithen, not according to what he interpreted from the holy book.

"How is this possible?"

"I told you ten years ago of a dream wherein I would have to make a choice. The time came and I chose."

"But you were dead! They buried you."

She stiffened. "They did."

"Are…are you dead? Are my eyes cheated that I am actually beholding a corpse?"

She hesitated before replying. "I am not entirely sure."

Enough conversing, wretch! Kill him!

She twitched and shuddered, as if the spirit was trying to subdue her. But that would mean she had some control of her body. And if that was the case, then she was indeed alive.

Hope flashed to the forefront of his mind, but it was immediately choked by reality. She chose this.

"Why?" Ninthalas asked. "Why would you not break free? What spirit could possibly take you? You were valiant and true, like none I had ever known."

"Do you think this is some simple possession? I can do nothing apart from what my possessor demands."

"No! I cannot believe it! How can this be reality? The Athlaya I know would not succumb to some lowly spirit."

"He is no lowly spirit, Ninthalas."

He opened his mouth to speak, but immediately shut it. No lowly spirit. What did that mean?

"Who is he?"

Athlaya sighed, closed her eyes and tilted her head back. When she opened her eyes again, the strands of green were nearly gone.

"Go on, possessor. Tell him who you are and why you have me."

I take no orders from you, Athlaya child.

"I am not Athlaya!"

She coughed and keeled over, groaning.

"Stop it! Stop. It!"

Ninthalas stepped forward. She held up her sword, the tip pointed at his chest.

"Do not interfere, Ninthalas."

"Please, let me help you. Let me pray—"

"You cannot free me," she rasped. "Not even Shadai can save me. He tried, but…" Her voice trailed off.

"Please."

Her face twisted into a sneer, the green strands in her eyes disappearing altogether. "*Get away from me!*"

She kicked his knee. Ninthalas screamed and crumbled to the ground.

"Say goodbye to your lost love, fool! Once you are dead, only one other stands in my way of complete dominion over her."

Her sword fell swiftly…

Blinding light exploded between them. Ninthalas flew backwards and hit the rock wall. Lights sparkled in his vision. His back burst with pain. Gasping for air, he lifted his head. Where he once stood light shown like a star, and there in its midst stood Shadai.

He gaped. This was no simple messenger from Yahlirin's realm. This was a *hallon*, one of the great protectors of the First Age.

"Curses, Shadai!" Athlaya yelled.

She staggered to her feet from a pile of carcasses, blood smeared on her armour. Before she could lift her blade, Shadai reached out and took hold of her hands. She screamed.

How many times must I prevent you from harming this man?!

"Curses, the foul!"

Too long have you dwelt in that body. And alas, for the woman's strength is waning! Yet a time is coming when your stronghold will be cut off. Indeed, it shall be brought to nothing.

"No!"

Ninthalas scrambled forward and clutched Shadai's robe.

"Do not harm her! Please, my lord Shadai, do not hurt her!"

Back with you, Líran, Shadai rebuked. *Do not come near. She is already afflicted.*

"But I love her!" Ninthalas exclaimed. "How long did I cry and the ache in my heart would not fade. I believed her dead and yet here she is, Athlaya Kírin Lothlúrin, alive. Only now she is cursed!"

Peace, peace, brother Líran, said Shadai. *Go now. You must not fight this woman or you shall surely die.*

Ninthalas refused. But he didn't have a choice. Bellim was at his side, pulling him to his feet. The trades captain dragged him to the landing.

"No!" Ninthalas cried. "Athlaya!"

Bellim hauled him out of the Death Chamber.

———◉———

Athlaya had known pain, known it in every form. From lacerations, to broken limbs, to sickness, to poison, she had encountered it all. Yet there was one pain she could not handle. That was the touch of death. As Shadai held her hands in a firm grip, all she could do was endure. Agony gnawed at her limbs. Despair flooded her mind, drawing her into a void from which she could not escape. She saw nothing save the face of Shadai, looking down at her in a tunnel of darkness.

Sister Athlaya.

The voice was calm, but the language that followed was foreign. Words enfolded her, held her in an embrace so loving and caring she could cry. The light of Shadai grew, drowning out the darkness and repressing the charred vines of the touch of death.

"Shadai?"

It was not him. She looked up into another face, one unknown, but she knew it somehow. Yet how could she? She'd never seen him before. Who was this man who could bring death to life?

Be of courage, my daughter, he said to her. *Your time is coming. Indeed, it is coming quickly!*

The man transformed into the face of Shadai. Shadai the Watcher. Now Shadai the Healer. He let go of her, letting her slump to the floor. Ehnthatúlen returned quickly, her captor from whom she would never be free. Yet she had been healed.

No more, Ehnthatúlen, Shadai commanded. *I hereby lay curse on you. Never again shall you take lives. Not by your hand, nor by the hands of those you possess. No more shall you kill, for now and for eternity.*

Ehnthatúlen cursed. Athlaya couldn't stop him from speaking through her.

"*You will not win. There are worse things than death. I shall yet deal with that weakling of a man you protect.*"

Athlaya's eyes widened. "No! Dethshaiken!"

Four swords thrust through Shadai's body. The *hallon* looked over his shoulder at the giant, indifferent that he had just been impaled.

At last you show yourself, Dethshaiken. You cannot kill me. I am like Morkhen, you know. After all, he is my brother.

"Damn you, Shadai!" Dethshaiken swore.

He hacked at the hallon, but his swords, one for each of his four hands, passed right through his glowing body. They left no scratch. Eventually, the Third gave up and simply stared at him with an evil glint in his eye.

"You'd best be wary, *hallon*," the giant said. "If Kírin can't kill that pathetic excuse for a man, then I will."

"Dethshaiken—"

"Quiet, wretch!"

You cannot kill the blessed of Yahlírin, Shadai stated. With that, he vanished.

Dethshaiken turned to Athlaya.

"You pathetic child! Now I have to finish him myself. Be happy you're too valuable to dispose of."

Athlaya didn't say anything. She watched as her master burrowed underneath the stair.

Left alone. In a sea of corpses. How fitting for someone who had lived with death all around her for ten years of her life. Now, it was all she knew.

"Is there no hope for me?" she whispered.

Only silence answered.

Athlaya, alive. Athlaya, after all these years, was alive. Tears streamed down Ninthalas' cheeks, his weeping echoing throughout the cavern, interrupted by short, heaving gasps of air. His heart burned with such an ache as he had never known.

"It cannot be!" he cried in True Faithen. "It just cannot be!"

Athlaya, the one whom he was once smitten for in the confusing emotions of first love. A forgotten memory of the past come back to haunt him. Once a pure, valiant spirit who defied every trait deemed feminine in True Faithen society. Now, the bearer of war and suffering. And by the possession of a powerful spirit! How was this reality?

"You knew her, didn't you?" said Bellim.

Ninthalas simply nodded. He couldn't speak. The words wouldn't come. Yet no conversation could ease his remorse anyway. He was done. Finished. What was the sense in living knowing that Athlaya had turned evil and wanted to kill him?

"But why kill me?!" he exclaimed.

"Easy, friend. No use putting out questions when there aren't any answers."

They groped their way through the tunnel until they reached the fork. Not long after, they came to the shaft.

"And now the climb," Bellim muttered.

"I cannot…" Ninthalas managed to get out.

"Put it aside Shadai. We gotta get out of here before that woman comes after us."

"True. She is indeed hunting me. But why?"

He looked up the dark shaft. A faint flicker of a torch high above marked the door that led to the back of the mountain. The rest of the way was dark. Levin had taken their only source of light. How he'd managed to carry both Amon and a torch in his hand was up to question.

"Climb…?"

Bellim leaned him against the wall and squatted.

"Jump on my back. I can carry you the rest of the way."

"Are you sure?"

"You're slimmer than a twig, Shadai. Probably lighter than my son."

Ninthalas didn't argue. He scrambled up and Bellim began the ascent. Where steps were missing, the trades captain managed to jump over the cracks. Ninthalas simply clung to his back and marvelled at the man's strength.

"You amaze me, Bellim Farthorn."

"Being strong comes in handy," he replied. "I keep it up to protect the weak."

"Such as myself."

"You've a different kind of strength, Shadai."

His words were cut off by a massive quake. The shaft rumbled.

"That does not sound good," Bellim remarked.

A crack sounded to their right and another on the opposite wall of the shaft. Ninthalas peered down into the abyss, black and endless like the gaping agony in his heart. Shadows mixed with shadows, but they began to change.

"The walls!" he exclaimed.

"What?"

"The shaft is closing in on us!"

Without a word, Bellim sprang up the steps. Ninthalas kept his eyes on what was happening below. The shadows grew lighter, clumping together into a mass of grey. As the torchlight from above grew brighter the higher they went, it was clear that the walls were caving in. Where the abyss once lay, now grey remained, squeezing and crumbling together. The walls grew narrower...

And narrower...

They reached the torch and the door.

"It's coming...coming faster," Ninthalas breathed.

Bellim put him down, grabbed the door handle and heaved.

"Drat! Door's jammed!"

Ninthalas kept his eyes on the closing shaft. He lost his balance as another tremor shook the platform they stood on. Pain exploded in his knee.

"*Ai!*"

"That's broken if I knew a brake," Bellim said. He peered down. "Holy *spizzaz* dolls! We're gonna get crushed!"

"To the throne room!" Ninthalas exclaimed. "Quickly!"

Bellim took his arm and they hobbled up. Ninthalas gritted his teeth against the pain.

"Levin!" the trades captain called.

The shaft continued to shrink.

"Levin, damn it! Where are you?"

The scraping sound of moving tiles sounded above and light from the throne room streamed down. They were almost there. Ninthalas kept his gaze fixed on the opening. They would escape. They *had* to!

The walls were only two arms' length away now.

Bellim picked Ninthalas up and pushed him through the opening. Two soldiers were there to pull him out and drag him away.

Crack.

A scream penetrated the air. Ninthalas glanced back.

Most of Bellim had escaped. His legs, however, were stuck encrusted in solid rock.

"Bellim!" Levin cried. "Guards!"

The soldiers dropped Ninthalas and he crumbled to the floor. He couldn't think, could barely hear as Levin yelled at the soldiers amidst Bellim's wailing and screaming.

He used what strength he had left scrambled out from behind the curtain. That was as far as he got. His agony outweighed him, both in his limbs and in his heart. His mind began to cloud over. He wept, but his tears ran dry.

Two arms wrapped around him and pulled him close. He lifted his eyes to see Ailene. Her mask was gone, replaced by a sympathetic expression that sought to comfort him. Yet she couldn't. Ninthalas' life had ended there.

Peace, peace, brother Líran.

As unconsciousness pulled him under, an image of Yosef flashed in his mind.

"Please, Yahlírin," his son prayed. "Bring my da back to me because I love him and I don't wanta be alone ever."

'You won't be alone, my son,' Ninthalas wanted to say. 'I will never let you be alone.'

CHAPTER THIRTY-FOUR

Lost Hope

Yosef's head pounded. He'd watched the whole thing. Or felt it. They were only the presence of feet, but he knew who they were. He found the Black Assailant first. She and one of the kings were under the mountain. Ninthalas and the others soon joined and then it was just three of them. He tried to pinpoint where the giant was, but the silence kept his sense on one location.

No, the silence told him. *Don't engage him. He's too powerful.*

So he kept focusing on Ninthalas and the Black Assailant. He didn't know what happened exactly, but he knew Ninthalas had been injured. Bellim dragged him out of the Death Chamber and down the narrow tunnel where the kings had fled earlier. He was about to break the sense when another looming presence found his. The giant. It was like a mountain within the mountain, a force so strong and fierce Yosef tried to pull back.

No, said the silence. *He needs you.*

The earth bent and twisted and the tunnel began to crumble, walls crushing and squeezing. The shaft was beginning to close. Yosef never knew something like that was possible!

No! he exclaimed.

The giant paused. One enormous silence collided with Yosef's small, fleeting sense.

You again, korme'khím! the giant boomed.

Leave them alone! Yosef yelled.

Laughter rumbled in Yosef's gut.

You care for that True Faithen, do you?

He's my da, Yosef replied.

Then watch him die!

The giant resumed closing the shaft, the walls crashing in faster than before.

Ninthalas!

The giant continued to laugh.

No! Yosef wouldn't have it! He lost one father. He wasn't about to lose this one, too. He grabbed hold of the sense and pulled hard.

Resistance! the giant bellowed. *The boy has spirit! Now I see why she wants you. The blood of the shapeshifters lives in you. Your efforts are useless, though.*

Yosef didn't care. He pulled as hard as he could.

The shaft shrank…

And shrank.

Ninthalas and Bellim weren't moving fast enough.

Yosef wouldn't let them get crushed. He had to save them, but he was too weak on his own.

Yahlírin! He cried. *Help! Please!*

The walls shuddered. Something like water dripped down the cavern walls. The narrowing didn't stop, but it began to slow.

How?! the giant demanded.

Yosef didn't waiver. He pulled until his head hurt. He pulled until he couldn't pull anymore.

Suddenly, the silence let go. Yosef snapped back like a spring. He was falling, faster and faster until he pounded into his physical self. For a moment, he lay petrified, breathing hard.

Then the headache came.

I told you, said the silence. *There are consequences.*

"Why?" Yosef whined. "Ninthalas!"

The name drew out into a moan and then ceased altogether. The pain was too much. Just when he thought it would let up, it came back even stronger, more excruciating.

"Make it stop!"

This is what happens when you focus too hard.

"You told me to!" Yosef yelled.

And you succeeded. Thank your friend.

How long he lay on the floor he didn't know. All he could feel was his pulsing, aching head. All he knew right then and there was agony. It blotted his vision completely and drowned out all sound. How much longer?

"Make it go away! Yahlírin, make it go away!"

He spent long moments in excruciating pain. How long, he didn't know. The headache eventually lessened, but it didn't fade completely. His vision cleared and he found himself in a cosy bed. A woman hovered into view.

Yosef squinted. "Mrs. Farthorn?"

"Oh, thank Yahl!" she exclaimed.

He looked around. Eera was there, as was Fehnan. Both wore concerned looks.

"Where's my da?" Yosef asked.

"Still in the City," Fehnan replied. "What happened to you? Found ya flat on your back and holding your head like you'd been hit with a mallet."

Yosef didn't answer. He looked at Eera. The fish boy nodded slowly and muttered a marine-sounding word. He tapped his head twice and said the word again. Did he understand? Did he know what the sense did? But that would mean he had it, too. He could feel the earth. Or, since he was aquatic, perhaps he could feel the water.

Thank your friend.

"You helped me, didn't you?" he said to Eera.

Eera simply looked at him. He didn't understand Common, but Yosef knew it had been him. The Ndaljú had helped slow the crumbling walls of the shaft.

His head swelled and he closed his eyes.

"I want my da."

"He'll be back, sweetie," Mrs. Farthorn said. She brushed her fingers through his hair. "Don't you go worrying yourself silly. He'll come."

Ninthalas did return, along with the largest procession of carriages Yosef had ever seen. By that time, Yosef's headache had cleared enough that he could get up and go outside. He was visiting Eera by the riverside when he saw the line of carriages and Ninthalas sitting at the front of the first one, the High Cleric

Ailene by his side. His dad's arm hung in a sling and splints secured his leg.

Yosef ran to the carriage, climbed up and embraced his father. Tears streamed down his cheeks.

"Why'd you go, da? Why'd you leave?"

Ninthalas didn't speak, but hugged back. They remained for long moments in that embrace. Yosef didn't want to let go. He'd never let his dad go again. Next time Ninthalas faced her, Yosef would be right there with him. Yosef would protect him. He'd use the sense no matter how much of a headache it gave him.

Ninthalas released the embrace. "Are my belongings ready?"

"You can't go travelling like that!" Ailene protested.

Ninthalas held up a hand. "I already told you I am going and I am taking my son with me. I aim to get as far from this country as I can."

"I got everything," said Yosef. "I'll get Fehnan to help me bring it out."

He ran to the house and found the teen in his room, reading a book as always. Fehnan looked up from the pages.

"Hey, *souther*—Yosef! I mean Yosef. Sorry."

"Can you help me pack up Hallas?"

Fehnan leapt off the bed. "Shadai's back?"

"Yeah, and we gotta go soon, so could you help me?"

"Of course."

They took one load down and outside. Ninthalas was on his feet, crutch in hand to support himself. He scratched Hallas behind the ears and spoke softly to it in True Faithen. The horse replied in it's own squeaks and neighs as if sensing the severity of its master's injuries. It was a serene scene of affection between man and beast, and Yosef didn't want to disturb it.

Fehnan, however, did.

"Where's my pops?" he asked.

His mother's cry answered his question. The teen's face went ashen. He dropped the packs and ran off in the direction of the cry.

Yosef watched him go, then brought the packs to Ninthalas, laying the items down with care. When he came back out with the second load, Ninthalas was directing some peasant on how to strap things on. Ailene stood close by. Her expression could only be described as pity.

Yosef approach with the last few things.

"You can't go—"

"High Cleric Ailene, we have discussed this time and time again," said Ninthalas sternly. He sounded like Kai-Tsúthlen. "I must continue on my journey—if not for my own escape, then for your own safety. She will kill you if I stay here."

Ailene shook her head, tears streaming down her cheeks. Ninthalas took her hands in his and looked straight into her eyes.

"Whatever blessing is upon me, let it be on you as well. May you have safe passage to Serenestí. I hope to see you again, and when I do, we shall both have stories to tell."

With that, he called Yosef over to him, they both mounted and rode away. Yosef strained his neck and watched Ailene fade into the distance. He wondered if he'd ever see her again. Apparently Ninthalas seemed to think so. Yet with the Black Assailant hunting them, Yosef couldn't tell.

Two days they travelled, due south following the river. Ninthalas was silent the entire time. Yosef wished he would talk, wanted him to say something, anything that would get his mind off of whatever it was he was thinking about. Yet he never spoke. He just cried. Yosef had never seen him cry. He wished he never had the opportunity to see it. His insides twisted and churned like swirling whirlpools. He tried to speak, but words failed him. What could he say that would make his father feel better?

Dusk consumed the sky and night came as a cold, unwelcome guest, forcing them to rest not far from the nameless river. Ninthalas let Hallas roam to the water for a drink and sat down.

"Would you mind getting us some wood for a fire, my son?" he asked, his voice high like a song sung in minor key.

Yosef silently trotted to the nearby trees and eventually returned with an armful of twigs and short branches. Through much effort, Ninthalas got a fire going and together they sat gazing into the flames. Again, Yosef tried to speak, but he had no idea what to say. Instead, he inched closer to Ninthalas and put a hand on his knee. The True Faithen looked down at him and forced a smile.

"My dear Yosef," he said, kissing Yosef's brow. "I am so fortunate a man to have found you, so blessed a soul to have come to know you."

Yosef didn't respond. He simply waited.

"I suppose I must speak, must I?" Ninthalas went on.

"You know her," said Yosef.

"Indeed, I know her, or I used to at least. She was very dear to me. I thought her dead, for she was buried many years ago."

"But she's alive."

Ninthalas shifted his gaze back to the fire. "She is alive."

"But the spirit thing controls her."

The fire crackled, sparks flying into the air. As the sky changed from dark blue to black, the stars unveiled their brilliance, dazzling the black canopy overhead with colourful sparkles. The air grew chill and Yosef huddled close to Ninthalas for what little warmth his slim frame could offer.

"Is that why you have the dagger?" Yosef asked. "To remember her?"

Ninthalas nodded. He pulled the elegant blade from his pack and unsheathed it. "The inscription reads '*Ninthalas'esh Athlaya*'. Me and her. I had her fashioned a short sword for her thirteenth birthday which bore the same engraving and tree design. The idea was that the roots would be our bond which would grow deep and become intertwined like an unbreakable cord. The sword was buried with her. I wonder if she still has it."

"She has two swords. She only used one when she killed the grey thingers."

Ninthalas chuckled and stroked Yosef's hair.

"What?" Yosef asked.

"Even in the midst of sorrow, you still give me joy. Come, my son, let us sleep. Tomorrow we must ride again, and the riding will be long."

Yosef frowned, but obeyed. As he lay down, exhaustion settled in, pulling him into a deep sleep.

"Ninthalas! Da, wake up. He's here!"

Ninthalas shot upright. It was still night. The moon shone bright in the sky, casting a pale glow on the ground.

Yosef pulled at his shirt, sending shots of pain through his arm.

"*Ai*, Yosef, that stings!"

"He's coming! We have to go *now!*"

A hoarse cry sounded from afar. Hallas whinnied in reply. If the horse was frightened, then that was reason enough to flee. He scrambled painfully to his feet and he and Yosef clambered into the saddle. Off they galloped just as another cry rose behind them.

The ground shook. A rock wall shot up right in front of them and it took Ninthalas' quick reflexes with the reigns and Hallas' cunning not to hit it. Hallas galloped around as as the earth rumbled again. Suddenly, the earth opened up in front of them. Ninthalas hauled on the reigns. Out of the ground emerged a dark, bulky form—a four-armed giant.

"Dethshaiken!" Ninthalas yelled. "Fly, Hallas! Run hard!"

Hallas bolted and the giant pursued. Ninthalas glanced back to see the massive form of the malshorth closing in behind them, though he only ran on two legs.

So fast! How was that possible?

The chase dragged on, every moment a question of whether or not Hallas would slow from fatigue. The horse burned on adrenaline alone as it weaved around trees, scarce obstacles that became numerous, monstrous pillars. The sky began to brighten. Dawn was at hand.

Up ahead, the tree line broke. Ninthalas pulled hard on the reigns and Hallas skidded into the shallows of a vast lake. Dethshaiken slammed into the steed at full force, sending both riders crashing into the water.

Ninthalas struggled to stand, his knee throbbing, arm stinging. He barely drew one of his swords before the giant attacked him. With one blade Dethshaiken struck. Then another. These Ninthalas managed to block. Then a third came at him at blinding speed which he somehow evaded.

Too fast!

The fourth sliced from the side, ripping his shirt and drawing blood. The cut was shallow, but Ninthalas buckled. So much pain. Too much pain.

"Is this really the man who weakened Kírin of Ehnthatúl?" Dethshaiken bellowed in a raw form of True Faithen speech. "What a pathetic excuse for a man! For what is a man if he can't fight?"

The giant kicked Ninthalas underwater and stomped down on him, forcing the air out of his lungs, holding him under. Ninthalas flailed, frantic. But then he remembered his dagger, drew it, and stabbed the foot pinning him. The giant cursed, lifted his foot just long enough for Ninthalas to scramble away. He came up gasping for air.

Furious, the giant ripped out the dagger and flung it aside. He raised his two upper arms, the sword points aimed to kill...

"Leave him alone!"

Yosef stood knee-deep in the lake, throwing rocks at the malshorth. Every stone bounced off the giant's tough skin.

"Oh ho!" Dethshaiken laughed. "Here is the *korme'khím* at last! Feisty fellow. You'd make a good malshorth, what with that sense of yours. Just like my old kin."

"Yosef, run!" Ninthalas cried.

He clumsily reached for his short sword, but wasn't quick enough. Dethshaiken shoved him under again, pinning him. Ninthalas' lungs burned. Only his willpower kept him from inhaling water.

Yet just when he thought he would give, the pressure lifted. Several hands grabbed hold of him, pulling him to the surface. He scrambled over to Yosef, wheezing.

"Da, you okay?"

"What is happening?"

"It's the fish people. They've come to save us!"

Wailing war cries rang like a roaring river. Ninthalas looked over to see Dethshaiken fighting a new foe. Several new foes, all of them *Ndaljú*. There must have been at least fifteen strong. They attacked, dealing swift, efficient blows. Enraged, Dethshaiken fell back. The *Ndaljú* drove the Third onto the shore.

"Curse you, son of Shadai!" Dethshaiken roared.

He disappeared into the trees.

Ninthalas collapsed to the ground, exhausted, his pain unbearable. He heard Yosef calling to him, but the voice came muffled, fading. Unconsciousness swept over him. Only a single voice spoke into the despair of his mind. He recognized it, knew it well. He'd heard it his entire life, though it spoke words he'd rather not hear.

Finally, brother Líran. The darkness has found you in the night and taken you. You are now mine, dear brother, to make me whole.

Laughter rose, ripping his sanity in two. One half was a fraction of hope dying from infection. The other was a man looking right back at him. Though the eyes were blood red, Ninthalas' jaw dropped and horror flooded his entire being as he gazed at the familiar sight.

He was looking at himself.

"Da!" Yosef cried. "Ninthalas! Wake up. Please wake up! Don't die on me!"

He shook Ninthalas' shoulders and yelled, but his father didn't wake.

"No," he whimpered. "No, da, not...you can't die. You can't die!"

Tears poured down his cheeks. Another father gone. He didn't remember the first one dying, but he didn't want to know the pain of losing this one, either. His chest burned. He buried his face in Ninthalas' tunic, sobbing.

"You can't do this to me." He lifted his face to the heavens. "You hear me Yahlírin? You can't do this to me! What kind of God are you?! I thought you were a father, but fathers don't kill their children. How could you?!"

He cried to the heavens again and again, but the heavens didn't answer back. He was alone. Alone like before. No one to take care of him. No one to comfort him. He wept as the sun rose into the sky, bringing the light of a new day.

Not new for Yosef. His life ended then and there. Again.

"Yozeb!"

A small head poked out of the water.

"Eera!"

Eera smiled. He floated deeper into the lake.

"Eera, where are you going?"

"*Ben'ag dahlíúr*," the fish boy replied.

"What does that mean?" Yosef asked, wiping the tears from his eyes.

The fish boy sank into the water.

"Don't leave me, Eera. Please, don't leave me here alone!"

A breeze blew dry the tears on his face. Along with it came singing, a sweet voice dancing over the water. Yosef squinted. The shape of a boat emerged from the morning mists, a single sail speeding it toward him. As it neared, the voice grew louder until Yosef could make out words sung in Common.

Brother Liran Shadai, they want him to die,
Die, yes die he shall.
Yet not for long fathoms in Feithna'him fashion,
For he is the blessed of Yahl.

Sweet brother Liran, I hear him breathing.
The Third thought he was gone.
No, not gone shall he be, you verily see,
He shall rise to a brand new song.

"Hello?" Yosef called.

He stayed by Ninthalas's side. The voice sounded nice enough, but he didn't want to take any chances. He had already witnessed a losing fight and he hoped whoever the voice came from wasn't some nasty malshorth in disguise.

It wasn't. When the boat docked, out jumped a pretty young girl Yosef's age and height. Her hair fell silvery white down her back like the silver-haired man's, her skin as white as Ninthalas'. Her eyes sparkled a shimmering blue, and freckles dotted her pale face. She wore short-sleeved and short-legged clothes foreign to Yosef, colourful blues and violets arranged in a flower pattern. Underneath were tight, long black sleeves and thick leggings, and soft leather boots bound her feet.

Yosef frowned. He had seen this girl before. But where? The memory tickled his recollection, but ultimately refused to be remembered.

"Hello, Yosef," she said, her greeting as much a melody as the song she'd sung.

"I know you," he answered.

"Indeed, you do. I know your blood father and I know you. And now I see you are in a similar situation as before."

"Before?"

"Oh, yes."

"You…you're the girl who took my memories, aren't you?"

She smiled and Yosef's despair almost melted away. He wasn't so sure if he wanted his old memories back anymore.

"I am," she replied. "And I have your memories. Forgive me. I only wish for you to be free of sorrow."

Yosef dropped his gaze to Ninthalas. "Can you help my da?"

"Yes, but I want you to do something for me in return."

"Anything! Just please bring my da back. Yahlírin let him die!"

She giggled. "Oh no, dear Yosef. Yahlírin does not let him die. Do you not know that brother Líran is the blessed of Yahl? No, by Yahlírin's calling, I am here that he may live. But Yosef, son of Micah of Limrak, adopted of Líran Shadai, you must sleep. Dream of good things, blessed things. Fun times with your fathers and better times with your mothers. And when you wake, your sorrows shall be no more."

She touched his forehead. Yosef's eyelids grew heavy and he couldn't stop them from closing. His body gave way as if he was falling. But he wasn't scared anymore. Yahlírin would protect him. Yahlírin would always protect him. This he now knew in his heart.

On the tip of his memory, the girl's song danced on the wings of his subconscious, then faded away along with the memory of her.

Epilogue

You wretch of a child! Ehnthatúlen raged.

Kírin twisted and turned. She could hardly breathe amidst her own screaming. Ehnthatúlen allowed her scars to swelter. Her back was a raging fire, burning under the sting of the Third's whip. She had failed her mission. Again. With every failure came a beating, and now the Second, too, was contributing in a frenzy of hate-filled insanity. Even after three days, Ehnthatúlen was still upset thanks to the curse placed on him by Shadai of the Halloneth.

"No more! No more!" she cried.

They heeded her cry. Kírin gasped for air, lying on the cold ground like a worm of a creature.

"*Gah*, that wretched Shadai!" Dethshaiken yelled.

"I told you...he could not...be killed," said Kírin between breaths.

"Those *Lúmbar'gím!*"

"You were driven...by the Lake Others?" She grinned despite the pain. "That must have been embarrassing."

"You sound pretty tough after just being beaten." He raised his whip yet restrained his hand.

"Do not...try your hand...at mockery with me," she said. "It will take time to recover."

If you recover, Ehnthatúlen noted. *This curse changes everything. If Morkhen infects you again, I will not to suppress it completely like before.*

397

Kírin licked her parched lips. "I can probably take a guess…as to who was the driving force behind the *Lúmbar'gím*."

"Oh?"

"It was the Chief Meddler herself…Endahlúmin Lúralí." She groaned, rolling onto her side. Her back was still sore, but it had eased a bit. Perhaps the healing of Shadai was still at work. *She cannot leave the safety of her forests for longer than two days.*

"Yet you and I both know there is thick forest on the other side of the lake," said Kírin. "And I imagine Serenestí is not as deterring as other places."

"Whatever," Dethshaiken scoffed. "We'll find out from Morkhen what to do next."

He should be here soon, said Ehnthatúlen. *What will I tell him, Kírin? That you failed to complete your task?*

"Let's hope he's in a tolerable mood," the Third remarked.

As he spoke, a deafening screech lit up the sky, and giant wing beats echoed from across the plains. A shadow appeared in the distance, growing nearer, larger, until it formed the shape of a giant lizard with a long, snake-like neck. Its wings spanned the length of its body. Its tail sported a club of spikes. The *ishmothe* loomed overhead, circled, and landed in front of them. Its fangs dripped with venom.

Off from the winged monster's back descended the Master. His clothes were darker than the night sky, his long hair stained black from corruption. His skin glowed lifeless like a corpse succumbed to cold, his figure slender as a man who had never known work. Kírin had always feared him. His charm could deceive the purest of souls, but the result of giving into his passions was fatal. This was the First, master of all malshorthath.

His eyes, stained red with the blood of his victims, looked down on them, scanning, searching. No one knew how he saw the world, if he still had the famed Eyes of the Ages, or if he simply saw things decay. What Kírin did know was that he anticipated the future and was always correct.

"I distinctly remember, Athlaya child," he said in his elegant, soothing voice, "that you swore by our Ruler's name you would be a suitable host. I remember your willingness to do the Great One's will."

Kírin looked up into the First's blood red eyes. He always referred to her as Athlaya despite her best efforts to clear that name from her history. Athlaya had been a woman of valour. Kírin was the ruthless judge of souls.

"So I vowed," she replied.

He knelt to her level, those eyes holding hers transfixed. They were so alluring, so inviting, yet she knew they were a lie.

"Yet you have upset him," the First went on. "Such disobedience does not go unaccounted for."

"Indeed, it has not," she said.

He grabbed her hands and she screamed. Her flesh burned icy cold under his grip.

"I was not referring to Dethshaiken's beating," the First sneered.

"Your punishment is just, my lord!" she cried.

He let go, his sneer vanishing quicker than she could comprehend. That was the real Morkhen under the mask. Under the smile, the coaxing words and the songs. The real First was a monster, and only his eyes gave hint to what lied behind the surface.

"You will not fail me again, Athlaya child," he said to her.

"Of course, my lord."

"As for my brother and sister," he added. "Your dealings with them shall be no more, your tidings laid to waste. I have replaced my curse upon you. May it stand for eternity. And you will be mine, my dearest, and make me whole."

She bowed her head, her hands now burning with charred inflammation. Hopelessness descended upon her like the weight of torrential rain. The touch of death would never leave her. She would never be free. For the touch of death from Morkhen the Infector was the end of life. Its darkness quenched all light. Nothing, not even Yahlírin, could save her now.

What of the son of Shadai? Ehnthatúlen asked.

Morkhen's face twisted into a grin. Kírin hated that smile. It was like a shadow of Ninthalas, what he could become should he fall into deception.

"He is already mine."

Appendix A

Character List - Serenestí

Family Shadai

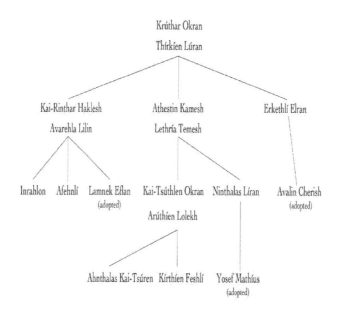

Krúthar Okran
Thírkíen Lúran

Kai-Rinthar Haklesh
Avarehla Lilin

Athestin Kamesh
Lethría Temesh

Erkethlí Elran

Inrahlon   Afehnlí   Lamnek Eflan
(adopted)

Kai-Tsúthlen Okran
Arúthíen Lolekh

Ninthalas Líran

Avalin Cherish
(adopted)

Ahnthalas Kai-Tsúren   Kírthíen Feshlí   Yosef Mathíus
(adopted)

Family Lothlúrin

Athlarek Dúrlen
Kavathíen Úlris

Athlaya Kírin

Tahlen Dían

Kírinfay Lathlí

Family Hashlen

Belthosh Metriank
Alshanda Íren

Elkeshlí Sen

Others

High Council

High Lord Tothran
High Councillor Afren
High Councillor Dúrlen

Denedrúath/Pellendrath
(Military Company/Squadron)

2nd Command Atheil Feiren
3rd Command Konran
Lothlúrin

The Messengers

Ahlinthrad Fin Thahlimon
Púrlon Shin Lavathkin
(Ahlinthrad's son)
Erehlin Kaneth Avathnon
Keflan Tek Aklanon
(Erehlin's brother-in-law)
Othlorin Fan Terahnokh

Family Farthorn

Bellim
Félía

Fehnan

The Kings of Hémon

Morin of Aerthkûn
Dellon of Helfohr
Levin of Dalfin
Amon of Feilan

Others

Meldesha, Dellon's High Cleric
Karvene, Levin's High Cleric
Amelí, Amon's cleric
Míral the cleric
Ailene, Levin's second cleric

Mallon, Bellim's friend

Village of Mor'Lûn

Rúter
Doken
Paden

Appendix B

Pronunciation Guide

While the *Plight* was in the making and I had beta readers and others perusing the (very) rough drafts of my work, several people stumbled over True Faithen names, particularly the name Kai-Tsúthlen. One person even suggested that I switch Kai-Tsúthlen's name to Okran instead. I was more than slightly perturbed by the suggestion. To me, the name just rolled off the tip of my tongue. I had no idea it'd be hard for other people to pronounce.

In the end, I didn't end up changing Kai-Tsúthlen's name, but I did create a pronunciation and style guide to help my readers out a bit. Hopefully, it will clear up some misunderstanding.

The Accents

í - sounds like "ee" as in "bee" or "keep" (eg. A'thería = ah-the-ree-ah)
ú - sounds like the "u" sound in "suit" or "lute" (eg. Kai-Tsúthlen = kie-tsueth-len)
é - like the French "é" as in "épée" or the "a" in "game" (eg. Hémon = Hay-mon)
û - sounds like the "oo" in "book" or "look" (eg. Mor'Lûn)
ah/eh - sounds like it reads. The "h" prevents the "a" or "e" from becoming a long vowel (eg. Ehnthatúlen = en-tha-tue-len)
kh - sounds like the "ch" in "Bach"
ai - most of the time, it's sounds like the "i" in "light". The word "Faithen" is the only exception, which is pronounced Fay-then.

The Apostrophe

The apostrophes in words and phrases came out of an obsession for creating weird spellings and punctuations when I was in my late teens and early twenties. A few of them still don't make sense, such as the apostrophes in A'thírin and A'thería. As for others, I've developed rules for their usage.

For comparison, let's look at English. Apostrophes are used to show possession (Yosef's book) and contractions (can't, don't, etc.). In True Faithen, apostrophes are quite versatile. One use is to connect an adjective to a noun. For example, *emkalaf'morlúrnaní* stands for "black assailant" (or "black attacker"). Another is to connect prepositional phrases to nouns that come before it. The Dead Forest is *Lotah 'an Morkh* (literally, "Forest of Death"). The apostrophe is also used to attach the subject article *'al* to its subject, and it is used to create compound nouns (*onen'menan*, meaning "only one" which is a term husbands sometimes use for their wives).

Like I said, versatile. But hopefully this little guide helps you out.

Forms of Address

You may have noticed that there are a variety of ways characters address each other in this book (i.e. what they call each other). Different cultures will refer to people in different ways. For most cultures, people may go on a first name basis, but in True Faithen culture, how you address a person depends on affiliation (their relation to you) and status. I've been told that this can be quite confusing, so here is a guide on how to address people according to the different cultures of A'thería.

Kislanía

Aside from their small linguistic mannerisms of adding -ish and -like to adjectives and stringing a number of nouns together, Kislaníans are quite simple when they speak to each other. They're all on a first name basis, so if you go there, you can just throw out names as you come to know them.

Hémon

Next on the list in terms of complication is Hémon. It's generally a first name basis unless the person holds a title such as "King" or "Cleric". (These are the only two used in the book, so there is no need to expand on other titles). Like North American culture, soldiers are addressed by their title and last name. The kings will refer to their subjects by their last name if it's known. People are often prone to calling others by their ethnicity, or geographical or religious affiliation. This is why Hémonians called Ninthalas "Faithen" or Yosef "souther".

Serenestí

True Faithen address is incredibly complicated. It's based on relation and status. The most respectful way to address someone you just met or your senior is by middle name, then last name. So if you're meeting Ninthalas for the first time, you would call him Líran Shadai out of due respect (and especially since he's from the revered family Shadai). If there is no middle name, then first and last will do, and if there is only a first name, then it is common to add "friend" or some other title or affiliation before the name. True Faithens will often do this for people of other cultures.

For those that hold a title, like an office such as High Lord or High Councillor, or if those who hold a military rank such as Captain, you always address them by their rank and middle name (hence Captain Dían). If you are introducing someone who holds office or a rank, then you may address them by rank, middle name, then last name (Captain Dían Lothlúrin), although this is optional. Ninthalas would call Tahlen Captain Dían Lothlúrin if he was holding Tahlen in high esteem, speaking of his prowess in battle, or introducing him to someone. He doesn't have to do this, but Ninthalas is one of the polite people you will ever meet and it's in his nature to hold everyone of higher esteem than himself (he's a humble fellow). This is an important point in True Faithen culture. Always hold others in higher esteem than yourself and treat them with respect, even if you don't like them.

If you have known the person, but are still on an acquaintance basis with them, or if you are friends but are wanting to point out a certain admirable quality about them (which Ninthalas would certainly do), then you would address them by their first name, then middle name.

This is a very common way to address people and when in doubt about whether to use the informal or middle address, it's best to go with this form.

First name basis is reserved for close friends and family. If you are not a close friend or family, then you had best avoid this informal address or you'll commit a cultural blunder. Of course, even if you do mess up, True Faithens are very forgiving. They will not hold you to the standards of their country, but it's good knowledge to have.

The most informal form of address is spoken by women only and that is nicknames they reserve for their husbands. Arúthíen, therefore, calls her husband Kai-Tsú, especially when she is being affectionate. This is a major *faux pas* if you shorten a man's name, so don't ever use it. A man would never use this and if he did, he would be shunned by True Faithen society, even if he was a foreigner. Yes, True Faithens are forgiving, but this is one thing you'd best not say.

On a side note, some names are taboo to say. True Faithens will not name Dethshaiken out loud, but call him the Third as he is described in the holy book. Dethshaiken is a loose example, however, because his name is mentioned so many times in the Fehlthan (holy book). True Faithens will almost never speak the names of the First and Second malshorthath. To a True Faithen, words hold power, and middle names of people and place names are often chosen with care. So uttering the names of the First and Second would be a curse.

All this talk of address in True Faithen culture can be confusing. When in doubt, though, you can always refer to someone according to their relation to you. True Faithens do this all the time, no matter the status. "My brother", "our good High Lord", "oh king", and "our host" are some good examples. If the person has no distinct relation to you, perhaps it is best not to refer to the person at all, unless of course that person is a possible threat. Then you might as well say, "Be wary of that man in the blue vest" or "do you notice how that bulky fellow in the shadows over there keeps staring at us?" Really, though, the possibilities of these kinds of address are endless.

Timeless Shadai

Ninthalas' guide, Shadai, is a *hallon*, which is an ancient guardian being from Yahlírin's holy realm. He, too, has a unique way of addressing people. Usually, he will say a name if it holds certain meaning. For example, he calls Ninthalas "brother Líran", understanding that Líran is derived from the True Faithen word *lí* meaning "life". He uses "brother" as a means of affiliation, but you'll read more about why there is a connection between him and the family Shadai in the next book.

About the Author

K-A Russell

I'm K-A Russell, full-time legal assistant, self-published fantasy author, wood burning enthusiast and all around creative. I'm also Canadian, a quarter Irish on my father's side, and have loved making worlds and other languages, and coming up with songs and odd, unconventional characters since I was young. Half of my life is spent being a constructive adult in society. The other half is spent in my imagination which is full of my own worlds and fanfic spinoffs of my latest craze.

A'thería's Wake began as a fanfic at the age of 19 and developed into its own self throughout my 20's. It is both a reflection of who I am and my growth throughout the past decade. *The True Faithen's Plight* went through at least 7 revisions during this time, and once it was published, I soon after wrote the Prologue, *The True Faithen's Dream*.

As I learn and grow, so does my writing, and since coming out later in life, that means it's gotten a little...queer, let's say. I draw inspiration from my life and cross-cultural experiences, my worldview as a result of those experiences, a passion for the "other", and the nature around me and its origins. I seek to challenge an inerrant view of the Bible, the way we treat people who are on the margins of society, and how we might embrace people of different faiths (or lack thereof), practices and cultural backgrounds. Saying that, this is more than just an epic fantasy. To me, it's a reflection of life. It's who I am and the evolution of how I interpret the world.

I hope you'll take the time to become immersed in these books and let them envelope you as they do me.

You can find me on Facebook at @karussell87 for latest updates regarding book progress.

Other Books

Return to Serenestí where the Shadai twins' journey began!

What if dream became nightmare? What if the nightmare never left you?

Ninthalas is out to prove his worth. He and his brother finally get to embark on the News Bearer errand without the guidance of their father. But as much as Ninthalas can't wait to get started, he is deeply troubled. For months, he has been having the same dream: that the city of Luthrey will be destroyed. And that dream won't let him sleep. As his enthusiasm wears in the first few days of travel, the nightmare becomes much more than just a dream. Will it drive him mad by the time he reaches the city he must warn? Will the people even listen to him?

Manufactured by Amazon.ca
Bolton, ON